OLYMPUS, HOME OF THE GODS—

Sometimes benevolent and ascetic, more often lustful and capricious, the Greek gods and their mythical exploits have entertained for thousands of years. From ancient Asia Minor to modern West Virginia, these original stories of the often very human Olympians will bring you divine enjoyment. . . .

"The Littlest Maenad"—Vicious gossip and backbiting have always been common at the Country Club, but when Dr. Dion Sonoma comes to lecture, he may inspire the leisure class to a less verbal form of bloodletting.

"To Hades and Back"—For golden Apollo, mortal women had never been much of a challenge, for they fell at his feet with one sight of his full glory. But times have changed, and Apollo finds himself at the mercy of a modern goddess: a wild, jaded rock star.

"The Sword of Herakles"—Many years after his labors, Herakles is living in obscurity on a misty isle. When jealous Hera tries to take his divine sword, Herakles attempts to hide it, but is confronted by a mysterious figure— Merlin. . . .

More Spellbinding Anthologies
Brought to You by DAW:

ZODIAC FANTASTIC *Edited by Martin H. Greenberg and A. R. Morlan.* Such top oracles as Mickey Zucker Reichert, Jody Lynn Nye, Mike Resnick, Kate Elliott, Michelle West, eluki bes shahar, Diana L. Paxson, and Elizabeth Ann Scarborough offer divine readings of the stars in such enlightening tales as: In a family of confirmed Capricorns was magic the only hope for a Capricorn-Gemini romance? Could a misprint in the horoscope column really become a matter of life and death? They were the avatars of the Zodiac, rulers of all they surveyed—at least until some of the other constellations decided to break into their club. . . .

THE FORTUNE TELLER *Edited by Lawrence Schimel and Martin H. Greenberg.* Seventeen masterful tales by such mesmerizing forecasters as Billie Sue Mosiman, Peter Crowther, Ed Gorman, Nancy Springer, Tanya Huff, Rosemary Edghill, Brian Stableford, and Michelle Sagara West—from a man caught between two worlds . . . to a gambler cursed with the ability to see possible futures . . . to a brand new Vicki Nelson adventure which reveals how dangerous it can be to meddle with a vampire's future.

WARRIOR ENCHANTRESSES *Edited by Kathleen M. Massie-Ferch and Martin H. Greenberg.* The rites of power, the arts of war are the subjects of fifteen original tales by such masters of spellbinding fantasy as Tanith Lee, Andre Norton, Melanie Rawn, William F. Wu, Rebecca Ore, Pamela Sargent, and Jennifer Roberson—from Kleopatra's bargain with a god on the eve of battle . . . to a princess who finds an unusual way to earn respect in a man's world . . . to a wife ready to call upon the powers of the earth itself to defeat the demon who holds her husband captive. . . .

OLYMPUS

Edited by
Martin H. Greenberg
and
Bruce D. Arthurs

DAW BOOKS, INC.
DONALD A. WOLLHEIM, FOUNDER
375 Hudson Street, New York, NY 10014

ELIZABETH R. WOLLHEIM
SHEILA E. GILBERT
PUBLISHERS

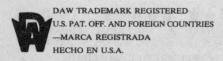

ACKNOWLEDGMENTS

Introduction © 1998 by Bruce D. Arthurs
Drown Night with Hope of Day © 1998 by
  Nina Kiriki Hoffman
The Littlest Maenad © 1998 by Esther Friesner
Flight © 1998 by Jane Yolen
Mantik Rites © 1998 by Jon DeCles
Harpies Discover Sex © 1998 by Deborah Wheeler
In the Quiet After Midnight © 1998 by
  Charles de Lint
The Sword of Herakles © 1998 by Irene Radford
To Hades and Back © 1998 by Karen Haber
In Re: Nephelegeretes © 1998 by
  Lawrence Watt Evans
Hekate's Hounds © 1998 by Diana L. Paxson
The Arrows of Godly Passion © 1998 by
  Mike Resnick & Nicholas P. DiChario
Traps © 1998 by Jo Clayton
February Thaw © 1998 by Tanya Huff
The Third Song © 1998 by Roberta Gellis
For a Transcript, Send Five Dollars © 1998 by
  Anne Braude
Kin © 1998 by Michelle West
The Divine Comedy © 1998 by Dennis L. McKiernan

CONTENTS

INTRODUCTION
by Bruce D. Arthurs

For thousands of years, the myths and legends of the Greek gods and goddesses have been an enduring part of literature and society. The stories of Hercules, Odysseus, Icarus, Prometheus, and others are almost universally known. The *Iliad* and the *Odyssey* are achetypes for war and quest stories. People have been intrigued and fascinated by the original myths for centuries. Repeated and passed on from generation to generation, they have come down to us remarkably unchanged.

But we're working on that. Greek myth has been a popular subject for films for decades. More recently, the television series "Hercules" has been placing the gods and heroes before an audience of millions of people every week. An opportunity to play on the slopes of Mount Olympus has an immense appeal to writers of every stripe; the initial proposal for this anthology provoked an overwhelmingly positive response from the writers contacted.

Those writers have provided stories ranging from slapstick-comedy-of-manners to darkest fantasy, and all points in between, and still only scratched the surface of possibilities for stories. I enjoyed having the opportunity to put this anthology together and to work with the writers involved. I hope that you, the reader, will enjoy it as much.

DROWN NIGHT
WITH HOPE OF DAY
by Nina Kiriki Hoffman

Nina Kiriki Hoffman has written numerous short stories, and
two novels, *The Thread That Binds The Bones* and *The
Silent Strength of Stones*. She brings a quiet compassion
to contemporary fantasy; this story is no exception.

Our lives are riddled with fragments of myths; Mer-
cury becomes enshrined in a car, later praised in
a song by a country singer; Pegasus gallops out of a
cloud before a movie starts; Hermes dances about hol-
iday bouquets of flowers, as if he has nothing better
to do than bring your mother a greeting; Mars sends
meteorites, perhaps rife with bacteria, to Antarctica;
Hercules stars on television; Eros, diminished but still
armed and dangerous, is everywhere on Valentine's
Day; Melpomene and Thalia masks frown and laugh
from the marquees of theaters. . . .

I had always considered myself a rational man, deliberate and logical in my thinking. These traits took
me far when I was a young and active archaeologist.
My precision in mapping sites, recording finds *in situ,*
measuring the distance from one fragment to the next
gave me the sense that I became part of history
through preserving it.

Yet here, becalmed all these years later in a throw-
away city where I saw pennies pounded into pavement,

still clinging to their purpose as the smallest unit of exchange, obsolete now in the midst of a mercurial commerce that hadn't time to pay attention to such paltry increments, I sat in my one-bedroom apartment, shipwrecked by my lack of faith in anything.

I have had a long life, and an adventurous one; have seen things in the night that filled me with fear, wonder, and awe. By daylight they proved prey to simpler explanations than the ones my midnight brain devised, and so I learned that fancy was folly rather than friend.

Yesterday I lost my job. It was the job of my old age, my retirement; my bones are too brittle to carry me across distant deserts any longer. Although winter in the city chills all the hollows in my soul and makes me long for the brassy, bullying sun of the desiccated places, I have learned I cannot live without mass transit and convenient healthcare. I depend on the corner grocery as well.

Yesterday I lost my job at the university, where as an occasional lecturer I had two feet of shelf space in the office of a lesser professor, access to his office and desk when he happened not to be using them, and a chance to speak a few times a term to anthropology students about the nature of digs and discoveries in the Ancient World forty years ago—only half my life away, yet forty years ago is almost as distant and strange to these youngsters as ancient Greece. No longer is this near distance relevant, according to the legislators who decide where budgets should be cut.

I came home with a small box of dusty papers and slender thumb-smudged books. I dropped the box as soon as I stepped inside my apartment, and fell into the one comfortable chair I own. I know not how many hours I sat and searched inside myself for reasons to continue my existence.

At last it came down to a slender vial full of mummified grain that I had taken from an excavated storeroom in the Great Temple of Aphrodite at Palaipaphos. How carefully I had weighed and measured and noted everything for the records of the British expedition I had been part of, and yet, in some mad moment, I had stolen this half-handful of antique offering. Unlike some of my colleagues, who had palmed whatever small golden trinkets they could escape with, I had chosen this.

Media of exchange: pennies, not worth enough to stoop and retrieve; a hundred seeds from a perished age that someone had once offered to the goddess, as prayer for a desired blessing, thanks for an end achieved, or just her due, I did not know. My sole legacy, aside from articles now out of date published in periodicals no longer printed, of my younger, adventurous years.

I sat with the glass tube of grain in my hand, staring at it. My heart was hollow and days stretched empty ahead of me. I did not believe I would be able to find another job that could offer me the Spartan but sufficient satisfactions of my last job; I was considered by most too old to employ. I had a pension that could sustain me. I had a library card, but increasingly these days my eyes betrayed me; print swam and squirmed and shrank.

On the bookshelf I had a chemist's mortar and pestle, purchased at a pawnshop when I was a younger man; to me it had been symbolic of an ordinary alchemy, that quotidian magic that one daily employs to change one thing to another: grinding, mixing, shifting, and altering a substance so that it serves a purpose other than its own. So the gods of Greece treated humankind.

I do not know whether it was exhaustion or inspiration that led to my next act. I poured Aphrodite's grain into the mortar. I fetched a paring knife from the kitchen and sat for a period with the mortar between my knees, grain once imbued with unknown purpose resting in its cavity. I tested words on my mental blackboard and finally had a set I liked.

I stroked the tip of the knifeblade across my palm and let the resulting sluggish welling up of blood drip into the grain, murmuring my prayer to a deity I did not believe in. Could fates be bribed? Could goddesses be bought? Could intention shape event? Now seemed as fine a time as any to test such a ridiculous theory.

I pressed a handkerchief against my hand to staunch the flow of blood. I gripped the pestle in my unmarked hand and ground grain and blood together, repeating the words of my desire.

I had been alone all my life, solitary in my pursuits and judgmental in my thinking. My heart had been wedded to my job, even when my job dwindled to nearly nothing. And now my job was as dust, leaving my heart behind, used hardly, hardly used.

When I finished, I had a dark, dusty paste in my mortar. I took it to the kitchenette and scooped it out into a bowl, moistened and thinned it with a little water. Cooking has never been one of my skills, but I imagined that something simple would do for my experiment. I perceived myself as the most untutored and rough of devotees, making do or doing without; would a goddess deny me because I did not know the exact forms of entreaty? Or would she listen because I was making an effort?

Perhaps, in this lack of preparation, I planned to fail.

I put a skillet over the gas flame, and poured a tot of red wine as a libation into the earth of the spider plant over the sink, invoking the goddess and asking her to watch over and aid me in my endeavors. When the skillet was hot, I poured olive oil into it, then added oregano for incense. *Let this my offering be sweet in your nostrils.* I stared at smoke, the conveyance of prayer, and breathed lightly so I wouldn't use up the spicy scent.

A moment later I poured my pitiful measure of grain-and-blood paste into the pan, where it spread out like a pancake and sizzled in the oil. Half a minute and I flipped it over; half a minute more, and it was just short of burning. I placed it on a plate.

It was a little larger than a silver dollar, this small dark mingling of ancient grain and fresh blood.

I wrapped it in a white paper towel and went out to seek my fortune.

The sun stood low in the sky when I stepped outside. A few brave and foolish flowering trees had cloaked themselves in pink-and-white blossom, though spring was technically a month away. I searched the after-work faces coming toward me along the sidewalk, wondering: Are you the one for me? Will you share this strange creation with me?

So few met my eyes, and those who did looked quickly away.

Goddess, give me a sign.

Would I know a sign if I saw it? Would I act on it if I knew it?

Afraid of seeing a sign in the face of another, I looked up at the faces of buildings. Gods and goddesses were everywhere; faces peered out of lintels and archways over windows and doors. They watched, and I had not noticed them until now. Usually I walked staring down at the sidewalks, studying oncoming shoes and dropped pennies.

They watched, but they did not smile or shift.

I walked in this way for a long while, now looking

at the faces of people, now at the faces of buildings and gods. Would I break out of solitude? I wondered. Brave ridicule and ask another soul to step into a circle with me?

A silver-haired woman with dark eyes stood at a bus stop. She wore a gray overcoat and had a green scarf tucked around her throat. I stopped beside her. For a moment we exchanged sideways glances.

"Do I know you?" she asked.

"No," I said. No one knew me.

"Why are you looking at me?"

"You're beautiful," I said.

Her eyes softened, and she smiled. Had it always been this simple?

"I'm Grace," she said.

"William," I said, taking her outstretched hand. Her grip was firm, her fingers warm. "Would you . . . ?"

"What?" she asked, still smiling faintly.

If I had been guided here by the goddess—if a goddess could achieve anything, and if she had listened to my prayers—this would work.

I reached into my coat pocket and brought out the white towel. "Would you share a tea-cake with me?"

Her eyes narrowed.

"Just a bite," I said, fumbling the towel open and displaying the small, burned cake. It gave no hint to its history: it looked like the mad creation of a sinister play oven. What a feeble, craven hope was this! A love spell! What had I been thinking? My heart shriveled within me.

"What?" she said. "No, I will not. Good heavens. A cup of tea in a restaurant, maybe. In the street? That? Forget it!"

I rewrapped my cake and stumbled away from her. I could have asked her to tea, but in the grip of my experiment it had not even occurred to me. It would never have occurred to me to speak to her if I had not been in the grip of my experiment. A world had opened and a world had shut in the space of half a minute.

I came to myself in the park.

I sat on a bench, the towel on my knee; I was pinching off rice-grain-sized pieces of my goddess cake and tossing them to the pigeons, who squabbled and pecked all around me.

No!

What was I doing?

Throwing away my chance at love!

Throwing away what made me appear crazy.

Throwing away that in which I had invested the rest of my life.

There was still half the cake left. I sat a moment with my hand cupped over it, thinking about years gone by, how all my choices had dwindled down to this: an old man on a park bench, feeding pigeons . . . on his own blood.

Well, the experiment was over. This avenue was closed to me; I would have to go home and make some other decision, always remembering that I had a gas stove and the apartment was small. I pinched off a piece of my pancake and tasted it: grit, dust, a faint note of grain; the blood I could not taste at all.

I fed the rest to the pigeons, who fought over it, flavorless as it was.

At home I made ramen for dinner and settled down to read about epic battles over stolen women. The print swam, and my interest wavered with it. I had pored over these matters before, and they were still distant in time and place, removed from all I knew. Tonight I could not lose myself in that beckoning distance.

*   *   *

Neither could I decide to make an end to everything. I still had food in the cupboards, and I was tired. I went to bed.

In the middle reaches of the night, a noise awakened me. I lay with open eyes staring at the faint line of light above the curtains and listened.

Tap. Tap. Tap.

It was not the drip of a faucet. I wondered if the young man in the next apartment had taken leave of his senses and was tapping a pen against the wall by my bed head.

Tap. Tap. Tap. Tap tap tap taptap . . .

No. It came from the window. Flurries of taps against glass. As though a regiment of incompetent burglars sought entry using blunt glass-cutters. Hail? Shrapnel? What?

I was afraid to look. The noise persisted and escalated. I sat up, turned on the light, and parted the curtains to see my own stunned night-shirted reflection, and the glint of a hundred golden, liquid eyes beyond the glass, the flash of fifty tapping beaks, the flutter of gray, brown, and white wings.

Pigeons. Pigeons hovered and beat upon my window.

Sickening memories of the Hitchcock movie swamped me. Birds had gone mad, and had come to peck me to death. I jumped to my feet and backed away from the window, my heart thudding, skin tightening on my skull. I could run—but what if they were tapping on every window in the building? What if the building were surrounded?

I took deep breaths.

Taptaptaptaptap.

I could hide in a closet; arm myself with my fire

extinguisher and make a run for it; wrap myself in all the clothes I owned and hope for the best. . . .

Pigeons. Pancake. The park. Aphrodite.

My goddess.

I crossed to the window, peering out at the flurry of birds. Wonder and fear warred within me. Had my prayer been answered? Had I cast true magic in the ultimate wrong direction?

My skin prickled. The pigeons tapped, stared, hovered.

What now?

Perhaps they loved me.

If I let them in, would they destroy me? Hurt me and leave me wounded? Or what?

Then again, I had been contemplating self-destruction. Perhaps this was a way to go.

Or I could close the curtains and try to sleep. Or leave the apartment, call animal control, see if someone could take care of this . . . problem.

I remembered tales of Aphrodite's anger. She was not a goddess you wanted to cross.

I wished I liked pigeons more.

My fingers trembled as I unlatched the window.

I opened it, and they flooded in, gray, white, brown, banded, cooing and squabbling. They drifted to the floor and furniture, settling like a quilt over the room.

"Uh," I said. "Welcome." I sat slowly on the bed, feeling dazed.

Those birds closest to me sidled closer, cocking their heads to stare at me.

Did I have anything I could feed them? A bag of cornflakes. Maybe they'd like that.

Before I could rise, pigeons settled on my thighs, shoulders, head. One stroked a soft wing across my cheek. They murmured and cooed, their toes making tiny pricks through the flannel of my nightshirt, their bodies warm.

Moving carefully so as not to dislodge them, I lowered the window until it was open just enough to enable them to go in and out. I could imagine the dropping-splattered room I would wake to in the morning, but even more I could imagine falling asleep now in the midst of this horde of warm, cooing creatures. Their throaty murmurs were soothing. The day had been long, and I was tired. I lifted birds off of me, arranged myself under the covers, felt birds mass over me in a warm blanket, and slid into sleep.

# # #

This morning I woke with a woman beside me. Her head hair is short and gray, more feathers than hair; wherever on a human woman there would be body hair, she has tiny, almost transparent feathers. Her eyes are large and golden. She cocks her head and looks at me sideways. In her gaze is fascination.

I remember that Aphrodite's chariot was drawn by doves.

Columba is quite satisfied with cornflakes for breakfast.

Today we are going to the library, where I will research as well as my vision allows ways to give thanks.

THE LITTLEST MAENAD
by Esther M. Friesner

Esther Friesner is considered one of the leading humorists in the fantasy genre, with such works as her (sadly out-of-print) *Harlot's Ruse* and the anthology *Alien Pregnant By Elvis.* Her short story, "Death and the Librarian" won the 1995 Nebula Award.

I believe that what I regret the most about the Club's latest *contretemps* is the fact that the best moral lesson I have been able to abstract from the wholesale slaughter is: *When your friends return from their travels, never ask whether they have brought home any interesting souvenirs.*

Which was precisely the mistake Bradley made at our little welcome-back party for Eames.

"Oh, this?" Eames held up the crystal pendant. He wore it as a watch fob. I could not quite make out the shape of the silver setting from which the stone itself dangled. "Just a trifle I picked up in one of those two-goat villages in the hinterlands of Athens."

Keats-Smythe laughed. "Crystals? It'll be hammered dulcimer music and bean sprouts next. And wine from California." We all shuddered at the thought.

"Now, now. I am beginning to think that there must be something to all this New Age nonsense," said

Benjamin Winthrop, our Richest Member. "All of those crystal doodads, well, they do seem to be good for *something*." He settled himself more comfortably in the buttery depths of one of our finer leather-covered armchairs and reached for the brandy at his elbow.

Note well that there was no brandy at his elbow when first he initiated that maneuver, yet by the time his fingers were within snifter-grasping range, the Club *factotum* Ashtoft had the glass bubble of fine spirits in place, awaiting Benjamin Winthrop's pleasure. Upon that dim and ill-starred day when the Club no longer exists and the fixtures must be sold to stave off baying packs of creditors, Ashtoft shall no doubt fetch his weight in rubies.

Or crystals of the mystic variety: quartz polyhedrons whose worth is measured in units more esoteric and less financially sound than carats. Yet I hesitate to confess that there are times on the links of life when the Monetary must allow the Arcane to play through, lest Madness follow as caddy to them both. I know whereof I speak, for that selfsame sort of crystal was the very agent which so nearly provoked the early, unlooked-for disaster I have just suggested, *viz*.: the permanent closure of the Club. Indeed, it has only been our general willingness to cooperate with the local police in their ongoing investigation of the carnage so tastelessly exploited in the local press that—

But I anticipate.

Benjamin Winthrop savored his brandy—he, like the rest of us then gathered in the library, blissfully unaware of the cataclysm on tap. "Yes," he went on, setting down the snifter upon a tooled leather coaster which materialized from the same omniscient Ashtoftian source as had provided the drink. "There most certainly is something to it—healing powers on some level or another. What do you gentlemen make of them, the crystals? For myself, I can no longer scoff."

There was the soft, hasty sound of many tongues being bitten. If our Richest Member found himself unable to scoff at the powers of externally applied minerals, none among us was man enough to counter him publicly.

"There—there might indeed be something to them," Bradley said hesitantly. "That is, I'm prepared to keep an open mind on the subject, until such time as evidence presents—"

"Evidence?" Benjamin Winthrop echoed. "I've evidence enough, if you'll hear it." We all encouraged him to enlighten us. He took some more brandy and folded his hands over his trim belly. "It concerns Amanda."

An uncharacteristically human sigh slipped from Bradley's lips at the mention of that name. If he heard it, Benjamin Winthrop no doubt put it down to dyspepsia rather than amorous devotion. The normally stolid Bradley was not known to cherish a passion for anything beyond the occasional round of cutthroat bridge.

Benjamin Winthrop ran his finger lightly 'round the rim of his snifter. "I needn't remind you how badly torn-up my poor child was by the death of her husband," he said, grim. There he spoke plain truth. We neither needed nor wanted to be reminded of the events linked to that sad occurrence.

A moment of silence was observed by all, the reverent hush broken only by the distant, muffled *click-click* of finest ivory billiard balls in the adjoining room. Amanda's late husband Piers had been our Oldest Member, a title which his demise had left by default to Benjamin Winthrop, who did not want it. Piers had seen us through the unpleasantness with Simpson's

Greek gift, and further weathered the storm of Young Chapin's tenancy and violent death. (Of both affairs, the less said here, the better. Amanda would concur, being as she was, to her shame, Young Chapin's relict. Having come to her senses, albeit tardily, she was eager to have all mention of that youthful *mesalliance* stricken from memory.)

Alas, Amanda had not long to enjoy the more staid delights of her second marriage. Piers' noble heart gave out soon after the birth of his predecessor's posthumous son. Some claim it was the infant's marked resemblance to Young Chapin and the thought of having to breed up the boy to the age of Reason (that is to say, Harvard matriculation) which caused a gallant spirit to throw in the towel.

"And how *is* Amanda?" Bradley inquired, breaking the solemnity of the instant. He wore an ardent, half-witted look such as I have only seen once in my life before, in circumstances involving the back seat of my first BMW and a Radcliffe English major to whom I fed four vodka screwdrivers and told that her poetry was evocative of Emily Dickinson.

"Astonishingly well, of late," Amanda's father replied, slapping the arm of his chair. "Never better." This was good news. In her zeal to have her first husband's tenure pass into the dreamy realm of myth, Amanda had set about bewailing her second mate's death with an intensity to leave most banshees looking like raw tyros. There had been days during the proper period of mourning when even the moony Bradley shuddered at the thought of being in the same room with her. "And it is all thanks to the very crystals we are presently discussing." Leave it to our Richest Member to refer to his lecture as if it were a dialogue. Rank has its privileges, but Wealth possesses *droit de seigneur*.

"I am glad to hear that she is better," Bradley said, his large, moist eyes aglitter with hope.

"Gentlemen, the change in Amanda's attitude has been nothing short of phenomenal since some happy accident a scant two weeks past turned her to the works of Dr. Dion Sonoma and she began her course of—um—ah—" Benjamin Winthrop groped for the *mot juste.*

"Treatments?" suggested Bradley.

"Therapy?" Eames provided. He had returned less than a month ago from his recent European trip strangely bitter. This was the first I had seen him smile. It was nasty.

"Self-knowledge," said Ashtoft, who endured almost physical pain whenever he beheld one of his charges groping for anything, be it potation or periphrasis.

"The very term!" Benjamin Winthrop snapped his fingers, looking as pleased as if he had thought of it himself. Ashtoft's self-abnegating, giocondesque smile as good as ceded all title to the phrase immediately. Contained within the economy of that expression seemed to be the implicit message that his will, his desire—nay, the very aim, purpose, and *sangreal* of his life was but to serve.

Before Winthrop could expand upon the precise means by which his daughter had achieved self-knowledge through large rocks, our mildly bibulous comradeship was interrupted by the entrance of Ashtoft. That is, I should more precisely say Ashtoft Junior.

Whereas our redoubtable *factotum* was a man well-stricken in years, the fires of youth prudently banked to embers, his son's whole manner implied that there had once been hotter fluids coursing through the family veins—coursed there still, in fact—of which the lad was walking proof. Only Ashtoft Junior never *walked;* he *erupted.* He was, in short, a genetic embarrassment.

"There's someone at the door to see Mr. Winthrop!" His handsome face flushed a tawny red as he blurted this advisory. In the six months since Ashtoft Senior had procured his boy the post of Club page, the poor youngster had been plagued by blushes. His fine, fair complexion changed color more readily than that of a Victorian heroine, and for reasons as frivolous. Mostly, however, he seemed to reserve his cardiovascular excesses for moments of impending embarrassment and paternal chastisement, such as this.

Impending, I say. Not that he *knew* he had committed yet another *gaffe servile,* but that his complexion appeared to have acquired the prognosticating talents of a Delphic Oracle. His face realized when he'd put his foot in it long before he did.

A hiss of air sucked in through serviceable dentures came from Ashtoft Senior. He crossed the room with silent, deliberate rage and hustled his son out through the huge burled oak doors. A moment later he returned to show us how it should be done. Taking his place at the rear of Benjamin Winthrop's chair he discreetly murmured in the Richest Member's ear that his presence was requested without, if it would not be too great an inconvenience.

As Benjamin Winthrop excused himself and left the library, Ashtoft Senior gliding after, Bradley remarked, "Well, *there* goes the perfect candidate for one of those New Age whatchamacallum's." He chuckled dryly, as always. Although he was not yet out of his thirties, Bradley had taken steps to accelerate the aging of his soul. Dry and stuffy by turns, he would make the perfect burial chamber for any Egyptian mummy worth its natron.

"What, Ashtoft? What's he want with a crystal?" Eames inquired, twirling his own.

"Not Ashtoft." Bradley sniffed. "*Ashtoft*. The young 'un. Take one of those crystals and use it to tune in on the great whozit of how d' you—? Of *Being*!" He pronounced this last word with force enough to let us all understand he meant it to begin with a capital letter.

"Now why in heaven's name would he want to tune in on anything like that?" Keats-Smythe yawned and stretched his feet to the fire. "The Superbowl, perhaps, but the great whozit of Being? Hardly."

A stern, determined look took over Bradley's features. It was the first time any of us had ever seen a headstrong bread pudding. "Don't you lot know anything? Crystals are the best way to summon up past lives or, failing that, to channel spirits."

"Speaking of which, did you know you can buy Courvoisier for quite a decent price when you zip over to France from England on that Hovercraft thingie?" Prescott piped up. Soon we were all locked in a fiery debate as to the best sources for duty-free goods.

"I meant it'd calm him down!" Bradley shouted, not one to allow his mystic observations to be ignored.

"Sounds like he's not the only one could stand a shot of tranquilizer." Eames chuckled. "He'd be a fool to take it, though. Ashtoft Junior may be bouncier than a Golden Lab pup, but that's not hurting him at all with the lady; that is, not unless her father finds out."

There are ways and ways of making general statements. It would be fruitless for an outsider to comprehend the innate telepathy at work among us when phrases such as "Not Our Kind" and "Not The Done Thing" are passed from lip to lip at the Club.

Details are extraneous; we *know*.

So, too, here: Not a hint was there in Eames' words to permit even Sherlock Holmes to deduce the identity of that tenebrous "lady" and her equally obscure "father," yet Bradley needed no further specification.

"Amanda?" he gasped. "*She* is seeing *him*?" A crisp Belgian linen handkerchief dabbed cold sweat from his brow. "*Socially?*" It was the ultimate horror.

Eames attempted to look contrite, but I could see his heart was not in it. "Well . . . yes." His fingers toyed with the silver-and-crystal fob.

"I take it that Benjamin Winthrop does not know," Prescott commented. It was a redundant observation. One had only to check the ceiling. Since it was still intact, obviously our Richest Member had no inkling of his child's latest ill-thought escapade in the realms of Venus.

Which orbit was approximately how far from Earth's atmosphere he would fly when he found out.

"He must be told." Bradley crumpled his handkerchief decisively between perfectly manicured fingers.

"Oh, go ahead and tell him, old boy." There was a jovially sadistic streak in Eames I had not previously noted, save in his choice of neckties. As this was his first reunion with us all since his return from better than two years abroad, it made me wonder whether I was only imagining the vitriol he so merrily let drip upon Bradley's head. "Yes, do tell him, but be warned. Either Amanda will deny it, in which case her father will freeze you like a slab of Chateaubriand, or else he will believe you."

"What is wrong with that?" Bradley looked like a hedgehog about to embark upon Crusade: prickly, inspired with a holy vision, and laughably small.

Keats-Smythe cleared his throat and in a diplomatic tone even Ashtoft would have admired said, "Are you familiar with the classic tradition of slaying the bearer

of bad news?'' Bradley nodded. "Benjamin Winthrop
has always been a great man for honoring the
Classics.''

It was piteous to witness the air going out of poor
Bradley's sails. "But—but it can't go any further—
ought not to be *allowed* to go any further—not after
the business with Young Chapin—not again—not
Amanda—not with a—with a—a *servant,* for God's
sake!'' We had never seen him so transported by
ardor. Some of us would be put off our golf game for
days after.

Keats-Smythe shrugged. "Hard to see how there's
any remedy. Perhaps it will burn itself out. These
things do.''

This might have been a source of comfort, had not
Bradley been aware—as were we all—that Keats-
Smythe's own mother had been a volleyball instructor
at the Caribbean resort at which his father and then-
bride Lucinda Keats-Smythe (*née* Carter) had spent
their honeymoon. The first Mrs. Keats-Smythe also
believed that all socially unfeasible flings run their
course. She did not realize that some courses have
their sequential finish lines at the divorce court and
the hymeneal altar.

"To let herself . . . *go* like that.'' It was the ultimate
faux pas in Bradley's book. Unbridled impulse, however romantic, had no place under the stringent leash
laws of his strictly ordered universe. He skewered
Eames with a hard stare. "How long has this been
going on?''

"Less than six months, surely. Ashtoft Junior wasn't
even on the premises any earlier.'' Eames tucked away
his watch fob. "How should I know? I'm as good as
a stranger here myself, these days. You of all people
should be aware of that.'' He gave Bradley a meaning-
ful look whose precise intent escaped the rest of us.

"There's been so *much* for me to catch up on." His eyes flashed.

Bradley was momentarily discomfited enough to avert his gaze. "Well, it won't do," he grumbled. "Steps must be taken."

"What sort of steps?" Eames inquired, a wicked smile making his thin lips almost visible to the naked eye.

"Why—why, whatever steps are necessary to nip this—this misbreeding in the bud. In the bud, I say!"

Eames chortled, a deep, rich, gloating sound that would have begged the question of justifiable homicide had Bradley been paying sufficient attention. "You make young Ashtoft and Amanda sound like a common mongrel and a pedigreed borzoi caught doing the dirty under the very eyes of the judges at Crufft's. What do you want done? Spaying all 'round?"

"Firing that upstart would do," Bradley growled, sounding for all the world like an AKC entrant himself.

"Fire Ashtoft Junior?" Eames smirked. Something sinister lurked behind his every variation of good cheer, from lip-quirk to broadest guffaw. I was beginning to think I liked him better morose. "Impossible."

"Why so? If Benjamin Winthrop learns what that blackguard's been up to with Amanda, we won't have time to open the front door before the scoundrel's pitched out ass over teacup."

"—to be followed, ankles over sugarbowl, by his father. Oh, yes, be certain of it: Dismiss Ashtoft Junior and Ashtoft Senior will take umbrage intense enough to leave Benjamin Winthrop's own paternal indignation panting in the shade."

Eames raised his glass to read the future through a film of Bombay gin. "Granted, our Richest Member will at first be glad for having been informed of his

daughter's capers. 'Whom do I have to thank for this?'
he will ask. And your name will be mentioned, no
doubt, and all will be beamish well-done-stout-fella as
far as the eye can see. But before he has gone a week
without the ministrations of our good Ashtoft—with
the first improperly chilled bottle of white wine, the
first snifter of Cointreau at his elbow when he called
for cognac at his fingertips—his gratitude will fade like
a rose on a griddle. The *second* time he asks, 'Whom
do I have to thank for this?' I should be in a distant
country, were I you."

Eames was in his glory. The well-tempered malice
now flowing from his every word struck me as
strangely arbitrary. "What's gotten into him?" I wondered, *sotto voce*.

Not quite *sotto* enough, for Prescott overheard.
"Don't tell me you've forgotten?" He adopted that
intense, confiding tone most used at funerals to comment on the lifelike appearance of the corpse. "Or
didn't you know—? No, you'd have to be a hermit
not to."

"Not to know what?" I replied, somewhat testily.
"Which scrap of utterly *vital* Club gossip have I over-
looked this time?"

There was no room in Prescott's mind for noting
sarcasm, or much else. "Sshh," he cautioned. Ashtoft
Senior had floated back into our presence, bringing an
abrupt end to all discussion concerning himself, his
offspring, and any Amanda-tampering the lad might
undertake. The others had turned to arguing the mer-
its of *la nouvelle cuisine* over real food. Using one
hand to shield his mouth so that our sidebar chat
might not attract attention, Prescott contrived to bring
me up to date: "*Everyone* knows why Eames flew off
to the Continent: Our cold fish Bradley's quite the

Wall Street shark, and he persuaded Eames to invest heavily in some properties over there."

"Heavily? How much was invol—?" A reproving look from Prescott brought me to my senses. I should have known better than to ask about specific sums.

"Heavily enough to necessitate that two-year jaunt of his, when the whole deal threatened to go sour. Bradley, *nota bene,* did not practice what he preached—invested nothing in the recommended venture, couldn't have cared less when things turned teetery."

"Yes, but to go abroad when there are other people to handle that sort of thing for one—!"

"Letting other people handle matters was what jeopardized Eames' finances in the first place. He would take no more chances, and he is a firm believer in the hands-on method of financial intervention— very literal, very direct; a little primitive, if you want my opinion." He sipped his drink and purred into the glass, "Alas, the lady of Eames' heart was also rumored to be a great advocate of the hands-on method."

"I never knew Eames had a lady."

"Not anymore he doesn't, thanks to Bradley. Absence makes the heart grow fonder, but it leaves the glands cold."

"Who was she? What became of her?"

Prescott placed his empty glass to one side. "Those secrets are Eames' alone. She married another, that much is sure. Whether she's dead, divorced, still happily wed, or off men entirely and turned to the D.A.R., your guess is as good as mine."

He picked up the fresh drink which the ubiquitous Ashtoft Senior had caused to replace his spent measure and added, "Carlysle might be able to tell you. He's the one found out the few bits we do know. He gathered them the day after Eames' return, when he encountered the poor fellow in the Club bar a tad, shall we say, in the thrall of the grape. You'll have to ask Carlysle himself if you wish to learn more. Or Eames."

Precious little chance I had of that. Eames left clams looking like magpies. Carlysle, however, was one of the party currently in the billiard room next door. I excused myself on a common enough pretense and sought him out while our resident gastronomes debated the life-or-death question of the proper wine to drink with a really bosomy Stilton. The Olympian eye of Ashtoft rested over all, taking in everything, betraying nothing.

"Eames' lady?" Carlysle thoughtfully chalked up the end of his cue. " 'Fraid you've got me there; sorry. I was lucky to get as much out of him as I did. He had his head down on the bar, spouting a lot of gibberish about frailty-thy-name-is and vengeance-shall-be-mine-anon. Actually said *anon,* he did, right out loud. He was clutching something in his right hand. Dropped it when he reached for another round, and it bounced under one of the tables. I wish you could've seen how he almost bowled me over, diving after it!"

"What was it?"

Carlysle shrugged and made his shot. He missed. "Damn. Damned if I know. Sparkly doodad. Soon's he got it back, he pressed it to his lips, mumbled something like, 'Call in one debt to pay another,' and laughed. That's what comes of majoring in the Humanities, I suppose. Join us?" He offered his cue.

I declined and returned to the library. In my absence, Benjamin Winthrop had returned, accompanied by a man whose tight curls of glossy black hair made a striking contrast to his pale golden-brown, almost yellow eyes. Whoever he was, he reminded one of a

predator—a charming predator, but a predator nonetheless. To my mind, he seemed entirely capable of
waltzing a debutante thrice around the dance floor
before she noticed the raw and dripping haunch of
something small and furry protruding from his mouth.
Even then, were he to offer her a nibble, she would
accept with rapture.

He was not conventionally attractive, after the fashion of Ashtoft Junior. Despite this lacking, there was
a hypnotic quality to him which made me fear that,
were he to prove to be an insurance salesman, I would
spontaneously fling myself upon him with the plea to
sell me as much additional whole-life coverage as he
saw fit.

Such men are dangerous.

Bradley sulked in his chair, nursing his single-malt.
Eames' cautionary words appeared to have had their
effect: He made no move to inform Benjamin Winthrop of Amanda's belowstairs alliance and feigned
temporary deafness as our Richest Member called for
our attention.

"Gentlemen, may I introduce Dr. Dion Sonoma?"
He presented him to us as proudly as Ashtoft Senior
displaying a carefully laid-up and cherished bottle of
Montrachet.

"Charmed." Dr. Sonoma spoke with an unplaceable
European accent and radiated hazardous levels of
Continental *savoir faire*. If he also clicked his heels
together in the Prussian manner, the effect was damp-
ened by his top-of-the-line running shoes. He wore
denim and leather exclusively, both well weathered,
yet he contrived to carry them off with a panache
that left the rest of us feeling decidedly shabby in our
bespoke Hong Kong tailored suits.

"You're the same Dr. Sonoma with the rocks?"

Keats-Smythe inquired when it was his turn to shake the man's hand.

"Yes, he's the one," Benjamin Winthrop said, clapping him on the back. Dr. Sonoma's secret smile was even more disquieting than Eames' smirk. "And what do you think? He's agreed to give one of his famous lectures right here at the Club next Wednesday evening, free of charge."

"Famous?" Prescott echoed, still behind the discreet shield of his hand. "The first I ever heard of the man was not fifteen minutes ago, in this very room."

As if Prescott had spoken aloud, Dr. Sonoma himself responded, "You do me too much honor, sir." Hood his eyes how he might, there was no way on earth Dr. Sonoma could look truly modest. "My fame is, as yet, strictly local. So it has always been, in the beginning. Yet the times change. The moment hangs upon the vine of Time, ripening as we speak. The—"

"If he starts in about the Harmonic Synchronicity of Thingummy, I'm leaving," Prescott whispered, causing me to miss the rest of what Dr. Sonoma was saying.

I could not miss our Richest Member's next declaration, though. "It's the least he can do," said Benjamin Winthrop, "seeing as how it's a personal favor for his future father-in-law." The wholehearted, incipiently familial manner in which he embraced Dr. Sonoma wiped clear all possibility of misinterpretation.

Bradley choked on a half a mouthful of Glenfiddich and spritzed the rest all over the library. We took it in turns patting him on the back while Ashtoft Senior materialized at once to blot up the widely asperged liquor with a sponge.

There were not sponges enough on the whole bed of the Mediterranean to absorb what would be spilled on Club property come Wednesday.

*   *   *

The turnout for Dr. Sonoma's lecture was all anyone might wish. I like to take the charitable view that
the full Club membership really did crave to hear him
speak on "Crystal Consciousness: Psychic Sham or
Speedway of the Soul?" and likewise panted like the
hart after cool waters to purchase autographed copies
of his privately published book of the same name. We
have always supported the Arts.

Cynics may say that Arts be damned, we showed up
out of well-considered fear of offending our Richest
Member. True, Benjamin Winthrop's money does un-
derwrite most Club functions involving mass quantities
of dance cards, crepe paper flowers, and gin.

One year a new member, one Thomas Yates, politely declined to allow Winthrop to play through on
the links. That was the year Mrs. Yates' candidacy for
president of the Ladies' Auxiliary Decorating Committee came a cropper because of a sudden and vehe-
ment lack of funds to support said committee's
projects. It was likewise the same twelvemonth during
which Yates' daughter could not "come out" at the
Amaryllis Cotillion, there unexpectedly being no Amaryllis Cotillion. (Cynthia did "come out" later that
same year, although not in precisely the manner her
parents had hoped. The consolation that the other
lady involved was a successful commodities trader
with an M.B.A. from Wharton did not assuage Mrs.
Yates.) Yates himself led a domestic life of purebred
hell from then on and gave up golf entirely. But to
put such things down to more than the veriest coincidence is unworthy of a gentleman.

Besides, Benjamin Winthrop might find out I said
anything about it.

Therefore it was standing room only in the Oak
Room for at least an hour before Dr. Sonoma

mounted the podium. The Ashtofts, Junior and Senior, were busier than a hostess who has lost her place cards at the last minute. Ashtoft Junior's face was a study in misery. His surging blood had surged its last, all inner hydraulics monkeywrenched past mending by the shocking announcement of Amanda's engagement. He could not have looked more dumbstruck had one of our members mistaken his head for a polo ball. My father wore just such an expression for the whole of Franklin Delano Roosevelt's incumbency.

I took pains to arrive early enough to command a good seat, one sufficiently to the fore to make my presence easily visible should Winthrop or Amanda choose to count the house, yet far enough back to permit me an unobtrusive lecture-long doze. I had hardly settled myself in when the place beside me was taken by Eames.

"A wise choice of seating," he said. "You always have been one for safety precautions."

"I don't see what you mean," I replied.

"You will." He raised his eyebrows and rolled his eyes to indicate the large EXIT sign prominently displayed above the French doors nearby. "Very soon."

"Eames, tonight I am not in the mood for hidden significance, and I have always hated cryptic utterances as a matter of policy. What in heaven's name *are* you nittering about?"

For once, Eames did not twist his lips into a wry-but-knowing grimace, but rather chose to sigh. "The first row. Why did it have to be the first row?"

Here was a statement both noxiously cryptic and fraught past the gunwhales with hidden significance. I ground my teeth. "Why did *what* have to be the first—?"

"It will only be the worse for her, once the bloodletting starts. She was always so fastidious about her wardrobe, too. It looks like . . . *could* it be that's a silk ensemble she's wearing? Oh, dear, even if she does speak to me again, she'll be in a snit. Still, when a man's just saved your life, you might be convinced to shelve the problem of stain removal, at least temporarily." He fiddled with his watch fob like a madman.

"Bloodletting?" I didn't like the sound of that— who would?—but in view of certain incidents in the Club's past history I had cause to like it less still. "Explain yourself!" I demanded.

"Oh, don't worry. You'll get out all right," was his inadequate reply. He laid the fob on his open program so that the light glittered off the crystal and glowed upon the exquisitely formed silver features of the leering, vine-wreathed face above. "The front row . . . tsk. And here I thought she was mad at Amanda. I *have* been out of the swim," was the only other thing he said.

Quickly I scanned the first row of seats, hoping to gather some clue to Eames' ravings from the persons seated there. Benjamin Winthrop and Amanda had the best seats, naturally, with poor Bradley not two places off. The gaze of pure, hopeless longing which he lavished upon her kept being intercepted by Gloria VanderSee.

Gloria was an old chum of Amanda's. Her divorce was the talk of the Club, as had been her marriage. That is quite the sort of thing one must expect when one weds in such haste as to overlook the fact that one's intended is in the ethnic habit of using too many spices and too few forks. Small wonder it scarcely lasted two years.

Two years . . .

There are times when the pieces of Life's little jigsaw persist in getting themselves lost between the sofa cushions, but there are other times when they all seem to fall into order as naturally as the Preakness follows the Derby. I seized the moment, along with Eames' wrist, just as Dr. Sonoma made his entrance. Eames' protests as I dragged him into the hall were muted by the usual prelecture susurrus in the audience. I am not remarkably strong, but four years of pulling for Harvard crew does leave one with residual upper-body strength convenient to have in an emergency.

I flung him down onto a satin-covered bench beneath one of our Founder's many portraits. "If there is to be any bloodletting upon Club premises," I expostulated, "it's going to be yours unless you tell me what little treat that love-addled brain of yours has cooked up, Eames."

Eames pretended indifference to my threats. "There's nothing you can do about it now," he said, cool as a *pamplemousse* sorbet. "The wheels have been set in motion."

I seized him by the necktie and practiced a choke-chain maneuver I'd previously employed to good effect with my pet Weimaraner, Sunnyland Wunderkind Otho II of Bickering-Wensleydale.

"Those wheels," I snarled, hauling him skyward, "are attached to the underbelly of a juggernaut that will squash you flatter than a Vassar girl's bosom. If you wish to kill Bradley, couldn't you have done it more discreetly? Good Lord, man, Gloria VanderSee is as tasty a finger sandwich as ever graced the brunch of Eros, but even for her sake, *must* you make your every vendetta a public spectacle?" I let him drop to the bench once more.

The charge of Causing a Scene (with Malice Aforethought) brought him up short, even before his rump hit the upholstery. Breeding is forever. Realization shamed him to the core. "What have I done?" he whispered.

"You tell me," I replied.

He detached his watch fob from its chain and pressed it into my hands. "It happened in that piddling village I mentioned," he said, much subdued. "The place where I picked up this very charm. Word had reached me in Athens of Gloria's marriage and I was heartbroken. I had to get away, out of the city, and an associate told me there were some excellent ruins to be seen in those parts. Anything to distract my mind! The natives gave me directions, but they wouldn't guide me to the site, for some reason. Just as well: Solitude was what I craved."

"So off you went to mope among the columns." I turned the pendant this way and that. There was a disturbing exuberance pent behind the silver features of that impish face, a malicious twinkle in the eyes not wholly attributable to reflections from the crystal shard below. "Go on."

"That was where we met, he and I." Eames looked up at me. "I don't recall exactly how it happened. I had—I had taken one companion with me to the ruins, and—"

"I thought you said you craved solitude?"

"This companion came in a bottle. A rather large bottle. The village I mentioned wouldn't attract the better class of bacteria, but for some reason the local wine was extraordinary. One moment I was by myself, simultaneously trying to pickle and shellac my liver in that resinous brew, and the next I was talking with this fellow." He nodded toward the closed doors of the Oak Room.

"Dr. Sonoma?"

"That's what he calls himself now. I never did get his given name. You know how it is when you've had a few: You gain a new cosmic perspective, you discover fresh priorities, you pass beyond the hollow social niceties—"

"You were blasted out of your mind, weren't you," I stated, returning the pendant to its owner.

"All the way to Albuquerque," Eames averred. "We soon learned we shared a common woe, he and I. I told him of Gloria's inconstancy, he bemoaned the fickle nature of humanity in general. 'How soon they lose faith!' he cried. 'Oh, once these woods rang with the wild, glad shout: *Evoe! Evoe!* But now the temple lies desolate, the rites forgotten, the maenads scattered. Even the raucous sileni have gone off, Zeus knows where, to seek a better life serving a more fortunate master.'" Eames sighed. "Well, right after he told me about those maenads and the lot, I began to suspect he wasn't just another misdirected tourist. I felt sort of sorry for him. I expect it's hard if you're a—a satyr, I suppose he is—and you're suddenly left out of work when the rest of your fellow employees desert the spiritual ship, as it were. It's refreshing to find a man who really cares about religion, these days. Can't say I'd fancy their idea of a church social, though. You *do* know what maenads do?"

"Get stewed to the eyeballs and run amok, ripping anything they catch into small, bloody gobbets." I had done fairly well in the Classics myself.

"Well, they're not the only ones," Eames said. "They're more like—like the cheering squad. Group participation's the thing, with everyone attending the rite supposed to pitch in and do his bit, especially when you find out the goat's a sight bigger than a handful of wine-soaked women can handle and—" He shrugged. "If you don't tear off just a *teensy* chunk of living flesh, it's a bit like letting the collection plate go by untouched during the Offertory."

My mouth was dry. Suddenly I understood Eames' cavalier use of the word *bloodletting*.

"At any rate, I proposed to him the advisability of a change of scene, with the added enticement of new territory where he might proselytize. At first he refused to believe that he would find any degree of popular avidity for getting drunk and subsequently tearing innocent passersby to gory pulp, but I took him to a video arcade as soon as he arrived in New York City and he confessed himself convinced."

"You paid for his passage?"

"That was not necessary." The crystal charm dangled from Eames' bony fingers. "He gave this trinket to me as we parted company at the shrine and told me to give him a call when I got home. One brief *evoe* in the men's room of the Harvard Club and there he was. However, I did buy him his first suit of clothes—can't very well be seen socially in a leopard-skin tunic these days or you'll be all over red paint from those environmental ninnies."

"So you were his ticket to fresher fields," I mused. "And in exchange he was to be for you—?"

"—the instrument of Bradley's destruction." Eames spoke diffidently. He was not a man given to second thoughts in matters of revenge. "Once he was here, we initiated my plan. It was all my idea, you know: The publication of his book, his infiltration of the Club, his courtship of Amanda. Charming girl, but extremely susceptible to suggestion, particularly when there is a good-looking man in the case. I saw to it that she received an autographed copy of Dr. Sonoma's *opus*. As soon as she saw his photograph on the dust jacket, I knew she would seek him out. The rest is hormones." He looked inordinately proud of himself. "I have played the spider, tugging lightly at the filaments of my web to make the poor flies dance."

"You have also managed to wrap said filaments nicely around your own neck in the form of a hangman's noose," I reminded him. "Your sole intended victim was Bradley. By having your—*creature* woo Amanda from him, you have dealt him a grievous wound, but if I know you, that will not suffice."

"Naturally not." Eames adjusted the Windsor knot securing his regimental stripe tie. "As a mythical being, Dr. Sonoma stands in possession of certain . . . powers. He told me he would use them this very day to destroy the man responsible for my unhappiness. At the same time, he promised to provide me with the opportunity to burst back into my darling Gloria's affections."

"What manner of opportunity is this?"

Eames pursed his lips. "He said I would have to leap to the fore and carry her off the moment the bloodshed begins. To her eyes, I would be the hero who saved her life. I think that should more than make up for my enforced two-year absence. She need never know that she was in no peril, nor was anyone else save Bradley."

"Bloodshed," I repeated. "Have you the veriest inkling of how your Dr. Sonoma intends to initiate this one-man massacre?"

"Well . . . no. Perhaps he'll pounce on Bradley and rip him apart with his bare hands at a good stopping point in his lecture. I think it's a sort of religious obligation with these people."

"Won't that look nice," I said with understandable bitterness. "So a brutal murder will take place on the Club premises, in front of countless witnesses, and at the hands of a seeming madman. Do you imagine there will be no investigation in the wake of such a debacle? Do you dream that no one will discover the person responsible for bringing the murderer into our midst?"

"You wouldn't—you wouldn't expose me?" Eames grasped at my lapels in a most piteous manner.

"My silence will avail you little. Eames, I am neither the Club fool nor our Brightest Member, but I managed to figure it out. Others will trace Dr. Sonoma's provenance back to you."

Eames' lips moved silently over Gloria's name. Like a knight of old taking courage from the thought of his lady, he found backbone enough to say, "Perhaps public slaughter won't be his method. I told Dr. Sonoma my wishes in strictly general terms. He might yet prove discreet as well as lethal. 'Leave everything to me,' he said. 'Soon we shall have all that we could possibly desire.' "

I disliked the sound of that 'we.' "And how *did* you phrase your wishes?" I inquired, feigning a calm I did not truly feel.

A sliver of the old surgical steel slipped back into Eames' smile. "I told him I wanted Bradley's liver on a plate. With onions."

"Eames, you idiot, creatures of myth are notoriously literal-minded. Ask for a man's liver and you very well might get it. And to avoid offending the procurer thereof, you will just as likely have to eat it."

"Good Lord, no!" Eames went all pasty in the face. "I didn't mean his actual liv— He mustn't—I couldn't—I would never— My word, which *wine* does one serve with—?"

"There, I suspect, you have brought along a higher authority than even Ashtoft," I said, and dragged him back into the room.

At the podium, Dr. Sonoma was discoursing upon the Freedom of the Spirit. "Every ill of modern life may be traced to our inability to truly let ourselves go," he said. (I saw several of our senior members wince as a helpless infinitive was split like an innocent babe upon the blade of one of Herod's Finest.) "All of our physical afflictions, from stress to sour stomach, are the result of our real selves yearning to *tear* themselves free from the encumbering body, to *rip* aside the burden of the flesh, to *shred* our inhibitions—!"

Eames and I sidled our way forward. We had an excellent view of the podium. It was a most disquieting one. Dr. Sonoma was working himself up into what my dear, departed grandmama generally called "a swivet." His eyes glowed the bright crimson of a fine old radioactive claret, his hands curled into the eager claws of the spotted pard, and his nostrils flared like a foxhound's scenting wounded prey.

Alas, he shared his swivet. I cast a glance over the audience and beheld a chilling sight: Every female, regardless of age or social standing, wore a look of absolute entrancement. Rapt, they leaned forward in their chairs, their bosoms rising and falling in perfect cadence, their lips parted, the color mounting to their cheeks. A fine dew of perspiration spangled each lily-white brow. Many of the more mature ladies were using their programs fanwise, but they only fluttered at the inevitable. Just looking at them, I felt an uncomfortable warmth welling up within me. I was about to commit the unthinkable—to loosen the knot of my necktie in public—when I made a supreme effort and snapped myself free of the spell.

"We are too late," I hissed. "He has cast his power over them. You were right, Eames: He will not soil his own hands with Bradley's blood. You have been so wrapped up in the fruition of your own desires that you gave no thought to where his might lie."

"His . . . desires?" Eames repeated the word as if

he had just heard it for the first time. "Well, I assume a satyr would like—"

"This is no mere satyr you have brought into our midst," I said. "Satyrs are his followers, his minions, his lackeys! Have underlings such power to command?" I waved my hand toward the podium. My gesture caught the speaker's foxy eye. He paused in mid-sentence. None of the entranced audience seemed to notice, prisoners of his spell. Amid the tangled glory of his curls I glimpsed the gloss of twining ivy and knew my theory to be true. "This is the deity of the vine himself," I breathed. "This is Zeus' child, foolish Semele's own son, the twice-born lord of wine, Dionysus!"

"Ah?" Eames remarked. "Oh. You're right, I suppose. Not very imaginative when it came to supplying himself with an alias, then, is he? Disappointing. Him being the patron of the old Athenian drama festival and all."

"We can report him for first degree transparency afterward," I gritted. "Look at him! He does not care how loudly I speak; none but you can hear me now. Our fellow members are in his thrall. He has them all in his pocket—if leopard-skin tunics *have* pockets. He can do with them as he pleases, and mark me well . . . he will."

"He oughtn't," Eames said, a trifle tardily. "I'll just have a word with him." He started for the podium.

Benjamin Winthrop rose from his seat and placed himself between Eames and Dr. Sonoma. "Stay back," he intoned in the accents of the better class of tomb. His suit had inexplicably assumed an airier cut and a wreath of vine leaves embraced his steel-gray temples.

"Yes, sir," Eames quavered, and shrank back.

"Man, are you mad?" I demanded, shaking him by the shoulder. "You must *do* something!"

"But—but that's *Benjamin Winthrop* up there," Eames protested helplessly. He needed say no more. It would take a backbone of adamant to face down our Richest Member before the assembled Club.

Yet I persisted. One cannot stand by in idleness when so much is at stake. "Eames, get a grip on yourself. Within moments, the distaff membership will be transformed into a troupe of sanguinary maenads, bacchantes flown with wine, deadly in their ecstasy! And in *this* room, of all places. My God, that's *white* woodwork."

"It will take a supplementary assessment of each member to cover the cleaning costs," Eames mouthed, trembling. "Heaven help me, I'll never be able to afford it without dipping into my capital." His hand closed around my wrist in desperation. "In mercy's name, what's to do?"

"We must intervene," I said. The words came out as scraped over sandpaper. "At best, we must prevent."

"I fear it's too late for that." Eames nodded toward the podium.

Our Richest Member no longer stood guard alone. Now he was flanked by Purcell and Keats-Smythe. The former was a gentleman much given to the seductions of the grape, and was often able to write the word *oenophile* by the light of his nose. His Brooks Brothers suit had gone the way of Winthrop's garb and was currently little more than a drape of undyed wool girt about his loins. He brandished a knotted club culled from the woody root of some ancient grapevine and made distinctly threatening gestures with same in our direction.

As for Keats-Smythe, his trousers had vanished entirely, but he no longer needed them. A fine crop of coarse goat's hair covered his body from naked waist to cloven hooves. For his sake, I hoped it was at least cashmere. He leered at us and tooted the opening bars of "The Whiffenpoof Song" on his reed pipes.

"Do not attempt to interfere," Dr. Sonoma drawled. "I would hate to have you become my first sacrifice."

"Of all the nerve!" Eames huffed. "Is this how you honor your sworn word?"

"To what did I swear?" the deity asked with a lift of one dark brow. His hand dropped to his side and a purring panther was suddenly there to have its ears scratched.

"Hmph! I wasn't all *that* drunk. I remember it precisely: You were so grateful to find a sympathetic ear after all those centuries that you promised to grant me my dearest wish. I can assure you, being torn to pieces by the ladies of the Club is *not* my dearest wish."

The panther's purr changed to an ominous growl. "You have a remarkable memory, my friend," said the god.

"I never forget a debt," Eames replied grimly. "What's more, you swore by—by—by some river or other— Sounds like Monongahela, I think—"

"The Styx," I supplied.

"That's the one!" Eames brightened. "I knew it couldn't have been the Hudson. And *that* was the exact moment when you gave me *this*!" He held up the crystal pendant for all to see. He was not to blame if no one present (except myself) was able to see anything save what Dionysus allowed.

The god scowled. "You speak the truth. I vowed by the awful name of Styx—which oath binds even the Olympians—and I will keep my word. But nothing in my oath prevents me from likewise achieving my own dearest desire."

"Oh, pshaw," said Eames. "What could a god desire?"

Dionysus' lips curved up like the business end of a tiger's claw. "A congregation. We shall accomplish our wishes together, my friend—you the destruction of your enemy, I the renewal of my worship."

"Too late," said Eames.

Dionysus' brows met. "I beg your pardon?"

"If that's all you wanted, you're there already. Years ago. Good grief, have you been walking about with your eyes shut all the time since I introduced you to the Club? Just look about you!" Eames' sweeping gesture encompassed the room. "The cocktail parties, the wine tastings, the before-and-after-dinner drinks that are *de rigeur,* the traditional potations of the nineteenth hole, the stirrup cup when we don't even have a stable, the deadly scorn that greets the Club guest unwise enough to request a Perrier after his twenty-first birthday— In the name of any decent Pinot Noir, if that's not worship enough for you, what is?"

"Truly?" The god's face was transfigured with a childlike awe. He gazed out over the glassy-eyed faces before him as if seeing them for the first time. He left his panther to warm the podium and descended to walk among his people, pausing here to sniff a breath, there to palpate a liver. His expression was radiance itself when at last he turned back to Eames and exclaimed, "They worship me! They really worship me!"

"So they do." Eames was pleased with himself. (There is no better way to defuse a demand than by granting it—except when one is forced to deal with trade unions.) "But they do so *discreetly.* The common ruck tears around the countryside hurling beer cans at stop signs, yet for all their unseemly brouhaha they never manage to consume a quarter as much of your sacred tipple as our frailest member once the sun tops the yardarm. And at any given hour the sun is above the yardarm *somewhere* on the globe." He gave Dionysus a conspiratorial wink.

"Beer is Demeter's department, strictly speaking," the god remarked.

"Do you want to quibble, or do you want to be adored by a better class of people?" Eames asked, a trifle peevishly.

Dionysus strode right up to him and gave him a hearty bearhug. I shuddered at this unseemly display of emotion and was quietly thankful that no one else was in any state to witness it. "You were right, my friend!" the vine-lord cried. "This is indeed the land of opportunity. You have given me what I have longed for these many years: a people willing to embrace my worship and all it entails. The joy! The ecstasy! The cirrhosis!"

"Well . . . maybe not the part about the goats," Eames said quickly.

The god did not appear to be listening. "I, too, can be generous," he said. "I know what it is you wish—the destruction of *that* man." He jabbed a finger at Bradley. "I will give it to you at once!" He raised his hands and the ladies slowly came to their feet. Some of them—I blush to recount it—were drooling. The panther let out a whimper of fear and bolted.

"*No!*" Eames dragged the deity's arms back down to his sides and held them there. "I think perhaps you might have . . . misinterpreted my wishes." In response to Dionysus' quizzical look he added, "His *physical* destruction will not be necessary after all. Certainly not here and now, at any rate. Why don't you just go ahead and marry Amanda. That ought to do him in just enough to suit me."

"Are you certain?" The god cast a doubtful look to where Amanda stood, side by side with Gloria VanderSee, awaiting further orders. "But I thought you also yearned to have the chance to reclaim that other young woman's affections by playing the hero. If you cannot save her life, then how—?"

"Oh, I suppose I'll have to buy her a sports car. *La couer a ses raisons que* my bank account will just have to accommodate. Now lift your spell, there's a good fella, and finish your little lecture, and we can go on as if none of this ever happened."

"I am afraid that is not quite possible," the god said with a smattering of regret. "You see, my spell, as you so lightly call it, is nothing more than the effect of divine intoxication conferred without benefit of actual drinking."

"Eliminate the middleman, eh?" Eames eyed the throng. "More than a few hangovers to be dealt with come the dawn, ho ho."

"Ho ho," Dionysus echoed, none too appreciatively. It struck me that the son of Zeus did not care for Eames' degree of familiarity. Gratitude has its limits and a mighty short memory. "What I am trying to tell you is that when I lift my hold upon them, those mortals here and now present will still be in the grasp of the vine. I suggest that you do your best to see to it that they return to their homes as soon as possible for a good, long rest."

"And miss the post-lecture reception? Pshaw," said Eames. "They can hold their liquor. After all, they belong to the Club." And he snapped his fingers in the god's face.

"So be it. You have been warned. I will not be responsible for the outcome."

"Well, no one said *you* have to hang about after the lecture," Eames responded. "Now get on with it."

The god scowled at being so summarily ordered about his business. An ivy-bound thyrsis sprouted from Dionysus' hand. He passed it over the heads of the assembly with a regal gesture. The bouquet of a fine Cabernet Sauvignon enriched the air. Keats-Smythe was instantly returned to fully human form—or at best to his original condition. Purcell and Winthrop were likewise restored. The assembled auditors blinked like bullfrogs and turned their heads groggily this way and that. Some of the ladies touched their temples and winced.

As for the god of wine, he was back at the podium delivering his concluding remarks. A patter of polite applause sealed the occasion. I breathed a sigh of relief; Eames had done wisely, if not as well as he had originally hoped. True, Bradley yet lived, but the look in that man's eye when Dr. Sonoma stepped down from the podium to take Amanda's arm gave Eames a healthy taste of revenge if not a glut.

As was customary, there were refreshments to follow. The Ashtofts, *pere et fils,* now appeared at the rear of the Oak Room, swinging wide those doors which led into the connecting Hunt Room where a light collation and full bar had been laid on. It would be churlish of me not to mention that Ashtoft Junior behaved admirably, his silent, efficient ministrations the very image of his noble father's. If heartbreak had begotten such superb service in the lad, I for one would employ a *corps d'elite* of Jezebels-for-hire to improve the quality of help one gets these days.

The crowd passed through the portals. As I entered, I happened to see Dr. Sonoma unthread his arm from Amanda's and excuse himself on the pretext that he had to see a man about a hippogryph. "Start without me," he said, smiling.

It began while I loitered near the buffet.

"Well, Gloria?" Amanda's voice had a sturdy, carrying quality to it, the product of elocution lessons at Miss Porter's. "What did you think of Dion's lecture?"

I glanced in the ladies' direction just in time to hear Gloria tersely reply, "It was bullshit."

Amanda sniffed. "You're just jealous because I'm getting married again and you couldn't even hold onto a man who unplugged toilets for a living."

"At least *my* husband was man enough to file for divorce. Both of yours *died* sooner than live with you, Pork Butt."

"Who are you calling Port Butt? From what I hear, your darling Billy-Joe-Bob-Guido skedaddled the day after you said you wanted to get on top for a change. He didn't want to be thunder-thighed to death."

Heads turned. Every eye in the Hunt Room focused on the hostile pair. I saw Benjamin Winthrop standing open-mouthed with shock at his daughter's language.

"Ah, close your trap before the flies get a head start," Keats-Smythe told him, giving our Richest Member a chummy elbow in the short ribs. "You know damned well Amanda's always been a bitch."

"Well, she can win Best of Show in my ring any day," Bradley announced for all to hear. "Woof, woof." And he made further unseemly comments concerning how he would like to partner her in certain intimate postures with canine implications.

"I wondered how long it would take before Gloria found out Amanda was the one who spread all those nasty rumors about her husband," the elderly widow, Mrs. Denning remarked, pursing her lips at the rim of an Old Fashioned glass. "I hear that's what really broke up the poor child's marriage."

"Oh, as if you weren't right in there repeating every scrap of slander to anyone who'd listen, you old windbag," her companion replied.

"Cousin Katherine, I never!" Mrs. Denning clutched her pearls.

"Ha! You forget, I *know* what you've never. I've

had to live with you all these years because I don't have two red cents to rub together. Trust me, if your father hadn't schneidered my father out of his fortune, I wouldn't be stuck in this jerkwater Connecticut town playing suckup to a swamp-thing like you. 'You've never' my *ass.*"

"I do not gossip!"

"You lie like a rug. *And* you've been secretly ogling that 'poor child' every chance you got, you lecherous cow. What, do you think she'd even *look* at you? Even when you had your own teeth?"

Mrs. Denning countered by ramming her cocktail glass straight into Cousin Katherine's teeth. The fine note of irony was drowned out, alas, by the turmoil fast rising all around them.

Turmoil, riot, devastation, call it what you will. By whatever name, words failed to encompass the full horror of the spectacle now playing itself out before my eyes. Oh, the havoc! Oh, the inhumanity! Oh, the bloodshed! Bloodshed of the very worst, bloodshed most discreet: Bloodshed without blood *being* shed. I have witnessed both, and say with authority that of the two, the honest flow of gore is easier to stanch than the flow of people—dare I say it?—*speaking their minds in polite society.*

Purcell, cousin to the displaced Lucinda Carter-Keats-Smythe, told Keats-Smythe what he really thought of the latter's whilom volleyball instructress mother ("Common little slut."). Keats-Smythe told Purcell what he really thought of Purcell's excellent work in the Episcopal church ("Can't keep your hands off those apple-bottomed choir boys, can you?"). Prescott told Carlysle why hardly anyone would play billiards with him ("You cheat and then you whine when you're caught cheating."). Carlysle coolly remarked, "You'd have to go all the way to Newport before you'd find a bigger cheater than Prescott." He said this to *Mrs*. Prescott, and he accompanied it with a list of female suspects and the name of a good private investigator. There was no telling where it might have ended.

I saw Eames standing with his back to the bar, panic in his eyes. I fought my way through the rabid mob to reach him. "Well, I hope you're satisfied," I growled. "This is where your petty vendetta has brought us!"

"It will be all right," he gasped, his fingers digging into the bar until the knuckles whitened. He did not sound convinced by his own words. "This is merely the effects of the wine—of the wine-god. It will wear off and no one the worse for it. To bring up this entire . . . *faux pas* afterward would not be the Done Thing. People will forget."

"I overheard Bradley telling Benjamin Winthrop that a number of people consider him to be an old fart. He mentioned your name among them. Do you think Winthrop will forget that?"

"Oh, God!" Eames moaned, his brow damp.

"Hey!" the bartender exclaimed. "Where's my knife? I can't slice limes without a knife."

I saw the silvery glint through the crowd. Impending death always manages to draw the eye. The implement was in Amanda's hand. She was breasting the crush with deadly purpose, her gaze fixed on Gloria VanderSee. I was not the only one to note this fresh variation on the disaster now playing itself out in our midst.

"Gloria!" Eames cried, and dove into the press of bodies.

"Amanda!" Bradley exclaimed, and tore himself away from Benjamin Winthrop's apoplectic company to intercept the lady.

"Son, see to that, will you?" Ashtoft Senior nodded toward the heart of the melee and Ashtoft Junior dutifully began to work his way in that direction.

The Fates might not have laughed aloud when all three of the men in question converged upon the embattled ladies at the exact same moment, but I did hear *someone* giggle.

Bradley seized Amanda's wrist and twisted it just as the knife was swiftly descending toward Gloria's heart. Eames flung himself in front of Gloria, shielding her body with his own and baring his chest to a stroke of steel that never came. Amanda let out a sharp cry of pain as the knife clattered to the floor. Her anguish struck Eames more deeply than her blade ever could.

"You cur! How dare you assault a lady?" he demanded, and he punched Bradley right in the nose. Hard.

The rest is history.

Club rumor has it that when Gloria VanderSee, with only self-preservation in mind, stooped to retrieve the fallen knife, her hand brushed that of Ashtoft Junior who was bent on a similar errand. Their fingers touched. Their eyes met. His color rose. They are currently cohabiting somewhere in the suburbs of Los Angeles, where people actually speak freely about their net worth and the only grounds for social ostracism is cellulite.

With the vanishment of Dr. Sonoma, Amanda found herself at liberty to express her thanks for Eames' chivalry to the fullest. The lady must have had quite a way with words, for Eames soon forgot his twice-shattered romantic plans for the proletariat-inclined Ms. VanderSee. Amanda prevailed upon her father to overlook any of Eames' past offenses—real or Bradley-spread calumny. They are to be married in the spring.

That is, they are to be married as soon as the police remove their most recent clutter of detectives from the Club premises. Ever since the unhappy incident in the Hunt Room—which of course no one speaks of— we have been plagued by more than our share of mysterious homicides. Mrs. Denning's Cousin Katherine has no idea how her dear benefactress fell on that fatal fishfork. We discovered Carlysle holding a pool cue in a most unorthodox (and mortal) manner. Purcell met his end when someone took a hymnal and— But it is too painful.

As for Bradley, the unwitting First Cause of these vicissitudes, he, too, is no more. They found his mangled remains in the Hunt Room. A perplexed investigating officer said the victim looked as if he had been mauled to death by some great cat—a lion, for example, or a panther. The gods never were famous for picking up after themselves.

We try not to dwell on it, reserving our ruminations for happier subjects, such as what to give our soon-to-be newlyweds. Silver? China? *Objets d'art?*

Crystal?

FLIGHT
by Jane Yolen

Jane Yolen is the author of almost two hundred children's
books, novels, poetry, and the editor of many anthologies.
She divides her year between Massachusetts and Scotland.

I cannot tell you when I first heard about the winged
horse. I can only tell you about the first time I
rode him. It was a dark, moonless night in Corinth,
for I dared not chance Athena spying me in her
horse's field. She is not the kind to let such daring go
unpunished. The gods only allow favors to those already favored, haven't you noticed? So what chance
had I, being neither well bred nor good looking but
rather scrawny, small, and poor. The gods swat such
mortals like horseflies.

The field was cut through by several streams. Later
it was said that Peg himself had stamped a foot and
forced a fountain. The fountain even had a name—
Hippocrene. Storytellers like to make specific what
they do not know. It lends a certain authenticity to
the tale. But even for a god's horse, that was assuming
much too much. He merely drank at one particular
stream more often than at any of the others, for it
had a well aerated flow of water. I expect the bubbles
tickled his nose. Horses can have a sense of humor,
you know, though that may be difficult for most peo-

ple to understand. Peg certainly did. He liked the kind
of jokes that manifested in snorting and drooling pro-
digiously over someone's new clothes, or dumping an
unsuspecting rider into a still-warm pile of droppings.
Not very sophisticated, of course. But he was only a
horse, after all. I have known shopkeepers and temple
virgins who had even coarser ideas of fun. And my
stepfather, cursed be, used to laugh uproariously
whenever he beat me, as if each stripe on my back
were a laugh line.

I found all the streams in Peg's field by wading
through each and every one unexpectedly. They were
cold and rocky, and my sandals were no proof against
either. But I had never thought that getting through
the night was going to be easy, so I didn't complain.
At least not out loud. I might have caught my breath
once or twice at the chill in the water, let out a whispered curse now and then when I slipped off a stone.
But my heart was already racing just by being in Athena's field uninvited. "No man who is not a god's son
may ride," was what was said about her horse. That
warning was even posted on signs at the field's perime-
ters. So what was a bit of wet, a bit of cold, a twisted
ankle, such minor shocks to the system, compared to
the things an angry goddess might come up with if she
caught you out?

After the fifth stream, I found myself in the main
part of the field at last. I stopped still and listened
hard. Horses are not quiet creatures, not even at night,
not even in sleep. I could hear the harsh rales of his
breathing from halfway across the green. I took my
bearings by that sound, as might a sailor by the
stars.

He could have heard me coming. He certainly
showed no fear. But as I drew closer, his breathing
never changed, though my own did. I could hear it

moving deeper and deeper into my chest. I tried holding my breath so as not to alarm him, though I am sure the *swish-swash* of the grass at my feet had already done enough to alert him. Still, I held my breath as I held my entire body, in a kind of watchful readiness.

And then, before I was quite prepared for it, I was by his side. He was a great furnace of a creature, his white body exuding warmth. Without moonlight he was still aglow, as if lit up from within. I hadn't seen that coming across the field, yet it was all I *could* see now. The whiteness of him. The purity. The glow.

I put out my hand to touch his white flank. He shuddered a bit under my touch, live flesh crawling. But it was just a momentary shiver, and then the skin was still.

His big head slowly turned my way, and he sniffed me all over, starting down at my knees and working his way up until we were finally nose to nose. I put both hands on either side of his big muzzle, and breathed into each nostril. It was something my stepfather, a horse coper, had taught me. Something the poorest of us knows and yet kings never seem to have heard of. Breath to breath with a horse, and he is yours.

Actually, he would *never* be mine. He was Athena's. And one day he would be a hero's. There was no denying that. But tonight—breath in, breath out—he belonged to poor, scrawny me.

He finished his examination at the top of my head, then took a piece of my hair—my long, stringy, no-color hair—into his teeth and yanked. See—that horse sense of humor again.

It hurt, of course, but I laughed. I had to. It really *was* funny. He whinnied back, appreciating my appreciation. Comics do like their bit of applause.

I ran my hand over his head, scratched behind his ears, stroked his neck. Then I spent long minutes untangling the strands of his mane, thinking as I did so how ill-kept this god's horse was when even the meanest of peasants will spend hours braiding his horse's mane for a fair.

"If you were mine," I whispered, "you would have blue ribbons every day and red ones for the holy days." Though of course I had no coins to do any such thing.

He nuzzled me as I worked and I began to sing, one of the old songs from before even Athena's time. My mother's mother had taught it to me. It had to do with the rule of women, and the chorus went

> *"Maiden came I and crone I go,*
> *The wisdom of water is what I know."*

It was not a song I dared sing at home, for it would have meant another beating. My stepfather was not a man who appreciated women, except in his bed. And those he liked well enough, as long as he could master them.

Peg seemed to like the sound of the song, though, and he leaned into me as I sang. Either that or he liked the feel of my fingers in his mane. Or maybe a bit of both.

When at last his hair was untangled, I braided it into twenty small braids, all by feel as there was no light but his own white coat to guide by. And then when he was ready, I led him by the forelock to a large stone I had stumbled over on my way across the field. He stood quietly while I climbed up, first on to the stone, and then onto his back. I was expecting an explosion once I was atop, for he had never been rid-den before, but surprisingly he did not move. He did not even tremble.

"Oh, mighty Peg," I whispered, leaning forward and putting my check down against the arch of his neck.

In response he lifted his great feathered wings till they stretched out on either side of us. He pumped them once, then twice. The wind from those wings was both warm and cold. Still wet from the streams I had crossed, I began to shiver.

But before I could dismount, before I could even *think* about dismounting, he had lifted up, straight up, hovering for a moment like a kestrel over a meadow. Then he took off into the air straight as an arrow. I had barely time to grab hold of his mane and wrap my legs tight around the great vaulted barrel that was his body.

We flew up and up and up above the field, a solid black space below us. Then we flew above the nearby mountains, their jagged peaks black against the blacker sky, with only the flickering stars showing the outlines. And then we were above the clouds themselves, the air about us so cold I could scarcely breathe. I could not call out his name. But I smiled and kept my fingers wound in his mane, my legs clamped to his sides.

The world, which I had always known as dangerous and mean, was far away. For the first time in my life I felt powerful and pure and out of reach. Tears froze on my cheeks, but still I smiled.

Then, suddenly, like a stooping hawk, Peg clipped his wings back and we fell straight down, down, down, the wind screaming against our ears. I thought it was to be my death, but for the life of me could not care.

At the very last moment, Peg unfurled his wings again, like a flag over battle. We floated down to land in the field, so lightly I did not really know when we had reached ground except that he flung his head back, neighed, then trotted over to the stone, to wait patiently for me to dismount.

When I got off, stunned and sore, there was Athena standing tall, grim, unsmiling, her baleful face furious. Even in the dark I could see how she looked, for it was as if she, too, were lighted from within, only it was with a goddess' righteous anger. I thought suddenly how easy and glorious it would have been to have died falling out of the sky and how painful and ugly it was going to be to die on the point of her spear.

"No man who is not a god's son may ride my horse," she said in her doom-filled voice. "I do not think you can make that claim."

I did not speak. Indeed I could not even if I'd wanted to. But Peg whinnied and moved his head close to my body. With his teeth he ripped down the top of my chiton. Another bit of his humor, I supposed as I shivered in the cold. This time I did not smile but put my hands up over my goosefleshed breasts.

"A girl!" Athena cried. "By my father, then you are no *man* at all, and so are under my protection." She had the grace to laugh. It was a golden sound, like a full descending scale on the lyre.

She disappeared, still laughing, leaving me to the cold and to a long, wet walk back over the field and streams to Corinth. I had plenty of time to make up an explanation for my torn chiton, but none came to me. I told my stepfather the simple truth of it but he, used to my lying, did not believe a word of it. Certain another man had had me, he died of his rage, face purple, head down in a manure pile.

I was never certain if that was part of Athena's protection, or her idea of a cosmic joke. She had her horse's sense of humor. But either way it served me well. And that was only my *first* ride.

MANTIK RITES
by Jon DeCles

Jon DeCles is the author of over fifty published works, including the fantasy novel *The Particolored Unicorn*. He has been working with the Greek mystery religions since 1972, and, under the name of Ramfis Firethorn, is the author of *Blindfold On A Tightrope: Men's Myths and Men's Mysteries.*

"Sing, Goddess, of the shortness of life, of the daughters of Night, of the sisters of Death, and how neither herb nor amulet may stay their hands. How Clotho spins a thread of surpassing beauty and strength, and how Lachesis measures it, and how Atropos cuts it off. Sing, Goddess, of the tragedy of life, for how else shall we seize and fix the excellence of a moment so brief?"

He saw me then, standing just inside the portico, dripping rain, and he stopped his singing and put down his lyre and got up from the couch on which he reclined. He came toward me, his lips curled in a smile of welcome that was twisted still by grief. The last time I had seen him he was like a god, golden as Apollon, agile as Hermes; now he seemed to carry his pain like the affliction of Hephaestos, as if it had been with him since birth. His shining hair was, of course, shorn short. His face was lined like that of a man past forty. His chiton, unpinned at the right shoulder, was gray and unornamented. He looked like a laborer who had come fresh from a funeral.

Thus, the Delphis I had known!

"Ion," he said quietly, standing just inside the door. "Take off your clothes and come inside. I will get you dry garments."

I nodded, took off my petasos, letting the rain fall on my head, stripped off my chlamys and chiton, my perizoma, and finally my sandals, then stepped into the shelter of the Hestiatorion naked. A slave had already rushed to the small chambers at the back and returned with a cloth to dry me, as well as a plain chiton with fastenings, simple dry sandals, and a himataeon, to warm me after my journey. I stood while the slave dried the rain off me, then rubbed my body with a fine sheen of oil.

The other men in the room looked at me casually, some wondering about my identity, some about my availability. The room was only half full at this particular time, just before noon. There was an empty couch next to the one Delphis occupied, and I took it. Delphis told the slave to get me food and wine and I pulled the himataeon close around me, for the rain had been cold.

"My friends," Delphis said to the others gathered to eat, "this is Ion, son of Eudamippus, of Alexandria in Egypt. He has come at my request to determine the cause of death of Idas."

There was an uncomfortable silence as the men looked first at me, then toward each other, then back at Delphis. Finally an old man who reclined near the back corner of the room sat up and spoke.

"Noble Delphis," he said. "It is admirable that your love for Idas ran so deep, like a vein of gold that plunges into the earth, so that none may know its extent without a lifetime of labor. But Idas is gone

among the dead, and not even Zeus Himself can
change that. The court of the Prytaneion, in this very
room, has debated the matter and made judgment
against the discus which slew him, and soon the mur-
dering weapon will be taken outside our borders and
broken in punishment for his death. It is time for you
to accept that verdict, and go on with your life. You
are to be married, Delphis, and you owe it to Praxilla
to think now of her, and the children she will bear
you, rather than the lover who is lost to you and who
wanders among the shades in the underworld. Soon
enough will you join him in lamenting the loss of shining life."

It was a harsh message, touching on things that were
not often said; but Delphis accepted it without reply,
as if he had heard it before and had given up on
answers.

I spoke to the old man: "My friend wrote to me
because the oracle told him to question one whom he
loved. Although some years have passed, and our lives
have become separate, he thought perhaps I might be
that one of whom the oracle spoke; for in truth, I have
served the God in that capacity myself, in temples in
several places."

"Ion has served even at Claros," Delphis said. "It
seemed to me that what the God was telling me was
that I must ask my question specifically of one whom
I loved, not merely of the person who was serving in
our temple at this time. Because Ion and I met in
competition at the games on Delos, and there grew
to love one another, I wrote to him and asked him
to come."

The old man sighed. A damp breeze blew in
through the open door and he pulled his himataeon
absently a little tighter, then he spoke to me: "It was
witnessed. They were in a field, just the two of them,

practicing the discus. Delphis threw, and somehow the discus turned in the air and struck Idas in the head. The youth was killed on the instant. Those are the simple facts. If there was aught beyond accident in the matter, it was as in the story of Apollon and Hyakinthos. The North Wind was jealous that the boy loved the God and not Him, and when the God threw, the Wind turned the discus and the lad was struck and killed. There is nothing to be done but lament and make offerings at the grave; yet Delphis pursues, like the Shining Ones after Orestes, seeking a cause beyond cause. What other cause can there be? The villain is either the Wind or the discus. We can punish the discus, but we mortals are powerless to do more than propitiate the Wind."

"There was no wind that day," said Delphis. "And I threw straight. Yet I saw the discus turn in the air, and my cry of warning was too late."

The old man's eyes met mine and he shrugged, then he reclined again. He reached out to the table next to his couch and took the last piece of barley cake from his plate, put it slowly into his mouth, and shook his head, as if inside a dialogue continued that there was no point in offering aloud.

The slave came in with a tray of food for my table, then went to the krater and dipped out a cup of wine for me. I tasted it and noted that the proportions of wine to water were a little stronger than was to my liking, then set the cup down next to a plate of broiled fish.

"It will do no harm," I said, "if I look at the matter once more. If what I see is what has already been seen, then perhaps my friend will take my agreement with the verdict as a seal upon the truth and accept his destiny. But should I find that there is more than has been seen, it will be no discredit to those who have already bent their minds to it. Both truth and justice are such shadowed gods that philosophers spend their lives in their pursuit. If the good people of this place will allow me, I will stay at the home of Delphis, take my meals with him, and offer my sacrifices at the Hearth of Hestia, and at the temple of your oracle and my God. Also will I fulfill whatever else is proper to a guest in your town, in thanks for your hospitality."

The old man fixed me with his dark eyes, then nodded.

"You speak yourself well, Ion of Alexandria," he said. "If by your investigations you can ease the mind of Delphis, who by virtue of his victories in many games we have given Sitesis here in the Prytaneion, then we will all be grateful to you. I will take it upon myself to offer you Xenia here until the Assembly can act upon the matter, so that the expense does not fall upon Delphis, who has other duties to consider. But I would like to know how long you think it will be that we will be feeding you; before you can come to some conclusion?"

"That I cannot predict," I said. "But rest easy regarding the expense. I am not without means, and neither the demos nor my friend will have to feed me. Reserve the Xenia for that time when I have been of use to you, and determined the matter one way or the other. For the moment only tell me what is appropriate to offer at the Hearth, and allow me to send a slave to purchase it."

The old man told me that the usual offering was a kind of incense which was kept in the Prytaneion, so after I finished my meal, I went out of the Hestiatorion, through the portico (where the rain had stopped), along the courtyard, and in through the second portico, to the chamber where the Hearth of Hestia was kept. I paid the attendant for a proper amount of incense, scattered barley grains upon the Undying Flame to bind me to the demos of the place, then made my offering.

"Hestia, Thine is always the First and the Last."

The home of Delphis was not luxurious, but it did befit an athlete who had brought to his people crowns of victory from two of the Panhellenic Games: those at Nemea and Olympia. The altar to Zeus Ephestios in his courtyard was built of fine white stone, finished smooth and carved with a relief showing athletes making sacrifice before the God. The scene was painted in the most beautiful and lifelike colors, and the crown upon the brow of Zeus was leafed with gold, as was the throne upon which He sat. The Hearth, beyond the altar and to the back, was equally well wrought, with a relief on the wall behind showing Hestia tending the Hearth on Olympus. The colors of that relief were more luminous as the rain did not touch them indoors. The stool on which Hestia sat was also leafed in gold, making clear the respect in which Zeus holds his elder sister; even as do we mortals.

Delphis gave to my use a room of goodly size and a slave named Euadne, who was quite beautiful and shy. She knew the town well and answered my questions without hesitation; but because of her shyness it was arranged that another slave, Moeris, should fetch anything I might need from outside the house. Both she and he made it clear that their bodies were available for my pleasure, considering the long journey I had undertaken: but as I was to seek the privilege of the mantik art, I was already entering into the period of abstinence which preceded the ritual. The only special services which I required of them centered on my diet, which from the moment of entry into the house

of Delphis I turned to one of fruits, vegetables and
grains, with only pure water to drink; and those inquir-
ies which I made concerning the life of my friend, and
which he might not understand, being the subject of
his own existence.

Alas, there was little to learn!

Delphis lived such a life as one might expect of an
athlete who was pious rather than ambitious. His days
were filled with exercise and study. Both his parents
were dead, a thing which had already touched him
with tragedy, and he was not yet married. He had not
fixed on one philosophy as yet, so there was no single
teacher who might be regarded as his mentor. Though
most schools were represented in the town, there was
no single philosopher of such skill or brilliance as to
stand out from the rest. It was natural enough that his
life should have been centered upon his lover, and
therefore that the death of that lover should have
struck him such a blow.

Delphis introduced me at the gymnasion where he
exercised and to some degree the old warmth that had
been between us at Delos was rekindled. We mas-
saged the olive oil on each other's skin before we
began, and each tossed the small handful of dust into
the air for the other, so that each might step through
the little cloud and acquire the light coating that
would absorb sweat and make the grip in the wrestling
less slippery. He still favored the red dust, and I still
favored the yellow, which some say has no particular
virtue to health but which makes the wearer look
good.

Delphis outdistanced me at the racing with ease. He
was *still* an athlete of some contention, whereas I had
long ceased to be a serious competitor. I managed to
come close to him with the akon, but I was pitiful
when we practiced the long jump. I was not surprised

that he asked to practice his discus alone on the field:
nor were any of the others who were present.

In the palaestra he came closer to his old self, our
bodies straining against one another in the wrestling
with that sublime tension of contact, that intensity,
that is a part of sex excerpted and elevated to an art
of its own. He was able to throw me, but not without
some effort; and I was pleased.

We scraped other's sweat and dust away, rinsed off
the residue, then relaxed in the hot water until the
euphoria of exercise had mellowed to that state of
tranquillity which only comes after the total engagement of the body.

"Would you like for me to meet Praxilla?" I
asked him.

"Yes," he said. "I would like that very much."

"If it would not displease you," I added, "I would
like to speak with her alone."

The beauty of Praxilla astonished me.

Her lustrous black hair was coiled atop her head
with ropes of white-and-gold beads such as were
traded by the Phoenicians in olden times. Her skin
was flawless as ivory from Carthage. Her features were
even, her nose straight, her cheekbones high; her eyes
glowed with the golden fire of dark amber, a brown
that has captured sunlight and made it the prisoner of
passion. Her neck was an Ionic column rising from
the elaborately worked peplos of white and gold that
graced her subtly rounded body. Her arms were like
strong white serpents, moving with easy grace under
the weight of golden bracelets set with polished jet.
The girdles that enwrapped her narrow waist were
woven of silver thread with just a touch of gold, and
fastened with clasps set with white opals. When she
walked, her feet appeared more graceful than the

prancing hooves of mountain does, her sandals mar-
vels of the leather worker's art, set with small pieces
of polished pink coral.

When she spoke, her voice was rich and flowing as
honey from Hymmetos, and I wondered what Muse
had been her mother.

"Delphis has told me that you have come to ease
his pain," she said, taking a seat on a stool opposite
the couch where I reclined.

"That is true," I said.

"Then tell me, if you will, what it is that you will
do to accomplish this thing."

"First," I replied, "I will see for myself all the circumstances of what came to pass, so that I will better
understand what happened. I have seen the field
where Idas was struck down. I have been to the room
where they usually honored Pan, and to the gymnasion
and the palaestra where they exercised. Today I come
to ask you if there was any thing which you noticed
which might have contributed to Idas' death being
other than an accident. I will then look upon the discus itself, and in the end I will use such tools as I
have learned to seek the truth of the matter."

"You will ask of the oracle?"

"I will *serve* the oracle," I said. "I have the training
to drink the waters and to let the God speak
through me."

She shrugged her lovely shoulders and looked away.

"I do not understand," she said, "why it should be
necessary to question the oracle again. Once has my
Delphis asked his questions of the God, and the God
gave him reply. Is it not impious to press the question twice?"

I smiled.

"It may well be," I said gently. "But the God is not
noted for giving answers that are easily understood.

Apollon told Delphis to question one whom he loved, and he knew that I had served in mantike, even at Claros; so he took the answer to mean that he must question me, rather than that one who drinks the waters here."

She took her lower lip between her teeth as if she wanted to speak but held back her words.

"Come," I prompted. "If there is any small thing you observed, it may be of importance."

"Well, then," she said, "it is this: Delphis once told me that the Gods had blessed him above all men in giving him a youth to love more beautiful even than Ganymede and a woman to wed more beautiful than all save Aphrodite. Such talk I know to be only the delight of a young man in his good fortune; but the myths tell us that the Gods do not take lightly such boasting as may verge on hubris, which they hold to be the greatest of crimes against Their sovereignty. Might it not be that Delphis has offended the Gods, and that Idas' death may be a punishment?"

I shuddered with a sudden coldness that came of fear. Was it possible that my friend could be so completely without the law of common sense that he could make comparison between himself and the Gods? True, the form of the words which Praxilla related was such that Delphis held the Gods responsible, and in honor, for his good fortune; but who, other than Zeus Himself, could know the intent of the spirit dwelling in Delphis' breast that formed such words? Fair words might well be formed by a foul soul, and the form of the words not quite contain the soul's condition!

"Your words are such as to cause me some concern," I said soberly. "I thank you for what you have said, and I will seek to discover if what you suspect is the case. If it should be, then I will also seek to find what remedies may be taken; for you must remember that Apollon is a God of Reconciliation as well as of prophecy, and if it is within His power, He will offer some method of recompense whereby such offenses may be mitigated."

As I left the home of Praxilla's parents, I placed my hand upon the upright phallus of the Herm before their door, and prayed that Hermes might guide my steps upon the unclear path that I pursued.

The Assembly of the town gave its permission for me to examine the guilty discus before its exile and destruction, so I returned to the Prytaneion in the company of the old man, who, as I had suspected, was an Archon. The Priestess of Hestia was present, to be sure no pollution occurred through the presence of the convicted murderer, and there were slaves present as well, to hold up lamps that were lit with fire other than the pure fire in the Hearth of Hestia.

The discus had been wrapped carefully in silk. Not the fine silk made by the unwinding of the cocoons of the silkworms, but the coarse kind that is produced by worms fed on oak trees in the islands; the kind that is carded like wool and woven the same way. It is still silk, and it still has the strength to insulate those powers called magical, whether for good or ill.

They put it on a small table and unwrapped it so that I might see.

There was nothing whatever remarkable about it, save the stain. It was a common clay discus, like those that can be bought near any gymnasion. Handling it with a fold of the silk, I turned it over, but found nothing unusual on the reverse either.

"Bring the light closer," I said, bending to examine the stain more closely.

"Take care!" warned the Priestess. "It has done

murder, and if you touch it, you will have to be purified!"

I knew well the apotropaic rites that I should have to undergo if I should become polluted by the evil thing before me, so I was most careful not to touch it. Yet upon close examination I noticed something odd about the stain. At the edge of the clot of blackened blood and hair there was a smudge of red. A red such as might be mistaken for blood if the blood were fresh.

"What is this color?" I asked. "This red beneath the blood? Is there one in this town who marks his work with such a color?"

My question caused consternation. The Archon and the Priestess both bent carefully to look at what I had described, but neither could fathom the meaning of it.

"I shall ask at all the shops where discoi are made," the Archon said at last. "It may be nothing. But as you have called it to our attention, our attention it deserves. Word will be sent to you if something is discovered."

Neither the Archon nor the Priestess, nor I, had any idea what the red smudge might mean; but so far it was the only thing I had found that was in any way different from what was already known; and therefore that *might,* indeed, provide a source for Delphis' concern, beyond his grief.

I was introduced to the woman who served as the voice of the God at the local oracle, and to the thespode who put the words that came from her mouth into verse. She served, as well, as priestess, for the town was not large and there was no need for a large staff. She told me the details of the cultis practice, most of which were familiar, and I began the preparation necessary to open myself to that mind which alone knows the mind of Zeus.

I bathed alone at dawn but left off the oil. I put on a chiton of clean white linen and went to the temple, where I was shown to a small room containing only a low cot and pitchers of pure water, and a simple altar for the offering of incense. I made my preliminary sacrifice of fresh leaves, from the daphnoi which grew at the back of the temple, then I began my fast and my meditations upon the God.

At Claros the statues of the Gods are gigantic. That of Apollon depicts the God seated, naked, and with His lyre. The statue in the small temple in which I meditated was of the ancient style, standing upright with one foot forward, the nude form of the sublime athlete with a joyous smile upon his countenance. It was that form which I held in my mind for the most part, though other depictions from other places also came into my consciousness as I waited through the day and the night before the ritual.

Eventually, as will always happen, the image of the stone figure transformed in my thoughts to that of the God Himself, that living, breathing entity Who is the inspiration for each artist in stone or paint or poetry; that One Who casts the shadow which poor mortals vainly seek to duplicate. He is a God of light, and when He comes, it is like the sun appearing out of dark clouds or the heat of a blazing fire appearing out of winter ice.

There is no other need or substance to the time in which a God comes into one's spirit. It is sufficient.

But eventually the priestess came to my chamber to tell me that Delphis had made his sacrifice of a young bull, and had fulfilled the full purifications that would allow him to enter the outer cave during the ritual. I rose and followed her into the chamber where the statue stood, looked up at Him with ever renewing wonder, then went out to the altar that stood before the front steps.

The crowd which dined upon the larger part of the sacrifice fell silent when I appeared. I took the branch of daphne which the priestess held in hand and added it to the sacrificial fire, then the priestess led me down the steps and to the side of the temple, where the thespode waited with my friend; though by this point I barely recognized him through the distance that grew between my mind and my surroundings.

The priestess opened a low door in the stone base of the high temple. Into my mind came the image of a similar aperture at Claros, where one entered a passage so low that one had to bend double to traverse it. At Claros the passage was vaulted with sky blue marble, and twisted seven times before one reached the first chamber. In the town where now I stood there was nothing so elaborate. One bent a little to walk the tunnel of gray stone, and it turned at angles three times before we reached the cave, where a single stone bench allowed the petitioner to hear whatever transpired at the spring.

Delphis sat on the bench and stared at me, hard. The priestess opened another door, and I went through, followed by her and the thespode, who carried the small oil lamp which lit our way, as well as his wax tablet for writing. The priestess closed the door, leaving Delphis outside in the dark, and I seated myself on a low, three-legged stool, the ritual tripod of this place.

The spring was edged with fitted white stones and a wooden cup sat to one side. I took the cup and drank deep of the water of the spring while the Priestess fed leaves to a small charcoal fire in a miniature tripod to the side. I inhaled the sharp smoke and drank again, and focused my mind on the light of the God. I opened my mouth and relaxed my throat, letting the breath move in and out of me the way a singer breathes before giving voice.

A guttural sound came out of my throat, and I knew what words to say, and then I began to speak.

It is thus: At first you are present, and you wonder whether the words are only things you *want* to say, whether your own mind is speaking rather than that of the God. You can hear and you can feel and you can think about what is happening. But after a while you are no longer present, and what is proceeding is at a distance, as if you are in a place with thin gray draperies that separate you from your body and your mind.

In the end you are not there at all. And when you return, those things which you were sure were part of your own thinking are gone, remembered only as patches of mist from a drifting dream, and then only briefly. By the time you have come to yourself, those fragments of memory which remain are only of the substance of things remembered from long ago, like the shadows of toys from childhood, or the kiss of one whose name has vanished.

I became aware in the small room at the back of the temple. I was sitting on the low cot with a low table in front of me, and there was food, and wine. The priestess sat beside me, her arm wrapped around my shoulder, tucking the folds of a heavy wool himataeon about me to drive off the icy cold of my limbs.

"What did the God say?" I managed to choke out, when I felt at last that my voice was again my own.

The thespode, who stood near by, gave troubled answer: "The same words as before. That Delphis must question one whom he loves."

*   *   *

There is more than one kind of mantike. The oracles of Apollon most usually give voice, and speak through a seer. The oracles of Zeus are often issued through a sign; the movements of birds, the entrails of a sacred victim. Those of Aesclapius come to the sick in dreams, when they sleep in the temple of the God; so that in the morn the priest may interpret, and prescribe what treatment the God has recommended.

But there are always exceptions, when a God will choose another way of setting forth a truth; and that night, in the temple of Apollon, I dreamed.

Beneath the full moon a woman runs down a dusty road. Dogs run beside her, and stags, and bears. She wears the short chiton of a youth rather than the proper peplos of a woman, and she has a hunter's horn slung over her shoulder by a thong. In her hand is an unstrung bow.

She comes to a place where the road forks. Three roads lead off from this place, and in the center stones are piled. Another woman waits, and she, too, has dogs. She, also, is beautiful, but she wears a dark peplos figured with a pattern of barley sheaves worked in pearls. She points to the sky.

The huntress strings her bow and lets fly an arrow. Swift as an eagle it wings toward the moon. Against the brightness the arrow strikes, and down falls—a discus!

I am standing beside the road. Next to me a bearded man with red hair laughs. He offers me a branch, a wand with leaves. I stare at it, recognize the herb.

I awoke.

I knew by her eyes that Praxilla comprehended the nature of the thing which Delphis held toward her. I knew by *his* eyes the terror he felt at holding it. Praxilla's parents stood in mute rage to either side of her, while the Archon and I waited beside Delphis for the ceremony to be fulfilled.

"Apollon has said that I must question one whom I love," Delphis said miserably.

"And Hermes," I added, "has said that whoever is questioned must be compelled to tell the truth."

Without waiting, Delphis reached out the branch and touched Praxilla's shoulder with it, and the power of the herb was engaged.

Tears made the girl's eyes glisten. They were more like jewels than ever. But jewels are not soft, they are hard, and they can be sharpened into points for spears or made into blades for daggers.

"Very well," Praxilla said, lifting her head with a bitter pride. "You compel me, and so I will give you a truth which the philosophers can never reason out. Most women are content to share the love of men; but some are not! Some women wish with all their hearts to possess the man they love as surely as he possesses the horses which draw his chariot in a race, or the home in which he seeks to house his wife. I have witnessed the anguish of my mother on those nights when my father dines with other men, discussing love and such things thought too important for his wife to share!"

"Praxilla!" her mother cried out, trying to stem the flood, but it was useless.

"I have witnessed the limits which my father places on his love for her, because custom demands it, and he cannot fight against that which he approves!"

"Praxilla!" her father said, his face a mask of shock.

"You have said that you love me, Delphis! But when you spoke of beauty, you spoke of Idas as one as beautiful as Ganymede, the favored lover of Zeus; yet of me you made comparison as *second* to Aphrodite, not as equal! No more could I tolerate that,

Delphis, than I could tolerate sharing you with a con-
cubine. Oh, Delphis, foolish man! Can you not see the
passion in my heart for you? Can you not see a
woman strong in her desire for you as Medea was for
Jason; and as willing to use the powers of Heaven and
Earth to secure you?"

The herb dropped from Delphis' hand to the floor,
but it was no longer needful.

"With the thick black blood of the blasphemous
dead did I anoint your discus, writing on it the name
of Idas! On a plate of lead also I wrote his name, and
smeared it with the poison of serpents that I killed
upon the tombs of those who died unnatural deaths!
Unbinding my hair, I drove a nail through that leaden
charm, and buried it at a triple crossroads, that I might
conjure Hecate to my aid in the enterprise. I covered
the writing on your discus in the red dust you wear
at the palaestra, that you, yourself, be compelled to
loose the curse! Then I prayed to Artemis by the
Moon, that Her wild hunt would bring down mine
enemy, whom you loved more than me! All this,
Delphis, have I done, and would I do again, to make
myself the single subject of your love!"

So confessed Praxilla.

And yet I did not see before me a monster, but
rather, a beautiful young woman with tears flowing
down her cheeks, as much the subject of the tragedy
as was Medea in whose name she spoke.

Delphis sank to his knees, weeping.

Praxilla's mother turned and left the room, her face
still and white. I could not imagine what emotions
must flow through her breast. Praxilla's father also left
the room, but from his expression I feared more rage
than anguish.

"I will go," said the Archon, strangely restrained
considering what he had heard. "I will return with

men to take her to a prison, to await her trial." Then
he, too, left the room.

There was quiet but for the weeping, then Delphis
stood and another kind of quiet seemed to seize him.

"You must know, Praxilla," he said, "just what the
limits of my love for you have been, and what they
have not. If you stay here, they will kill you for the
murderer you are. I would not live to see that happen.
You must go, and quickly. In my house there is
money. You know where I keep it. Go there and take
it, and disguise yourself as something you are not. A
slave. A traveler of some kind. Your skills will teach
you. Leave the town quickly. Go by unknown tracks.
My love cannot help you beyond your freedom, but
you will know at least that it was truly love, even to
giving you your life despite the death of Idas."

Praxilla looked to me, but I had no comfort for her.
She looked again to Delphis, but what she sought in
him she had already sacrificed. She nodded once, then
went out through the door her mother had taken.

What arts the woman practiced none may know,
nor where she learned them. Such knowledge is more
common than is thought, and far more widely spread.
Her arts sufficed, and she was never found, nor was
any of the money that Delphis proffered her taken
from its cache.

The Archon's offer of Xenia in the Prytaneion was
never fulfilled, but then, I did not expect that it would
be. Neither Delphis nor I had satisfactory explanation
when questioned about Praxilla's disappearance. It
was enough that the Assembly did not pursue the
matter.

Praxilla's parents moved away within a few days,
and I have never sought to know where they went or
how they fared.

Delphis had a hero shrine built at the grave of Idas, and the last time I saw him, he was there, making offerings.

I do not know if there was hubris in his breast when to Praxilla he boasted of the good fortune the Gods had given him, but I spent much time as I returned to Alexandria meditating upon the matter, and to this day I still do.

HARPIES DISCOVER SEX
by Deborah Wheeler

Deborah Wheeler has been a frequent contributor to the *Sword and Sorceress* volumes and other anthologies. Her novels, *Jaydium* and *Northlight*, are published by DAW Books.

A ello, whose name means storm, floated through her dreams, swirls of darkness and light, earth and water, jumbled half-formed memories of the very beginning of time. The constant motion of the four Elements, forming and reforming, filled her with joy.

"Awake, snatchers! Awake, sisters of darkness!"

The voice, arrogant and male, shattered the tumultuous harmony. Vaguely, Aello sensed her body, the surrounding cave, her head tucked beneath one iron-pinioned wing. As she'd slept, her physical form became unstable, as it tended to do when she immersed herself in primal chaos. Quickly she reabsorbed the ass' ears and jellyfish tentacles. With a vulture's razor talons, she clenched her twisted olivewood perch. Deep scratches, accumulated over the centuries, marked the pale wood.

The sun rose beyond the eastern rim of the Cretan hills, revealing the modern world in all its static form: rocks, dried weeds, sky, the whitened bones of some pathetic hero or other, come to slay the monster Harpies in their den.

"Awake!"

At Aello's side, Celeno, whose name means darkness, ruffled her feathers and opened sleepy, disgruntled eyes.

Against the waning blackness of the cave, a shimmer of gold appeared, condensing into the shape of a swan. For an instant, the bird's head turned to that of a bull, horns sweeping wide.

Zeus.

Aello blinked. The god took on his usual form, this time naked except for blue flowers threaded in his beard and a tiny silver thunderbolt dangling from one ear.

"Drat!" Celeno muttered under her breath. "What does *he* want?"

He would want something, Aello thought. These new upstart gods always did. Why they couldn't settle for being elemental forces, she'd never understood, perhaps because she herself was so close to the origin of things. That crowd on Olympus were bent on separating *this* from *that,* man from nature, male from female, nothing but difference and distance.

Zeus glared at Aello's chest and cleared his throat. She looked down at the purple warts which had sprouted in her sleep.

The humans depicted the Harpies as having the talons of vultures and the faces and bared breasts of women. It was certainly what people had come to expect. Aello and her sisters couldn't very well come swooping down as butterfly hummingbirds and get the same terrified reaction. Once they'd tried something more creative, a concoction of scorpion pincers, sea cucumber bodies, and clusters of giant eightfold spider eyes. Very admirably it had worked, too, except the priests complained to Zeus and he'd forbidden any more experiments.

Now Aello altered her wonderfully textured and colorful warts to resemble human breasts. Underneath the curved pink flesh lay pouches for carrying away food, one of the ways Zeus commanded the Harpies to harass the disobedient.

Zeus smiled and waggled his eyebrows at her. "I've got a job for you."

"Someone else to harass for breaking some law which should never have been made in the first place," Celeno grumbled. "Why don't you do your own dirty work?"

"You *are* my dirty work!" Zeus smiled even more broadly. "Why else do you have such a stench?"

At least, Aello thought, Zeus was in a good mood today. He'd probably caught whatever unfortunate female creature he was running after with those ridiculous flowers in his beard.

Sex again! Dividing everything into "innies" and "outies"! What was the point of it all?

"Let's get on with it," she said. "Who do we go after this time?"

"Phineus, the blind King of Eastern Thrace, has been a naughty boy."

As Zeus filled in the details, it sounded to Aello like the usual story of bestowing prophecy on some poor fool, as if that somehow balanced out the loss of vision, and then placing all kinds of restrictions on what he was allowed to say without telling him what they were.

"What did Phineus do that was so awful?" Aello asked.

"He revealed that which only the gods should know." Zeus repeated the traditional formula.

"So what was it?"

"The recipe for apple strudel."

It took a lot to astonish Aello. She baited, her wings

churning the air. "But the Greeks don't *eat* apple strudel."

"Not yet, they don't." The god frowned. "*I* get to say who eats apple strudel and who doesn't."

"You'll want the usual treatment, I suppose?" Celeno said. "Screeching, laying waste to croplands, carrying off banquets, befouling what we leave behind?"

"You got it, sweetie." Zeus pointed a finger at Celeno and winked. Then his form dissolved into a curtain of confetti.

With a clashing of metallic feathers, the third Harpy flew into the cave. Ocypete, whose name means speed, glanced nervously from one sister to the other.

"Uh-oh!" Ocypete said. "Zeus again?"

"Who else?" Aello shrugged.

"Well, he can wait for his petty revenge," Celeno said. "I want to know how the plans for the cousins' reunion are coming along."

Aello had mixed feelings about family gatherings, as she had about just about everything else. Iris was a sweet creature, if untidy, scattering her rainbows everywhere, but the other relatives could be temperamental when provoked.

"Scylla absolutely insists we hold it at her place," Ocypete said. "Charybdis is in one of those *moods* again and refuses to travel."

"We had it there last time," Celeno whined. The mermaid Sirens hadn't minded, as anywhere near water and handsome sailors suited them just fine, but the Gorgons had put up an immense fuss and almost ruined things for everyone. There were few things as off-putting as the sight of a headful of sulking snakes.

"Let's worry about the reunion later. There's work to do," Aello said, spreading her wings. Celeno and Ocypete followed.

Aello loved flying. The sky lightened to that pellucid shade which held all colors. Her wings beat strongly, sending their rhythm through her body.

After the bright surging foam of the sea, the rocky coast seemed dreary, giving Aello the itch to mix things up. The place could stand an infusion of Water and Fire. Inland had once been fertile, vineyards and strips of golden wheat, but now lay waste. It looked suspiciously as if the landowners had decided that having a prophetic king was enough in itself to ensure prosperity, and had simply abandoned their fields.

They reached the city of Salmydessus. Instead of gleaming white walls and neat tile roofs, beds of bright green rosemary and oregano, a heavy veil of dust, dead vines, and spiderwork cracks dulled every surface. The palace roof was in terrible repair. From inside, Aello caught the smells of roasted goatmeat and pastries, fermented fruits, and toasted nuts.

Ocypete made a quick circuit and decided that the windows were a bit narrow for a suitably spectacular entrance.

"Then we're stuck with the crash-through-the-roof maneuver," said Celeno, whose feet always hurt afterward. "On the count of three—"

Together they hurled themselves at the weakest point of the roof and burst into the central hall, shrieking political slogans in Neanderthal. Sometimes Celeno got a little confused and switched to Esperanto, not that the humans noticed the difference. They gibbered and cowered just the same.

In the hazy dust-laden light, Aello spotted King Phineus sitting at the head of the banquet table. A strip of linen embroidered in crimson-and-gold thread covered his eyes. He himself could have benefited from a little culinary restraint earlier in life. Missing a banquet or two wouldn't hurt him a bit.

A pair of armed guards rushed forward, poking

their spears upward. Laughing, Aello dodged their thrusts. She was tougher than a few bronze points. Meanwhile, Ocypete stuffed food into the pockets beneath her breasts with her usual speed and Celeno took out her temper on the servitors, slashing at them with her talons. Within a few minutes, the room emptied of all except the Harpies and the hapless king.

"My doom has come upon me!" Phineus flailed about with his arms. "Cried the Lady of Shalott!"

"Look, Kingie," Aello said, settling on the whole roasted kid and inserting chunks into her chest pouches. The inner linings flooded the air with pleasure pheromones. Phineus covered his nose and mouth. "You might as well get used to it. You've managed to piss Zeus off, and *we* are what happens."

"Liberté! Egalité! Fraternité!" cried the hapless Phineus.

His utterances made a bizarre kind of sense to Aello. After all, wasn't prophecy the ability to see into the future. Zeus just hadn't said *how far* or *which* future. Phineus' subjects, being human, would undoubtedly manage to make sense out of whatever he said.

"Are we done yet?" Celeno demanded. The walnuts in the *baklava* gave her hives and she was anxious to dump it in the first available ocean. She ruffled her wings, releasing more gusts of pheromones. By now, every bit of food left on the table reeked.

"Tomorrow and tomorrow and tomorrow, creeps on this petty pace," Phineus moaned.

Aello launched herself into flight. "Sit tight, Kingie. We'll be back!"

"Sink the *Bismarck!*" was the King's reply.

Ocypete shot Aello a quizzical expression as they sped back toward Crete. "And this is going to go on for a long time?"

"Until Zeus says enough," Celeno grumbled.

"Or we find some way out of it," said Aello. For the first time, she resented the shared origins which made her subject to the will of the gods. Division and separation seemed like an excellent idea.

The commute itself quickly became tedious, even for hyperactive Ocypete, so they moved to the mainland, where Celeno discovered a new allergy to blooming rosemary. For a time, Aello diverted herself by sorting Phineus' utterances by chronological period, although she never could decide where to put "Ba Ba LOO."

Then the heroes came, as if Torture by Harpy were a magnet for their kind. They were mostly bearded and half-naked, hoping to win Phineus' kingdom and his daughter's hand in marriage, only Phineus didn't have a daughter and by this time the palace was in truly decrepit condition. The Harpies' daily forays through the roof and back out again, chest pouches bulging with whatever the kitchen had concocted that night, had enlarged the opening considerably.

The heroes bore the usual swords and shields, which they applied vigorously and with no particular degree of accuracy. They also swaggered, used bad language, and had obviously not bathed in far too long.

"And they say *we* smell bad," Celeno muttered as they rested beneath the crumbling Bronze Age tomb that was their temporary den, discussing the latest forays.

Aello closed her eyes and pretended to be sleeping. Ocypete had gone off to calm Scylla about having to put off the reunion yet again. As long as the heroes kept coming regularly, they couldn't reschedule. By the time Zeus relented or Phineus died of starvation, they'd all be downright happy to hold it in Hades.

She sensed a disturbance in Salmydessus. The clashing of swords and body armor, the tramp of sandaled feet. And food—a shipload of supplies. A new band of heroes had arrived. It was time to get back to work.

As Aello and Celeno neared the town, Aello noted the difference in this bunch. She wondered if they'd come to rescue Phineus like the others, or to consult him about a noble quest. Something shone from within the intruders, a glimmering like gold; two even bore the unmistakable stamp of godly ancestry. She'd never felt anything like them, as if a cold, delicious wind lifted her pinions. Part of the wonderful sensation was the *response* it evoked within her.

She said as much to Celeno as they circled above the ruined palace. Celeno snorted, in a worse mood than usual because they had to cover for Ocypete's absence.

Aello swooped into the hall, her eyes adjusting instantly to the dim light. Phineus cowered in his throne, now a pathetic wreck of a man. Even the bandage over his eyes had turned dingy. But this time he was surrounded by a band of warriors in gleaming breastplates.

"Jason! They've come!"

"Defend the King!"

Swords leaped from scabbards. Celeno screeched and dodged the nearest blade, talons extended.

"Behind you!" the one named Jason shouted.

In a single graceful movement, the Greek raised his shield. Celeno swerved just in time. Nimbly, she dipped to gather up a basketful of dried figs. Pheromones from her chest pouches filled the air. The men's faces contorted, but they held their positions.

"Workers of the world, unite! You have nothing to lose but your chains!" Phineus gibbered.

Aello grabbed a pile of round loaves of bread and assessed the situation. Clearly, this was not a disorderly band like the others. Golden-headed Jason gave his orders in a calm, ringing voice and was obeyed instantly. Within moments, two of the heroes had raised their shields to cover Phineus from attack. Others moved around the table in a coordinated maneuver, setting the pattern for the defense. Unenthusiastically, Aello started another run at the table.

A hero appeared before her, his bared arms glimmering like marble. She backstroked, scenting immortality in his blood. His face, although contorted in battle fury, was comely, the silvery curls forming a halo. But the most astonishing thing was that he had thrown back his short cloak to reveal . . . wings.

Wings?

Out of the corner of her eye, Aello noticed a second winged warrior bearing down on Celeno, but dared not stay to watch. Her own pursuer was closing fast. She dodged sword thrust and stayed just out of reach. Her heart beat unaccountably fast.

"What manner of man are you?" she cried.

"I am Zetes, son of Boreas, the North Wind!"

Aello had heard rumors, mostly from the Sirens, about Boreas' exploits among the nymphs, but she'd never encountered one of the inevitable results. She had no time for any questions now, for Zetes appeared to be in deadly earnest about his mission to protect Phineus.

Fine. She'd let him chase her off and then complain to Zeus there was nothing she could do about it. They'd be off the case and enjoying the cousins' reunion within the week. Celeno must have had the same idea because she bolted from the palace, the second winged warrior practically on her tail feathers.

Aello's wings beat strongly, carrying her toward the roof opening. Zetes followed a heartbeat behind. She burst through the clouds and into crystalline blue sky. Hovering, she turned to face Zetes again.

Suddenly, Aello forgot poor Phineus, forgot Zeus and his peremptory commands. Let Jason go on to whatever glory awaited him. She had far more interesting things to consider.

The hero before her was neither man nor god, but a glorious combination. Gleaming wings stroked the air rhythmically, a drum beat. Wisps of clouds clung to him like bits of dream-stuff, air and flesh and water churning most enticingly. He was born of the union of air and nymphly flesh, just as she was the product of earth and sea. She had never felt so fully herself and at the same time so unique.

Ever since the Olympus gods had started separating *this* from *that,* rupturing the patterns of elemental chaos, she had resisted the very concept of difference. Resisted it. Resented it.

It had never occurred to her that *difference* might be the basis for attraction. Or that without separation, there could be no coming together, no completion of one another.

Maybe, Aello thought, there was something to this male-female business after all. Curious, she drew closer.

Something in her responded to Zetes like a resonant chord. The flesh of her body, malleable, began to take on a complementary shape. Without her conscious will, she shifted form, chest pouches into voluptuous breasts tipped by rosy nipples, and softened the contours of lips and cheek.

"Begone!" Zetes shouted again. "Begone, foul destroyer . . ." His voice trailed off.

"Yes, men call me foul when I carry out Zeus' foul orders," she pointed out.

"But you are not foul, as the legends say. You are fair, O most splendid winged one, so fair . . ."

As they talked, they drew closer, wings fluttering. Aello's body continued to change, to . . . *respond*. Curves matched to his, softness to his hard muscle. His breath stirred the delicate feathers on her neck. He touched one of her breasts confidently, but with wonder. The most delicious sensations flooded through her, so unexpected that she knew she could not have imagined them. Smiling, she enfolded him in her wings.

Together they possessed three of the four Elements, Air and Earth and Water, aching to be recombined.

They would make their own Fire.

IN THE QUIET AFTER MIDNIGHT
by Charles de Lint

Charles de Lint has been producing finely crafted novels of
contemporary urban fantasy for years now. He is a resident
of Ottawa, Canada, the setting for many of his stories. His
latest book is *Trader.*

I'm fifteen when I realize that I don't remember my
mother anymore. I mean, I still recognize her in
pictures and everything, but I can't call her face up
just before I fall asleep the way I once did. I used to
tell her about my day, the little things that happened
to me, all the things I was thinking about, and it made
the loneliness seem less profound—having her listening, I mean. Now I can't remember her. It's like
she isn't inside me anymore, and I don't even know
when she went away.

I still remember I had a mother. I'm not stupid. But
the immediacy of the connection is gone. Now it's
like something I read in a history book in school, not
something that was ever part of my life, and it scares
me because it was never supposed to go away. She
was always supposed to be with me.

It's a seriously hot day in the middle of June, and
I'm walking home from school when it hits me, when
it stops me dead in my tracks right there in the middle
of the sidewalk, near the corner of Williamson and

Kelly. I can't tell you what makes it come to me the way it does, so true and hard, bang, right out of nowhere. But all of a sudden it's like I can't breathe, like the hot air's pressing way too close around me.

I look around—I don't know what I'm looking for, I just know I have to get off the street, away from all the people and their ordinary lives—and that's when I see this little Catholic church tucked away on a side street. Kelly Street was a main thoroughfare years ago, back when the church was really impressive, too, I guess. Now they're both looking long neglected.

I don't know why I go in. I'm not even Catholic. But it's cool inside, dark after the sunlight I just left behind, and quiet. I sit down in a pew near the back and look up toward the front. I've heard of the Stations of the Cross, but I don't know what they are, if they're even something you can see. But I see Jesus hanging there, front and center, a statue of his mother off to one side, pictures of the saints. I wonder which one is the patron of memory.

I bring my gaze back to the front of the church. This time I look at the candles. There must be thirty, forty of them, encased in short red glasses. Only five or six are lit. They're prayers, I'm guessing, or votive offerings. Whoever lit them doesn't seem to be around.

I slouch in the pew and stare up at the vaulted ceiling. It's easier to breathe in here, the world doesn't seem to press down on me the way it did outside, but the sick lost feeling doesn't go away.

I don't know how long I've been sitting there, when there's a rustle of cloth behind me. I turn to see a hooded man kneeling, two pews back, head bent in prayer. He's all in black, cloak and hood, shadows swallowing his features. A priest, I think, except they don't dress like that, do they? At least none of the ones I've ever seen—on the street or in the movies.

Maybe he's not even a man, I find myself thinking. Maybe he's a she, a nun, except they don't dress like that either, do they? I guess I'm thinking about him so hard that my thoughts pull his head up. I still can't see anything but the hint of features in the spill of shadows under the hood, but the voice is definitely male.

"A curious sanctuary, is it not?" he says, sitting back on the pew behind him.

I have no idea what he means, but I nod my head.

"Here we sit, neither of us parishioners, yet we have the place to ourselves."

"The priest must be around here someplace," I say, hoping it's true.

It's suddenly occurred to me that this guy could easily be some kind of pervert, following young girls into an out-of-the-way place like this and hitting on them. I'm very aware of how quiet it is in here, how secluded.

He shakes his head. "They are all long-gone," he says. "Priest and parishioners all."

Now I'm really getting the creeps. I don't want to turn my back on him, so I gesture with my chin toward the front of the church. I clear my throat.

"Somebody lit those candles," I say.

"At one time," he agrees. "But now we see only the memory of their light, the way starlight is but a memory of what burns in the heavens, crossing an unthinkable distance from where they flared to where we stand when we regard them."

"My, um, dad's expecting me," I tell him. "He knows where I am."

As if, but it seems like a good thing to say. I might be alone in here, but I don't want him thinking I'm

an easy mark. I sit up a little straighter and try to
look bigger than I am. Tougher. If worst comes to
worst, I'll go down kicking and screaming. I may be
small, but I can be fierce, only ferocity doesn't seem
to be the issue since all he's doing is sitting there
looking at me from under the shadows of his hood. A
footnoted script would be good, though, since nothing
he's saying really makes much sense.

"What is it you have lost?" he asks.

The confused look I give him isn't put on like my
bravado. "What do you mean, lost?"

"We've all lost something precious," he says. "Why
else would we find ourselves in this place?"

Maybe I'm not a Catholic, but I know this conversation has nothing to do with their doctrines. I should
get up and see if I can make it back out the door.
Instead I ask, "What have you lost?"

"My life."

Okay. Way too creepy. But I can't seem to get up.
It's like it's really late at night and I know I have to
get up for school the next day, but I still have to finish
the book first. I can't go to sleep, not knowing how
it ends.

"You don't look dead," I say.

"I don't believe in death," he tells me.

There's a glint of white in the shadows under his
hood. Teeth, I realize. He just smiled. I don't feel at
all comforted.

I clear my throat again. "But . . ."

I can't see his eyes, but I can feel the weight of
his gaze.

"I have lost my life," he says, "but I cannot die."

He shrugs, and I realize there's something wrong
under that hood of his, the way the folds of the cloth
fall. He's bumpy, but in the wrong places.

"And you?" he asks.

"My mother," I find myself saying. I remember what he said about the candles and starlight. "The memory of my mother."

I don't even know why I'm telling him this. It's not the kind of thing I'd tell my dad, or my best friend Ellie, but here I am, sharing this horrible lost feeling with a perfect stranger who doesn't exactly make me feel like he's got my best interests at heart.

"Some would embrace the loss of memory," he says, "rather than lament its absence."

I shake my head. "I don't understand."

"Remembering can keep the pain too fresh," he explains. "It is so much easier to forget—or at least it is more comfortable. But you and I, we are not seeking comfort, are we? We know that to forget is to give in to the darkness, so we walk in the light, that we hold fast to our joys and our pains."

At first I thought he had a real formal way of speaking, but now I'm starting to get the idea that maybe English isn't his first language, that he's translating in his head as he talks and that's what makes everything sound so stiff and proper.

"There was a glade in my homeland," he says. He settles farther back against his pew and I catch a glimpse of a russet beard, a pointed chin, high cheek bones before the hood shadows them again. "It had about it a similar air as does this church. It was a place for remembering, a sanctuary hidden in a grove where the lost could gather the fraying tatters of their memories and weave them strong once more."

"The lost . . . ?"

Again that flash of a smile. There's no humor in it. "Such as we."

"I just came in here to get out of the heat," I tell him.

"Mmm."

"I was feeling a little dizzy."

"And why here, do you suppose?" he asks. "I will tell you," he goes on before I can answer. "Because like us, this place also seeks to hold onto what it has lost. We help each other. You. I. The church."

"I'm not . . ."

Remembering anything, I'm about to say, but my voice trails off because suddenly it's not true. I am remembering. If I close my eyes, I know I can call my mother's face up again—not stiff, like in a photo, but the way it was when she was still alive, mobile and fluid. And not only her face. I can smell the faint rose blush of her perfume. I can almost feel her hand on my head, tousling the curls that are pulled back in a French braid right now.

I look at him. "How . . . ?"

He smiles again and stands. He's not as tall as I was expecting from his broad shoulders.

"You see?" he says. "And I, too, am remembering. Reeds by a river and a woman hidden in them. I should never have cut a pipe from those reeds. Her voice was far sweeter."

He's lost me again.

"I can pretend it was preordained," he says. "That the story needed to play out the way it did. But you and I, we know better, don't we? The story can't be told until the deed is done. Only the Fates can look into the future, and I have known them to be wrong."

"I'm not sure I know what you're talking about," I say.

He nods. "Of course. Why should you? They are my memories and it is an old story, forgotten now. But remember this: there is always a choice. Perhaps destiny will quicken the plot, but what we do with the threads we are given is our choice."

I've taken this in school.

"You mean free will."

He has to think about that.

"Perhaps I do," he says finally. "But it comes without instruction and the price of it can be dear."

"What do you mean?"

He shrugs. "I can only speak of what is pertinent to my own experience, but if there were any advice I would wish I had been given, it would be to believe in death."

"How can you not believe in it?" I say. "It's all around us."

There's a tightness in my chest again, but this time it's because I can remember. It's because my memories are immediate and clear, the good and the bad, the joy of my mother's love and the way she was taken away from me.

"It was not always so," he says.

"Then it was a better time."

"You think so?" he asks. "Consider the alternative. Imagine being alive when all consider you dead. You walk through the changing world as a ghost. You can touch no one. No one can see you."

I could really use those footnotes now.

"But—"

"Be careful with your choices," he says and turns away.

I hear the rustling of cloth as he moves, the faint click of his heels on the stone floor, except they don't sound like leather-soled shoes. There's a hollow ring to them, like a horse's hoof on pavement. He turns to face me again when he reaches the door, pushes back his hood. He has strong, handsome features, with a foreign cast. Dark, olive skin, but his hair is as red as his beard, and standing up among the curls are two small horns, curled like a goat's.

"You . . . you're the devil," I say.

I can't believe he's here in a church. I want to look up above the altar, to see if the statue of Jesus is turning away in horror at this unholy invasion, but I can't move, can't pull my gaze from the horned man. I feel sick to my stomach.

"Where one might see a devil," he says, "another might see a friend."

I'm shaking my head. I may not be much of a churchgoer, but even I've heard about what happens to people who make deals with the devil.

"Remember what I said about choices," he tells me.

And then he's gone.

It's forever before I can get up the nerve to walk back out through that door myself and go home.

2

They'd all gotten together at The Harp to share a pitcher of beer after finishing the evening classes they taught at the Newford School of Art. After the quiet of the school, the noisy pub with its Irish session in full swing in one corner was exactly what they needed to wind down. They commandeered a table far enough away from the music so that they could talk and hold forth, but close enough so that they could still hear the music.

They made a motley group. Jilly and Sophie, alike enough in the pub's low light that they could be sisters, except Jilly was thinner, with the scruffier clothes and the longer, curlier hair; Sophie was tidier, more buxom. Hannah, all in black as usual, blonde hair cropped short, blue eyes sparkling with the buzz her second glass of beer was giving her. Desmond, dreadlocked and smiling, dressed as though he was still living on the Islands, wearing only a thin cotton jacket, despite the below-zero temperatures outside. Angela, the intensity of her dark eyes softened by her pixie features and a fall of silky Pre-Raphaelite hair.

It was Hannah who'd come up with the question—"What's the strangest thing that ever happened to you?"—and then looked around the table. She'd expected something from Jilly because Jilly could always be counted on for some outlandish story or other. Hannah was never quite sure if they were true or not, but that didn't really matter. The stories were invariably entertaining, everything from affirmation that Bigfoot had indeed been seen wandering around the Tombs to a description of the strange goblin kingdom that Jilly would insist existed in Old Town, that part of the city that had dropped underground during the Big Quake and then been built over during the reconstruction.

And, of course, she told them so well.

But the first story had come from Angela and instead of giving them a fit of the giggles, it made them all fall quiet. Her calm recitation created a pool of stillness in the middle of the general hubbub of the tavern as they regarded her with varying degrees of belief and wonder: Jilly completely accepting the story at face value, Desmond firmly in the rational camp, Sophie somewhere in between the two. Hannah supposed she was closest to Sophie—she'd like to believe, but she wasn't sure she could.

Angela smiled. "Not exactly what you were expecting, was it?"

"Well, no," Hannah said.

"I think it's lovely," Jilly put in. "And it feels so absolutely true."

"Well, you would," Sophie told her. She looked around the table. "Maybe we should order another pitcher so that we can all work at seeing the world the way Jilly does."

"We'll be needing a lot more than beer for that," Desmond put in.

Jilly stuck out her tongue at him.

"So?" Angela asked. "Was he the devil?"

Desmond shook his head. "As if."

"What do you think?" Hannah asked.

"I have no idea," Angela replied. "I was young and impressionable and certainly upset at the time. Maybe I saw what I thought I saw, or maybe I imagined it. Or maybe he was suffering from one of those deforming diseases like elephantiasis and those weren't horns I saw coming up out of his hair, but some sort of unfortunate growth."

"I'll side with Desmond on this one," Jilly said.

Everyone looked at her in surprise. Jilly and Desmond never agreed on anything except that their students needed a firm grounding in the basics of classical art—figure studies, anatomy, color theory and the like—before they could properly go on to create more experimental works.

Jilly rolled her eyes at the way they were all looking at her. "I mean that Angela didn't meet the devil," she said. "Or at least not the devil according to Christian doctrine. What she met was something far older— what the Christians used as a template for their fallen angel."

"I definitely need that beer," Desmond said and got up to order another pitcher.

"But in a church?" Hannah found herself saying.

Jilly turned to her. "Why not?"

"Who exactly are we talking about here?" Sophie asked.

"Well, think about it," Jilly replied. "You've got him talking about chasing a nymph into the reeds and making music that can't compare to her singing. He had goat's horns and probably goat's feet—Angela says his footsteps sounded like hooves on the floor."

Angela nodded in agreement.

"And then," Jilly went on, "there's this business of being dead but living forever."

She sat back, obviously pleased with herself.

Hannah shook her head. "I still don't see what you're getting at."

"Old gods," Jilly said. "She met Pan. Like it says in the stories, 'Great Pan is dead. Long live Pan!' "

"Not to be picayune," Sophie put in with a smile, "but I think you're quoting the Waterboys."

Jilly shrugged. "Whatever. It doesn't change anything."

"I thought about that, too," Angela said, "but it makes no sense. What would Pan be doing here, thousands of miles from Arcadia, even if he ever did exist and was still alive?"

"I think he travels the world," Jilly told her. "Like the Wandering Jew. And besides, Newford's a cool city. We all live here, don't we? Why *shouldn't* Pan show up here as well?"

"Because," Desmond said, having returned with a brimming pitcher in time to hear the last part of the conversation, "Roman gods aren't real. Aren't now, never were, end of story."

"He was Greek, actually," Sophie said.

"Whose side are you on?" Desmond asked.

He poured them all fresh glasses, then set the empty pitcher down in the middle of the table.

Sophie clinked her glass against his. "The side of truth, justice and equality for all—including obstinate, if talented, sculptors."

"Flatterer," he said.

"Hussy."

"Men can't be hussies."

"Can too!" all four women cried at once.

3

The talk went on for hours along with another couple of pitchers of The Harp's draft lager. By the time Sophie said they should probably call it a night—"It's a night!" Jilly pronounced to a round of giggles—Hannah was feeling dizzy from both.

She and Angela had the same bus stop, so after a chorus of good-byes, they left together, slightly unsteady on their feet, breath clouding in the cold air. Happily the bus stop wasn't far, and there was a bench where they could sit while they waited. Hannah settled back in her seat, not really feeling the cold yet. She looked up at the sky, wishing she was out in the country somewhere so that she could fully appreciate the stars that were cloaked by the city's light pollution. That was one of the things she missed the most about having moved to the city—deep night skies and country quiet.

"Did that really happen?" she asked after a moment.

Angela didn't need to ask what.

"I don't know," she said. "I can joke about it, but the truth is, that was a pivotal moment for me—one of those crossroads they talk about where your life could have gone one way or the other. It doesn't matter to me whether it was real or not—or rather if I had some extraordinary experience or not. I still came away from it with the realization that I always have to think my choices through carefully, and then, when I make a decision, take full responsibility for it."

Like moving to the city, Hannah thought. It was no use bemoaning the things she missed, though of course that didn't stop her from worrying a half dozen times a week over whether or not she'd made the right decision. She wanted to be a painter and the community and contacts she'd come here to find were what she needed to be able to do it—not to mention the fact that back home she could never make her living with the odd sorts of jobs she held here: art instructor, sometime artist's model, waitress, messenger, the occasional commission for an ad or a poster. Maybe when she was somewhat better established she could afford to move back to the country, but not now. Not and feel that her career was actually moving forward.

But that didn't stop her from missing everything she'd left behind.

"Think it through first," Hannah said, "but then don't look back."

Angela nodded. "Exactly. If you embrace the decision you've made, everything seems that much clearer because you're not fighting self-doubt."

"You got all that when you were fifteen?"

"Not the way you're thinking. It wasn't this amazing epiphany and my whole life changed. But I couldn't get him—whoever or whatever he was—out of mind. Nor what he'd told me. And whatever else happened, I had my mom back." Angela touched a mittened hand to her chest. "In here." She got a faraway look in her eyes. "Jilly's always saying that magic's never what you expect it to be, but it's often what you need. I think she's right. And it doesn't really matter if the experience comes from outside or inside. *Where* it comes from isn't important at all. What's important is that it *does* come—and that we're receptive enough to recognize and accept it."

"I could use a piece of magic to change my life," Hannah said. "I seem to be in this serious rut—always scrambling to make ends meet, which also means that

I never have the time to do enough of my own work to do more than participate in group shows."

"Well, you know what they say: visualize it. If you see yourself as having more time, being more successful, whatever, you can make it happen."

"I think if I'm going to visualize magic, I'd rather it was dancing on a hilltop with your horned man."

Angela's eyebrows rose.

Hannah smiled. "Well, that's what I think magic should be. Not this." She waved a hand to take in the city around them. "Not being successful or whatever, but just having a piece of something impossible to hold onto, if only for a moment."

"So visualize that."

"As if."

They fell silent for a time, watching the occasional car go by.

"Did you ever see him again?" Hannah asked.

Angela smiled and shook her head. "I think it was pretty much a once-in-a-lifetime sort of experience. That piece of something impossible you were talking about that I only got to hold onto for a moment."

Her bus arrived then.

"Can you get home okay?" she asked.

"I'm not that tipsy," Hannah told her.

"But almost."

"Oh, yes."

Her own bus took another five minutes to arrive.

4

Later that night, Hannah lay in bed, studying the splotchy plaster on her ceiling, and let her mind drift. Visualize, she thought. How would she visualize Angela's mysterious visitor? Like that painting in *The Wandering Wood,* she decided. The watercolor by Ellen

Wentworth that depicted the spirit of the forest as some kind of hybrid Greek/Native American being— goat legs and horns, but with beads and feathers and cowrie shells braided into the red hair and beard, even into the goaty leg hair.

She smiled, remembering how she'd copied the painting from out of the book when she was twelve or thirteen and had kept it hanging up in her room for ages—right up until her last year of high school when the sheer naiveté of its rendering finally made her put it away. She was doing such better work by that time. Her grasp of anatomy alone made it difficult to look at the piece anymore. What had become of it?

She got up out of bed, but not to go searching through stacks of old art—most of that early juvenile stuff was still stored in boxes on the farm anyway. No, she'd had a cup of herbal tea when she got home and now she had to pay the price with a trip to the bathroom. She got as far as putting a thick flannel housecoat on top of the oversized T-shirt she slept in before being distracted by the scene that lay outside her bedroom window.

There was nothing particularly untoward to catch her eye. Back yards and fences, half of the latter in desperate need of repair that they'd probably never get. Narrow lanes made more narrow by garbage cans, dumpsters, and snow banks. Above them, fire escapes and brick walls, windows—mostly dark, but a few lit from within by the blue flicker of television screens— rooflines, telephone poles and drooping wires crisscrossing back and forth across the alleys and lanes.

The snow covering softened some of the usual harshness of the scene, and yes, it could be almost magical during a snowfall, the kind when big sleepy flakes came drifting down, but it was still hard to imagine the city holding anything even remotely as en-

chanting as Jilly's stories of gemmin, who were a kind
of earth spirit that lived in abandoned cars, or Angela's mysterious goatman—even if such things were
possible in the first place. If she were a magical being,
she wouldn't live here, not when there were deep for-
ests and mountains an hour or so's drive north of the
city, or the lake right smack at the southern end of
the urban sprawl. She'd run through the woods like
one of Ellen Wentworth's elfish tree people, or sail
off across the lake in a wooden shoe.

She smiled. Leaving the window, she went and had
her pee, but instead of getting back into bed, she
pulled on a pair of jeans under her housecoat, stuck
her feet into her boots, and left her apartment. She
took the stairs up to the roof. The door was stuck, so
she had to give it a good shove before she could get
it open and step outside into the chilly air.

She wasn't sure what time it was. After four, at any
rate. Late enough that you could almost tune out the
occasional siren and the vague bits of traffic that
drifted from the busier streets a few blocks over. The
wide expanse of the rooftop was covered with a thin
layer of snow, granulated and hard, clinging to the
surface of the roof like carbuncles. Her flowerboxes
were up here, a half-dozen of them in which she grew
all sorts of vegetables and flowers—a piece of the farm
transplanted here so that she didn't feel quite so cut
off from the land. The dirt in the boxes was all frozen
now and snow covered them. She'd pulled most of the
dead growth out in the autumn, but there were still a
few browned stalks pushing hardily out of the snow
that she hadn't gotten to. Cosmos and purple cone-
flowers. Some kale, which was better after a frost anyway, but it was finished now.

She shivered, but didn't go back inside right away.
She looked out across the rooftops, a checkerboard of

white squares and black streets and yards. There was a sort of magic, she supposed, about the city this late at night. The stillness, the dark, the sensation that time seemed to have stopped. The knowing that she was one of a select few who were awake and outside at this hour. If you were going to discover a secret, if you were going to get the chance to peer under the skin of the world, if only for a moment, this was the time for it.

Are you out there? she wondered, addressing the mysterious man Angela had met in a church long before Hannah had even thought of moving to the city herself. Will you show yourself to me? Because I could use a piece of magic right about now, a piece of something impossible that shouldn't exist, but does, if only for this moment.

Her straits weren't as desperate as Angela's had been. And compared to how so many people had to live—out of work, on the streets, cadging spare change just to get a bowl of soup or a cup of coffee—what she had was luxury. But she still had a deficit, a kind of hollow in her heart from which bits and pieces of her spirit trickled away, like coins will from a hole in your pocket. Nothing she couldn't live without, but she missed them all the same.

She wasn't sure that magic could change that. She wasn't sure anything could, because what she really needed to find was a sense of peace. Within herself. With the choices she'd made that had brought her here. Magic would probably confuse the issue. She imagined it would be like an instant addiction—having tasted it once, you'd never be satisfied not tasting it again. She didn't know how Angela did it.

Except, not having tasted it created just as much yearning. This wanting to believe it was real. This asking for the smallest, slightest tangible proof.

She remembered what Angela had said. Visualize it.

Okay. She'd pretend she was thinking up a painting—a made-up landscape. She closed her eyes and tried to ignore the cold air. It wasn't winter, but a summer's night, somewhere near the Mediterranean. This wasn't a tenement rooftop, but a hilltop with olive trees and grape vines and . . . the details got a little vague after that.

Oh, just try, she told herself.

Some white buildings with terra-cotta roofs in the distance, like stairs going down to the sea. Maybe some goats, or sheep. A stone wall. It's night. The sky's like velvet and the stars feel as though they're no more than an elbow-length away.

Where would he be?

Under one of the olive trees, she decided. Right at the top of the hill. Starlight caught on the curve of his goat horns. And he'd be playing those reed-pipes of his. A low breathy sound like . . . like . . . She had to use her father's old Zamfir records for a reference, stripping away the sappy accompaniment and imagining the melody to be more mysterious. Older. No, timeless.

For a moment there, she could almost believe it. Could almost smell the sea, could feel the day's heat still trapped in the dirt under her feet. But then a cold gust of wind made her shiver and took it away. The warm night, olive trees and all.

Except . . . except . . .

She blinked in confusion. She was on a hilltop, only it was in the middle of the city. The familiar roofs of the tenements surrounding her apartment were all still there, but her own building was gone, replaced by a snowy hilltop, cleared near the top where she stood, skirted with pine and cedar as it fell away to the street.

She shook her head slowly. This couldn't . . .

The sound she heard was nothing like the one she'd been trying to imagine. It still originated from a wind instrument, was still breathy and low, but it held an undefinable quality that she couldn't have begun to imagine. It was like a heartbeat, the hoot of an owl, the taste of red wine and olives, all braided together and drawn out into long, resonating notes. In counterpoint she heard footsteps, the crunch of snow and the soft sound of shells clacking together.

"Dance with me," a voice said from behind her.

When she turned, he was there. Ellen Wentworth's forest spirit, horns and goat legs, the hair entwined with feathers, beads and shells. She seemed to fall into his eyes, tumbling down into the deep mystery of them and unable to look away. He was a northern spirit, as much a part of the winter and the hills north of the city as a wolf or a jack pine, but the Mediterranean goat man was there, too, the sense of him growing sharper and clearer, the deeper she was drawn into his gaze.

"You . . . I . . ."

Her throat couldn't shape the words. Truth was, she had no idea what she was trying to say. Perhaps his name—the name Jilly had given him.

She let him take her in his warm arms and felt ridiculous in her tatty housecoat, cowboy boots, and jeans. He smelled of pine sap and cedar boughs, and then of something else, a compelling musky scent she couldn't place, old and dark and secret. His biceps were corded and hard under her hands, but his touch was light, gentle as she remembered the brush of wildflowers to be against her legs when she crossed a summer meadow.

The music had acquired a rhythm, a slow waltz time. His music. He was dancing with her, but somehow he was still making that music.

"How . . . ?" she began.

His smile made her voice falter. The question grew tattered in her head and came apart, drifted away. Magic, she decided. Pure and simple. Visualized. Made real. A piece of impossible, a couldn't be, but here it was all the same and what did it matter where it came from, or how it worked?

He led beautifully and she was content to let everything else fall away and simply dance with him.

5

She woke to find that she'd spent the night sleeping on the landing outside the door that led out onto the roof of her building. She was stiff from having slept on the hard floor, cold from the draft coming in from under the door. But none of that seemed to matter. Deep in her chest she could still feel the rhythm of that mysterious music she'd heard last night, heard while she danced on a hilltop that didn't exist, danced with a creature that couldn't possibly exist.

She remembered one of the things that Angela had said last night.

Jilly's always saying that magic's never what you expect it to be, but it's often what you need.

Lord knows she had needed this.

"Hey, *chica.* You drink a little too much last night?"

Mercedes Muñoz, her upstairs neighbor, was standing on the stairs leading up to where Hannah lay. Hand on her hip, Mercedes wore her usual smile, but worry had taken up residence in her dark eyes.

"You okay?" she added when Hannah didn't respond.

Hannah slowly sat up and drew her housecoat close around her throat.

"I've never felt better in my life," she assured Mercedes. It was true. She didn't even have a hangover. "For the first time since I've moved to this city, I finally feel like I belong."

It made no sense. How could it make her feel this way? A dream of dancing with some North American version of a small Greek god, on a hilltop that so resembled the hills that rose up behind the farm where she'd grown up. But it had all the same. Maybe it was simply the idea of the experience—wonderful, impossible, exhilarating.

But she preferred to believe it hadn't been a dream. That, like Angela, she'd met a piece of Old World magic, however improbable it might seem. That the music she was still carrying around inside her had been his. That the experience had been real. Because if something like that could happen, then other dreams could come true as well. She could make it here, on her own, away from the farm. It hadn't been a mistake to come.

Mercedes offered her a hand up.

"And now what?" Mercedes asked. "You going to try sleeping in a cardboard house in some alley next?"

Hannah smiled. "If that's what it takes, maybe I will."

THE SWORD OF HERAKLES
by Irene Radford

Irene Radford lives in Oregon and is the author of the Dragon Nimbus trilogy (*The Glass Dragon, The Perfect Princess,* and *The Loneliest Magician*), published by DAW Books.

The woman breathed delicately into his ear. His senses swirled, then centered on the seductive scent of her. Earthy, clean, irresistible.

"Come with me. Give me what I want," the woman whispered, placing her hand upon his sword hilt.

Herakles clamped his own hand atop the woman's, suddenly alarmed. He shifted his stance, angling his hips slightly away from any direction her knee could reach. A head shorter than he, she seemed firmly muscled and agile.

"Who are you?" he breathed back in her ear, careful not to let his words carry further. The sea was calm tonight. Sound carried far across the bay, a beacon to any enemy that lurked there.

"I am the companion you hired for tonight," she replied petulantly. Her fingers flexed beneath his, still grasping the sword hilt.

He knew all the women attached to this small army—knew them intimately. She was not one of them. Any experienced camp follower would wait for a man to finish his patrol before approaching. Punishment for a man deserting his post would extend to the woman.

The small, sheltered fire he kept to ignite signal torches cast disguising shadows across her face. Her simple gown shimmered in the moonlight. The finest silk, almost transparent. She was much more than a common campfollower.

Her breath fanned the fires of his desire. The stirring in his groin demanded attention. He looked deeply into her eyes, seeking answers.

Such beautiful eyes, as blue as a peacock's feathers. He knew her now. Her eyes always gave her away. His desire vanished as quickly as it had come.

"Give me . . ."

"You're cheating, Hera." Herakles shifted his grip to pinion her arms at her side. She squirmed and kicked for release. He twisted quickly, turning her to lock one arm across her throat while keeping her immobile with the other. "I'll tell Lilith that you are impersonating one of her succubi." He allowed himself a low chuckle.

"You wouldn't dare!" Hera jerked upward and forward unable to break his grip on her. Suddenly she sagged against him.

"Wouldn't I?" He had evaded his stepmother and her schemes for centuries and didn't believe for a second that she had accepted defeat so easily.

The sea pounded the parapet at his feet. He listened with part of his attention, still aware of his duties.

After decades of wandering the Earth as a mercenary—always one step ahead of Hera—he'd landed far away from his native land. He found the high-spirited natives in this remote island fascinating. They were a race who produced minor heroes, celebrated in song and lore, on a regular basis. Given time, they might spawn the next great civilization to rival Greece.

Herakles hoped to help them along. No one else was left to do it. The legacy of Prometheus had to continue, even if Herakles' efforts were insignificant compared to the renegade Titan.

"How would it look in Olympus, Hera, if the others learned the patroness of fidelity and marriage had tried to seduce her own stepson?" She'd done worse trying to retrieve the artifact he guarded.

"The others won't listen to you. You forsook Olympus. Why are you so concerned with these barbarians? You should let their enemies slaughter them, one and all."

"I didn't forsake Olympus. I chose to continue as the protector of humans. These people deserve my help." Help he wasn't giving if he gave Hera all of his attention. The bay was vulnerable on this moonlit night.

"We could end this game once and for all. Give me the sword!"

"Why?"

"I'll give it to one who will murder Zeus' latest playmate—a blonde nymph he found flitting about the northlands." Hera's hands clenched into tight fists. "A blade forged by Hephaestus is the only weapon that will break through the defenses my husband has set around her."

"You know me better than that, Hera. No ordinary man should have the sword; its wielder is invincible. What mortal can appreciate its dangers?" Herakles asked. He shuddered at the thought of one of the bloodthirsty sea raiders turned loose with the sword. Any spark of civilization would be swallowed up in the larger conflagration of chaos and destruction. He looked over his shoulder toward the bay, making certain none of their ships entered the quiet bay.

"The last time you stole the sword from me, you gave it to Attila the Hun," Herakles reminded Hera. "The death and destruction he caused—was it any wonder I stole the sword back and left Olympus?"

"I gave Attila the sword so he could ruin that bothersome Christian movement that's getting so popular. He almost succeeded."

"The sword was given to *me,* so I could free Prometheus. No other weapon would break his chains. He had to be freed so humans could use his gifts to grow. You had no right to use it for your petty schemes."

"If it weren't for Prometheus, we gods would have destroyed humans centuries ago. They are a pestilence. They breed and multiply like rats—especially the ones Zeus seduces."

"Like my mother." Bitter silence stretched between them. He didn't need to mention his wife and children. Hera had induced madness in him and he'd murdered those he loved best. If he vented the rage that boiled in his blood every time he remembered Hera's treachery, he'd lose control. Hera might steal the sword back while he wreaked his own swath of destruction.

He thrust her away and turned his back on her before he let his hate get the better of his good sense.

Hera pouted prettily. "Give me the sword, Herakles. Give it up, and all your dreams and desires will come true." Her gaze rested on the pommel of the crude weapon on his hip. "You can go back to Olympus. Or I can make you mortal again. You could walk the Earth as an ordinary man, marry, and beget children."

"Why? So you can force me to murder those I love?

Or trick my family into killing my mortal body again?"

"I'll leave you alone forever if you give me the sword now." Hera grabbed the hilt again in a movement so swift only a god could execute or anticipate it.

Herakles clamped his hand on her wrist, squeezing hard on the vulnerable bones. He smiled at her error in judgment. "You don't think I'd wear such an important weapon on an everyday patrol, do you?"

"What have you done with the real sword?" Hera stamped her foot and tried to wrench away from him.

After a moment, he deliberately thrust her away from him. He wiped his hands upon his clothing as if she had soiled him with her touch.

"You are a disgrace to Zeus, who sired you, and the gods who nurtured you." Hera paced the rampart where he stood watch. The rock work trembled under her step. "How can you waste your strength and talents on these barbarians?" She waved her hands wildly and tore at her hair.

Herakles ignored her ranting and turned his attention back out to sea. A quiet moonlit night. Would the wily raiders take advantage of the illumination and good weather? They were unpredictable. He couldn't outthink them. But he'd pledged his help to the natives here. Many of the soldiers called him "friend." He returned their affection.

"Don't you ever long for the warmth and sun of Greece?" Hera's tone now relied on nostalgia rather than sex. "Remember the scent of olive trees and juniper on the hot wind? The rolling hills? The dry air that let you see forever under a deep blue sky? The beautiful sea, warm enough to bathe in?" She leaned on the parapet looking southeast across the water, toward Greece, toward home.

"I like it here. I like these people." They had fire

in their thoughts and dreams. A fire the Greeks had let die out. A worthy hero for the sword might grow out of this environment.

"It's so damp here. Only barbarians would like this climate!"

"Barbarians who love life and carve out their own destiny without your interference."

"I'll trade you the safety of these people for the sword." Hera pointed out to sea.

Thickening clouds threatened to obliterate the moonlight, but not before he caught a glimpse of a sail and the silhouette of a long, low boat.

"I can make Aeolus shift the winds and drive them back to their homeland." She drew a lazy circle with her finger. A puff of wind followed her gesture. She increased the speed of her circling finger. The wind intensified, driving the enemy toward the shore.

"I have to light the bonfire. Alert the others." He dashed to the stash of torches and the small hidden fire.

Hera sent the torches flying over the wall into the sea. Her circling wind extinguished the fire. "Give me the sword, and I'll send the raiders home."

"Your price is too high!" He raced for the camp. "Sound the alarm! Raiders by sea!" He grabbed a dying torch from outside an officer's tent and raced back to the unlit bonfire on the slight rise west of camp. He thrust the weak flame into the heart of the kindling.

Hera appeared at his elbow. "You can't protect both the sword and these humans, Herakles. I'll find your hiding place while you fight off the invaders."

"You'll need more time than that!"

"The sword needs a hero to wield it. The days of great heroes are over. You were the last, until the mortal half of you died. Now you are little more than a ghost drifting through time," Hera screamed, sounding very much like the rising wind.

She was right.

"You don't have to do this, Herakles. Give me the sword, and I'll never bother you again. You can go back to Olympus."

He glared at her, waiting for the torch to ignite the damp kindling.

"You won't have to watch your mortal friends age and die. You will no longer be the only one who remains forever young while the rest of the world grows older, more feeble."

Herakles blotted Hera's pleas from his mind. He didn't have time to listen.

Finally, the flames from his meager torch licked the heavier wood of the bonfire. They shot upward as the larger branches ignited. On the next hilltop, a league away, another bonfire flared to life. The next signal fire was beyond even Herakles' immortal sight.

Within minutes, every fighting man available would be mustered and ready to meet the enemy as they landed.

Hera dematerialized. Herakles doubted that she actually left him. She needed more information to find the sword on her own.

Strength flowed through his muscles and sang in his blood as he ran for the beach. This was his destiny. To defend the weak against aggressors, to guard them against the interfering whims of greater powers, like Hera.

Hours later, when there were no more enemies, Herakles lowered his club and sword and looked around. Four ships sailed away. Two more burned on the beach and broke apart as he watched. The last ship listed heavily to port in the surf where a submerged rock had pierced its hull. He'd help beat off this attack. How long would the raiders stay away this time? How many friends and comrades had died?

"The world needs a hero to wield the sword for justice, not destruction like this!" he shouted into the wind. "But where will I find him?" he asked himself in a softer voice. Quickly he sorted through the current leaders. Most of the petty kings were too self-serving to draw together the varied peoples of this land. The High King of the tribes was a good general with strong leadership. Could he master the sword?

Not just any warrior could maintain control of a weapon forged by a god. Not just any warrior could put the needs of his army and his people above the absolute power the sword could give. The man who wielded the sword needed to be honorable, just, fair, and a little bit humble.

"You're right, that isn't any sword Hephaestus forged." Hera rematerialized and pointed disgustedly at the chipped and bloodied blade in Herakles' right hand. "Only your skill and strength kept that weapon intact. Where is the real sword?"

"You'll never find it, Hera. I'll destroy it before I give it to you." Something he should have done centuries ago—if a weapon forged by Hephaestus could be broken. But it was such a magnificent weapon, a symbol of justice and freedom. If he destroyed it, would those qualities of life disappear?

"You could have helped, Hera." Even now, he doubted any of the mortals could see her.

"Why would I do that? Unlike you, I don't like humans. I won't stoop to interfering with the natural course of events." She sniffed haughtily.

"First time you've ever wasted an opportunity to meddle. You want to give the sword to someone who will abuse its powers. We can't predict if the man will stop his murder with the nymph—whose only crime, like my mother and many others before her—is to be beautiful.''

For the first time in decades, Herakles used his immortal powers. He dissolved his body, just as Hera had done before the battle. He had to move fast and free to stay ahead of her now. She could follow his trail across time and space, but it would take time.

Dark mist boiled over him. Cold pierced his body until his joints ached. Time and distance folded and collapsed into tiny pinpricks of light akin to the distant stars in the heavens. Each point of light winked at him in a different color. He reached for an obscure one that sometimes looked white, other times, blue and sometimes a pale pink. Time and distance lost meaning.

Sunlight burst around him, dazzling his eyes and warming his body after the chill darkness. Trees and rocks took form. Birdsong and the sound of a gentle breeze in the tree tops whispered to him. At last the earth became solid beneath his feet. He stood on a rocky ledge before a narrow crack in a mountain wall. Low shrubs and rubble hid the rest of the opening from casual view. A sparkling, clear lake stretched out from the outcropping where he stood. Its beauty drew the ordinary seeker away from the cave entrance.

He ducked into the low opening. On a ledge to his left, he found the candle stub and flint he had left there. He struck a spark from the flint against the rock wall. The candle leaped to life.

A few steps farther into the cave and the candle flame exploded into a million points of light. Bright crystals clung to the ceiling of a huge cavern and filled its walls. In the center of the cave, a long narrow stone, seamed with marble, stood solitary vigil over the wonders displayed in the crystals.

Men called Druids had worshiped here last. They

were all dead now. The altar abandoned, as lonely and useless as Herakles had felt when he realized what he had done to his family after Hera's fit of madness left him.

Where was the sword now? It should be resting atop the altar. Panic shot through him like Zeus' lightning. Hera couldn't have found this cave in a forgotten corner of Britain so soon.

If any mortal had stumbled upon the cave, the hallowed position of the sword on the altar should have discouraged trespassers from touching the relic.

"Looking for this?" Echoes distorted the voice of the questioner.

Herakles whirled around. His rapid movement sent the candle flame sputtering and waving. Shadows flitted across the crystals in demonic shapes, defying his eyes to keep up with them.

A hunched figure, cloaked against the damp chill of the cave, stood up from behind the altar, holding the sword aloft in his left hand.

This wasn't Hera. She hadn't had time to follow him.

No trace of rust dulled the ancient blade. The star-iron glowed softly in the crystal's prismatic light. Shorter and thicker than modern weapons, the edge glinted with a keenness only Hephaestus could hone.

"Yes. It belongs to me," Herakles replied, assessing the distance between himself and the shrouded figure. He automatically judged the strength of the arm that still held the sword aloft and the skill of the hand that clasped the hilt.

"I knew you'd come eventually. This is too powerful a weapon to leave unguarded for long. Some men would sacrifice the lives of their entire army to hold power like this in their hands." The figure lifted his head. A rather full and shaggy white beard poked out from beneath the folds of the cloak.

"It must never fall into the hands of one who would sacrifice so much for the sword and the power."

"Agreed." The man moved around to the front of the altar. He shifted the sword to rest horizontally across his hands, almost offering it in peace.

"Then I will dispose of it safely." Herakles took another step forward. The man appeared old, very slender. He couldn't carry much muscle on so spare a frame. "You can't hope to protect it."

"I have my ways, though I find myself a little stiff and sore traveling forward through time to meet you. Only a few months, but enough to weary a body. You, I think have traveled farther than I, a decade or two at most. Tell me about the sword."

"I do not know you. Why should I trust you?" The old man had come forward through time, as Herakles had done. Such power shouldn't belong to an ordinary mortal.

"Among my people, I am known as The Merlin."

Herakles halted in mid-step. "I know of you. Last of the Druids, gifted with power and wisdom. This was once the cave and altar of your people. But I thought you dead, or a fanciful tale. Did your power draw me here?"

"Possibly. The patterns of past and future create strange coincidences. You left a wondrous sword here. I—no, Britain—needs such a sword. You and the sword belonged together."

"You say the sword *belonged* with me?" Herakles found himself liking this old man. Not many mortals would face a man of Herakles' size and appearance, an immortal, without any trace of fear.

"Aye. *Belonged.* It will belong to another soon enough. One who can use it to save Britain." The

Merlin swung the unsheathed weapon testing its balance. It sang as it cleaved air. The crystals picked up the hum and passed it around the cavern.

"The sword is too dangerous for an ordinary mortal."

"The man who will inherit this sword will have to earn it. And he will be no ordinary man. As you are no ordinary man, Herakles."

"How do you know my name?"

"I learn many things. I know of your exploits, but I thought you dead, or a fanciful tale." The Merlin yanked a hair from his long beard. He grimaced at the slight pain, then tested the edge of the sword by splitting the hair.

"In many ways I am dead. In other ways I can never die. I cannot fully withdraw from life until humans are safe from the temptations of a sword such as this."

"Agreed. But I have plans for the sword and the future that will fit your ideal."

"Such as?"

"I have found a hero. A hero who will bring law, justice, and peace to Britain. He will need a sword such as this."

"Who is this mighty man, and why have I not heard of one worthy of the sword and my trust?"

"He hasn't been born yet, in the time you came from. But he will be. Shortly, nearly two decades before the time we are in now. I know that he will be worthy of the sword and your trust, as well as mine."

"Even the gods of Olympus can't see into the future." If only the old man's words were true. He wanted to believe The Merlin.

"The future is a shadow among many shadows. Those who know how and where to look can catch glimpses of shapes and patterns. I saw a sword in the patchwork of time. Look into the crystals. I will show you."

Herakles looked. The lights and shadows from the candle shifted into symbolic shapes and rhythms. He recognized Hera's peacock blue eyes, searching, ever searching. Another shadow, fleeing her. Fleeing toward something bright. A bright sword blade. He also saw a cloaked figure, prematurely gray of beard and hair, hiding a second sword in this very cave.

Hastily, Herakles looked toward The Merlin to make sure the old man hadn't tricked him with reflections and shadows. Merlin stood off to one side, head bowed, the sword resting quietly in his hands.

"I sought the pattern," The Merlin said, as if sensing Herakles' gaze. "That is how I found your hiding place. I sought a place to secrete a different sword and found a better weapon for my purposes. But for its full potential to be unleashed and controlled, it must be given, not stolen."

"I can't allow the sword loose into the chaos that rules the world in the time I left. I do not foresee an early end to the swath of destruction left behind by the sea raiders."

"The sword does attract a great deal of notice." The Merlin chuckled as he hefted the weapon, assessing its balance. "Clever of you to hide it in the future, at a time when it can be used for good. I sense someone seeking it even now. She? She has ties to you and through you to the sword. This power within the blade is easily recognizable. Reforging might shift the pattern enough to disrupt her search. Can you reshape the blade? Something longer and more slender? The kind of warfare my hero wages will require a longer reach and a shift of the balance."

"I have been many things, including a blacksmith.

But this sword was forged by Hephaestus. I'm not certain anyone but a god could change it."

"Was it the forger, or the nature of the star-iron itself, that makes this weapon so formidable?" The Merlin asked, raising one white eyebrow. "You are Zeus' son, the strongest man on Earth. If anyone can work this metal, it is you."

Reforging might alter the pattern of power within the blade enough to divert Hera for a little while, give him time to find a new hiding place. Or working the blade might show him a way to destroy it. "I will try, though I am but half a god. Do you have a forge?"

"This altar stone will suffice for an anvil."

"The altar will splinter at the first strike of a hammer."

The Merlin smiled with half his mouth. His eyes danced with mischief. He was younger than his white hair suggested. "I think not. I have hidden sea coal, tools, and water buckets deeper in the cave."

"Then let us to work." Herakles stripped off his shirt and stretched in preparation for the hard work.

Very quickly, heat from the burning coals filled the cavern and coursed through Herakles' veins. He thrust the sword into the brazier much as he had thrust the torch into the signal fire. Tiny flames licked at the black lumps of coal within the makeshift forge. He watched for what seemed an eternity. The sword was slow to take the heat. Its tip remained bright steel gray. He added more coal. The tiniest bit of red glowed at the sword point.

"The fire has to be hotter," he said. He couldn't fail now.

The Merlin knelt beside the brazier and blew at the base of the fire. His breath came longer and steadier than an ordinary man's. A cloud of sparkling mist surrounded the coals, then sank into them. Instantly the fire blazed hotter. The old man sat back on his heels, blinking tiredly. "That should help," he said.

The glow of red crept up the sword blade. The crystals reflected the heat and light, adding to the burning coal. Gradually the red blade turned white. A sense of triumph bloomed inside Herakles. With The Merlin's magic and his strength, they just might achieve the impossible.

He moved the sword onto the altar and raised the hammer. He closed his eyes as he swung, expecting the stone to shatter. He heard only the resounding ring of metal against metal.

Another blow and another. He watched the sword carefully as the blade flattened, thinned. Each blow of the hammer changed the pitch of metal clanging against metal. Gradually the sound sweetened to a pure tone of music.

Pound, reheat. Pound, reheat. Dust rose from the altar stone and filled the air under the force of Herakles' blows, but still it did not shatter. Endlessly, Herakles worked the blade. Fatigue crept into his arms. His legs trembled from the strain. Dust clogged his senses. He hadn't felt this tired since the twelve labors.

At last the sword took shape, long and slender, layered with tensile strength. The beauty of the blade took hold of his senses. Balanced, keen, perfectly proportioned. He wouldn't destroy it. He had to find another solution. Perhaps The Merlin's hero was truly worthy of the blade.

Herakles reached for the tongs, ready to plunge the blade into the lake outside the cave for the final cooling and tempering.

"Let me finish this," The Merlin said as he sloshed a bucket of water over the blade where it lay on the altar stone. Immediately, the cloud of dust swirled together and dropped onto the sword. It combined with the cold water, cloaking the sword in a sheath of white stone; only the hilt remained free. The thin layer of dust hardened rapidly around the blade. The soft patina of dressed marble settled around it.

"Don't!" Herakles stayed The Merlin from dousing the altar with another bucket of water. "The blade is now a part of the altar. It looks sculpted from the marble."

The Merlin smiled. Mischief brightened his eyes. "Now for the final deception." He slid the metal blade out from beneath the marble casing. A perfect replica of a sword sheath lay atop the altar. Then the magician retrieved a second sword from the folds of his cloak. He slid this weapon under the marble sheath. "Uther Pendragon's sword of state. The sword that other kings will recognize as belonging to the next High King. Our hero will be the only man among them who can draw it forth. A useful weapon, but not an artifact of power and destiny. *Our* sword will come to our hero later, when the time is right."

Another slosh of water extended the marble casing over the hilt.

"Where did you get Uther's sword?" Herakles asked.

"I have kept it safe during his last illness. It will be here, awaiting our hero when he is ready to claim his heritage. You almost hid the sword in this cave too late for him to claim it upon Uther's death."

"Tell me, Merlin, how you work this magic. Are you a god?"

"No. Every person can work magic if they want. Not all have the patience to bring it forth from the depths of their souls. Not every one has the courage to work magic only for good. Few have the wisdom to know the difference between good and evil."

Herakles looked from the true sword to the replica

on the altar. Both resonated a kind of power, reflections of the original weapon. Had he diminished the sword?

Hesitantly he touched the blade with one finger. Energy snaked up his arm to his shoulder, infusing him with new strength. Changed, not diminished. The lightning of Zeus and the invincibility of Hephaestus still resided in the metal.

Together they hid the tools and other evidence of the transformation they had worked.

"I must go now." The Merlin tucked the sword within the voluminous folds of his cloak. "I have had the rearing of our hero. He will be worthy of this blade when it comes to him."

Herakles grasped the sword hilt within The Merlin's cloak one last time. "Promise me that he will know humility."

"I'll do my best." The Merlin bowed his head. "I would give him a perfect life if I could. But I can't alter the future, only perceive it."

"I trust your promise, Merlin. Now I, too, must go." He knew a satisfying sense of completion.

Herakles looked up, startled by the sound of a determined step at the cave entrance. The Merlin seemed to fade into the shadows and reflections of the crystal as he took a step back toward the wall.

"Looking for this?" Herakles asked Hera as she ducked into the cavern. He pointed to the sword replica upon the altar.

"What have you done to it?" she screeched as she ran to the stone. She wrenched at the sword hilt, trying to free it from the marble.

"Hera, the sword is beyond you." Herakles chuckled. "The time has come for us to leave Earth to younger powers." Out of the corner of his eye he saw

The Merlin. No more than shadow, the old man seemed to flow toward the cave entrance.

Hera looked only at the sword sculpture. Defeat dragged her shoulders down. She hung her head and dropped her hands away from the marble altar. "How did you make it more beautiful than Hephaestus could? I will find a way to retrieve it."

"No, Hera. Other powers govern it now."

"Who? Who dared help you deface the sword of a god?" Hera whipped her head around searching every corner. She spied the movement of shadow on shadow. "Stop!" She lunged for The Merlin. He evaded her grasp and ran.

Hera followed. Herakles strode after.

"I command you to stop!" Hera screamed.

The Merlin continued running. He escaped the cave and dashed toward the lake. Dawn sent ripples of fiery light across the smooth water. The Merlin skidded to a stop at the water's edge. He jumped back, just a little, as if the water were poison or he feared to trespass.

Hera latched her hand around The Merlin's wrist. She yanked at the sword.

Herakles grabbed Hera around the waist, lifting her away from the magician. "Cease, Hera. You can't win this battle," Herakles said, keeping her arms pinioned and her feet off the ground. She kicked him. He tightened his grasp.

"It takes a woman to keep an artifact away from a woman. I consign its care to the Lady of the Lake. It has been foretold that she will bestow this sword on the proper hero." The Merlin laughed out loud as he raised the sword and invoked the Lady. He hurled it far out into the lake. It tumbled end over end, spinning in the growing sunlight, reflecting it back more brightly than any crystal in the cave.

"Noooooooo!" Hera screeched. "You can't! I need the sword."

A graceful feminine arm, clothed in white samite, reached up from the depths of the sparkling water and grasped the hilt of the sword. The delicate fingers wrapped possessively around it. "I name thee Excaliber!" The Lady of the Lake's triumphant voice echoed up and out from her watery home. Then she pulled the sword beneath the surface of the lake.

"It's lost forever." Hera sagged limply in Herakles' arms. "She'll never give it up."

"Not forever," The Merlin said with a smile. "Only until the Lady finds a hero worthy of its power."

"That will be forever," Hera sobbed.

"Perhaps." The Merlin smiled knowingly.

"The Lady of the Lake alone will make that judgment." Herakles stood between Hera and the lake, making sure she didn't dive after the sword. "Go, Hera. Go home now. You have lost this battle."

"Hmf," she snorted as she snapped her fingers and disappeared.

"I'd better follow her. Someone has to keep her—and the others—from meddling where they don't belong. Good-bye, Merlin." Herakles wrapped the darkness of time and distance around himself and reached for Olympus. The sword was safe now, his work on Earth finished.

TO HADES AND BACK
by Karen Haber

Karen Haber lives in Oakland, California, with her husband
Robert Silverberg. Her most recent novel, *Sister Blood*, is
part of her "War Minstrels" series from DAW.

"Thank you, Cleveland, good night, and good
luck getting laid!"

Amber, fabulous Amber, the Gothic Queen of Rock
and Roll, stood in the burning spotlight and gave the
finger to her adoring fans. She grinned at their roars
of approval and, with a final wave, strode offstage,
trailing diaphanous yards of transparent silk the color
of the sea around the sacred isle of Delos.

Apollo, watching from the wings, pounded his hands
together with the rest of the crowd. She had performed gloriously, a wild thing transfixed by the white
eye of the spotlight, howling at the center of her own
self-generated sound storm.

Sweet Amber! She of the Attic-blue eyes, the wine-
dark hair, the alabaster complexion, the ten platinum
records and Grammy awards. From her throat came
the voice of angels and harpies, intertwined. The
thought of her, of all the exciting things that she was,
brought an amorous tear to the god's eye. He reached
out to make her his own.

But as the lights dimmed onstage, Amber swept past

him—him, Apollo, god of music, light, and prophecy, to whom the oracle at Delphi whispered her awful truths, Phoebus, master of the chariot of the sun and the great steeds that drew it—and instead selected one of the nearby long-haired mortals wearing a suit of black-stained cow skin.

Apollo was not amused. He had sworn to woo and win the queen of Goth Rock. How could she pick another? Perhaps his robes of gold had blinded her. Well, if she preferred the skin of cows to his magnificent tunic, so be it. In a moment his fine-spun garb was gone and in its place he sported a dark confining hide jacket and pants studded at irregular intervals with pieces of silver.

"Hey, Spartacus," a roadie said. "Nice leathers, but those sandals really don't make it."

It took a moment for Apollo to realize that the comment was intended for him. He gazed down at his feet, the priceless golden leather sandals, his lordly toes. "No?"

"Boots, man. Gotta have boots."

Ah. In a flash the god of light understood. Dark garb required dark footwear. He made it so. Black ostrich skin boots with silver tips and heels.

"Better," said the roadie, showing his thumb in a manner reminiscent of Caesar in the Coliseum.

"Thank you," said the god, returning the gesture.

But Amber wasn't paying attention. Instead she had retreated to a back room where she was busily digging into a platter of cold meat, stuffing her mouth full of slices with a vigor that would have put warriors such as Ajax and Achilles to shame. And why not? Why not, indeed? Apollo mused. She had labored mightily and deserved this respite. It would only add to her vigor later. He smiled at the lusty thought.

Amber's glance fell upon him. She frowned. "Hey, Goldilocks, you're new. Who are you?"

"Apollo, god of light, and your true love." He raised his arms. The sound of a holy lyre filled the air with liquid notes. He smiled, hoping that the revelation of his true nature would not be too much for Amber to bear.

"Yeah?" she said. "Well, I'm the Queen of Sheba."

Apollo paused, momentarily flustered. The queen, as he recalled, had been dark-haired, of dusky visage, and looked nothing like Amber. But he recovered quickly and decided to play along. "How delightful, Your Majesty. Then I'll worship at your feet." He knelt, bowing low.

She stepped over him and reached for a pack of cigarettes. Selecting one, she stuck it between her rosebud lips and lit the tip. With a gesture of her hand she cleared the room. They were alone. "Am I really supposed to call you Apollo?"

"Well, some people call me Chrysocomes," he said, turning his head in becoming modesty to show off the golden curls from which the name sprang.

"Chriso-what?" She inhaled deeply and exhaled a cloud of malodorous smoke directly into his face. "So is your name Chris or Al, or something else?"

"Whatever you wish to call me, fabulous maiden." Apollo got to his feet, standing at his full magnificent height.

"Maiden?" Amber snorted. "It's been a while since anybody called me that. You're funny, Goldilocks. Where did you say you come from?"

"From Olympus."

"Is that in Greece? You're pretty light-skinned for a Greek, aren't you? Got a Swede in the woodpile?" She snickered. Apollo smiled uncomprehendingly. At least she was smiling at him.

"So Chris-or-Al, what've you got for me? Some blow?"

"Pardon me?"

"Y'know, white powder, cocaine." Her tone indicated considerable pique.

Apollo rushed to reassure her. "Oh, no, sweet one. I have nothing of the sort."

"Well, could you get me some?"

"Of course. I am a god, you know."

"So you said." Amber settled into a sling chair, kicked off her shoes, and rested her right ankle upon her left knee. A tattoo on one thigh said, "Right Side." On the other leg, the tattoo read: "Suicide." But most thrilling of all, Amber wore no undergarments. Apollo could see her private parts, right up to the mount of delight. He was enraptured by the sight, although he noted, with some slight disappointment, that she was not a natural redhead.

Was this an invitation? he wondered. No, too soon. He would bide his time, making the rewards that much sweeter. Meanwhile, she wanted something called cocaine. He dimly recalled it: the powdery residue of the sour coca leaf. So be it.

A pile of cocaine appeared at Amber's feet.

Her eyes lit up. "Not bad. Not bad at all." She leaned over, dipped in a pinky and licked it. "Very good, in fact. So, Chris, aside from the blow, what else are you good for?"

"Pardon me?"

"I mean, I've got a regular supplier. I assume you want to sell me something or screw me. What's your gimmick?"

"But I told you, I'm the god of light—"

"I know, my own true love." Her imitation of his voice was creditable. "Look," she said. "I've done them all. Mick, Bill, k.d., Rodman. Animal, mineral, vegetable."

"I'm afraid I don't understand." This was not going as Apollo had expected. Once he revealed himself in his full magnificence, the maiden, overcome, usually submitted or fled. But the fabulous Amber was doing neither. She looked positively unimpressed. Well, he would show her.

He clapped his hands together and sang one note that encompassed every scale, every chord, every sound in the known—and unknown—universe.

The room was filled with a wild spray of light, bouncing from wall to wall, golden and silver and every color of the spectrum. Pink flowers rained from the ceiling and became lavender butterflies before they reached the floor. A fountain erupted from the center of the room and began to fill the air with its heady, astonishing perfume.

Apollo clapped his hands once more.

The room was silent, the illusion gone.

Amber smiled. "Very nice, very cute. I can use that. Maybe we can even incorporate it before Denver." She gave him a sly look. "Chris, you didn't tell me you were an f/x expert. I've been looking for one ever since I sacked the last creep. And you provide good blow, too. Okay, you're on the payroll as of now."

"Payroll? I want no payment. No tribute, save one. You."

"Sorry, I never sleep with the help. Policy."

"But Amber, blessed lady—"

She waved away his objections. "I know, I know, it's tearing you up inside. I'm your reason for living. Do you know how many times I've heard those lines? If I slept with everybody who wanted me, I'd never have time for anything else. Nope, sorry. You've got to give me a good reason—a damned good one—for violating my own policy."

"Let me take you on a tour of wonders such as few mortals have seen."

"Namely?"

"I'll take you to fair Olympus itself."

"Greece? Sorry, no time. And I hate retsina."

"Well, then, to Poseidon under the sea—"

"No Poseidon adventures for me, thank you. I saw that old movie. Besides, I can't swim anyway."

Apollo paused, wondering what to offer. Then he knew. Of course. "A trip to Hades."

"You mean Hell?" Amber's eyes widened. "Get-outtahere. You're kidding."

"A god never kids."

"Hangin' in Hades." Amber rocked back in her chair. "Yeah, I can see it. Amber: the Hades Tour. What a kick. Can I videotape it? I'll only go if I can videotape it."

"Whatever you wish, if you'll be mine."

"The trip first, then we'll see."

"Done."

"You promise?"

"Yes." He reached out. "Take my hand."

His chariot came for them in a flood of light and a fierce arpeggio of notes. Swept up in glory, Apollo and his passenger descended into the earth.

* * *

The rock-walled chamber was long, windy, and it had no end. Shadows of departed souls blew through the air, moaning, weeping, crying out. It was not and never had been a pleasant place, nor was it meant to be.

Amber stared around her, and her look was one of

triumphant satisfaction. "Wait until Cher sees this. She'll pee in her pants." She picked up her camera and the thing began to whine as she filmed, turning slowly. "But where're the boiling tar pits, the souls in agony, the fires of Hell?" She shivered. "It's actually cold down here. Last thing I expected."

"This is the land of the dead. It is as it is."

"Okay. Whatever." Amber paused. "So do you think I could, like, talk to Jim Morrison? Or Kurt Cobain?" She hugged herself. "Imagine, Amber and Kurt, together after death!"

"Summoning individual spirits is difficult."

"Are you saying you can't do it?"

"No," Apollo said. "But the spirits are often unwilling to come. They are not as they were in life."

"Cool. Then Marie Antoinette might, like, actually be holding her head under her arm?"

Apollo sighed. "Possibly. I do not know. For this we must consult Pluto. He rules here with his wife."

They neared two thrones of stone with two dark figures upon them. A hideous creature, three-headed, hyenalike, with six opaque eyes, guarded the thrones.

Apollo saw that, as usual, Pluto's face and form were terrible to behold. At his side, Persephone, his bride, cast her somber gaze upon the visitors.

"Why have you come?" Pluto asked. His voice rumbled like distant thunder.

Apollo bowed to his uncle and nodded his head ever so slightly toward Amber. "A brief visit."

"See that it is very brief," Pluto said. He turned away.

"Who was that?" Amber whispered. "Your old man?"

"My uncle."

"He owns this place?"

"Not exactly."

"And is that his pet?" She reached out a hand to the awful monster that guarded the rulers of Hades. "Nice doggy. Scratch your tummy?"

Cerberus took a hesitant sniff of her hand and backed away, whining from each of its three terrible mouths.

"Hey, c'mon, pooch!" She reached for its studded collar, grabbed it and pulled.

The whine became an agonized howl.

"Cease," Pluto thundered. "He is not for the living."

Frowning, Amber released Hell's guardian. Her glance at Apollo was filled with reproach. "I thought you told me I could do whatever I wanted here."

"Well, almost anything."

"Nephew, why have you brought this troublesome mortal to my realm before her time?" Pluto's face was livid.

"A whim, Uncle. I promise you, we'll make no further disturbances." Apollo took Amber's arm and hustled her away from the lord and lady of Hades. "Let us go over here, shall we?" He pulled her toward a dark and sinuous river. Its opaque waters lapped at the colorless shore with the sound of endless sighing.

"You're not just kidding me, are you?" Amber said. "This is the real thing, isn't it, not just some theme park or George Lucas-type virtual reality?"

"This is Hades."

"Brutally cool. I'll bet even Diamanda Galas hasn't been here yet." She skipped along the cold stone riverbank until they came to a ferry crossing. The boat was just pulling in from its journey to the other side. The boatman, old Charon, eyed Apollo and his charge with a grim, resigned air.

"The fare is an obol," he said.

Amber grabbed the ferryman's oar. "Let me steer

the boat. Ooh, can I take some dead souls across? Can I?''

"But she's not dead yet," Charon said.

Apollo nodded in apology. "I know."

"This is not part of my job," Charon said. He crossed his arms. "I have nothing to do with the living. Until she leaves Hades, this ferry is closed." He put down his oar and sat, motionless, head averted. The oar, clattering down against the boards of the boat, dark with river mud, spattered the hem of Amber's dress.

"Shit! Look at that stain. This dress is a Versace! Are you going to pay for its cleaning? It's ruined. I'll probably have to get an entire new dress!"

Charon heaved a sigh. "Mortals!" He put his cloak over his head and settled into silence.

On the far shore of the dark river a queue of spirits was massing. Apollo could already hear the sighs and whispers of the disgruntled shades.

"Come," he said. "Let us visit the Plain of Asphodel. I can show you the burning river Phlegethon."

"I'd rather see Elvis. Or Marlene Dietrich."

The god of light felt distinctly nettled. "Have I not explained already? There are no people here, only pale shades and a few fading memories."

"Then what good is it? Where are the fires, the souls in torment, the devils with pitchforks?"

Apollo shrugged, confused. "I have no knowledge of such things."

"I thought you said that you were a god!" Amber's eyes flashed. "Don't gods know everything?"

Apollo saw that he was failing to impress her. "Well, we know *many* things." To his relief he saw a distraction ahead. "Look. A famous shrine of this place."

Rugged stones, cast up like jagged teeth, formed a half circle near the shore. At the center of the arc on a low stone outcropping sat a large silver salver cradling a freshly cut pomegranate. Lucious red seeds spilled into a ruby pile, glinting against the shining metal.

"Ooh, yum!" Amber reached for a bright red morsel.

Apollo barely stopped her in time. "I don't think that would be a good idea."

"Why not?"

"The last woman who ate a pomegranate seed here was forced to return to Hades every six months."

"No lie? She needs to get a lawyer."

"There are no lawyers in the underworld."

"I thought that's where they all came from."

Apollo felt his spirits lift. Amber was smiling again. A moment later he felt even better. A pale wisp bloated toward them. "Look," he said. "A dead soul approaches."

"Ooh!" Amber squealed. "Who is it? Cleopatra? Janis Joplin?"

Apollo squinted and finally closed his eyes, attempting to hear the phantom's thoughts. "It tells me that it is a former ruler of an island nation. Henry. The Eighth."

Amber's smile faded. "Oh. Big effin' deal. Just some fat old guy in tights who killed off his wives one by one so he could get married again." She sized up the shade. "Doesn't look much like a king now, does he?"

"I told you—"

"Tell that male chauvinist pig to get lost. Let's go to the Elysian Fields."

"We can't get across the river without the help of Charon."

"That asshole at the ferry?" Amber shrugged. "Forget him. Hey, what about the damnation of souls?

This is hell, right? Do they get judged or condemned or what?"

Apollo nodded, brightening. "Yes, that's right. Of course they do."

"Cool. Let's go see that."

"I must consult my uncle—"

"And do they scream as they're plunged into the horrible depths of the earth?"

"Well, actually, the depths of the earth are reserved for the Titans, who are guarded by the hundred-handed."

"The who?"

"Three giants with fifty heads and one hundred arms."

"Mega-cool! I'll hire them. They can carry my sedan chair onstage."

"I do not believe that they can be hired."

Amber ignored him. "Just let me talk to them."

"They will not see you. It is a place of eternal night. Even I may not venture there."

The queen of Gothic Rock's face darkened. "Hades is really a drag, y'know? I used to think that New Jersey was bad, but this place even beats Newark."

Apollo felt slightly winded. The excursion wasn't turning out at all as he had intended. He settled onto a cool stone surface for a moment and felt a sudden relaxation steal over him. Yes. This was better, much better. He leaned back against the high wall behind him and closed his eyes. A blessed mist settled over his senses. He didn't care why he was there, who he was with . . .

A powerful hand seized his wrist and yanked him upright. Apollo stared at the dark and glowering face before him. He had a feeling that he knew him, somehow.

"Nephew," Pluto said. "Beware the Seat of Forgetfulness." His voice had the quality of long-suffering impatience.

Oh. Now Apollo remembered.

He followed his uncle back to his throne room, wondering what to do next.

Before Pluto could remount his throne, Amber hopped up onto it. "How do I look? Videotape me here, okay?" Oblivious to Persephone's glare, she slung one leg over the armrest and waved.

Apollo gave his aunt and uncle a sheepish look. "Perhaps it's time to leave."

"But I was just getting comfortable," Amber said.

Pluto took a step toward Amber. "I rarely allow mortals to come here before their time, but in this case I might make an exception. There's still room in the deepest pits."

Without hesitation Apollo summoned his chariot.

* * *

He and Amber were below the earth and then they were above it, back in the world of sunlight and living mortals.

Amber stared at him, a pouty look upon her lovely face. "But I wasn't ready to leave yet."

"It was time."

"How did you do that, anyway?"

"One must be a god."

She grinned. "Okay, then make me one. That way I could visit Hades whenever I wanted to."

"I'm sorry, fair lady. Many have longed for what you desire. But you're either born a god or you're not."

"Oh, come on. You're Apollo, right? God of lightshows and peroxide, or whatever. You can bend the rules for me."

"I already have." Apollo wondered what price Pluto would exact from him for his trespass into the lower world.

"That's just for starters. Look, I've been thinking. This god game looks pretty good. It'll give me something to do when I'm older, like twenty-six or twenty-seven, and don't want to tour any more. So make me a god and we'll see about that roll in the hay you've been after."

"I can't do that."

"What about a demigod? I guess that would be all right. I could still have a temple and priestesses, couldn't I? And maybe even sacrifices."

"Sacrifices?" Apollo didn't like what he was hearing.

"Yeah, you know. Blood. Guts. It'll look great in my next video."

Amber stared at him. She seemed extremely pleased with her latest notion. And there was a new fire smoldering in her eyes. "Hmmm, you're really cute, y'know?"

"Yes," Apollo said.

"Yeah. We'd make hella beautiful babies together. And we could videotape the entire process, start to finish." She held up her hands. "I can just see it: Amber, goddess, mother to gods. I like it."

"I told you—"

She talked right over him. "So as soon as you make me a goddess, we can start screwing." She held out her arms.

Apollo backed away. "Uh, will you excuse me for just a moment?" Before she could answer he thinned himself upon the air. But as he faded away, he heard her wail, "You promised, dammit! A deal's a deal."

Even in his insubstantial state, Apollo sighed. She

had him there. He *had* promised her whatever she wanted.

He was in big trouble.

* * *

The skies above Mount Olympus were a perfect blue. Beneath them the gods and goddesses cavorted. All, that is, but Apollo. He was looking for his father, Zeus.

The throne room was empty. So, too were the holy bedchambers. The silken sheets were empty. Zeus wasn't in the wine cellar, nor was he in the kitchen. Finally, in the gardens by the oracle pond, Apollo saw a foot clad in a solid gold sandal. It was sticking out from under a pile of nubile handmaidens. The foot had a familiar look to it, especially around the toes.

"Father?"

"Mmmph?" came the muffled reply.

"Father, I need to talk to you."

"Not now. Can't you see that I'm busy?"

The maidens giggled.

"Please, Father!"

"Oh, all right." Snowy white hair, ruddy face, and various godly body parts were suddenly visible in the gaps between wriggling pink female flesh.

"Girls, I'll see you later." Zeus dislodged his company and blew them kisses as, still giggling, they retreated. Turning a frown upon Apollo, he said testily, "What seems to be the problem that couldn't wait?" He did a double take. "What in Tartarus are you wearing?"

Apollo looked down at his black leather getup. He had almost grown accustomed to it. Suddenly it felt confining, suffocating. Wearily, he replaced it with his fine robes and sandals. Zeus grunted in approval.

"Father, I've gotten myself mixed up with a mortal again. She insists that I impregnate her."

"Well," said the elder god. "What's wrong with that? Sounds like fun to me."

"I don't think it's such a good idea. But I promised her whatever she wanted if she'd sleep with me."

"And now that's not a good idea? Why didn't you think of that in the first place?"

"She's so beautiful, Father. So fiery and exciting."

Zeus chuckled. "You young rams. In too much of a hurry. Now a seasoned god takes a different approach. Some gifts. Some honeyed words. But never promise anything. Merely imply."

"Yes, yes, I tried all that."

Zeus shrugged. "And?"

"All she wanted was a trip to Hades."

"Hades?" The father of the gods looked as though he had swallowed a sour quince. "Most odd."

"So I took her there."

"You did." Zeus nodded, then seemed to actually comprehend what his son was telling him. "You did? I'm sure my brother Pluto had some interesting words for you. What happened there?"

"She frightened Cerberus."

"Frightened the guardian of the infernal gates? Unusual. Still, she's a mortal woman, yes? And she wants to bed you?"

"Oh, she demands it," Apollo said. "On videotape."

"Splendid. Bring me a copy, and we'll show it at next Sunday's foot races."

"Father!"

"Well, what's the matter? Why all this hesitation?"

"Father, I'm just not in the mood any more. She's so—ferocious."

"Not in the mood? What kind of new-fangled notion is that? I never heard of such a thing. Since when did mood have anything to do with sex? You've been spending too much time in the twentieth century."

Apollo leaned closer. "Well, to be honest, I was rather hoping that you'd take this on for me." The sun god smiled the smile that had charmed dryads out of the trees.

"Me?" Zeus looked surprised. "Well, I don't know about that. I'm pretty busy just now."

"As a special favor to your favorite son?"

Zeus cuffed him gently. "And by whose account are you favorite? Well, I suppose I *could* fit her in between nymphs."

Apollo made a great show of bowing. "Father, I would be in your debt."

"Promise me that you'll swear off these flibberty-gibbet celebrities. Stick to milkmaids."

"Whatever you say."

Zeus rubbed his palms together. "Just move aside, sonny, and let me show you how it's done." He blinked.

* * *

He blinked again. He was in the bedchamber of the mortal, Amber.

Amber stared at him. "Where did you come from?"

"Never mind," Zeus said. "Don't be shy."

"Where's Apollo? And whose grandpa are you?"

"Snow on the mountaintop, fire in the belly." The god's robes disappeared. "Forget about Apollo. I'm here now."

"Well, gramps, I'll say this for you, you certainly come well-equipped."

Zeus chuckled. "Don't be skittish, m'dear. Come along and lie down. You remind me of—oh, what was her name?—Danae. Don't make me turn myself into a shower of gold."

"Golden showers? No way. I'm *really* not into that."

Zeus clapped his hands. A snowy bed as wide as a hayfield appeared. Grasping his by now erect member in one hand, he reached for Amber with the other. "Come to me."

"Now wait just a minute—" She slid out from under his arm and pointed at his majestic erection. "Haven't you ever heard about foreplay?"

"Pardon?" Zeus blinked.

"Y'know. You touch me. Then you touch me some more, here and there. Maybe you lick me. Tease me. Please me." She grinned. "Never heard that tune, did you? You're positively antediluvian."

"Yes, that's true," Zeus said proudly. "But what does Atlantis have to do with bed matters?"

"What I mean is, no lickee, no tickee." She waggled her fingers at him and made a lewd gesture with her hips.

Zeus was beginning to see the world through a red haze. He'd been warned by Hera that this was a dangerous sign—that his temper was about to erupt. If only the girl would be quiet and lie down—

"Why don't you just put that thing away until you figure out how to use it?" Amber said.

Zeus lost all semblance of control. "Vixen!" he snarled. "I'll teach you to toy with the master of Olympus."

He clapped his hands. The sound was like a hundred thunderbolts.

Where, a moment before, Amber's dark copper tresses had curled around her face, a hundred stone-gray snakes now writhed and spat, hissing madly.

Amber clutched her head and cried, "What the fuck have you done, old man?"

"Revealed your true nature."

Cursing, she raced out of the room.

Zeus listened carefully, anticipating heartfelt screams and delicious pleas for pity.

All was silent. The top Greek god heard nary a wail, not even a satisfyingly wrenching moan.

Had she died from fright? Swallowed her tongue? Eventually, curiosity got the better of him. Zeus went to the doorway and peered out into the hall.

Amber stood before a round and beveled mirror, still as a statue, staring intently at her reflection. The snakes coiled and uncoiled.

Perhaps, Zeus thought, the wench had been struck dumb. He fervently hoped so.

Just then she spoke, in a husky whisper. "Cool. Brutally, totally cool."

The perversity of this mortal! "You won't enjoy it so much when your visage turns men to stone," Zeus snapped.

"You mean it?"

"Of course."

"Mega-cool."

Zeus made a vow that in the future he would never again fool with his son's girlfriends. Apollo's taste in mortals left a great deal to be desired, and he would tell him so just as soon as he saw him. With a snort of disgust, the lord of Olympus blinked and vanished.

Alone in her chambers, Amber contemplated her new coiffure. The gray snakes slithered and spat in ceaseless motion.

It was really too bad about Apollo, she thought. But she would survive without becoming a goddess. She stared into a golden hand-mirror, contemplating her reflection.

The snakes writhed, never still, angry, terrifying.

"Perfect," Amber said. "Just wait until those record label slimeheads want to decrease my royalties. I'll turn their secretaries to stone. But first maybe I'll take care of a few music critics."

* * *

Safely tucked away in his chambers on lofty Olympus, Apollo watched the fading reflection of Amber in his magic pool. He felt no remorse, nothing except relief. She had been dazzling, yes, and very sexy, but a flawed vessel, unworthy.

He turned his attention to a new image now coming into focus. Blonde hair, sturdy jaw, serious demeanor. She reminded him a bit of his sisters Athena and Diana. For a moment the thought quelled his rising interest, but then he saw a flame of passion burn in her eyes. She was queenly, magnificent. He must have her.

He knew that his father would frown, but at the moment Zeus was taken up with family matters, namely, a harangue by Hera.

Tiptoeing out of his temple, Apollo prepared himself for the coming challenge. He groomed his golden locks, bathed in mare's milk and annointed his lordly body with sandalwood. He wanted to be at his best, his most awesome, when he revealed himself to Hillary Rodham Clinton.

IN RE: NEPHELEGERETES
by Lawrence Watt-Evans

Lawrence Watt-Evans is the author of the "Brown Magician" trilogy, along with numerous other novels and short stories.

   Where Karen Haber's story dealt with gods pursuing mortals, Lawrence Watt-Evans chose to deal with the consequences of such a pursuit. . . .

"The son of a bitch just up and *left* me!" the blonde wailed; Benny Perelman resisted the temptation to cover his ears. Her voice wasn't bad, but the volume was more than his tiny office could handle, and her accent was the worst of everything California had to offer, blending midwestern twang, Hispanic lilt, and that distinctive Valley Girl rhythm. "He didn't even *pretend* it was anything else," she said. " 'It has been a delight,' he says, 'nay, a myraid delights, but it's time I returned to my wife. . . .' " Her expression shifted abruptly to astonished fury. "I didn't even know the bastard still *had* a wife!"

   Benny tried to smile sympathetically, but the resulting expression was closer to a wince. Unless there were something more to the story, this dumb broad's dreams of collecting palimony for her six-week fling with someone else's husband were on a par with Benny's own hopes of winning a few million in Vegas, the chief difference being that Benny *knew* he was never really going to hit the big jackpot.

There might be a chance at an out-of-court settlement, though—or less politely, a little blackmail—if the male in question was rich enough, and sufficiently desirous of keeping his reputation unsullied.

"So what's this guy's name?" he asked.

"Zeus Nephelegeretes," she replied, somehow managing to produce the entire sesquipedalian surname without stumbling. Benny supposed she'd practiced it—he could imagine the poor bimbo standing in front of the mirror with a white dress, trying out "Mrs. Nephelegeretes" for size.

At least Benny thought it had to be a real name—*nobody* would have come up with a fake like that! That would make finding the guy easier.

She was looking at him expectantly, as if waiting for a comment. "Greek, huh?" Benny asked.

Her expression changed to utter disdain. "Well, *duh*!" she said.

"Is he rich?" Benny asked, dispensing with subtlety.

"He's *Zeus*, for heaven's sake!"

Benny decided not to admit his ignorance of just who this Nephelegeretes character was; he didn't want to look stupid in front of a potential client, and he could always look the name up later.

But it sounded like the guy *was* rich.

"So tell me about it, Ms . . . uh . . ." He had already forgotten the name she had given him; he hadn't expected the interview to get even this far.

"Darwin," she said. "Bambi Darwin. I told you."

"Of course, Ms. Darwin. So how did you and, um, Zeus . . ." Benny wasn't about to attempt that last name after only hearing it once. "How did you meet?"

"I just stepped out my door one morning and there he was, waiting for me in the driveway," she said. "Not that I knew it was him, or anything; all I saw was a Harley. I thought someone must have left it by mistake, you know? Though I don't see how they could have . . ."

"Wait a minute," Benny interrupted. "He was on a motorcycle? If he was still there, why'd you think someone had left . . ."

"He wasn't *on* a motorcycle," Bambi interrupted right back. "He *was* a motorcycle. A big, beautiful Harley-Davidson, standing there in my driveway, all gleaming chrome and black leather . . ." She sighed.

Benny blinked. "I don't get you," he said. "Was he on the Harley or not?"

Bambi stared at him.

"You really *don't* get it, do you?" she said. "He's *Zeus*. Olympian Zeus. King of the gods. That Zeus."

Puzzled, Benny said, "You said his name was Neffle-something."

"Nephelegeretes. It means 'cloud-gathering.' That's what Homer called him."

"Homer who? Simpson?"

"Homer the blind poet who wrote the *Iliad*. Jesus, how'd you ever get through law school?"

That was a new one on Benny; he stared at Bambi Darwin, the starlet with peroxide hair and spectacular bosom, the absolute epitome of the California blonde, who was calling *him* dumb.

She stared back for a moment, then sighed.

"Okay, look," she said. "You ever study Greek myths in school? Maybe saw *Clash of the Titans,* that Ray Harryhausen flick?"

"Sure," Benny said.

"So, you remember Zeus, the king of the gods? Big guy, threw lightning bolts like javelins, had the hots for anything with tits?"

Benny vaguely remembered some guy sitting around on clouds in *Clash of the Titans*. "Sure," he said. "Who played him? This Neffle guy?"

Bambi looked ready to strangle him.

"No," she said, biting off short whatever word had been about to follow the negative. "I mean the *god himself.*"

Benny stared at her. It was April, but three weeks past the first, and she looked completely serious. He protested, "But those guys lived thousands of years ago! Besides, they were just myths!"

"Gods are *immortal,* you bo . . . Mr. Perelman. A couple of thousand years is nothing to them. Believe me, I *know.*"

Benny continued to stare at her, and the truth gradually penetrated.

Ms. Bambi Darwin genuinely thought she had been boffing a god.

This led him immediately to the conclusion that Ms. Bambi Darwin was crazy as a bedbug.

"Anyway," Bambi said, settling back, "if you remember the stories, Zeus used to turn himself into stuff in order to get the women he wanted. He turned into a swan to seduce Leda, and a shower of gold for Danae. For me, he turned into a Harley-Davidson." She shrugged. "I've gotta admit it worked. It's the fastest way anyone's ever found to get between *my* legs."

Benny winced. "If we ever get to court, don't even *think* of repeating that," he said.

She sat up angrily. "Hey, do I look . . ." She stopped, and the anger vanished. A bit sheepish, she said, "Well, yeah, I suppose I do look it, but just take my word for it, Mr. Perelman, I am *not* stupid."

Just nuts, Benny thought. He nodded. "Of course not," he said.

"So anyway," she continued, "there was the Harley sitting in my driveway, and there wasn't anyone else in sight, so I went over to take a look at it, and, you know, I just sort of wanted to try it out. So I climbed on, and I swear I didn't touch the key, which was right there in the ignition, but I did *not* touch it, and it started up, and next thing I knew I was halfway to Redondo Beach, and I figured what the hell, I'd just take a look at the ocean and then head back. So I got down to the beach, to the state park, and stopped the bike and sort of settled in, looking out at the Pacific, all sparkling in the morning light—it was beautiful, you know? And the Harley was all hot, and the vibration, and everything . . . Anyway, I leaned forward over the handlebars—and wham, there I am sitting astride Mr. Cloud-Gatherer, with my hands in his hair and his face in my cleavage, and . . . well, right there on the beach—I mean, he was *so* hot. It was pretty clear how he got all those women in the stories." She blushed slightly, and Benny was charmed; he hadn't seen a woman blush in years.

She'd presumably screwed *someone* for all those weeks, even if it wasn't the King of the Gods; maybe he could get her some sort of settlement just out of sympathy.

"So afterward I wasn't about to say no to anything, you know?" she continued. "Except he didn't want me to tell anyone about him, and I couldn't help saying something to my mother—I tell her everything. But other than that I went along with whatever he wanted. He moved in to my place in Gardena, and I thought we had a pretty good thing going, and then this morning wham, he says good-bye and walks out, and I was pretty upset, but then I remembered something I'd read about where demigods come from, so I stopped by the drugstore for a home pregnancy test, just in case. I was taking precautions, you know, but the stories . . . well, damn it, the stories were right!" Her eyes began to cloud up. She swallowed, and said,

"My mother warned me. I was on the Pill, but hey, gods are, y'know, *divinely* potent. I knew right away I wanted to sue the bastard, and I have friends who recommended you, so I called you, and here I am."

"Child support?" Benny brightened. That had *much* better odds than palimony. "Or are you going to get rid of it?"

"I don't think I *dare* get rid of it," she said.

"Um," Benny said, remembering her delusion. He supposed aborting a god's kid wouldn't go over very well. Then he brightened. "Well, we can say you have religious reasons for keeping the child."

Bambi smiled weakly—the first time she had smiled since arriving in his office. "You got it," she said.

It was Benny's turn to frown deeply as something occurred to him. He thought he had a case here; if the broad really was pregnant he could probably turn her obvious derangement into a few extra grand in every payment—but first he had to find the defendant.

"So . . . if he walked out on you, and the two of you only saw each other at your place in Gardena and on the beach, how're we going to find him? I tend to think process servers aren't exactly welcome on Mount Olympus."

She grimaced. "Yeah," she said. "I know. But he's got a few temples still, in Greece and Italy, and he gave me a fax number . . ." She fumbled in her purse, then handed Benny a slip of paper.

Benny took it. "Olympus has a fax number?"

"Hey, *everybody* has a fax number these days," Bambi said. "Why shouldn't they?"

Benny couldn't answer that. He looked at the paper, and saw that it was an overseas number; he didn't recognize the country code.

"Worth a shot," he said. "We can't subpoena him,

but maybe once he knows there's a kid coming, he'll agree to a meeting."

*   *   *

He agreed. The return fax was in a bold Roman font, floridly worded, professing great affection for Ms. Bambina Muñoz-Darwin and acknowledging—hell, Benny thought, *boasting* of—the paternity of her unborn son.

"Of course it's a boy," Bambi muttered. "Damned old-world sexist pig."

The fax also agreed to a meeting, with the understanding that all cooperation was entirely dependent upon no mention of Ms. Muñoz-Darwin's condition or recent involvement being made in any wedding chapel or other temple of Hera anywhere on Earth, nor any further faxes being sent.

"Well, I'll be damned," Benny said, as he read the document through for the second time. *"He* thinks he's Zeus, too."

*   *   *

Benny had to admit that the guy looked the part of a god—tall, majestic, magnificently broad-shouldered, his face calm and unlined. He wore his white hair and beard long, and arrayed in ringlets; the contrast with his smooth, youthful complexion was striking.

He was dressed in an impeccable gray suit, and filled the conference room doorway quite convincingly, almost hiding another figure who stood just behind him—a shadowy figure, almost as tall. The white-haired man announced, "My brother has chosen to accompany me. I trust you have no objection."

"Of course not," Benny said. "We have nothing to

hide." He gestured at the waiting chairs. "Come in and make yourselves comfortable."

The two men entered and seated themselves, Zeus striding boldly, his dark brother moving silently, almost stealthily. Benny stared at the brother, but seemed unable to see him properly; he got an impression of someone large, dark, and forbidding. . . .

Uncomfortable, he tore his gaze away and looked around the table. "Well, we're all here," he said.

Then he noticed that Bambi wasn't listening. She was staring at the dark figure.

Benny frowned and turned to Zeus. "I'm sorry, I didn't get your brother's name . . . ?"

"Hades," Zeus said. "I had thought you would recognize him."

"Hades?" Benny looked at the dark figure and paled slightly under his tan. Whoever and whatever that guy was, Benny didn't want anything to do with him.

"If you're trying to intimidate us, it isn't going to work," Bambi snapped. "I'm not scared of *him*."

Her voice didn't sound entirely steady, and Benny glanced at her.

She was still staring at Hades. From her expression, she really *wasn't* scared.

That didn't mean she wasn't reacting, though.

Benny suppressed a groan; he leaned over and muttered, "Hey, pay attention. We have business to conduct." Then he leaned closer and whispered, "What *is* it with you? You have a thing for gods? That guy gives me the creeps! And if you act like a round-heeled slut, it isn't gonna make my job any easier!" He glanced at the two gods—somehow, here in the room with them, he was having much less difficulty in believing they were indeed gods—and wondered whether Zeus had brought Hades along deliberately, knowing Bambi would find him attractive.

Tall, dark, and handsome, yeah, but still, Benny wondered, what did Bambi see in *him*?

"Sorry," Bambi said, turning away from that ominous figure. "Guess maybe I *do* have a fascination with the divine." She giggled nervously and stole a quick glance at Hades. "Or maybe a deathwish."

"Well, whatever it is, it can wait," Benny said. Then he turned to Zeus and spoke up.

"In your fax you acknowledged impregnating my client," he said. "May I ask what your intentions are toward the child and mother-to-be?"

"I have no intentions," Zeus replied. "The child is mine, and will be a mighty hero. When he is grown, he may come to me as a son comes to a father, to be recognized and accorded the treatment he deserves."

"Hm." Benny cleared his throat. "I'm afraid that isn't sufficient. Under the laws of this state you have an obligation to provide for the feeding, clothing, shelter, and education of your offspring. If you are unable to do in person—as I understand to be the case here, since you're married—then you must make support payments to the mother until the child is grown."

"Payments? I do not traffic in earthly wealth." Zeus, already dominating the room, seemed to swell. "I am not bound by Man's laws, nor do I recognize this state of which you speak."

"You damn well *better* recognize the State of California!" Bambi said, suddenly angry. "This isn't your precious Greece! This is *my* place, my family's homeland, where *our* rules apply and you old gods don't count for anything special!"

"California?" Zeus glanced at Hades, who shrugged. "I have kept up with the times in many ways, but these western lands are still strange to me.

The legendary isle named for the Amazon queen Califia—is that what you claim this place to be?"

"You're in Orange County, in the State of California, yes," Benny said.

"I had not troubled myself to learn the local
names," Zeus remarked. "Interesting. Califia was dei-
fied, was she not?"

"I haven't . . ." Benny began.

Bambi interrupted him. "You *bet* Califia was dei-
fied—you're not the only god around here, Zeus!" As
Benny tried unsuccessfully to quiet her, she shouted,
"Maybe you'd *better* trouble yourself a little more in
the future. You think you can just go where you want
and do as you please, and not pay any attention to
the consequences? Well, think again! I'm not just any
bimbo, Mr. Lightning Bolt, I'm a true Californian and
proud of it—a daughter of Califia!"

"And I am King of the Gods, the lord of Olympus,"
Zeus said in reply—not shouting, but firmly, in a voice
that brooked no dispute. "I *will* do as I please. And
I accept the consequences of my actions. You say the
laws of your people require me to support my son; it
is a just law. I will see that he is provided for. I cannot
make payments in your currency, however. I have no
earthly wealth."

"Uh-huh," Benny said. "And just how will you provide for him, then?"

"That is what we are here to resolve." He turned
to Bambi. "Beloved treasure," he said, "what would
you have of me? I give you my blessing; good fortune
shall be yours. What more do you ask?"

"I've got all the blessing I need from my mother,"
Bambi grumbled, her arms folded across her chest.
"What I *want* is someone who'll help me raise the
kid—but *you,* you're going back to your wife!"

"I must," Zeus said. "Hera is not to be dismissed,

not even by me. And for your own safety she must never know of our liaison; she would take vengeance upon you, and upon the child, for she has not the power to strike against me directly."

"So I get to raise a demigod by myself. A single mother in a tract house in Gardena, no support payments, gotta get daycare whenever I'm working . . ."

"Perhaps other arrangements can be made," Zeus said thoughtfully, with a glance at his brother.

"Like what?" Bambi demanded, before Benny could intervene. "You going to take us back to Olympus with you?"

"No; Hera would find you. But perhaps there's another possibility." He gestured at Hades.

Benny and Bambi both turned to stare at the dark brother.

"Him?" Bambi said. "What, *he's* going to come live in Gardena and play babysitter?"

"No. But for half the year you could live with him, in his own shadowy home, as his honored guest, your every need attended."

"*Half* the year?" Benny asked.

Zeus nodded. "In the summers, when his own wife is away visiting her mother in the daylight lands. In the winter Queen Persephone is at home, and were she to know of this arrangement she might well let a word slip—if not to Hera herself, then to Demeter, or some other."

"And you don't think your brother himself might blab?" Bambi asked.

"As you may have observed," Zeus said dryly, "he does not speak o'ermuch. That was why I trusted him to accompany me here, as adviser."

"So you didn't already have this planned out?" Benny asked suspiciously.

"Do not question me too closely, mortal," Zeus said mildly.

"How do we even know he agrees?" Bambi asked.

"I agree," Hades said, in a voice that sent chills down Benny's spine—but which apparently touched Bambi somewhere else, as her mouth came open slightly, her breath quickened, and her eyes grew big and dark.

"So do I," she whispered. Then she shook herself. "But my mother's gonna hate it," she said. "She *hates* it if I go out of state, even for a minute."

"Don't agree to anything yet," Benny warned Bambi. "We're still talking." He thought, but did not say aloud, that the suggested arrangement didn't cover his fee, and he wasn't about to consider *anything* settled until that was taken care of.

But the rest was simply details.

* * *

Hades was waiting by the ferryboat as Bambi hurried down the ramp dragging an immense suitcase. Benny was a few steps up the slope, making sure everything went off as arranged; he took the suitcase and accompanied her to the boat.

She was just beginning to bulge a little around the middle, but was still gorgeous; her golden hair stood out like a beacon in this rather gloomy place.

"Your mother's not seeing you off?" he asked, as he handed the suitcase to Hades.

"No," Bambi said. "She's too upset. I'm sorry about that; you'll have to live with whatever she does about it."

Benny had yet to meet Bambi's oft-mentioned mother, and had no intention of changing that any time soon, so he thought he could bear up under her displeasure—especially since he had, indeed, negotiated himself a good fee, in the form of certain divine assurances of good fortune.

"I'm sure she'll be fine," he said.

"Well, I've warned you," Bambi said doubtfully, as she took Hades' hand and stepped onto the ferry.

"Sure," Benny said. "What's your mother's name, so I'll know if she calls?"

Bambi stared at him open-mouthed. "Didn't I tell you? I'm *sure* I did, when I got so mad at the meeting!"

"I don't remember it," Benny admitted.

"My mother's name is Califia," Bambi said as Hades pushed the boat off.

Benny blinked.

"See you in six months!" Bambi said with a wave, as the ferry vanished into the shadows.

"Six months!" Benny called after her. "Have a good time!"

Then he turned away and walked slowly up the ramp, out of the dim netherworld into a California May . . .

Where it was already starting to snow.

HEKATE'S HOUNDS
by Diana L. Paxson

Diana Paxson has written a number of meticulously re-
searched historically- and mythically-based novels, including *The Serpent's Tooth* (King Lear retold as a tale of Iron
Age Britain) and the *Wodan's Children* trilogy (the Sigfrid
and Brunahild myth). She is currently working on an Arthu-
rian novel.

Caria, Asia Minor, 363 AD

"The Emperor is dead!"

Diotima dropped the turnip back into the
farmer's basket and turned to stare down the narrow
street that led from the market square, hardly big
enough to merit the name of forum, to the harbor.
Heads appeared at upper windows and people popped
out of doorways and ran toward the docks, trailed by
barking dogs.

"Julian has been killed in Persia!" Other voices carried the news. The beloved of Apollo is no more!"
Wails of grief echoed from mud walls.

But as the word spread, new cries were added to
the clamor.

"The spawn of Satanas is dead! The Lord has punished the Apostate Emperor and redeemed his people!" Jubilation clashed with mourning as the local
Galileans joined the crowd.

Diotima's vision darkened, and she wondered detachedly if she were going to faint. A true philosopher, said her father, was unaffected by the reversals of fortune. A true philosopher would note the vicious satisfaction in the Christian rejoicing with unconcern.

But then Diodatus did not believe that a woman could be a true philosopher. She took a deep breath, blinking as returning sight showed her the crowd recoiling toward the square in the wake of the messenger.

It had not been an assassination—everyone's first suspicion in these troubled times—or if so, it was not an open one. The Emperor had been wounded in a battle in Persia and died shortly thereafter.

"You see—" jeered the Christians, "your gods are false and without power!" And in this moment of disaster, it was hard to call them wrong.

The emperor's successor was somebody called Jovian who was, despite his name, one of the Galileans. Prayers of rejoicing were commanded, but she noticed that the proclamation was somewhat vague regarding to which god they should be addressed. In nearby Didyma, where Julian had been consecrated as one of Apollo's prophets, the mourning would, no doubt, be more sincere.

"At last!" cried a woman stretching her arms to the heavens in exultation, "our Lord has triumphed!" Diotima recognized her as the local bishop's housekeeper. Her name was Rachel. In another moment she realized that the woman had recognized her as well. "Surely now you will accept Him, sister—" Rachel held out her arms. "The way to salvation lies open to you now!"

"The emperor who is gone allowed you to worship your god in peace," answered Diotima. "That is all I ask of those who shall come."

The woman shook her head in sorrow, but in another moment she had been swept away by the press of people coming in to hear the news.

As the swelling crowd filled the square Diotima was forced backward and stumbled into one of the newcomers.

"Idolatrous bitch!" he spat, recognizing her as the philosopher's daughter, "your devils didn't help your emperor, and they won't help you!"

Diotima recoiled, pulling her veil across her face with a prayer to Hekate, but the man's laughter followed her as she fled down the alleyway.

Several of the dogs loped after her, grinning like Chaldean daemones, ignoring her when she tried to shoo them away. Her father considered dogs to be the minions of Physis, a lesser aspect of Hekate who ruled the irrational soul, and had taught his daughter to consider them dangerous and unclean. Fortunately, when she reached the crossroads and turned up the road to the hills they lost interest and lay down panting in the dust.

The villa where the philosopher Diodatus had made his home was set amid acacia trees at the edge of the hills above the town. When Diotima returned, her father was in his study, her uncle meditating in the garden. She knew better than to disturb them, but old Lilias in the kitchen shook her head at the news.

"The poor young man! Do you remember how his face shone when they made him priest of the oracle? I am glad we journeyed to Didyma for the rites. We shall not see his like again."

"I remember . . ." said Diotima.

The oracle of Apollo at Didyma was a woman, but the priests who interpreted her words to the people were male. The Emperor's inauguration had sent the entire province into a frenzy of celebration. Her father and uncle had been given honored places among the philosophers and she had been privileged to accompany them, with old Lilias as chaperone. She remembered Julian, thin, intense, his eyes luminous with divine ecstasy. For months after the visit that face had haunted her dreams.

And now he was dead without an heir, and in an Empire ruled not by Hellenes but by Galileans, no man would dare to wed the daughter of a pagan philosopher who had little dowry but her intelligent face and shining dark hair. She would spend the rest of her life keeping house for her father and uncle, with no hope for husband or child. She reflected bitterly that her father, who believed that the soul's descent into flesh was a misfortune anyway, would not complain.

But her lack of a husband was likely to be the least of her worries. Frowning, she told Lilias how the Christian had cursed her.

"You should have let me go to the market!" The old woman shook her head. "It is not right for a maiden of good family to go out alone—"

Diotima looked at her old nurse, who could hardly hobble from the garden to the kitchen without wincing, and sighed.

"Lilias, it is not the insult that disturbs me. You didn't hear them—I think we are all in danger now!"

She repeated her warning when her father and uncle joined them for the noon meal.

"The Emperor dead?" For a moment she saw in her father's eyes the disbelieving stare of a hurt child. Then Diodatus blinked, and his features regained their customary calm. "It is Rome's loss, indeed, but we should rejoice that he has left this world behind and ascended to the true realm of the soul."

He cleared his throat and continued, "As for us, I think, daughter, that you overestimate the threat."

"There is much to be admired in the Christians," said her uncle Theophilus. "They are men of pure life, denying the flesh. Bishop Nennius has in his household four virgins and lives with them as sisters."

"Virgins!" Diotima snorted. "Virgins who come to old Lilias in the dark hours of the night seeking herbs to cast out unborn babes. Do not widen your eyes at me, uncle. I was with Lilias when the woman came!"

The old man shook his head sorrowfully. "I am saddened to hear it, the more because I know how guilt must tear the bishop's heart. The flesh is loud in its claims."

Diotima stared. And what about the woman? What must she feel, bound to bear not only her own guilt but the burden of being an occasion of sin, as the priests of the Christians would say?

"Be that as it may," said her father, "we fared well enough under Constantine, and though the temples will no doubt lose much of their prestige without the support of the Emperor, does not Plotinus tell us that the gods should come to the wise man, not he to the gods?"

Her uncle Theophilus put down the egg he had been peeling. "But Iamblichus teaches that each man must come to the gods in his own way, some through pure meditation, and others through ceremony. The strength of the Galileans is that they welcome everybody. Where will the people worship if the temples are abandoned? And how can society be healthy if it is cut off from the gods? We may be enlightened, brother, but I think we will be very lonely if that should come to pass."

Her father, brightening, countered with another quote from Plotinus. Diotima sat back with a sigh, recognizing the first moves of a philosophic duel that could continue until night fell. Exasperation warred with affection as she watched them argue, her father wiry in body, balding, with a beak of a nose that quivered with intensity as he spoke, and her uncle, a more attenuated version of the same pattern, with gentler eyes.

It was Theophilus, the follower of Iamblichus, who encouraged his brother not only to talk about the gods—theology—but to engage in the magical workings of theurgy. But they would still rather debate than eat. She tried to tell herself it did not matter; the danger, if there was one, was not immediate. Her father and his brother could remain in their world of Ideals a little longer.

Hekate Enodia, Lady of the Crossroads, she prayed as she went into the kitchen to help Lilias, *show us our way*!

But it would appear that Diodatus, despite his philosophic demeanor, had not discounted his daughter's words entirely. On the following day, he directed her to prepare the upper room they used as a temple for a working in honor of Hekate, the patroness of theurgy.

That day Diotima sprinkled and swept with especial care, for a dirty house and a troubled mind were alike a barrier to divine communion. She polished the holy vessels and set them ready on the altar, laid the fire, put out the bowl of barley and made sure the lamps were filled with oil. When all was readied, she took her place on the stool by the door.

When she reached womanhood, her father had hoped to train her as a seeress, but she was, she sup-

posed, too much his daughter to relinquish consciousness, even for the gods. It was Theophilus, her uncle,
who was their medium, while Diodatus conducted the
rituals and Diotima kept the lamps filled and watched
the door.

Her father entered first.

"Hekas, o hekas, este bebeloi— Let all that is pro-
fane be far from here!"

The lamp flames flickered wildly as he moved coun-
terclockwise around the chamber, sweeping away any
psychic impurities with the branch of cypress in his
hand. Theophilus followed him, the white woolen
folds of his mantle drawn over his head as if he already stood in the presence of the gods.

The purification complete, Diodatus laid the branch
across the threshold. Diotima handed him the basket
of barley and the three returned to the altar, where
each in turn scattered a few grains upon the marble
surface.

"Children of Earth and starry heaven, why have you
come here?" Diodatus turned to them.

"We are here to honor the gods and goddesses,"
they replied.

Diodatus nodded gravely, touched a long waxed
reed to the lamp that burned in its niche behind the
altar, then touched it to the fire. In a few moments
the fragrant scent of cedar filled the room. Diotima
handed him the flagons of water and wine which he
mixed in the krater and then poured out the libations,
first to Hestia and then to Hekate. Diotima took back
the flagons and offered him the vial of oil. A philosopher did not shed the blood of living beings, but the
oil was spikenard, quite costly enough to be a worthy
offering. The heavy sweet odor mingled with the
harsher scent of the myrrh that was cast onto the
flames after the oil.

"Hekate, accept and delight in our offerings—"

Diotima put out her hand as her uncle swayed, and assisted him to sit down. He smiled at her, blinking, and she saw that his pupils were already dilated with the onset of trance. Diodatus stepped back from the altar, lifting his hands in salutation, and launched into the hymn—

"Hekate I praise, who with your bright torches lit the way when blue-robed Demeter searched for her daughter . . ."

Diotima, kneeling beside her uncle, felt a wave of dizziness and shook her head to clear it, catching phrases and fragments of her father's song.

"Upon the waves you walk, and lie down with the gods who dwell in the depths of the sea . . ."

She sat back on her heels and rubbed her eyes, wondering what sudden wind had sent sparks showering from the altar fire and shadows scampering like playful dogs about the room.

". . . the moon blazes from your torches; you know the secrets of the starry heavens.

Lady of the three ways, looking in every direction equally, you see what has been, what is, and what will be . . ."

From her uncle came a formless moan. His mantle had fallen back and his darkened eyes gazed unseeing before him. Diodatus glanced at his brother and spoke more quickly.

"Wide-wandering Hekate, there is no road you have not walked, no mystery beyond your knowledge;

Workwoman of the cosmos, bestower of life-bearing fire,

From your right flank the Primal Soul flows forth abundantly,

Your left enshrines the Source of Virtue undefiled . . ."

He was leaving out large portions of the hymn, hurrying to finish before the goddess actually arrived.

"Giver of gifts, we ask your blessing; Be not distant from us, oh goddess! With your bright torches light us to wisdom!"

From the pouch that hung at his waist Diodatus drew the *iynx-wheel*. Taking his stance before Theophilus, the priest pulled out the loops of cord so that the pierced golden disk was suspended, the Chaldean characters with which it was incised glinting in the lamplight. Then he began to whirl it, twisting up the rawhide cord, pulling it out, and letting it wind itself up once more. As he pulled, the *iynx* hummed softly. When it began to run down, he whirled it again.

Diotima, kneeling behind Theophilus and holding him, fought to keep her own breathing even. She was no medium, but there had been times when awareness altered and she felt the pressure of the unseen like a heat upon her skin. The experience had always been frustrating, because her fear of losing herself prevented it from going further, but now, hearing the whirling *iynx* roar as if a lion prowled the room, she felt her senses expanding until there were no boundaries between her own spirit and her uncle's. She saw, as he did, the lightnings that played about the temple, wandering fires that formed in swift succession the shapes of children, a horse, a pack of black and cheerfully grinning hounds.

"Hekate, Hekate!" Diodatus cried, ignoring the apparitions. "Goddess be with us! Enodia, Kleidukos . . ." Hearing came and went as the priest called out the holy names. "Hekate Soteira . . . Lady of Salvation, hear and appear, hear and appear to us now!"

And then there was only a bright darkness that overwhelmed all other senses. The air grew heavy, as if something too great for mortal comprehension were attempting to fit itself into the room. Diotima felt an odd tickling and shook her head. It did no good—the feeling was *inside* her mind. In panic she thrust it away.

In the next moment she felt her uncle's body go rigid beneath her hands.

"Lady, I conjure you, be gentle to this mortal—" Diodatus spoke firmly, but his features were strained. "Whisper your wisdom in his ear, that he may speak your will. . . ."

Gradually, the awful rigidity began to ease, though Theophilus still quivered like a bent bow. Then that, too, passed, and he sat upright as an image, eyes closed.

"I have come . . . hearing your eloquent prayers . . ." It was like hearing a statue speak, for only his mouth and the muscles of his throat moved. ". . . which the nature of mortals discovered in the counsels of the gods." The voice seemed to come from some great distance, unhuman, but unmistakably female.

Diotima drew a deep breath. The pressure was gone, but the tension remained, focused in the slight figure before her.

"What is it," said the goddess through his mouth, "that you desire to know."

"How shall we guard ourselves from the evils of the world?"

"Being dressed in the full-armored force of the re-sounding light, equipping the intellect and the soul with the weaponry of three-barbed strength, you must wander amongst the fiery rays not in a scattered manner but with full concentration."

Diotima frowned. The armor of intellectual light might ward the spirit from stain, but would it protect the body from stones flung by a Christian mob? She had noticed that the answers one got from an oracle, or a deity, were usually in the same style as the question.

"Will we escape the snares that blind the spirit and attain to the radiant Gnosis of the Father?"

"Open the immortal depth of the soul," came the answer, "The Divine is not easily accessible to those who think about the body. Do not incline toward the somber world, delighting in images without intellect."

"But I do think about the body!" exclaimed Diotima. "If the Christians destroy us, who will pour out the wine and the oil for you?"

Though Theophilus did not move, Diotima felt the blind gaze of the goddess turn toward her, and trembled.

"That which was not born of the world cannot be destroyed by it. The Supernal Fire transcends the darkness. But in the world of forms there are many whose spirits are shadowed. Beware . . . Beware. Beware!"

The Voice roared through the room like thunder. Then it was gone, and the goddess with it, and Theophilus collapsed into Diotima's arms.

"You fool!" Diodatus glared at his daughter over Theophilus' head as he felt for his brother's pulse. "He could have died if you had angered Her. Only the priest understands how to put the questions!"

But does he understand what questions to ask? she thought rebelliously. Then Theophilus began to stir, and while Diodatus poured the final libations and thanked the goddesses, she applied herself to tending him.

The problem with oracles, no matter what god or goddess gave them, was in the interpretation. In the endless discussions of theurgy that went on over meals in the house of Diodatus, Diotima had learned that the ability of a spirit to communicate was limited by the concepts and vocabulary available in the mind of the medium. Theophilus had steeped himself in the works of Plato and his followers. It was not surprising, therefore, that the goddess who came to him discoursed in the language of Neo-Platonic philosophy.

It was not surprising, she thought as she cleared away the remains of the melons and bread on which they had breakfasted, but it was not very useful. Her father and uncle had been arguing since dawn about the meaning of Hekate's words, and Diotima, still in disgrace because of her interruption, dared not offer an interpretation. Still debating, the two men returned to their studies.

She was helping Lilias to shell peas when she heard someone coming up the path. Her belly clenched with anxiety, but surely a mob of angry Galileans would have made more noise. Still holding the bowl of peas, she went to the door. Not a mob, she thought as the woman entered, but a Christian, the girl Rachel from the household of Bishop Nennius who had come to them by night once before.

"So, my child," said Lilias, evaluating her color and her waistline with an experienced eye, "is all well with you?"

"Yes, yes!" Rachel looked over her shoulder nervously, "But I can't stay— I've come to warn you!"

Diotima and Lilias exchanged looks, and the older woman pulled up a bench for their visitor to sit down.

"What have you heard?"

"Men came last night to the Bishop," said the girl, "I heard them talking when I served the wine. They said that God has struck down the Apostate Emperor and now it is up to us to cleanse the sin of idolatry from the land. Pagans of the common sort will be encouraged to seek instruction in the true faith. But they blame the philosophers for counseling the emperors to persecute us in the time of Diocletian—" She shook her head in distress.

"But that was a generation ago!" exclaimed Diotima. "The Emperor Julian restored the worship of the gods, but he did not persecute Jews or followers of the Galilean way—"

They had laughed, she remembered, at the disappointment of those Christians who had expected an imminent martyrdom to wash away their sins. Julian's worst act against them had been to "bring the religion into disrepute" by inviting priests from different Christian sects to debate for the entertainment of his court.

"The Lord is a jealous God," said Rachel. "But you helped me. If you will not convert, you must flee. I have stayed too long—" She got to her feet, wrapping her mantle around her. "May whatever gods you follow have mercy on you, for you will get none from Bishop Nennius and his men!"

"My father should have named me Cassandra!" exclaimed Diotima furiously, gazing at Diodatus' shut door. "Why won't he listen to me?" She had gone to him, certain that the Christian girl's warning would convince him of their danger, and he had responded with words of philosophic detachment and turned away.

"Because you are a woman," said Lilias. "But we women have magic of our own. It lacks a week till the new moon, but I think the goddess will understand. Come, child, we will make an offering to Hekate that maybe she will like better than your father's philosophy."

They spent the evening making their preparations, and just before midnight crept out, mantles drawn over their heads, and latched the gate quietly behind them. Once or twice a dog barked as they passed other houses. Diotima looked at her old nurse with new respect as a word from Lilias silenced them.

The moon was dark and the stars were partly veiled by high clouds. A restless wind whispered in the tree-tops and rustled the drying grass. Diotima's steps lagged as she paused to listen, thinking she heard words. She shivered involuntarily and reminded herself that it was not the evil spirits of the night she had to fear, but the evil in the hearts of mortal men. Lilias' bent figure was disappearing into the shadows ahead. Whispering a protective charm, Diotima hurried after her.

The midnight stars were overhead when they came to the place where the road from the hills joined two others, one leading to Miletus, and the other to the town. As they approached, they slowed, looking about them nervously, for only thieves and murderers had business abroad at such an hour.

And witches . . . Diotima thought wryly. *And any man who disturbs us here had best beware of Lilias' spells!*

Quickly they arranged the offerings of eggs, salted mullet, and lamb cooked in honey by the side of the road, and poured out the libation of resinous wine. About the round cake three lamps were set burning, and Diotima lit charcoal in a large potsherd and sprinkled it with myrrh and frankincense, sage and storax, until the sweet-scented smoke swirled out across the road.

The old woman hobbled to the center of the place where the three roads met and knelt there, lifting her hands in salutation to each direction in turn.

"Hekate Enodia, Lady of the Crossroads, Mistress of the Daemones who wander between earth and heaven, watch over us! You who guided Persephone back from Hades' realm, guide us! Mighty Mother, your daughters seek safety—be our Salvation!"

Three times she prayed, rocking back and forth on her knees, and three times she sang out the mighty names of the goddess, some of them familiar to Diotima from her father's teaching, some of them ancient in this land which was Hekate's traditional birthplace, when Rome was only a gaggle of mud huts in the Tiber's swamps.

Diotima joined Lilias in the road and called softly, "Goddess, we have set out this supper for your pleasure. Save us from those who would forbid your worship! Send us an omen of your protection!"

They waited, hearing the night creatures who had been frightened by Lilias' incantations begin to give voice again as silence fell. Crickets chirred from the grasses, and a frog in the ditch was answered by another farther down the road. Diotima fixed her gaze upon the old woman, whose dark figure appeared and faded again as the clouds covered the stars. And presently she realized that she was hearing soft footfalls, and breathing that was neither Lilias' nor her own.

Then the clouds moved onward, and she saw the gleam of eyes. A dozen or more dark dog shapes were sitting in the road. Abruptly she became very, very still. These were no spoiled and scrap-fed animals to be frightened with a word, but feral scavengers haunting the borders of human habitation, more dangerous than any wolves.

"... *for being earthly, difficult dogs, they are shameless, and charming souls they constantly drag them away from the rites.*"

The remembered fragment from one of the Chaldean Oracles made her smile in spite of her fear. Slowly she rose to her feet.

"Chariotress of the aery, earthly, and watery dogs," she whispered, "if these be your minions, let us depart without receiving any harm."

For a long moment they only looked at her, and she had time to reflect that she had not intended to escape the stones of the Christians only to be eaten by dogs. Then, tails wagging and tongues lolling, they moved past her. Carefully, Diotima helped the old woman to her feet. In silence they retraced their steps down the road. Behind them, they heard the dogs consuming the offerings.

For three days nothing happened, and Diotima began to believe that their offering had indeed bought them Hekate's protection.

On the fourth day, news came that the Christians of Didyma had risen up and slain Apollo's prophet, perhaps blaming his Order for the counsels to Diocletion which had instigated the last great persecution some sixty years before.

"I shall be sorry to leave this house which, though simple, has sheltered my search for wisdom," said Diodatus, "but it does not become a philosopher to attach himself too much to earthly things. I believe that the time has come for us to depart."

"But brother, where shall we go?" said Theophilus, looking like a lost child, "and how?"

Diotima looked at the two men, both past their prime, weakened by a way of life both sedentary and austere. She had counseled this, but now she wondered the same thing.

"We shall become peripatetic philosophers," Diodatus forced a smile, "with a mule to carry our library."

"One mule can hardly carry it all," said Theophilus dubiously.

"That is true." For a moment grief aged Diodatus' features, then he regained his mask of calm. "We must select the most valuable. . . ."

Diotima cleared her throat. "If the mule draws a cart, you can take more scrolls, and Lilias will be able to ride. Or did you plan to abandon her too?"

For a moment Diodatus looked taken aback, then he smiled. "Of course, a cart! You must go purchase one while we pack up the scrolls."

With my dowry, thought Diotima. But that hardly mattered now.

It seemed unwise to attract attention by going into town, but for a good price, she was able to persuade a local farmer to sell her his mule and the cart in which he drove to market. Her father and uncle were still packing books when she returned just as darkness was beginning to fall.

It was the mule, head up and long ears swiveling, that gave them warning. Diotima put the bag of scrolls she was carrying in the wagon and went to the gate. Through the trees she could see a rosy glow. Was the town on fire? No, for the light was moving. Men were coming with torches.

Her first reaction was anger—at Bishop Nennius' fanatacism, at her father's unworldliness, at the farmer who had sold her the mule and then, perhaps, betrayed them, and at herself, for not pushing harder and so avoiding the confrontation that was coming now. Then she heard the ominous murmur of the crowd, and began to be afraid.

She called out, trying to think of a place her father and uncle might hide. But she had grown up on stories of the last days of Socrates. As they came out onto the porch she realized that rather than be caught cowering beneath a pile of turnips or wedged in the pipes of the hypocaust, they would face whatever might come, even death, with dignity. But Diotima was not resigned, or detached, or accepting; she was frightened and furious.

The torches surged toward the gate; there was a pause, as if the leaders were remembering the respect in which the philosophers had always been held, then one of the Christian deacons stepped forward.

"Julius Diodatus, stand forth to answer for your crimes against God!"

"I am here," came the answer, "but as for crimes, if I have sinned against the true God, surely it is for Him to judge me."

Diotima looked at her father with unwilling admiration, but the calm response seemed to enrage Bishop Nennius, who pushed his way to the forefront of the crowd.

"I speak in the name of the Lord, and I say that you are of the breed that turned the emperors against us, and we will have none such in our community!"

"Thirty years and more we have dwelt among you," said Diodatus, and in his voice Diotima heard the pain. "What household have we wronged? What man insulted? We have no wealth for you to envy. Our only treasure is wisdom, and for that we have given all."

"Your disbelief insults God," said Nennius, his beard bristling. "You must swear to abjure Apollo and Hekate and all your devils and seek instruction in the true faith."

Diotima had never quite believed in evil daemones, but she saw them now in the torchlit faces of these men. *Hekate, Mistress of Daemones,* her spirit cried, *send them away!*

"All my life I have searched for truth," Theophilus moved to stand with his brother. "I would be lost indeed were I to forswear the truth that I have seen."

Diotima looked desperately at the sickle moon that hung in the sky. *Goddess, do not forsake these men who have served you so faithfully!* A wave of dizziness made her sway.

"You stand there so calm—" cried the deacon. "The priest of Apollo screamed before he died, and you will, too!"

"You can only kill our bodies, and they are dross . . ." Diodatus straightened, gathering strength for what must come. Some of the townsmen began to pull stones from the old wall.

"No!" Diotima shook her head, trying to clear her vision, but the torches cast lightnings across the ground. She tried to hear what they were saying, but her ears throbbed to a deep thunder. She told herself she must not faint, but the earth was shifting beneath her feet. "No—" she cried again as a stone sped toward her. She turned to avoid it, turned, turned like the *iynx-wheel*, consciousness wheeling away.

"NO!" She spoke a third time, but it was not *her* voice, and not her will that formed the word. Diotima's own awareness fluttered like a storm-tossed bird as the power of the goddess swept in. "These souls are Mine! You shall not harm them!"

"And who do you think you are, the Empress?" one man laughed.

"She's a pagan whore who has no husband," said another. "Have you been consorting with devils, girl? Have you been casting spells?" He snatched up a stone and flung it.

Diotima glimpsed it coming, felt her arm lifting and saw the stone shatter against her hand.

"I am the Mistress of Magic," she answered in a

mighty voice, "the fount of all enchantment. Beneath the earth I have power, and on it, and in the moon's radiant sphere. At midnight I pass, black dogs baying around Me; in My train the spirits of the dead come dancing. I open the doors of the womb that the child may come into the world, and I open the doors of the grave when men pass out of it."

Diotima felt as if she were looking down from a great height. What the crowd saw she did not know, but many of them were dropping their stones, their faces grown pasty with fear.

But the bishop was too angry to be afraid. He waved his staff in the magic sigils of the Christians, conjuring her in the name of his own spirits to be gone, exorcising her—*Her!*—as if she were some ignorant ghost or wayward daemone that had taken to haunting a farm.

"Yapping dog! I will exorcise *you*!" She pursed her lips in a whistle that shrilled through the shouting.

"Now from the depths my dogs I summon, my brood of black puppies, from the earth come bounding! Soul-devouring daemones, filth devouring, here is a feast for you. Come to Me, come to Me, come to Me now!"

She swept down her arms, and in the sudden silence men heard a distant howling. Louder and louder grew that dreadful singing, and in the next moment the hounds of Hekate came bounding up the road. Half-starved and slavering, feral dogs from the countryside leaped over the walls; watchdogs and farm dogs came after them, deaf to their masters' cries. Tonight, every dog in Caria belonged to Her.

The pack-song changed to a chorus of snarls and growling as the dogs got in amongst the crowd, but louder still was Hekate's laughter. Sharp teeth nipped at calves and ankles, worried at trailing mantles, and

the mob disintegrated into a rabble of fleeing men.
Even the bishop ran, leaving his crook clenched in the
jaws of a huge sheepdog, who laid it at the feet of the
goddess and sat down, red tongue lolling from sharp-
toothed jaws. Some of the others danced around her,
but the rest of the pack was chasing the crowd as dogs
will chase cattle sometimes just to see them run.

Theophilus had sunk down upon a bench, but Diodatus still retained his feet, though he was holding
onto one of the posts that supported the grape-arbor.

"I am She whom you have called on many times in
your temple—" the goddess laughed again, but more
softly. "Why are you afraid?"

"That is true, but I have not before seen you in
such guise. Be gentle, I beg you, to the human whose
form you wear, for she is dear to me."

"Is it so?" asked Hekate. "Then you must take care
of her. My dogs will chase your enemies back to their
homes and hold them there until morning. You must
be long gone by the time the sun rises. Go forward
boldly, for My power will protect you throughout the
hours of night."

Diotima woke slowly, wondering why her bed was
so lumpy, and why the earth shook so. It took her
some time to realize that she was lying wrapped in a
cloak atop the bundled scrolls in the wagon. Rubbing
her eyes, she sat up and looked around her.

To either side rose the dim shapes of hills. Behind
her it was dark, but the sky ahead had a gray pallor
that brightened with each moment that passed. Lilias
sat on the wagon box, driving the mule, and walking
beside it she saw her father and Theophilus.

"Where are we going?"

"Toward Chaldea, the source of wisdom," said her
father, setting his hand on the edge of the wagon as

he looked up at her, "but where we will come to rest is in the hands of the gods."

Diotima nodded. Fragments of memory were beginning to come to her now, along with more twinges and aches than could be accounted for by her strange bed. A flicker of movement to one side caught her eye and she squinted. Along the slope above the road a black dog was trotting, keeping pace with the mule. Looking to the other side she saw another, and more beyond it, slipping like shadows through the grass. Her father did not seem to notice them, and as the sky paled they faded.

But if she tried, she could still see them. She understood then that they would always be with her now. Smiling, she reached out to touch her father's hand, and they gazed eastward toward the rising sun.

In the Empire, the time of the philosophers was done. But it is said that in the border city of Carrhae which is now called Harran, a Platonic tradition survived for seven centuries longer, and through the philosophers of Arabia was passed down to the modern world.

THE ARROWS OF GODLY PASSION
by Mike Resnick and Nick DiChario

Mike Resnick has won a number of Hugo and Nebula Awards for his work. His novel *Santiago* has been optioned for film.

Nick DiChario is a Hugo and World Fantasy Award nominated author whose short fiction has appeared in several major magazines and anthologies.

Arrow of Deception

Mitch Sierra sat at his desk and looked out at his hardworking Customer Service Support Unit. Mitch was Air Sterling management—*upper* management—which meant he had plenty of time to look. He spent most of that time inside the glass bubble that surrounded his office up on the twenty-seventh floor of the Sterling Building in downtown Chicago, checking out the pretty women.

When Mitch first saw the new girl sitting in row 4, seat 12, he knew immediately he'd seen someone special.

"Haswell, sit down," said Mitch. "We've got some urgent business to discuss."

Mitch's male secretary sat in the chair opposite Mitch's desk, and sank himself deeply into its soft leather. "Row 4, seat 12, right?" said Haswell. "Her name is Artemis."

Mitch smiled. "That's what I like about you. You can read my mind."

"Your mind isn't especially difficult to read when it comes to urgent business like this." A cynical response . . . but then Haswell was always cynical when Mitch was on the prowl. Which meant Haswell was always cynical.

"Artemis," repeated Mitch. "Seems to me I've come across that name before."

"She's never worked for us before."

"The name, not the girl."

Mitch stood up, clasped his hands behind his back, and marched to the glass partition that fronted his office. Here, he was every bit as visible as an actor, on stage from nine o'clock in the morning until five at night (or sometimes two or three in the afternoon if he had an early range time at the archery club), so he always wore his finest suits, fresh from the cleaners with nary a wrinkle. His black shoes were polished, his thin necktie cut at a perfect angle down the front of his trim but muscular torso, and his cap lay perched on the edge of his desk, showing off his company wings. He didn't like to wear his cap unless he had to, because his hair was of the thick-wavy-blond variety, a perfect complement to his hale features.

He knew that the women of Air Sterling wanted him—*all* women wanted him, come to think of it—but such had been the story of Mitch's life, so he had learned to be selective. His ego was much more gratified knowing that he was wanted by all but had by few.

Mitch glanced out of his glass office, looking discreetly for his woman-of-choice. "Is Artemis her first name or her last name?"

"Who knows?"

"I'd rather hoped *you* would," said Mitch.

Haswell shrugged. "As far as I can tell, officially and legally, her name is just plain Artemis."

"Intriguing."

"Why do I think you'd find it intriguing if her name was Fungus?"

Mitch ignored Haswell and ogled the woman as inconspicuously as possible. She was talking to a customer on the telephone. He found it almost impossible to look away from her. Her appeal went far beyond the natural beauty some women were blessed with and the tricks of the trade others developed over the years, tricks of makeup and hair style and clothing that flattered one's virtues and concealed one's flaws. Artemis' hair was the rich color and texture of sable. She not only possessed the golden glow of a healthy young woman in her prime but had the look of an athlete—lean, hard, vibrant, graceful, hungry. Her clothing was extraneous, her mannerisms and style spare but reflective of an almost courtly elegance. She was a true combination of wholesome comeliness and a certain majestic grandeur that only the finest breeding proffered. Hell, even Haswell seemed impressed by her, and *nothing* ever impressed Haswell.

"I'd like to learn more about her," said Mitch.

Haswell sipped at his coffee, unsurprised; it was strictly routine. "Shall I pull her personnel file for you?"

Mitch rarely saw his employees before his Human Resources department hired them; such was the procedure at Air Sterling, and Mitch liked it that way. If he wanted to know a little bit more about a woman, he made it a point to find out. Otherwise it was business as usual.

Mitch sat down, satisfied. "You're a credit to your gender."

Haswell got up and started to leave the office. "Someday, Mr. Sierra, if there's any justice in this world, a woman is going to hit you like a ton of bricks," he said with a sigh and a shake of his head.

Mitch, alone once more, looked out again at row 4, seat 12. One more casual glance in her direction couldn't hurt.

Artemis.

Before he knew it, lunchtime had arrived, and Mitch had spent the entire morning staring at her.

Mitch ate lunch at one of his regular places: Gerardi's Bistro—exquisite antipasto, posh furnishings, ivy curling around Roman sculpture, and discreet Italian waiters who understood English perfectly (but couldn't speak a word of it). He often used Gerardi's as a place to entertain the women he was pursuing in order to impress them with his *savoir faire,* but this afternoon he needed to be alone to study the Artemis file, and he felt reasonably certain that no one else from the company would dine here at midday.

He opened the manila folder and scanned its contents:

Artemis had worked for several different airlines over the years. She'd been a stewardess, and she'd been in several different areas of customer service. She'd never been fired or laid off—quite the opposite, in fact. All of her employers begged her to stay. She'd been offered any number of managerial positions and had refused them all. Apparently she liked to move around every year or so. She was smart as a whip, with a degree in aerospace engineering from Colorado University.

Mitch paused, impressed, and tried to imagine why

anyone would turn down all those promotions. After a moment he read the next accomplishment from the file: she was the NCAA women's champion in archery for four consecutive years.

Mitch whistled between his teeth. A woman as strikingly beautiful as Artemis, not only of superior intelligence, but interested in archery? This was far too good to be true. Not that her brains or her interests would have mattered in the end. The fact that she had equaled, or perhaps even bettered his Boston University education, was merely a perk, and the archery a fortunate coincidence. For Artemis, Mitch wouldn't have cared if she had failed a high school equivalency exam, or if her hobby happened to be rifling flea markets in the heart of the ghetto.

He took another look at the file. Artemis had excelled in every position she'd ever been given. She was liked by all, criticized by none, lauded for her professional qualities, extolled for her virtues, and sought after by rival airlines.

Mitch could hear laughter from other conversations, and plates and silverware clanking. The smell of garlic wafted from the escarole soup he hadn't sampled yet.

"What about her personal life?" he mused beneath his breath, and turned to the appropriate page.

Single. No recorded birth date or birthplace. And something else of interest, under the unlikely heading of religious preferences.

She had always made it a practice to inform each of her employers, Air Sterling included, that she was a devout practitioner—if so active a word could be used for so inactive a belief—of celibacy.

Mitch decided it was high time he became a more personable manager. He started walking the floor a bit more, smiling, shaking hands and patting backs, saying his "good mornings" and "good afternoons" and "how-are-yous?"—all of it done solely to impress Artemis.

Oddly enough, the fact that she was celibate did not dissuade Mitch in the least. If anything, it fueled his fire. Rumors had begun to circulate among the male employees of Air Sterling that Artemis was a virgin. The mere thought of such a beautiful creature untouched by human hands was enough to make Mitch shiver in anticipation, and spend several restless nights dreaming about being the first to take the plunge.

Mitch always made sure he had a pleasant word or two each day for Artemis. They were not easy words. Mitch had never been tongue-tied in the presence of a female, but with Artemis he felt foolish, clumsy, confused, and exposed. Their contact was always too brief and frustrating for Mitch, who could never say exactly what he'd intended to say.

Mitch was ruggedly handsome, thirtyish, a man accustomed to seeing gorgeous women not just in an office environment but up close and personal, in just about every compromising position imaginable, pretty much whenever he pleased. It was Mitch's common practice to pick the most beautiful, the most intelligent woman he could find—someone worthy of his own high standards—and take her. Her circumstances never mattered. Married, single, divorced, engaged. Whenever Mitch picked a woman, she could not resist his looks, his charm, his position, his brains, his style, and, ultimately, his body.

But Artemis, for lack of a better turn of phrase, had gotten under his skin. She had the air of an untamed lioness, with all the texture of a Michelangelo masterpiece, and, perhaps her most disarming quality of all, she didn't seem to notice her own power over men. The staring, the gawking, the posturing and pan-dering that went on around her nearly every minute of every day, did not affect her in the least.

It was enough to drive a man insane.

Mitch hated conceding the upper hand in any personal relationship, whether that relationship was casual or intimate, and he knew that if his fumbling went on much longer, he might very well frustrate himself into social paralysis. He'd seen it happen often enough to lesser men. Mitch decided that the time had come to make a play for her, before he made a complete fool of himself while skirting the issue.

"Miss Artemis," he said, "may I have a word with you in private?"

"Of course, Mr. Sierra."

Mitch led Artemis to his glass office. She was a tall woman, almost as tall as he. "Please, sit down."

"Thank you, Mr. Sierra. Nothing is wrong with my job performance, I hope."

"Oh, no, absolutely not. You're doing a marvelous job." Mitch began to sweat. He knew he'd better get right to the point before he started stammering. "I hope you don't think this too forward of me, but to reward you for the quality of your work I was hoping to ask you out to dinner this Saturday evening. I know a wonderful little Italian restaurant that serves the best antipasto in Chicago."

"Oh, thank you for asking, Mr. Sierra, I'm touched."

Mitch's heart leaped for joy.

"But I'm afraid I can't."

Mitch's soul flickered out like a spent candle. For the first time in his life, all words failed him. His mouth hung open. His legs trembled. He wanted to sit down but he couldn't move for fear of falling.

"It's nothing personal," she said.

"Perhaps you don't like Italian food," Mitch suggested. "It might interest you to know that I have a membership at the archery club on Parkway and Harvard. I happened to notice in your personnel file that you're quite an accomplished archer. Possibly you'd like to meet me at the club. I could show you around, we might have a little lunch—"

"That's very kind of you," she said, her smile as steady and unreadable as that of a Russian spy. "But I'm afraid I just don't think it's a good idea for management to fraternize with staff. It doesn't look professional. Besides, I've got the weekend all planned out. I'm headed off Saturday morning, all by myself, to the mountains of West Virginia. I've got a small cottage there. Every once in a while I just like to get away from civilization."

"Oh," said Mitch. "Pity."

"Well, I'd better get back to work. We don't want to keep our valued customers waiting." She stood up, breezed past him out the door, and returned to her work station.

Mitch took out his handkerchief and dabbed the perspiration from his brow. He sat down at his desk and turned his back to his employees.

He felt light-headed.

He felt weak.

He felt deliriously happy.

Mitch knew he hadn't been rejected—no, just the opposite! True, Artemis had said no to him. But then she had told him she was heading to West Virginia for a weekend in the mountains . . . alone. Yes! *That* was an invitation. It *had* to be. Why else would she have mentioned it?

A cool, clean feeling of relief and renewed hope cut through Mitch like a jet stream off Lake Michigan. It had been ridiculous of him to think for even a moment that anyone, even someone as ravishing and perfect as Artemis, could resist his charms. After all, he was ravishing and perfect, too. Artemis was a more sophisticated woman than most, and hence she played a more sophisticated game, a game of clues and innuendo and unspoken challenges. Mitch liked that. She was challenging him to come after her.

All right, I'll play it your way, he thought. *I'll follow you to West Virginia, and then I'll have you. I'll have you, Artemis. I promise.*

But her name continued to haunt him. *Artemis.* He decided to do a little research on the Internet. He seemed to remember the name Artemis from college, but he couldn't quite remember where. His web-crawler found 8,114 references. The first was the best:

Artemis, it seemed was a Greek goddess. Specifically, she was the beautiful child of Leto. Adopted by Zeus, the Lord of Olympus, Artemis was worshiped as the Mistress of Wild Things. Although she would roam freely among the cities, she would always return to the solitude and natural beauty of the mountains.

When Zeus adopted Artemis, she asked him for a special gift. She wanted a golden bow, with golden arrows, and a golden quiver. Zeus was so taken with her beauty that he granted her this wish. With her bow, legend maintains, Artemis protected her maidenhood—by which, the Internet pointed out, it meant her virginity.

There were a lot of parallels. One by one Mitch knocked them down.

Archery? Mere chance.

Celibacy? Hell, lots of people were celibate in this day of AIDS.

Her name? Maybe her parents were Greek, or maybe they named all of their kids after Greek gods.

The only one that bothered him was the little kicker

in the *second* reference: according to myth, anyone who spent time alone with Artemis would end up sharing her commitment to celibacy.

Mitch? *Celibate?* He threw back his head and laughed aloud, then logged onto his computer, referenced Air Sterling's confidential reservations data, and booked himself on all the same flights as Artemis (first class, because Artemis was flying coach and he did not want to be seen before he was ready).

This was going to be a wonderful weekend.

Arrow of Desire

Mitch stood in the small country kitchen in Artemis' cabin. He glanced out at the hardy mountain terrain. He and Artemis were rather high up in the West Virginia mountains, somewhere east of Charleston. He could see nothing but miles and miles of blue-green trees, hills reaching up into the clouds, and slopes falling headlong into dark, misty valleys. It was November, and about an hour ago it had begun to snow, not heavily, but in large, soft flakes.

Mitch poured two steaming mugs of hot chocolate that he'd just boiled atop Artemis' tiny cabin stove, and brought them over to the table where Artemis sat gazing out the picture window. She was wearing blue jeans and a heavy flannel jacket. Her hair was pulled back, her face radiant.

"I've been all over the world," said Mitch, "and this is some of the most beautiful scenery I've ever laid eyes on." He was talking about Artemis, of course, but he decided she didn't need to know that just yet.

"I love it here," she answered. "It rejuvenates me."

Mitch wasn't quite as nervous with Artemis as he had been back in Chicago. He was feeling more confident, partly because his plan, thus far, had worked to perfection. He had followed Artemis unnoticed until she reached the Charleston airport. There he approached her, pretended to be changing planes— "What a coincidence meeting you here!"—and struck up a friendly conversation. He'd told Artemis that he was en route to a conference in New York, but that he had a day and a half to kill before he was expected. "Would you like some company, Artemis? I'd love to see that cabin you were telling me about."

"I don't know if that's such a good idea," she had said.

"Why not?"

"There's nothing up there for you to see, I'm afraid, except the wilderness and the mountains. I think a man like you would be bored to tears."

"Not at all. I love the outdoors. Besides, I would be with you. Nothing could be more delightful."

Mitch had every reason to be pleased with himself. It had all been so easy. A woman as smart as Artemis should have seen clear through him. That could only mean, as Mitch had told Haswell back in Chicago, that Artemis had wanted him to follow her.

Mitch sipped at his hot chocolate.

"It's dusk," said Artemis. "Just look at that amber sky, the orange sun creeping behind the mountains."

"Romantic," Mitch said, placing his hand on her forearm. It was the first time he had touched her, and the thrill of it sent his heart racing.

She turned and looked into his eyes. "I think I'd better go outside and get some wood for the fire. It can get awfully cold at night up here in the mountains. We wouldn't want to be cold tonight, would we?"

The seductive tone of her voice promised something more than burning wood. Her eyes glistened, reflecting the waning light of day. At last the subtle maneuvering was over. Artemis had acknowledged his intent and was taking the game to the next level. She was marvelous!

"Let me get my coat," he said. "I'll help you."

"No, you stay here," she answered. "I don't want you to catch a chill we can't get rid of."

When she stood, oh-so-slowly, she placed her left hand firmly on his shoulder, and Mitch could feel the heat pass between them as blistering as jet fuel.

She didn't come back.

For a little while Mitch wasn't worried, but as darkness closed in, he started getting nervous. How far did Artemis have to go for firewood? Shouldn't she have had a stack of it near the cabin, cut and ready for the fire, or a small shed full of pine kindling? She hadn't gone off with an ax to chop down a tree, for godsakes. Could she have fallen and gotten hurt? Or maybe her absence was part of the ultimate challenge Mitch was to face tonight. Maybe she wanted him to come looking for her.

Mitch donned his coat and stepped out into the brisk mountain air. The snow was still falling. He could see Artemis' footsteps in the frost. He followed her tracks around to the back of the cabin. They led to the woodpile, but no farther. Artemis was nowhere in sight. It was almost dark now, and Mitch could not see very far into the woods. He called her name, but she didn't answer.

Mitch walked through the snow to the nearest rise. He didn't want to walk too far, afraid that he might lose sight of the cabin. The ground was slushy. He wasn't wearing boots. He hadn't been planning on taking a stroll.

"Artemis!" he shouted. No answer. He leaned against the thick trunk of an old tree and scanned the terrain again. There was no seeing much of anything through the trees, the shadows, the encroaching night.

Mitch figured he should probably head back to the cabin. Getting lost in the woods wouldn't do either of them any good. Who knew what she was up to? Perhaps she had changed her mind, and this was her way of backing out of their tryst. She probably knew of another place nearby where she could spend the night without him. Mitch wasn't used to women treating him this way. He didn't like it. In fact, it made him angry. He didn't mind giving chase, but he expected to catch his prey.

He had just started back to the cabin, thinking about how he was going to handle Artemis after this failed rendezvous, when he saw something move out in front of him. He stopped and watched for the movement again. There, just beyond the cabin, a flash of white that looked like a body moving quickly from behind one tree toward another.

"Artemis!" he whispered, edging closer.

Another movement. There was definitely someone out there. He edged closer.

There she was again—yes, a woman, he was certain—dashing behind the rocks a little farther out. It was Artemis. He'd seen enough of her that time. She was naked.

So this was how she liked it. Out in the woods like a wild animal. She wanted to be hunted down and taken. As cold as it was outside, Mitch felt a rush of heat pump through his veins. He'd never been this excited in his entire life. What a prize Artemis would be!

When Mitch reached the rocks, Artemis was gone. He'd expected as much. She wasn't going to make this easy on him. *All the better,* he thought. *All the better in the end.*

Another movement to the left, another to the right. Mitch followed, ran, slipped and fell, followed again. *There—behind him!* He whirled around. No, out in front of him.

"Artemis!" he yelled, unable to contain himself any longer. "I'll find you! I'll find you!"

"No," came Artemis' voice. *"I'll find you!"*

Mitch looked up. There, on the ridge above him, no more than twenty or thirty feet away, stood Artemis. She was completely naked except for a quiver of arrows slung over her shoulder, and a golden bow sparkling in her grip. Her beauty was no less than perfect in every way: the smooth cut of her trim body; the strong, slim legs; the muscular yet sensuous shoulders; the firm, round breasts. She was a vision of absolute eroticism and carnality. Mitch froze. He could not find his breath.

"You should not have come," Artemis said. Her voice was music in his ears, the sound of angels. "I am a goddess, Mitch Sierra. I am Artemis. I defend my maidenhood with the golden bow of Olympus, and after my arrow strikes your heart, you will be celibate for the rest of your pitifully short human existence."

There was no bitterness in her words, there was only truth, justice, and the unearthly music that held Mitch frozen in the snowy hills of West Virginia.

Artemis slowly drew a golden shaft from her quiver, notched the arrow, took aim, and fired.

Mitch saw the arrow hurling toward him. Her aim was true. The arrow, any moment now, would cleave his chest asunder and bury itself in his heart. Mitch Sierra would be celibate forever. Or just plain dead. Same difference. Strangely, the thought of it did not terrify him half as much as he suspected the reality of it would.

But the arrow was moving . . . *slowly.* Mitch wondered about that. He wondered why. The distance and motion that held the arrow aloft seemed to be swallowed by an eerie swirl of space and time, and the shaft's trajectory became bent and twisted into a surrealistic arc of elongated duration, a much more complicated illusion than the typical archer's paradox known to gently warp an arrow's pattern of flight. It seemed to Mitch as if he had plenty of time to get out of the way. But he didn't move. He watched the arrow come closer. . . . No, he *let* the arrow come closer.

What was happening here? He experienced a crisp moment of lost identity, of truncated yet stark amnesia. Who was he? Why was he here? What world, what life had come before him? *Artemis,* he thought. *I know you.*

Then, when the shaft was nearly at his heart, he reached up with his hand and plucked it easily out of the air. Time and space, distance and motion, returned to its normal state of passage.

Artemis lowered her bow and stared at him. Her face changed into an architecture of wonder. She stepped forward, climbed down the ridge, and stood before him, staring into his eyes.

"It's you!" she said. "By Zeus, it's really you! I've found you. After all this time I've finally found you."

Mitch stared at the arrow in his grip. Suddenly he was not a man. He was something more, something greater. He felt eons grow within him, and recede. He felt ages past and future move through the history of his body, living entities, first born, then blossoming, then dying a thousand deaths. He felt the wrath of gods known and unknown. He felt the eternal freedom of immortality, and the prison walls that held him inside it.

"Who am I?" he mumbled. "Who the hell am I?"

They made love all night long—outside under the cold stars although they felt no chill, inside beside the crackling fire, in the small warm bedroom of Artemis' smoky cabin. Greek gods required no respite from love or war, from treachery or delight.

"Dear, sweet Eros!" Artemis said. "The other Gods were so envious of you. Maia, Hermes, Apollo, Dionysus, Orpheus, Atlas, even the mighty Zeus could no longer bear your relentless passion. They drugged you with an evil potion, robbed you of your passionate soul, and buried it in the heart of Man. I've been searching for you ever since. I remembered how much you adored to fly, so I kept searching for your lost soul among those men on earth who pursued the industry of flight. I was certain that someday I would find you. I vowed never to give up."

"We won't tell them you've found me," said Eros. "We'll live here forever on this earth. There are places here that defy the beauty of Olympus." Now that Artemis had touched his heart, Eros remembered who he was, and where he'd come from. He remembered the emptiness at the beginning of time, and how he emerged from Chaos, one of the first three immortal beings. There was Gaea, the Earth Mother; Tartarus, ruler of the Dark Underworld; and Eros, God of Love and Desire, known to the Romans as Cupid, enabler of all creation. The spell of the jealous gods of Olympus had been broken. "We'll live in peace, in love. We'll live forever."

Artemis curled up against him. Sparks flared between their earthly bodies. "Wherever you are, sweet Eros, there will always be beauty to defy Olympus."

Arrow of Fulfillment

They watched the sun rise slowly over the mountaintops. For the first time in a long time, Mitch—Eros—felt contented in the arms of a woman. He thought of

Haswell, and the words he'd spoken: ". . . like a ton of bricks." A wise man, thought Eros, for a mere mortal.

"The beauty is not in me," said Eros. "The beauty is in the passion. The beauty is in the desire."

"No, sweet Eros, I beg to disagree." Artemis gently kissed his tender lips. "The beauty is in us, together, forever."

There in the mountains, where the world of men reached weakly up to grope at Olympus and the Realm of Immortals, all the love in the world once again belonged to the gods, as it had so long ago.

TRAPS
by Jo Clayton

Jo Clayton is the author of the Diadem series and many other works. Her most recent novel is *Drum Warning*.

1

Though the sun was only a vermilion bead between two peaks of the mountains called The Chine, the burgeoning day was already warm. Estila Kair Fonazous loosened the black shawl she'd wound around her head and shoulders and dabbed at her sweaty face with one of the ends as she moved into the shadow under the olive trees, whispering olive hymns to focus her mind on the Genethial rites that rededicated her to the Mother of Olives.

When the cleansing and oiling of the altar and of Athena's Eidolon was done, when the fire was lit in the stone bowl of the sacrifice lamp and the last of the sacred songs was finished, Estila lowered herself onto the broad stone set before the altar, her knees resting in hollows worn by generations before her.

She barely had time to settle there before she was jolted from her peaceful contemplation by a blue-white flare from the Eidolon.

Trouble, Bond Daughter.

Observe.

Serve the Witch.

The mindvoice was deep, rich, powerful, one she'd heard every Genethia since her grandmother had brought her here and bonded her to the first of the olive trees—Athena her Bond Mother speaking with an unfamiliar urgency. Commanding her. Trouble? Serve the Witch?

Tenaron burst from the trees, riding one of Kitryes' prize black geldings. Estila dropped into the shadow of a clump of polebeans until he spurred the laboring beast onto the wooden bridge that crossed the Aftisteri.

On the far side of the undersized river the land turned wild and wet—the Tsikalia, a shallow sheet of water standing over sand and sawgrass, curling round hummocks of gravel and earth with clumps of trees, thickets of redwire brush, tall fronds of bracken. Half an hour's walk from the Aftisteri, the Black Tower rose from the largest of those hummocks, its ancient stones rain-rotted and mottled with the black and poisonous moss that gave the Tower its name.

The Witch lived in Black Tower House.

Serve the Witch?

On her sixth Genethia and many days thereafter, year after year, Estila had stolen away from the altar clearing and climbed into the oak so she could spy on the Witch, a thin, tall woman with dark gold skin who dug in the flower beds or the herb plantings, and raked the gravel paths. Or worked at training Witch Willows to grow flat against the walls, their thin, chartreuse leaves a vegetative calligraphy scrawled over the rough black stone.

The Witch had a ghost twin, a semblance in fine crystal who followed her around, tending the garden with her, singing work songs to make the time pass.

That was odd, but not especially disturbing. One expected Witches to have spirits hanging about.

Serve the Witch.

Athena's whisper was prickly with impatience.

Estila got to her feet, drew the hem of her black skirt between her legs, behind and over her wide black leather belt, baring her legs so she could run without tripping on her hem. A moment later she was racing south along the bank of the river, heading for The Splash, a broad, shallow ford where she could cross without wetting her knees—and with luck reach Black Tower House before her brother did.

2

Marousia wriggled her shoulders and danced her hooves on the oak planks, drawing a satisfactory boom from the workroom's floor. An impatient mutter from her sister made her laugh and stamp a few more times, but when she walked to the long narrow window, she was careful to go quietly.

Stubborn and fierce as she'd been all her life, Matya was trying to read her way through the Tower's library, searching the grimoires and handbooks for some way to reverse what had happened, to free them both from the Mortal Trace, to restore flesh and blood to the spirit body that was all Marous had now.

She retrieved the comb she'd left on the sill and began teasing sleep knots from her mane. "Matya, give it a rest, hm? My gut is growling, so I know you're hungry."

"A moment . . ." The word was swallowed by a yawn and the creak of ancient parchment as her sister unrolled a new page of the scroll.

Marous clicked her teeth. "You won't get much

sleep today if you don't stop soon. It's already stifling."

"Mmmm. I hear you, Hon—a moment . . ."

Creaks and thumps as the scroll went back in its urn—

Patter of felt-shod feet—

Matya slipped the comb from her ghost twin's hand. Humming a centaur song about sun and running, she teased loose one lumpy tangle in the mane, then went to work on the next.

Sighing with pleasure, Marous crossed her arms, rested them on the sill, stretched out as far as her back legs would reach.

She glanced out the window, snorted with disgust.

"That Mortal's back again. Spying on us."

Oak bark digging into her knees, Estila crept through heat-wilted leaves until she reached her usual place and stretched out to scan the garden through the thin skim of foliage at the end of the limb.

A centaur came prancing around a far corner of the hexagonal tower. Knees lifting high, iron-shod hooves beating a lively rhythm into the earth, she whirled and danced to music from the alto flute that floated behind her, held in the hands of the revenant twin.

The Gate Bell's harsh clangor broke into the dance and the music. The centaur squealed and reared; her forelegs crashed down, her form wavered until she was mostly a shiver of blackness.

The blackness steadied.

The Tower Witch stood on the gravel path, her mouth grim, her orange-brown eyes cold with an anger that hadn't changed a nuance when she switched from four legs to two.

She crossed to the Gate, slid the bars from their iron hooks, and turned them vertical. Stepping back several paces, she folded her arms across her ample breasts. "Enter."

Leading the exhausted gelding, Tenaron walked in; he dropped the reins and swaggered along the gravel path to stand looming over the Witch. "They say if you take a notion, you can compound poisons that even a touchstone won't read."

In her deepest, iciest contralto, the Witch said, "They? *They* say a lot of things, most of them lies."

"My stupid brother Kitryes has found a suitor for our sister Estila." He spat. "He'll have the coin from the brideprice in his hands; the rest of us won't get a smell of it."

"So?"

"You sell, I buy."

"I don't have what you want."

He kicked at a clump of grass beside the path. "He's cutting my allowance by half once she's married off. Humiliating me in front of my friends."

"I don't have what you want."

He thrust his hand inside his shirt and brought out a bulging purse. "Name your price."

"I don't have what you want." She spoke slowly, emphasizing every word. "Open your ears, Rockhead. *I do not deal in poisons.*"

"They say—"

"They lie."

Estila drew her tongue across dry lips; her choices for her future had shrunk suddenly to a desperate few and none of them were happy ones.

The Witch thrust her hands behind her back. "Spells and potions I will sell you. Poisons? No! I give you this much time to get out of my face." She brought her right hand around, snapped thumb against fingers.

"If you don't like that, you can join these." She thrust her left hand at him and as it neared his arm she was suddenly holding half a dozen vipers. Their harsh snaky smell filled the garden.

Tenaron screamed and ran.

The Witch sent the black gelding hobbling after his rider and rebarred the Gate. A centaur again, she stomped over the grass patches and gravel paths, venting her anger on the air. "Marous! Did you see that cretin? Did you hear him?"

She threw her head back and screamed, a harsh, terrifying sound that filled the skycurve. Then she went spronking about the garden, blowing off anger, fear, frustration, and excess energy in a series of leaps and contortions.

"Miatseya, calm down. Matya. Sister. Hoo! Go quiet." The revenant's voice was lighter and brighter than the Witch's contralto, a pure tone with very little vibrato, rather like the angelic clarity of a boy's soprano before his voice broke.

"You want to know about dead? Dead is a stone that even water can't wear away."

Estila bit down on her lip. Is that what Athena meant? I'm supposed to get the Witch free of some trap? How does *she* need serving when she can turn people into snakes? The Tsikalia is full of snakes. Foh! More snakes than there are folk in Dimaristopol.

Matya stopped her careening, stood with her legs trembling, her sides heaving like bellows; she snorted uncertainly, shook her head, held it quiet for a moment, shook it again and trudged over to her ghost twin.

For a long time they stood in a loose embrace, as if that brushing touch comforted both of them, then both twitched, wavered, changed. Arms resting about each other's waists, they vanished round the corner of the tower where they'd first appeared.

Estila rose onto hands and knees. "Athena. Mother. What do I do now? Ring the bell? Go home? What?"

No answer.

Estila sighed. "Since it's my call . . ."

She crawled to the trunk, swung down and trotted back to the altar clearing at the heart of the olive grove; if nothing else, she owed the Mother of Olives a day's worth of contemplation and worship. Today was, after all, her eighteenth Genethia.

3

"Who comes so early to disturb my sleep?"

"Estila Kair Fonazous. I ask only for time to state my case."

"Your case or your brother's?"

"Mine." Estila's voice shook as she went on. "Yestereve one Yianik Dia Yisiris dined at Fonazous House. During that meal my brother Kitryes sold me to him. All that remains is the writing of the Contract."

"I don't understand. What do you expect from me? Everything you've said follows the custom and law of your people."

"Yes." She'd meant to wait till she was inside to explain what she wanted; instead, the words came pouring out of her in an anguished whisper. "My mother . . . hates me . . . she told me . . . things. I'd expected to . . . to endure . . . his attentions and find my . . . my peace with Athena and my olive grove. Kitryes made me . . . serve him . . . Yianik the Beast . . . I managed to keep away till I . . . had . . . I had to serve the brandy . . . he touched my arm. . . ." Estila pressed her hand hard against her mouth and set her head against the night-cooled planks of the Gate. It was several minutes before she felt enough in control of herself to go on.

"My mother . . . when he was gone, she told me . . . like I said . . . things . . . about Yianik Dia Yisiris. I'd be his fifth wife. The other four are dead. Childbed. Strangled for adultery. Poisoned . . . that was suicide my mother said. Drowned. That was called an accident. . . .

"There's more. He's rich and respectable, the most powerful man in Dimaristopol. Kitryes is bursting with the need to strut and preen, to boast his connection with that power, but he is also terrified of the man; even he knows about Yianik's Shadow . . . marauder on sea and land . . . slaver . . . blood on his hands . . . on his soul . . . he touched my arm . . . I can't . . . help me. Name your price and help me."

The silence on the other side of the planks grew thicker as Estila faltered through her plea, but when she finished and fell silent, the Gate swung ponderously open. A dark figure waited on the path. "Come inside. Were you followed here?"

"I was, but I came through the olive grove. The trees . . . they . . . um . . . dealt with him." Shivering nervously, Estila pulled the shawl more tightly about her shoulders and stepped onto the gravel path.

The Witch set her hand on Estila's arm, her touch light and warm. "Good. When she takes a proper notion, Great Athena can butcher with the best."

The Tower Witch's consulting office was midway up the hexagonal tower. The room was small and austere, lit by a bronze-and-crystal lamp in the center of a narrow worktable and by the wick trailing in the reservoir of a silver statue of Artemis set up on an altar at the other end of the room. Estila sat at the table, her hands flat on the cool wood. The Witch and her ghost twin were seated across from her.

"We can deliver you to your brother when he comes for you, or shackle you and return you to your House." As Estila started to protest, the Witch lifted a hand, tapping her thumb against her middle two fingers, the simple gesture sealing the Mortal's lips momentarily shut. "Or we can do what you ask of us—once we find out what that is."

The Witch leaned back in the chair, tented her hands; fingertips resting on her lips, she contemplated her visitor. "So. Is it poison? With your kind that's the usual . . . ah well, never mind. A dead brother . . . hm, especially an elder brother . . . no weddings till your mourning year is done."

"No poison." Estila shivered. "I don't dare stay where Yianik can put his hands on me. He . . . custom . . . law . . . he'd brush them away . . ." She stroked her throat, fingers trembling. "Cobwebs . . . ?"

"You're wasting my time and yours. What do you want us to do?"

"I'm bonded to the olive trees on my Marriage Portion land. That bond will be broken and the land will pass to my sister Vangelio when I forfeit my ties to it. Which I will do if I . . . if you could help me to keep the bond . . ." She passed her hands across her eyes. "But that's more meandering . . . I know I can't keep everything. What do I want? I want to be safe from Yianik. Whatever it costs."

"Costs who?"

"Me, you—what does it matter? I'll use anything, with or without its consent." She laced her fingers, stared down at them; it was easier than looking at the Witch. "Guards. That's what I need. Guards to drive off ambush bands of Yianik's Chosen. I want you to get me to the Artemision by Dimaristo. Once I reach the Grand Eidolon, I'm safe. Even Yianik isn't so imperious . . . should I say mad? Roaring mad? I don't know . . . so veiled from god-anger that he'd dare interfere with a Hyerotee. And you're the only folk I can trust to keep your word to me and not go soft in the spine at the first glare from that old Monster."

"We can get you to the Pool, but not to the Eidolon. You have to manage that yourself."

Estila's eyelids drooped shut, and a sudden flood of fatigue sent tremors through her body. "I thought . . . I wasn't sure," she said. "It doesn't matter. I accept." She passed her tongue across her lips, the soft rasp of flesh against flesh the loudest sound in the room.

Matya looked thoughtful. "Have you ever wondered if you might be able to bond with other trees? Willow as an example?"

"Witch Willow?" Startled, Estila lifted her head. "Change my dedication from Athena to Hecate?"

"Yes."

"Why?"

Matya set her hands on the table, the pouch of coin between them. "Name your price, you said. This . . ." She touched the leather with her thumb, applied more pressure and tipped the pouch over, spilling a few of the coins onto the wood. "Gold has no value in our . . . ah . . . present dilemma. If you can bond with Willow and use Willow to reach Willow's Patron and help us open a Gate. . . ."

The Witch leaned back in the chair, her eyes closed, her face stern, the age lines cut into the dark gold skin deepened by the shadows form the flickering lamplight. "I will explain what I can. There is too much we don't know, my sister and I.

"We were—remote? unmindful? apart from? the right word eludes me—outside of Mortal Time and

Mortal Place—the Mortal Trace is what the Gods call it—

"Living in Elsewhere—sun blessed, swept with the warm rains of spring—moving from spring to spring, sometimes into summer, even into the harvest season—but never touching winter—we didn't like cold—my twin and I. We could be anywhere and anywhen at the merest twitch of desire—

"Then Marous my sister—a faun pricked her with his teeth and she died—all that was Mortal melted from her bones. Then even her bones were gone—a faun with a viper's bite and a face wrinkled with evil—he bit and was gone before I could reach him—a faun like none I'd seen before—they're usually playful and happy—innocent—and not accustomed to thinking beyond the moment— This one had the shape but not the temperament—someone molded him from poison and mildew and all ugliness—someone sent him to kill us—us, yes—he came back for me, he was there when—

"I ran to my sister—it took forever—as if I ran through quicksand—the faun was there—he came at me—but I'd had time to think what I should do—I swung round and kicked him with my hind feet—I broke every rib in his evil body—yessssss—I turned him into a bag of flesh and bone bits, yesss—

"Time's Everwhen Flow stopped for us—the Elsewhere was closed to us—is closed even now—I have tried—by Will and Wizardry—and failed—Black Tower House and the Mortal Trace is our prison—we are frozen here—no escape—an hour is an hour—marching single file—Apollo rules—the metronome clicks—day follows day follows day—"

Matya straightened; her eyes snapped open and she brushed at the pouch of coin. "Our price? Our freedom. Reopen the Gates of Elsewhere."

Estila rubbed at her eyes. "But I don't know. . . ."

"All you need do is agree to try."

Estila thrust her hand across the table, palm up. "Agreed," she said. "Let the bargain be sealed."

Matya set her darker hand on Estila's. "Done. I am Miatseya, use name Matya, and my sister is Marous—"

4

At the top of the six-sided Black Tower, three ribbons of silver a handspan wide were laid into the slabs of roof stone—the TriVia sigil sacred to Hecate. At the center of the sigil there was an ancient Eidolon of the Goddess, the iconic three faces gazing along the Crossways from deceptively mild, intelligent dog's eyes.

A master sculptor had carved that Eidolon from the trunks of three black poplars, the wood darkened by age until it was nearly as black as the Tower stone.

Estila dipped the hairy gray moss into the stone bowl, swirled it through the weakly poisonous infusion of yew.

"Lady of the Crossways," she sang. "Great Hecate."

She squeezed the cold clear liquid onto the carved hair and watched it flow down over the three faces, the age-hardened poplar glistening like smoked glass in the dim starlight.

"What I am now, what I shall be," she sang.

The overflow of the infusion dripped from the wood and gathered in the grooves that ran along the silver ribbons of the TriVia sigil and soaked the worn black wool of her robe as she knelt and washed the Eidolon's feet. She dropped the tattered moss into the basin, sat on her heels, and held out her hands, palms up.

"I hold that here in my two hands; it is my gift to thee."

There was no response.

The black wood was Dead. Empty. Not even a Curse. Only the Outline of a place where a Curse might have lain. It was as if the Hecate Paradigm had been attacked and destroyed to the point that the Goddess could no longer indwell. And what would do that? What *could* do that?

Another God?

Not working alone.

A cabal of Great Gods in a secret war? In the *Chronicles of Becoming* there were stories of past wars as Titans and Ouranians struggled for power, stories of alliances and millennial feuds that changed every relationship and lifted first one group then another into the Ruler's Rank.

I don't know. How could I know?

The answer to the Witch's problem was clear now— as Lady of the Crossways, Hecate was the Gateway to Elsewhere and Hecate was locked away from the centaurs. All Estila had to do was find the key that would open the Way.

She sat on her heels and looked up at Matya, wincing as she saw hope flare in the centaur's eyes, then fade as she kept her silence.

"It's almost sunrise," she said finally. "It won't be long before my mother finds me gone and rouses the House. You'd best be ready for Kitryes and my cousins and a declaration of feud if you don't hand me over."

"We're ready."

5

A muscle twitched beside Estila's mouth as she saw a head appear, black against the yellow of the rising sun. Her cousins were coming over the wall to get her, and this one—she thought she recognized him—yes, it *was* Wertin, Old Methualogin's youngest. Wertin had a pash for Vangelio, followed her around like a milky pup. And of course he'd be too eager to wait for Kitryes' signal. Idiot.

Fire leaped in a colorless curtain between her and the climbing man. Wertin shrieked just once, then his body blackened, the howl stopped, and the crisped form vanished.

All along the wall men screamed and crashed down, the screams stopping with the same terrible suddenness.

Estila covered her eyes with her hands, shoved hard against them as if somehow she could force out of her mind what she'd seen and heard.

Snakes in the water, snakes in holes on the hummocks.

Calcined bones on the ground outside the walls. Prime fertilizer. No wonder Witch Willows grew so thick and strong around Black Tower House.

The Witch and her ghost twin needed no help protecting themselves.

Ignoring the noises outside the walls, Matya strolled around the tower, a ruminative half-smile twisting up a corner of her mouth, a braided wand of Willow withes molded from the softest of silvers swinging between the thumb and forefinger of her left hand.

When Estila started to speak, the Witch stopped her with a shake of her head and a flip of her hand. She led Estila to the nearest of the Willows and bent the braided silver of the wand about her wrist, silently smoothing the delicate Willow leaves flat against the skin.

The papery, fibrous bark tickled Estila's palms as the tree came alive under her hands—prickly, quick, squirmy, like a juvenile hedgehog half-enchanted by her touch, half-frightened.

=Hecate's Daugher,= the Willow sang to her. =We bend to you, beg of you, help us.=

Estila drew her fingertips along the graceful, twisting trunk, troubled because she wanted desperately to help but didn't know how. With a sigh, she completed the bond, then moved to the next tree, then the one beyond that, forging bonds as long as she had the strength to complete them, moving through a golden haze of fatigue and muted happiness until strong hands took hold of her and led her to a sun-warmed stone bench.

Matya touched Estila's face. "Hot. Like a fever. Does that mean anything? Did you . . . was there any . . . ?"

Estila shook her head.

Matya pressed her lips together, her face grim with her disappointment. "I'd hoped . . . maybe it's all this sunlight. The Lady of the Crossways prefers night and cloud cover. Rest here and wait for me. I'll be back in a moment."

Estila closed her eyes and slumped against the back of the bench, expecting a resurgence of the fatigue she'd felt so many times before.

Hot, wild energy raced through her.

Startled, she jerked upright and was standing before she was aware of moving. An odd semistiffness spread along her body, an even odder multiplicity of image sprang into her field of vision, a multiplicity of sensation flowed into her from the six arms that dangled from six delicately boned shoulders.

Matya's words hung in the air before her. Hecate was the Lady of the Crossways, the Daughter of Night and Shadow. Sun and Daylight were Apollo's Realm. The two of them at the best of times were Unfriends and Enemies in harder days. Why a cloudless sky and light as hard and burnished as the edge of a damascus blade had worn the Curse Spell thin enough to let Night's Hecate break it so . . . so easily. . . .

Hecate's essence flooded into her, filling and over-filling her with the full power of a goddess, power that had been dammed away from this place for so many centuries that the life and land within the walls of Black Tower House had built up a NEED—a powerful craving that summoned a Godwind—a storm blowing from Elsewhere in wild whirling gusts—snatching her into the air—swinging her round and round the six-sided tower—

Dropping her into the Deadness—the Emptiness at the heart of the Silver TriVia—

Estila flung her arms about the Eidolon—Image clinging to Mirror Image—Hecate's Paradigm, the Master Pattern of the Goddess—which oozed out of her, curdled into a *shape* flattened between the Eidolon's carved wood and Estila's Mortal flesh—a *shape* that flowed into the ancient wood, black poplar, Hecate's Wood, impregnating it with the life force of the goddess—

The Spell dissolved. The Curse was gone.

6

Estila twisted around, frowned at the Black Tower rising dark and ominous against the violet dusk staining the eastern sky. "What happens when we're gone and there's no one to guard the House?"

=No need for guards.= Hecate had taken her horse form, a bitter-dark kafé-brown Mare with three white feet and a white slash down the front of her face. =Wait wait wait. Now! Whistle. Song.=

The reflection of the crescent moon running before

her in the clear, shallow waters of the Tsikalia, Estila played the song that Hecate had etched into her mind—until a glittering burst of whiteness behind her erased the dark and faded the lunar light to a faint glow.

She dropped the willow whistle, twisted round once again.

Her eyes went wide with surprise as she saw a dome delicate as a soap bubble rising above the treetops. "What's that?"

Hecate's Mare snorted, bobbed her head up and down, then settled to a long, steady lope—a gait so smooth the Mare's hooves slid in and out of the water with barely a splash.

A sudden, warbling whoop, loud and raucous.

War cry. The centaurs.

Matya galloped faster and faster, her form elongating with the increasing speed. A breath later and she was gone, melted into Elsewhere.

A silver streak followed her, Marous leaping immaterially through the Gate that Hecate had opened for them.

A short while later Estila heard a sudden flurry of shouts and screams coming from one of the hummocks some distance ahead of them—thud of hooves, splashes of Tsikalia swamp water, more screams, these noises swallowed after a moment by sounds of flight.

A streak of darkness slipped from Elsewhere, slowed, and recaptured form. Matya loped among the hummocks as she had before, her gleaming black mane and tail like silk flags caught and lifted by the wind.

A streak of silver followed the darkness from Elsewhere, acquired a crystal presence. Kicking up sheets of water and foam, a fine mist settling on her and turning her to a living statue of acid-etched glass, Marous once again took her place at guard.

Hecate's Mare laughed—silent mind-laughter it had to be, but also a full free burst of gaiety that coursed warm and comforting through Estila's body.

It was an extraordinary sensation for what was essentially a gauntlet of death where every hand was turned against her, where netmen were set to gather her in and take her to a prison cell she could never escape, a dungeon where torture was bread and anguish the wine she'd drink to wash it down.

The Mare's laughter bubbling in her blood, tickled along by the absurdity of the high-flown phrases whirling through her head, Estila pressed her hand against her mouth, swallowing bursts of giggles.

As the moon's lowest cusp slid behind the western horizon, the land rose and dried out, the clumps of trees thinned and vanished, replaced by pillars and piles of basalt, thickets of thornbush and desiccated weeds.

Hecate's Mare left the Waste and loped along the Market Road that ran the length of Dimaristopol; it was a ragged, rutted Road, red dirt pounded by hooves and wheels into a paving almost as hard as stone and covered with thick and thin layers of fine red dust. Caught by the hot dawn winds, clouds of that dust seethed and swelled, twisted and whipped about, billowed up under the hooves of the centaurs and of Hecate's Mare, stretched out behind them like fingers the earth was pointing at them.

Long after sundown, the Market Road turned south, following the curve of the cliffs that circled Maristo Bay and led to the City of the citystate, Dimaristo.

Matya and Marous were kept busy by a series of

ambushes planted along the Road ahead of them, ambushes that weren't meant to succeed as attacks. Cloaked by the noise and tension from this incessant sniping, a dozen of Yianik's Chosen came in a silent rush from the strip of Waste that ran beside the Road—men in black leather masks shaped and dyed like lizard heads, bronze-clawed gloves and boiled leather cuirasses, each of them carrying small round throw-nets and a half dozen bob-tail lances.

Hecate's Mare glowed darkly as if a hidden wick had been lit inside her.

She *CHANGED*.

Hecate's WolfHound whirled and leaped at the net-men, her mindshout dropping Estila flat along her spine.

The eerie, semisolid light that surrounded Hound and Rider lifted the first of the throw-nets just enough to let it skim across Estila's back, flipped away the next and the next—

Three mouths dripping drool, three sets of yellow fangs snapping in threat, Hecate's Wolfhound swung her heads, slashing at the Chosen, tearing flesh, drawing blood, her limber, powerful body twisting and leaping, avoiding the jagged points of their lances, lunging in rough circles so she could keep close to the Road as she fought and mangled the attackers, turning their ambush into a scramble of self-defense.

Silvertip arrows whirred past Estila, arcing over one or another of the three heads of Hecate's Hound. She glanced over her shoulder, saw the Tower Witch and the ghost twin scrambling toward her.

The Chosen broke off their attack and fled into the rough pastureland beyond the fringe of Waste that bordered the Road.

Pilgrim Avenue.
The Approach to the Artemision.

Hecate's Mare turned between two soaring, free-standing columns of marble so white it glowed with a numinous phosphorescence as magical as the light from a Hunter's Moon. Columns crowned with the Crescent Moons dedicated to the Virgin Huntress.

The Mare leaped into the air above the Sanctuary Pool, reared, bucked, shook Estila from her back into the middle of the Pool, landing her in the center of the reflected image of the moon.

Bugling her triumph, Hecate's Mare whirled, leaped, and vanished into Elsewhere.

Echoing that shout, Matya and Marous leaped after her, finally going home.

As if Hecate's sky-filling Outcry had summoned him, Yianik came striding round the Grand Eidolon of Artemis and stepped into the moonlight to stand with his legs planted wide, his hands clasped behind him, his head thrown back, his eyes fixed on Estila with anticipation and greed—and a smugness born from the knowledge that there was no way she could escape him, not this time.

Fragments of the reflected moon breaking and re-breaking over her, Estila churned toward the Isle, paddling awkwardly as she fought the drag of sodden wool and the stinging slaps as strands of her hair wrapped across her mouth and eyes. When she lifted her head to gasp in more air, she saw Yianik standing between her and the Eidolon of Artemis.

Despair leached strength from her arms and legs. For a few breaths she floated motionless in the dark water.

She had to get past him. Somehow.

Coughing and sputtering, she wallowed into a wider curve, forcing her arms and legs to keep moving despite the drag from her robe and the chill that threatened to freeze her into immobility.

Loud splashing, pressure of water slamming into
her.

Thick black arc of an arm swinging up, swinging
down.

Pain. Exploding against her jaw.

Nothing. . . .

7

Matya shouted with excitement and pleasure, spun
on her hind legs and bounded through centaur Airs
while her ghost twin played a song like liquid laughter
on her long gold flute. Ghost twin and live twin chased
each other, dancing, leaping galloping, working off
eruptions of exuberance. The moment the Gate had
opened for them, Estila, the Black Tower, the Mortal
Trace were wiped from their minds.

Abruptly, Hecate's Eidolon loomed stiff and black
in front of them, blocking the center of the Ride.

"What? Wha . . ."

Marous' eyes popped wide; the flutesong broke off
and the flute went flying from her hands.

Hecate's Eidolon turned in a slow circle.

"Skatch!" Marous swung down and snatched the
instrument from the tuft of grass where it had landed.
She straightened up, stood brushing absently at the
smooth gold. "What is it, Hecate Mother? We did
what we contracted to do."

The Eidolon halted.

Five arms were folded neatly into the folds of the
sparely carved robe; the sixth hand held a short lance
which pointed at an oval shimmer, a mirror of sorts
with moving images passing across its face.

Yianik brought his fist around and slammed it
into Estila's jaw. He grabbed her hair, scowled

at the leader of the Chosen standing on the back of a marble bear, watching him. "Kuvinny! Get over here."

Kuvinny looked at Estila's limp body, looked at Yianik, then lifted his eyes to the gold-and-ivory face of Artemis. He shook his head.

"I'll have your hide!"

Kuvinny shrugged, jumped from the bear's back and vanished into the darkness beyond.

Yianik's face blackened with rage. Thick legs shoving against defiant water, he hauled Estila toward the Isle, bellowing orders as he moved. "Kruo, Sponker, get him. Alive if you can, dead if you have to. If he's still walking free come sunrise, you'll be kissing Old Savo's scourge. Padoc, where are you? Ah! Kuvinny's place is yours if you have the nous to take it."

Padoc oozed from the shadows round the Beast statues, a narrow man with the suppleness of a viper and a hungry gleam in his eyes. He sprang into the water, snatched at Estila's tangled, floating hair and leaped for the black basalt of the Isle.

"Fool! Don't let her touch the Eidolon." Yianik scrambled after him, too lost in the buzz of his fury to care about his own movements. "Pick her up, you're bruising her, you could break bones dragging her like that . . ."

Matya raised her brows.

Marous grinned at her. "Tyché's Blessing. Clean shots and confusion to the Enemy."

The centaurs raced along the narrow strip of grass, moving faster and faster until their legs blurred. The final leap turned them to twinned streaks, dark and light, as they plunged through the Aspect of the Gate that took them back to the Mortal Trace.

As Matya slowed, she laughed and pranced, brandished her bow in comic threat, mocking the Chosen who thought they lay hidden among the beast carvings.

One of the Chosen shouted his rage and flung his bob-tail lance at her; the whistling point gouged a strip of flesh from her haunch an drew a squeal of pain with the blood. She flipped an arrow from the quiver buckled to her harness, nocked it, then saw that the man who'd wounded her was already dead, one of Marous' silvertips skewering his heart.

Matya shouted her thanks and marked another target. Padoc.

Pull. Release.

Arms flung out, hands slipping from their clutch on Estila, Padoc arched backward, dead before he hit the wet black stone.

Pull. Release.

Matya swore as Yianik dodged with unexpected agility and her silvertip tore through the bulge where his arm and shoulder met instead of cleaving his heart. "I'll have you, Monster, Tyché Bless."

Dazed, head throbbing, jaw aching, Estila dragged an arm up and pushed it around in front of her; after a tedious interval her hand jammed against the Isle's black basalt, tearing one of her nails loose. Finger throbbing painfully, she wedged her hand into a crack, pulled her aching body up onto her elbows; panting with the effort, she lurched out of the water and managed to drag herself closer to the Eidolon, collapsing as the embroidered hem of the golden stolé brushed the top of her arm, a band of weathered ivory with sacred signs inlaid in soft gold.

With the last of her strength, she swung her arm in a clumsy arc.

Her hand closed round the Eidolon's ankle.

"Artemis!" She coughed, panted, brought her other arm around and fumbled for a grip, the ivory worn smooth and treacherous by centuries of suppliants' hands. "Shield me."

Yianik roared his frustration and rage. He ran 'round the statue, yipped as another of Matya's silvertips cut off the top of his ear, then dropped behind Estila, using her body as a shield.

He wrapped his arms about her, flung himself backward as he sought to use his weight to break her grip on the ivory.

She ground her teeth, focusing all of her will on maintaining her grip. "Artemis, Mother, help me!"

He twisted one hand into the wool of her robe, buried his other in her hair. Hugging her tight against his massive body, he arched his spine, focused on his purpose and threw himself backward.

The force of his effort hurled him away from her, broke his grip and sent him rolling down the broken rock toward the water. Cursing her, shouting the punishments he'd administer himself, he curled onto his feet, started for her again in a stuttering run that took him to the far side of the Grand Eidolon and brought curses from Matya as she missed him again.

He bent toward Estila—and froze, staring at the tongues of blue fire flickering along his forearms.

Between one breath and the next he was a torch, tainting the air with the sweetish reek of roasting meat.

Out in Maristo Bay, Poseidon rose in his glory from the night-dark water.

On the cliff the Grand Eidolon of Artemis glowed with captured moonlight.

The Great Paradigms glowered at each other, challenge in the blind ivory eyes of the Eidolon, threat in the glassy green stare of the God, godpower sparking from Mortal-carved Ivory and Immortal godflesh.

Matya held out her hand and Marous closed her fingers about it, her grip warm and strong.

The mystery of the Curse was laid clear before them.

Godwar.

The secret, intricate plotting. The maneuvering and manipulation. The Oblique attacks—weeding out the supporters of the enemy with disease, poison, or hunting bow. Or persuading them to change sides.

Matya unstrung her bow, clipped it to her harness. "That pair may not know it, but the war's over."

"Looks like." Marous twitched the loose skin on her flanks, arched her neck. "And far as I can see, it's us who won. Let's go home."

Coughing, nauseated by the stench from Yianik's immolation, Estila uncramped her fingers from their deathgrip on the ivory ankles. Using a fold of Artemis' golden stolé, she pulled herself onto her feet, the tattered black wool of her own robe falling away until she was nearly naked.

Pulling together the edges of the largest of the rips, she stared up at the sky where Hecate and the centaurs had vanished. There was nothing to mark the spot, not even the faintest of stars. Absurd that so momentous a departure should leave no trace behind. And frightening. A sign—if she ever managed to read it.

"Hecate Mother," she cried. "Blesséd you be.

Matya and Marous, all that I have, all that I am, this is yours."

A hand closed on her shoulder. "Bless our Virgin Huntress instead, Aspirant."

Too exhausted for fear to touch her, Estila turned her head, saw a tall, gray-haired woman standing beside her. "Who are you?"

"Doskalarché Dymna. I teach Aspirants what they need to know. You desire Sanctuary?"

"More. I offer service."

Doskalarché Dymna nodded. "Many do. We'll ask again a year from now. Follow me." She turned and stepped onto an elegant wrought-iron bridge that ran from the Sanctuary Isle to a Trilith Gate at the eastern end of the pool.

"Follow. . . ." Estila could see the peaks of the temple's golden roof rising above obsidian cliffs, but the place where the centaurs had vanished was lost; that she'd never find again.

The sign.

For Estila, nothing was unchanging, eternal. The future she expected would never be, and the one she got would have no rules except watch your back and keep your eyes open. And there would be no markers to guide her. All she'd have was the wit she was born with.

She smiled. *The wit I was born with.* Laughing aloud, she ran onto the bridge and hurried after the Doskalarché.

FEBRUARY THAW
by Tanya Huff

Tanya Huff lives in Ontario, Canada. Her most recent DAW
book is *Blood Debt,* fifth in the "Vicki Nelson" series of
occult adventures.

Scuffing across the rec room floor in a pair of well-
worn fuzzy slippers, Demeter, Goddess of the Harvest, pulled open the door to her small wine cellar,
took a bottle of wine from the rack and held it up to
the light. A Tignanello, 1990; lovely vintage. Most of
the family didn't think much of Dionysus, but she
rather liked him. Not only did he do very nice things
with the grapes she provided but, in his other guise
as God of Theatrical Arts, he saw to it that she got
complimentary tickets to all the big shows.

She'd seen *Cats* half a dozen times before the novelty wore off.

Tucking the bottle under her arm, she scuffed back
to her chair and settled into the overstuffed cushions
with a satisfied sigh. One thumb popped the cork—
there were perks to being an immortal goddess after
all—and she settled back with a glass of wine in one
hand and the television remote in the other.

Demeter loved winter. Not so much because she
had nothing to do after the rush of planting, tending,
and harvesting, but because her house was her own

again. She could eat what she wanted, she could drink what she wanted, she could wear what she wanted, and, most importantly, she could watch what she wanted. During the winter, she wore stretchy fabrics and watched absolutely nothing with socially redeeming value.

"I admit it," she announced to the fat, disinterested tabby sprawled in the middle of a braided rug. "I was an overprotective mother. Well, what do you expect? I was a single, working mom. *He* was never around. Still . . ." She took a long, contented swallow of the wine and turned on the first of the afternoon's talk shows. ". . . if I had it to do over, I'd give them a nice set of salad bowls and my blessing."

"Mom?"

Having just taken another drink, Demeter choked.

"Mom? Where are you?" Fashionably high heels ringing against the worn carpeting on the stairs, Persephone descended into the rec room to find her mother dabbing at the stains on her turquoise track suit with one hand and trying to fish a tissue out of the box with the other. "Mother! Honestly!" She shoved a tissue into Demeter's searching fingers. "It's the middle of the afternoon!"

Wiping at the wine dribbling out her nose, the goddess glared up at her only daughter. "What," she demanded, "are you doing here? There's two more months until spring."

"Two more months?" Persephone repeated, volume rising with every word. "Two more months? I couldn't stay with that man two more minutes!"

While she had every intention of being supportive, Demeter couldn't help looking a little wistfully toward the muted TV as she asked, "What did he do?"

"What didn't he do?" Throwing herself down on the sofa, Persephone ran a slender hand through cornsilk blonde hair. "He leaves his socks and underwear on the floor, he never gets any exercise . . ."

Just why the Lord of the Underworld, who was not only slender bordering on downright skinny but also an immortal god, needed to exercise, Demeter had no idea.

". . . he spends all his time playing poker with Minos, Rhadamanthys, and Aeacus, he lets that stupid dog up on the furniture."

"Sephie, these don't sound like reasons for you to leave a god you've been married to for millennia. In fact, they sound an awful lot like the things you complain about every spring." She leaned forward and patted her daughter's knee with one plump hand, trying to sound more sympathetic than she felt. "What's the real reason you're here when you shouldn't be?"

In the silence between question and answer, the cat wisely got up and left the room.

"We had a fight."

"What about?"

"Pomegranates."

"What, again?"

"This was a different fight." Her face crumpled. "Hades doesn't love me anymore!"

Picking up the box of tissues, Demeter moved to the sofa beside Persephone. "Of course, he loves you, sweetie."

"No, he used to, but now he doesn't." She blew her nose vigorously. "And I'm never going back to him."

"Never?" Demeter repeated. She reached for her wine.

Outside the cozy, country cottage, the snow—currently, the goddess' preferred symbolism of her time off—began to melt.

* * *

"Is that what you're having for breakfast?"

Demeter sighed and paused, fork halfway to her mouth. "What's wrong with my breakfast?"

"Eggs, sausages, and homefries? Not to mention toast and beans? Mom, you've got enough bad fats in front of you to kill you, and trust me, I *know* what can kill you." Before Demeter could secure it, she whisked the plate away. "I'll make you some whole grain porridge, just like I do in the summer. No saturated fats, plenty of fruits and vegetables; we'll get that extra weight off you in no time."

"Sephie, I'm the goddess of the harvest, I'm supposed to be ample. And trust me, you can't get ample on fruits and vegetables."

Persephone shot her a glittering smile. "Isn't that a bit of a contradiction?"

"Trust me, dear, I've learned to live with it."

A sheet of snow slid off the steeply raked roof and landed on the burlap wrapped foundation plantings, crushing them under the wet weight.

Demeter stared into her whole wheat pita stuffed with alfalfa sprouts, hummus, and god knew what else, because the goddess certainly didn't. "I wonder what Hades is eating right now."

"I don't care."

"Probably something greasy and bad for him."

"I know what you're trying to do, Mom, and I appreciate it, but my marriage cannot be saved." Persephone bit the top three inches off a raw carrot with more enthusiasm than was strictly necessary. "After we eat, I've got a new low-impact aerobic workout that I want you to try."

"Sephie, I usually rest in the winter."

"If you mean you usually spend the winter in front of the television, well, that's not resting."

"It's not?"

"It's vegetating. And you won't have to do it this winter because I'm here. Think of it, we'll have such fun. Just like we do in the summer."

"Oh, I'm thinking of it, sweetie. . . ."

Out in the garden, a confused iris stuck its head above ground.

"I'm going for a walk, Mom. Do you want to come?"

"No, dear. I thought I'd . . ." Demeter racked her brain for something that her daughter couldn't object to. ". . . chop up some vegetables for a salad."

Persephone sniffed disapprovingly. "How can you stand being stuck inside on such a beautiful day? You're not like this in the summer."

"It's not summer, Sephie."

"Hades and I walk all over the Underworld in the winter: through the Asphodel Fields, along the Styx, and back home to Erebus by way of the Lethe. We walk . . ." The second sniff was much moister. ". . . and we talk and then, later, we curl up in front of the fire."

Encouraged by the longing in Persephone's voice, Demeter dared to suggest that her husband probably missed her very much.

"Good."

"Maybe you should just talk to him."

"No."

"But . . ."

"You don't understand, Mother."

Demeter smiled tightly. "That's because you haven't told me anything, dear. If I knew what the fight was about, maybe I could help."

"It's between Hades and me, Mother." Throwing an elegant sweater over slender shoulders, Persephone opened the back door. "I'm going for my walk now."

"Put on a coat, Sephie."

"I don't need one."

Glancing over at the calendar, Demeter sighed.

A few days later, standing in the kitchen making a cup of tea while Persephone went through her winter wardrobe and got rid of everything comfortable—as Queen of the Underworld, she favored haute couture—Demeter stared out the window at the bare lawn and wondered what she should try next. Nothing she'd said so far had made any difference; although she cried herself to sleep every night, Persephone was not going back to her husband and that was that.

"There's a robin on your lawn."

Sighing deeply, the goddess dumped an extra spoonful of sugar in her cup and turned to face the man sitting at her kitchen table. "I figured it would only be a matter of time before you showed up."

Zeus squared massive shoulders and laid both hands flat on the tabletop. "Spring seems to be early this year."

"No shit. What was your first clue?" The head of the pantheon was still an impressive looking god and certainly well suited to populating Olympus, but, in Demeter's opinion, he'd never been that bright.

"In fact, spring appears to have arrived two months early."

And he had a way of making pompous pronouncements that really ticked her off. "Persephone's had a fight with her husband and come home."

"I cannot allow the seasons to be messed up in this manner." Folding his arms, Zeus leaned back in the chair, gray eyes stormy. "Send her back."

"It's not that easy. . . ."

"Why not?" he demanded. "You're her mother."

Demeter smiled and stood. "You're her father. You

send her back." Pitching her voice to carry to the second floor, she headed for the rec room, ignoring Zeus' panicked protests. "Persephone! Your father wants to talk to you!"

She kept the volume on the television turned low so she could listen to the ebb and flow of the argument. It seemed to be mostly ebb. A very short time later, quick, angry footsteps headed upstairs and slow, defeated ones headed down.

"Well?" she asked.

"She said no." Zeus dropped onto the recliner and dug both hands into the luxuriant curls of his beard.

"She said no?" Demeter repeated with heavy sarcasm. "The Father of Heaven unsuccessful with a woman?"

"She cried, Demi. What could I do?"

"Did you ask her what was wrong?"

He looked indignant. "You told me they had a fight."

Demeter sighed. "Did you ask her what the fight was about?"

"What difference does that make?" His full lips moved into what was perilously close to a pout. "She has to go back, and I told her so."

In spite of his many opportunities for practice, Zeus had never been, by any stretch of the imagination, a good father. More of a realist than most of the pantheon, Demeter recognized that they were all in part responsible for that. He'd been the youngest in a wildly dysfunctional family and they'd all indulged him. She'd been just as bad as the rest of their siblings but she'd long ago stopped indulging him where their daughter was concerned. "Well," she said dryly, "that was stupid, wasn't it?"

All things considered, he took it rather well. Thunder rumbled in the distance, but nothing in the immediate area got destroyed.

"Demi, it can't be spring yet. When it's this early, it screws everything up."

"Zeus." She leaned forward. She would've patted his leg except that he took physical contact as an invitation and this was not the time for fertility rites. "I know."

"What are we going to do now?" he sighed.

Demeter grabbed her favorite lamp as it blew by on the gust of his exhalation and placed it on the floor by her chair. "We?"

Heaving himself up onto his feet, the ruler of Olympus had grace enough to look sheepish. "Deal with it, would you, Demi?"

She sighed in turn. "Don't I always?"

Having sloughed off responsibility once again, Zeus grew more cheerful and his step was light as he headed for the stairs. "You should visit Olympus more often. We miss you."

"No, you don't. Whenever I'm there, Hera and I fight, then you go off and do one of those swan, shower of gold, quail things, and we all know how *that* ends up—Hera blames me since she can't seem to blame you, I get annoyed and crops fail over half of the southern hemisphere. Better I just stay here."

He threw her a brilliant smile. "*I* miss you."

"No, you don't." In spite of everything, she couldn't help adding, "But it's sweet of you to say so."

At the bottom of the stairs, he paused and half turned back to face her as another thought occurred to him. "Oh by the way, what's Iaachus up to these days?"

"How should I know, I'm only his mother." And her son was a great deal like his father. "If you see him, tell him to call."

* * *

"Sephie, what are you doing?"

Persephone rubbed at a smudge of dirt on one peaches-and-cream cheek and looked up at her mother, her other hand continuing to vehemently, almost violently, poke seeds into the ground. "Planting radishes."

"Now?"

"We've got the year off to an early start." She frowned, suddenly noticing the jacket and boots. "Where are you going?"

"Eleusis," lied the goddess. "For the Mysteries."

"Now?"

"You've got the year off to an early start," Demeter reminded her. "We've had to make a few changes because of it." The Eleusisian Mysteries had always been a convenient way to ditch a grown, and often disapproving, daughter for more, as it were, fruitful company. Being Mysteries, they never had to be explained. Patting Persephone fondly on one shoulder, she continued down the garden path. "I won't be long."

"Evenin', yer Ladyship." Boat at the dock, Charon rested on his oar as Demeter approached. "Haven't seen you in these parts since the wedding."

"I try not to interfere in the lives of my children." She glanced down at a full load of the dead. "Do you have room for one more?"

"Well now, I'd have to say that depends."

Demeter sighed and rummaged through a change purse full of breath mints, jiffy pots, and wildflower seeds, finally pulling out a coin. The ferryman reached for it, but she held it back. "When we reach the other side."

"Good enough, yer Ladyship." Reaching down, he

grabbed his nearest passenger by the head and tossed him overboard. "Fool already paid me," he explained as he held out a hand to help the goddess over the gunnel.

It was a quiet trip across the Styx. Charon didn't encourage chatter, and Demeter had a lot on her mind. Not far from the landing, she frowned, suddenly unable to ignore the tormented screaming any longer. "Is it just me or are the cries from Tartarus louder than they should be?"

"They're louder," Charon agreed. "He's been depressed since she left. Makes him cranky."

The newly dead, sitting shoulder to shoulder on a triple row of uncomfortable benches, shuddered as a group.

Stepping out onto more or less dry land—it squelched underfoot a great deal less since she'd recommended they have it tile drained—Demeter braced herself.

"Down, Cerberus! Down! Good dog." She scratched the center head behind the ears as the other two stretched around her body and snarled at the disembarking spirits. When one or two hung back, Charon smacked them with his oar. "Oh, for pity's sake," she snapped. "Cereberus won't bother you if you're supposed to be here. Who's a good boy? Who's Demeter's favorite puppy?"

Tail whipping from side to side, the tapered back end of his body moving back and forth in time, Cerberus drooled happily on the goddess' feet.

Glad she'd worn her boots, and beginning to realize why Persephone didn't want the dog up on the couch, or on anything else that couldn't be hosed down immediately afterward, Demeter gave all three heads a final scratch and started toward the Asphodel Fields.

Winter or not, she didn't intend staying in the Underworld for too long. Cerberus bounded along beside her for half a dozen steps, then the wind shifted and he took off downstream, howling, snarling, and barking furiously.

Pulling her jacket more closely around her, she hurried along the path toward Erebus trying to ignore the gray and boring landscape and the incessant twittering of the undistinguished dead. Although a few of those who'd known her in life waved a limp hand in greeting, most ignored her.

Most.

"Greetings, rich-haired Demeter, awful goddess, lady of the golden sword and glorious fruits."

"Hello, Orion." The ghost standing on the path before her, the son of Poseidon and the gorgon Euryale, had been the handsomest man alive until he'd taken up with Artemis and run afoul of an overprotective Apollo. As she'd often thought it unfair the way the Olympian powers fell, Demeter smiled kindly on her nephew. "Still hunting the shadow deer?" She nodded toward his bow.

"The hunt is all I have." He paused and then continued ponderously, "The Queen is gone early from Erebus."

"Yes, she is, isn't she."

"She has returned to your hearth?"

"Oh, yes." *My cold hearth,* the goddess added silently. *And I still don't believe gas fireplaces give off unhealthy fumes.*

Orion nodded. "Good. I am glad she is safe. Do you now descend to see the Lord Hades, your brother?"

"Not exactly," Demeter told him tightly. "I descend to see the Lord Hades, my son-in-law."

The hero's eyes widened and his Adam's apple bobbed in the muscular column of his throat. "Oh," he said, and stepped off the path. "Look, uh, don't let me get in your way, Aunt Demi." He faded back toward the trees. "And, uh, if there's anything I can do, don't hesitate to call."

Picking up her pace again, Demeter rolled her eyes. *Honestly; men,* she thought. *Even dead ones. And Hera wonders why I never married.*

There were gardens down the middle of the wide avenue that led to the palace. In spite of the inarguable presence of the pomegranates, Demeter hadn't expected that. If they'd been in place during the wedding, she hadn't noticed them, but then, as mother of the bride, not to mention sister of the groom, she'd had other things on her mind.

All the flowers were black—except for one corpse-lavender rose she was fairly certain she'd seen in the upper world—and the beds had been edged in giant uncut diamonds. She could see her daughter's taste in the design. Persephone had always loved order. A closer look and she realized that the flowers desperately needed dead-heading and everything wanted water. Sighing deeply, Demeter reached under the lip of a black marble fountain and turned on the irrigation system.

"This is her garden," said a gardener, who'd been standing so quietly she hadn't noticed him. "His Majesty said we weren't to foul it with our touch."

"Hades said that?"

"Yes, ma'am."

Demeter smiled. This might be easier than she'd thought.

The palace was a mess.

Demeter had no idea how it could have gotten so bad in only eight days. Then she remembered how it had gotten at her house in those same eight days and tried to be less critical. It wasn't easy.

The servants, drawn from the ranks of the dead, huddled confused and insubstantial in corners. She could feel them watching her hopefully as she passed. Well, with any luck, their ordeal and hers would soon be over.

She found the King of the Dead in a small room he used for a den, slumped in a chair mournfully eating peanut butter straight from the jar. His clothes were wrinkled, he didn't smell very good, and it looked like he hadn't shaved in about three days.

He looked up when Demeter came in, too far gone in misery to be surprised. "Have you come for her things?"

"I've come for an explanation."

His gesture took in the drifts of potato chip bags in the immediate area as well as the chaos in the rest of the palace. "She's left me, Demi."

"I know that, you idiot. Where did you think she'd gone?"

"To you?"

"That's right. To me." She kicked a pizza box out of her way. "And do you know what happens up above when Persephone comes home to me?"

"The upper world is not my concern." If he'd intended to sound regal, he didn't quite make it past petulant.

"This time it is, because it's spring up there." Demeter's voice grew sharper as she put both fists on the back of the couch and leaned toward her son-in-law. "And it's not supposed to be spring for another two months! I want to know what happened, and I want to know right now!"

A single tear rolled down alongside Hades' aquiline nose. "She's left me, Demi."

Even the most gentle goddess had a line that shouldn't be crossed.

When the dust settled, He Who Has Many Names picked himself up off the floor and lowered himself gently back into his chair. "You blasted me," he said, shaking his head in disbelief, slightly singed black hair falling over his eyes. "In my realm. In my palace. In my den."

"That's right. And I'm going to do it again if I don't start getting some answers that make sense."

Scratching at the stubble on his chin, Hades sighed. "We had a fight," he said in a small voice.

"What about, and don't say pomegranates because I know that much."

"But it *was* about pomegranates, Demi. I had the tree cut down."

Demeter took a deep breath and counted to ten. "What tree?"

"The pomegranate tree." When she made it clear she needed more information and what the consequences would be if she didn't get it, he went on. "You remember back when I was courting Persephone . . ."

The goddess snorted.

A patch of color stained the son of Chronos' pale cheeks. "Yeah, well, do you remember how Zeus said she didn't have to stay with me if she hadn't eaten anything?"

"I remember."

Hades took a hint from her tapping fingers and began to speak faster. "Well, as it turned out she'd eaten those seven pomegranate seeds. Anyway, we worked all that out years ago and *I* thought we were happy, but in the midst of a small disagreement about saturated fats, one of the servants put a bowl of pome-granates on the table. She said I was trying to run

roughshod over her feelings just like before and I said
I wasn't. Then, to prove it, I had the gardeners cut
down the tree."

Demeter stared silently down at him. "The tree that
bore the fruit that she'd eaten from to become your
bride?" she asked when she finally found her voice.

"Well, yeah, but . . ."

"You putz! For her that tree was a symbol of your
union, and you got miffed and cut it down to prove
a point."

"I didn't want her to be reminded of less happy
times," Hades protested indignantly.

"Did you tell her that? Of course not," she went
on before he had a chance to answer. "No wonder she
thinks you don't love her anymore. That you regret
marrying her."

"How can she think that?" He started to pace, kicking accumulated floatsam out of his way with every
step. "Persephone is the only bright light in my world.
While she's here with me, she rules over all. Without
her, I dwell in darkness. I adore her. I always have,
and I always will." Face twisted in anguish, he turned
toward the goddess. "You've got to talk to her, Demi.
You've got to."

"Oh, no," Demeter shook her finger at him. "I'm
not the one who has to talk to her. You go up top
right now and you tell all this to my daughter."

Hades stopped pacing so suddenly Demeter thought
at first he'd walked through some spilled chip dip and
glued his feet to the floor. "I can't."

"You what?"

"I can't go up top. It goes on too far." Glancing up
at the ceiling, he looked beyond it to the arcing dome
of rock that covered the Underworld. "There's no
roof."

"Don't start making excuses, Host of Many, Brain

of Pea," Demeter snarled. "You went up there to get her originally."

"That was a long time ago."

"So?"

"I've got agoraphobia."

"So stay out of the marketplace. Or don't you want her back?"

"I want her back more than anything!"

Not more than I want to get rid of her. "Then get off your skinny butt and do something about it. And speaking of getting off your butt, why is this place such a pig sty? You've got servants."

"Persephone always dealt with them. I don't know what to say."

"She's with me half the year." Which was quite long enough. "You can't possibly live like this for all that time."

"She always leaves lists." The King of the Dead bent down and pulled a piece of cold pizza out from under the sofa cushions. "Very precise lists."

Demeter sighed. She knew she was enabling his helplessness, but she couldn't have her daughter return to this mess. "Would you like me to take care of it?"

"Could you?"

The goddess put two fingers in her mouth and whistled. Almost instantly, as though they'd been waiting for a signal, a crowd of worried spirits wafted into the room. Demeter waved at the mess. "Compost this crap," she told them.

Hades frowned as the mess began to disappear. "I'm pretty sure that's not how Persephone does it."

Remembering that his argument with her daughter had started over saturated fats and fully aware of what side of the issue Persephone came down on, Demeter looked more kindly on him than she had. "You're probably right."

"Did you have a nice Mystery, Mother.".

Demeter stuck her heel in the bootjack and pulled off her boot. "I planted a seed. Time will tell if anything comes of it."

"I hate it when you've been off talking to your priests," Persephone sniffed. "You get all obscure." She patted a pile of paper before her on the table. "While you were gone, I worked up a plan to redecorate the kitchen."

"But I like my kitchen."

"Our kitchen. It's hopelessly old-fashioned. The microwave still has dials."

"I only use it to reheat tea," the goddess protested.

"The kitchen in the palace has all the most modern equipment. Very high tech."

"Yes, well Hades is God of Wealth," Demeter muttered. "He can afford to get every new piece of junk that comes out."

Persephone ignored her. "And we'll have to get some servants." She smiled brittlely at her mother's aghast expression. "Mother, we're goddesses. Cookouts and things are all very well in the summer . . ."

Demeter had long suspected Persephone regarded the seasons spent with her as an extended visit to Guide camp.

". . . but it's not something we should have to live with year 'round."

"Sephie, when you're with me, it *is* summer year 'round."

"That's no reason why we shouldn't have servants. We can add on a wing out back." Rummaging through the pile, she held up a sheet of paper. "I drew a sketch. What the . . . ?"

Both women stared at the paper, trembling like an aspen leaf in Persephone's hand.

Suddenly concerned, Demeter reached for her daughter. "You're shaking."

"No, I'm not." A mug fell off its peg and crashed into a thousand pieces against the floor. "The whole house is shaking."

"Earthquake?" Demeter pressed her lips together. "When I get my hands on the god who's doing this, he'll get a piece of my mind and boot in the backside!"

"Not now, Mother." Grabbing the goddess' shoulders, Persephone pushed her toward the door. "We've got to get outside. This whole place could come down any moment."

"If it does," the goddess promised, "I'm going to be very angry."

They'd gotten only as far as the porch when the lawn erupted. Four black horses, nostrils flared and eyes wild, charged up from the depths of the earth pulling behind them a golden chariot. In the chariot, stood Hades, ebony armor gleaming, the reins in one hand, a black rose in the other.

Demeter had to admit the rose was a nice touch.

His eyes beneath the edge of his helm almost as wild as those of his horses, Hades turned toward the cottage. "Persephone, this time I do not pull you from your mother's arms but implore you for the sake of love to come home with me."

"Very prettily said. Almost classical." Demeter poked her daughter in the hip. "Well?"

Persephone folded her arms. "You cut down my tree."

"And I have caused another seven to grow in its stead. One for each of the seeds you ate so that you can see how much my love has multiplied."

"I ate?" Persephone repeated, her voice rising dramatically. "You fed them to me."

"I only offered them to you," Hades protested. "You ate them."

Her chin rose. "I didn't know what it meant."

"And now you do." He opened the hand that held the rose and, like drops of blood against his pale skin, were seven pomegranate seeds.

Persephone gave a little cry Demeter wasn't quite able to interpret but her eyes were dewy and that seemed a good sign.

"Please come back to me, Sephie. The Underworld is empty without you. All my wealth is meaningless. I'll stop spending so much time with the guys. I'll cut out saturated fats. I . . ." The horses jerked forward. Muscles straining, Hades brought them back under control. "I love . . . Damn it, you four, stop it! I love you, Persephone."

It could have been a more polished declaration, Demeter acknowledged, but not more sincere. "Well?" she said again, this time with a little more emphasis.

"But spring . . . ?"

The goddess smiled, trying not to let the relief show. "Spring can wait two months."

With a glad cry, Persephone ran forward and leaped into both the chariot and Hades' arms. Finding no hand on the reins, both of the god's hands being otherwise occupied, the team did what horses always do under similar, if less mythic, circumstances. Hoofs striking sparks against the air, they bolted down toward their stable carrying their two oblivious passengers back to the Underworld with them.

The last Demeter saw of her daughter and her son-in-law, they were feeding each other the pomegranate seeds and murmuring things she was just as glad she couldn't hear.

"Happy endings all around," she muttered, and added as she went to work tucking the spring growth back into bed, "I have no idea how Aphrodite puts up with this kind of nonsense day in and day out."

With Persephone back in the loving arms of her husband, it didn't take long for Demeter to return the season to normal. She felt a little bad about the radishes.

When Dusk approached, the goddess wandered down to the rec room and poured herself a glass of wine. The house was blessedly quiet. Even the cat had returned from wherever he'd hidden himself.

Slippered feet up on a hassock, she picked up the remote. Maybe she'd heat up a frozen pizza for dinner.

The lawn was a disaster. In the spring, the actual spring, it would have to be rolled.

It seemed a small price to pay.

Outside the cottage, it began to snow.

THE THIRD SONG
by *Roberta Gellis*

Roberta Gellis has been a leading writer of historical romance for many years. More recently, she has been establishing a niche for "mythological romance," using Greek myth as the basis for such books as *Shimmering Splendor* and *Enchanted Fire*.

He had lost his way somehow as dusk fell and it began to rain. But that was impossible. He had been treading a well-traveled road, singing softly to himself, expecting to see the walls and lights of Heraclea from the top of the next rise. Instead there was nothing but the road ahead, going down into the next shallow valley and then climbing the next hill. But surely from the last hilltop he had seen a glint of the sea in the distance and the faint haze in the air that comes from many fires.

Orpheus turned and looked back, but the road behind was exactly like the road ahead. Despite the slight drizzle and the deepening dusk, he could see the packed earth, lighter than the bordering trees, right to the crest of the last rise—and there was no branching, no place he could have gone astray. Should he go back?

For what? The farmer's cot where he had been assured that he would reach the town before dark was too far away for him to shelter there. And what good would it do him to catch another glimpse of the sea? He laughed a little shakily. He would not be able to see anything long before he reached that high spot; black night would cover all.

No, it was better to go ahead. The road was wide and rutted with use; it must lead somewhere. And wherever it led, he would find a welcome. Orpheus pulled the kithara in its oiled leather case from his back into his arms to make sure it was still dry and to shelter it better by a double fold of his cloak. For some reason the movement caused a string to sound. The note set off a cascade of others in his mind. Distracted, he sang the falling trill, modulated it into a melody which he began to repeat to commit to memory, but his voice checked suddenly as his eyes caught a gleam somewhere in the valley below.

For one moment Orpheus stared unbelievingly at the faint, flickering light; in the next he set out toward it with a lifting heart. From time to time as he walked, he wondered from where the light could be coming because he had seen no house nor even any cleared fields along the road. Probably, he told himself, it was only another traveler with no more hope of shelter than he had. Nonetheless, another traveler was company. He strode forward eagerly while he could.

The rain had stopped, but no light from moon or stars pierced the clouds. Soon darkness became near absolute and he was forced to moderate his pace, feeling for the difference between the bare earth of the road and the hillocky grass of the verge. Still the light served as a beacon and he continued toward it. He did think now and again of outlaws using a campfire to lure travelers—he had been warned often enough of the dangers of the road—and loosened his sword in its scabbard. But the light drew him, and he put that fear aside.

As he came closer, caution bade him move onto the grass verge so the sound of his footsteps would give no warning. He even stopped and peered around, a hand on his sword hilt. He saw and heard nothing. The small fire lit only its immediate area and showed only one slumped figure, which seemed too slight to be a danger to him. He stood irresolute, but he must have made some sound because the figure twisted toward him, the fold of the cloak that made a hood falling back. The face it exposed was as ancient as time, sunken, wrinkled, framed in sparse, straggling white hair. Orpheus bit his lip. If he had been frightened, how much more fearful must this frail ancient be. He stepped forward into the light.

"Forgive me if I startled you, mother," he said softly, "and for intruding on you, but I am lost and wet and cold. May I share your fire?"

The crone raised her eyes to meet his and Orpheus' breath caught in his throat. Those eyes were as young as morning, large and almond-shaped and of a blue that was startlingly bright even in the dim glow provided by the low-burning fire. Then she drew the cloak forward again into a hood and her face was hidden.

"I am old," she said, "but I gathered the dead leaves and sticks, I struck the sparks and blew upon them. Now the fire burns. What have you to contribute?"

Orpheus thought rather despairingly of the journeybread and cheese he had finished before sunset. If he had saved some for an evening meal, he could have offered it. But he had been so sure he would eat well and lie warm, so sure that Heraclea was just over the next hill.

"I could gather more wood," he said tentatively, "or if the moon rises, I could hunt."

She cackled with laughter. "By the time the moon rises, you will be warm and dry. If you hunt, why should you share your catch with me?"

"Because I said I would!" Orpheus snapped.

A clawlike hand came from under the cloak and gestured impatiently. "I have enough wood and enough food, too."

"Then I have only this." Orpheus opened his cloak so that the case of the kithara showed. "I can sing and play for you."

"Do you doubt your skill that you were so slow to offer it?" the old woman asked. She had raised her head again, but this time the hood was drawn well forward and showed only a bit of angular chin and sharp nose.

"I do not doubt my skill," Orpheus replied, his voice sharp with indignation. "I only thought an old woman alone on a dark, wet night might value firewood or food over song."

"Would you?"

The question was as sharp as his reply. Orpheus laughed aloud. "No, mother, but I do not have to make that choice. Song is always with me, for it fills my heart and mind even when my kithara and my voice are still."

"So . . . sit and play."

She gestured with one thin, crooked hand and with the other added two or three sticks to the fire. Instantly the blaze flared up and light flooded outward. Orpheus saw that the fire had been set into the angle of land made by the meeting of two roads. Oddly, the old woman sat on a tripod stool right in the crossroad. A chill not caused by his damp, cold tunic touched Orpheus' back, the rising of a buried memory. Nonsense, he told himself, that is a tale to frighten children. Why should the old woman not sit in the road? It was a good way to keep her skirts out of the wet grass, and she hardly needed to fear traffic at this hour.

His head had turned automatically in the direction in which she had gestured, and to one side of the fire Orpheus saw a fallen log he could use as a seat. He moved toward it, not surprised that he had missed seeing it before but suddenly very surprised that he had been able to make out from so far away the small flicker of light provided by the underfed fire. And how had the few sticks the old woman added made such a difference? Not only was there now light, but a pleasant warmth enfolded Orpheus as he sat down and made him very willing to throw back his cloak and uncase the kithara. His hand paused on the strap, but he shook his head slightly. Children's tales.

"Is there something you would like specially to hear, mother?" he asked.

"At my age, I can do without love songs." She cackled briefly with amusement. "What do the old desire?" she mused so softly that Orpheus almost missed the words. "Life." Her voice became stronger, less broken. "Sing about life."

While she spoke, Orpheus had been tightening the strings of the kithara. When they felt right, he plucked an arpeggio of scales, tightened a string, then another, played the arpeggio once more to be sure, then stilled his harp. Life. All songs were about life to some extent, but what life would be most familiar, most desirable because it was almost gone from her, to an old peasant woman? Softly, Orpheus began a simple melody, a child's jumping song and sang the words of that ancient game. Before it ended, he had enriched the single-note melody with others, a plowing song and the lilting notes of a girl calling goats from their grazing ground.

To the music he put words limning the rhythms of a village year, the planting in the spring, the hoeing in summer, the reaping in autumn, and the quiet tasks of winter. And into the rhythms of the year he wove the rhythms of the people from birth to death. It was an honest song, not scanting the harshness of the labor or the small reward or the pinched bellies of winter, but telling also of the joys, small and large, of the simple life.

Although neither voice nor fingers faltered, tears came to his eyes as the song he had made for the people of his village poured forth. He had not sung it for a long time. In the great houses and high courts where he performed for the noble and the royal, there was little interest in songs of planting and herding. They called for stirring epics of great deeds and high heroics. Now those seemed hollow and empty compared with the lives of the villagers.

Having worked through the seasons and within them the days of the villagers' lives, the song at last came to night and sleep. One by one the interwoven melodies were stilled until only the poignant single notes of the child's jumping song softened into silence. The old woman did not stir, and the fire slowly sank back to little more than flickering coals.

After a time, Orpheus said, "I hope I pleased you, mother." The hood turned toward him, but he could not see the face within. "I am afraid I have received my reward already," he added, smiling, "for I am warm and dry, but if you are not satisfied with a song of such simple lives, I will sing again of grander things."

She uttered a low chuckle. "Oh, I am satisfied, although if I were less honest than you, I would deny it so you would sing again."

The voice, deep and rich with no hint of cracking or tremulousness, was so different that Orpheus stared. But he could not see into the hood and for once the voice was less important than the words. The old, when they were in full possession of their minds and memories, as this beldame was, were often hard to please. They kept remembrance of songs and singers of the past, the songs growing more beautiful, the singers more silver-voiced and nimble-fingered with the passing years. Thus her approval was of special value.

Orpheus smiled. "If my song gave you pleasure, I will the more gladly sing again without need of further reward."

He lifted the kithara to playing position, but a pale hand slipped out of the folds of the cloak and showed a flat palm to stop him. "Not yet, I pray you. I need time to relish what I have heard. I do not wish that song to be overlaid by any other, even one more wonderful. And you must be hungry and thirsty, too."

Now the voice was hardly above a whisper, and Orpheus could tell himself he had imagined the full-throated tones he had heard earlier. He smiled more broadly. "Well, I am, but I am also what you said—an honest man—and my bargain was to share your fire."

The woman laughed aloud, tipping her head back to expand her throat. The fold of cloak slipped back onto her shoulders, and the smile froze on Orpheus' lips. The laugh was no aged cackle but a young woman's mellow gurgle of delight, and the cheek and chin off which the dim firelight glanced were soft, round, and smooth and shadowed by a wealth of dark hair.

"An honest man, indeed," she said. "But as host

here, it is my right freely to offer more. Come closer, and I will give you some bread and wine."

Because his heart was beating so hard in his throat that he could not answer, and also because he had to see, had to know, despite his fear, Orpheus rose and approached the woman on the stool. As if she understood without words what drew him, she again cast several sticks on the fire and light flooded the area. The woman turned her face toward him. Now there could be no doubt. The beautiful, smiling countenance was that of a woman in the prime of her life, mature enough to be knowing and young enough to be mischievous. Only her eyes, those blue eyes younger even than her new face, were the same. Orpheus went down on one knee, clutching the kithara for comfort.

The woman laughed. "Why do you stare so?" she asked. "Did I not ask for life? Why should you be so surprised when the magic of your music gave it to me?"

"Music, yes, but no magic," Orpheus whispered, shivering. "Beauty is not magic, lady. May all the good gods forbid. If my songs were magic, I would be trussed like a goat and sacrificed to Hades. The magic is in you."

"Perhaps." She was still smiling as she turned away and reached into the dark. When she turned back, she held a flagon and cup in one hand and a loaf of bread in the other. "Will you not come closer and take what I offer?" she asked.

She lifted the wine and bread slightly, but the offer in her voice and eyes had nothing at all to do with food or drink. Orpheus swallowed hard as a fire rose in his loins. However, he was almost as frightened as he was aroused—oddly, not because of the incredible change from age to youth but because he was unsure of his ability to satisfy such a woman. Barely a man, his experience was small—one of the bold girls of the village on his last trip home and a hetaera a patron had hired for him.

"You said you were too old for love songs," Orpheus said desperately, playing for time and also hoping that if he chose his song right and sang well enough, she would be too eager for a man, any man, to notice any deficiency in what he offered. "You are not too old now—not now."

"Oh, no." Another gurgle of laughter, so warm, so inviting, that Orpheus almost forgot his fear. "I am not too old now." She put the bread down in her lap, took the cup and filled it from the flagon, and held it out to him. "At least take some wine to soothe your throat."

When he touched her hand, heat again surged through him. He clutched at her fingers, but it was too late; all he gripped was the smooth goblet. He thought of putting down the wine, seizing her, but she was looking at him, her head tilted, smiling slightly. Had she looked away, like a modest Greek woman, he would have taken her in his arms. Flushing with shame and desire, he lifted the goblet and drank, hoping and fearing he did not know what, but he felt nothing strange or wonderful nor anything dreadful either. It was just good wine. Only, when he lowered the cup, which she took from him, the woman had pulled her cloak over her head again and the light from the fire was dying.

That made it easier. A singer must feel if emotion is to touch the listener, but too much feeling changed the voice and made the fingers less agile. Orpheus sang of love, a paean of praise of woman, of her body and its rich secrets, of the soft, smooth flesh of her breasts, the sinuous curve of her hips, the full thighs with between them the hungry, toothless, nether mouth, eager to engulph its willing sacrifice. His voice was warm and liquid; it touched and probed with immaterial caresses.

Even in the dim glow from the dying coals, Orpheus could see the darkness that was the cloak leaning toward him. He bent and laid the kithara down softly and stretched out his hand to the woman. A hand came out, paler, thinner than the strong hand with which the woman had handed him a cup of wine, but it did not meet his. It lifted, palm out, bidding him stay.

"Sing again, sweet singer." The voice was higher, lighter, a voice to match those young, young eyes. "Give me a third song."

"Indeed I will—a third song and as many more as you care to hear, but now I would only sing of you, and to sing of you I must know you."

In a single, fluid motion Orpheus rose, stepped forward, bent, and caught the robed figure in his arms. The hood fell back completely, showing the startled face of a scarcely nubile girl. There was nothing inviting in her expression. She looked angry and frightened and strained backward, crying, "Mother!"

Caught in the momentum of his action, Orpheus held her for a moment longer, then cried out himself and staggered back. Before his eyes the thick, black hair paled and thinned into scanty, straggling white, the flesh of the face writhed, lost substance, the cheeks falling in, the full lips flattening, nose and chin hooking forward. Only the eyes were the same, blue as a bright winter sky, young as morning.

Then the cold that had threaded along Orpheus' back when he first saw the old woman perched in the crossroad spread over his body and pierced inward, striking ice even into his heart. This was no children's tale.

"Hecate," he whispered.

Hecate of the three faces and three souls; Hecate who always came upon one at life's crossroads; Hecate to whom no one prayed because too often she gave—not what you wanted but exactly what you asked for; Hecate the mad, with whom, it was said, no one meddled, not even the king of the gods.

"Hecate," the old woman agreed with a cackle. "You should have sung the third song. Now you owe it to me."

Then it was all gone, the crossroads, the fire, the old woman, everything—except that his kithara was naked in his hands as if he had been playing. Orpheus found himself walking down the last hill with his shadow stretched long ahead of him in the light of the westering sun. Ahead of him also were the walls of Heraclea, gilded by the same light, and the sea sparkling beyond. Orpheus stopped, his heart pounding in his throat, but he did not look back.

Slowly, with shaking hands, he loosened the strings of his instrument, slipped the kithara into the case still hanging from his shoulder. His back was cold. If he turned, would he see night and a crossroad with a barely flickering fire? The cold slid up his back and tickled his ear.

"Because you did not ask," the dulcet, mocking voice of the lady murmured, "because you would not take even what was freely offered, because you deny magic—" a soft, inviting chuckle, "—you will have it. Your hands and voice will have the power to chain hearts and melt them."

"No!" Orpheus cried and spun around. But there was no valley full of night behind him. There was only the road, pale in the last of the light, going up the hill he had just descended.

He shuddered and a string of the kithara he

clutched sounded, recalling to him the cascade of notes that he had sung and the melody he had begun to form before he saw Hecate's fire. Complete now, it poured from his lips, and within him silver cords formed and coiled, cords with which he could bind men and women and even beasts to his will. Orpheus choked down the song.

"You owe me." The old woman's cackle whispered away on the wind. "All your songs are the third song now."

FOR A TRANSCRIPT,
SEND FIVE DOLLARS
by Anne Braude

Anne Braude was one of the founding members of the Society of Creative Anachronism, is a longtime student of medieval literature, and is an editor for and frequent contributor to the Hugo-winning fanzine, *Niekas*. She lives in a book-crowded home with her collection of moles and dragons.

MOLLIE: Hello, everyone! Welcome to "Focus on the Family Week" on THE MOLLIE! SHOW. I'm Mollie Drake. We conclude this series of programs with the most dysfunctional family who ever lived. You've all read about our guests in Bulfinch's *Mythology,* the *Oresteia* of Aeschylus, and of course the *National Inquirer;* now give a big MOLLIE! SHOW welcome to the House of Atreus!

(APPLAUSE)

MOLLIE: The crimes and sufferings of this family have inspired some of the greatest literature of the western world, as well as psychoanalysts, myth critics, anthropologists, and a couple of unsuccessful slasher movies. Fortunately, most of them are able to be with us today, despite having all died, mainly in creatively horrible ways, because they are all mythological characters. But let poets and dramatists contemplate their terrible fates with pity and horror; we're a talk show, and we say—these people need help! And today on

THE MOLLIE! SHOW, we are going to get them that help.

NIOBE: Actually, Mollie, a number of us are in therapy already.

MOLLIE: This is Niobe, who turned into a perpetually weeping stone statue after her children were slain by Apollo and Artemis because she boasted her superiority over their mother Leto. Just how do you fit into the family, Niobe?

NIOBE: I'm the daughter of Tantalus, and Atreus' aunt. And I've been seeing this grief counselor . . .

MOLLIE: We'll get to you later, Niobe. I want to take the family in order. Although it's called the House of Atreus, the founder—and the subject of the original curse—is Tantalus, the son of Zeus himself, who angered the gods by inviting them to a feast at which, as a test of their omniscience, he served up the boiled flesh of his son Pelops. Why did you do this, Tantalus?

TANTALUS: Oh, I just got tired of Dad always carrying on about proper nutrition, like he was the Ralph Nader of the nectar-and-ambrosia set. And Pelops was a real whiny kid.

MOLLIE: But you lived to regret it, right? Zeus placed you in Tartarus, up to the chin in water, with trees laden with luscious fruit overhanging you—but every time you try to take a drink or a bite, they recede.

ESME: Mollie, may I put in a word here?

MOLLIE: People, let me introduce our guest therapist, Dr. Esme Timberlake, the New Age therapist you probably already know from her popular Los Angeles radio show and her hot new bestseller, *Incest and Cannibalism as Alternative Family-Bonding Strategies*. Esme, was this good parenting on the part of Zeus?

ESME: No, Mollie, I must say that this is no way to deal with a child who is acting out. It's too destructive to the child's self-esteem. I mean, look at poor Tantalus; I've never seen a worse case of anorexia.

PELOPS: What about what he did to me? Are you saying that that's okay? If the gods *hadn't* been omniscient, I'd have wound up as everybody's inner child—garnished with parsley!

MOLLIE: But fortunately for you, Pelops, they didn't eat you, except for Demeter, who was so preoccupied with the loss of Persephone that she devoured a shoulder.

NIOBE: If she had only talked to my grief counselor . . .

MOLLIE: Later, Niobe. Pelops, the gods restored you to life, with all your original parts except the shoulder, which was replaced by an ivory one supplied by Demeter. Is there a question from the audience?

AUDIENCE MEMBER: Why aren't the gods here to tell their side? Could there be some kind of a frame-up by the authorities? Like with O.J.?

MOLLIE: We asked the Olympians to join us, but they refused. Hermes sent a written statement saying that they won't comment publicly until after Pelops' product-liability suit against Demeter has been heard.

TANTALUS: I told you he was a whiny kid.

CASSANDRA: Hermes is the god of lawyers, you know.

MOLLIE: Actually, he's the god of thieves and liars.

CASSANDRA: That's what I said.

MOLLIE: Later, Cassandra. We're a long way from your part in the story. Pelops, you did a bit of acting out yourself. You won a bride and a kingdom by cheating in a chariot race, and you murdered the charioteer when he demanded that you make good on the promised bribe. He was the son of Hermes, who invoked the curse upon your house all over again.

SAME AUDIENCE MEMBER (muttering): I knew there was a conspiracy.

MOLLIE: Your sons were Atreus and Thyestes, who did their own share of acting out.

NIOBE: What about me? I come in here.

MOLLIE: Yes, Niobe. Your story we know already. You say you're seeing a grief counselor?

NIOBE: Yes, she's wonderful. She's helped me so much. I'm feeling so much better that I'm thinking of turning back into flesh. And's she's gotten me a deal for a miniseries.

SECOND AUDIENCE MEMBER: According to the myth, your kids got killed because of your boasting. Don't you feel guilty about this?

ESME: Let me handle this one, Niobe. Guilt is such a self-destructive emotion that the only way to deal with it is to learn to leave it behind. Niobe was only giving her children positive reinforcement. It shouldn't have been an issue for Leto.

SAME AUDIENCE MEMBER: Are you saying that we shouldn't feel guilty even when we have really done something wrong? Isn't that why the gods punished these people? Isn't it sometimes right to feel bad about what you've done?

ESME: Oh, my dear! This is the nineties.

CASSANDRA (to AUDIENCE MEMBER): Right on!

MOLLIE: Later, Cassandra. We were about to talk with Atreus and Thyestes. There are multiple issues here. You got together to murder your half-brother Chrysippus. You fought over the throne, taking turns exiling each other, until the gods had to intervene. You, Thyestes, seduced your brother's wife, and later sent a son of his, whom you had raised as your own, to murder him. Atreus killed him, not knowing who he was, and later in revenge murdered your sons and

served them up to you at a feast. And there's much more. We'll be right back after these messages.
(COMMERCIAL BREAK)

MOLLIE: We're back, with Thyestes and Atreus. To make a long story short, we'll skip to Pelopea, Thyestes' daughter, whom Atreus married. She had a son Aegisthus, whom we'll meet later, whom Atreus raised as his own. Pelopea, who was Aegisthus' father?

PELOPEA: (Uncontrollable sobbing)

MOLLIE: Would you like a tissue, dear? (More sobbing) Esme, would you take her backstage and talk to her, please?

PELOPEA: I . . . I . . . I didn't know he was my father when I slept with him!

ESME: It's perfectly okay, Pelopea. Come on back with me. We'll talk. I'll give you a copy of my book. Everything will be just fine. (ESME and PELOPEA leave the stage.)

CASSANDRA: "Everything will be just fine"? She had a child by her father. She married her uncle. She killed herself. And Aegisthus wiped out all the rest of the family he could get his hands on!

MOLLIE: Later, Cassandra. Thyestes, you and Aegisthus later slew Atreus. How are you dealing with *your* guilt?

THYESTES: Atreus had it coming; I don't care what the gods say. As for Pelopea, she knew what she was doing. I'm not responsible for her guilt trip.

CASSANDRA: Bastard!

THYESTES: Bitch! What do you think you can do about it, anyway?

CASSANDRA: I gave her Gloria Allred's phone number during the break.

MOLLIE: Later, Cassandra. And speaking of breaks, it's time for another one. We'll be right back after this.
(COMMERCIAL BREAK)

MOLLIE: We're back, talking to Atreus' brother Thyestes. Thy, you say you feel no guilt over your murders, incest, and adultery. What about eating your sons?

THYESTES: That was a real bummer, Mollie. But I went to this great workshop last summer, on "Cannibalism and Co-Dependency," and it's really helped me a lot.

MOLLIE: I believe I've heard of it. Isn't it taught by John Bradshaw?

THYESTES: Yes, jointly with Wolfgang Puck.

ATREUS: You and your (bleep)ing workshop! You wiped out most of my (bleep)ing family, you and your (bleep)ing incestuous bastard! (Lunges at THYESTES.)

MOLLIE: People! People! Calm down, people! We'll take another break here. Go to commercial! Go to commercial! *Security!*

(COMMERCIAL BREAK)

MOLLIE: Sorry about that. During the break, the whole family started getting physical, so we've cleared the stage for the next generation. And Esme Timberlake is back with us. How is Pelopea doing, Esme?

ESME: She's still pretty upset, Mollie. Not only won't she stop crying, she won't even agree to be a guest on my radio show.

MOLLIE: She's obviously in really bad shape. But let's move on to our next group of guests, Atreus' son Agamemnon, his wife Clytemnestra, and Aegisthus—Thyestes' son, Clytemnestra's lover, and Agamemnon's murderer. We invited Agamemnon's brother Menelaus, king of Sparta, and his wife, Helen of Troy, but they couldn't be with us because of a scheduling conflict; their couples' group is having a marathon session. Clytemnestra, what happened between you and your husband? Was it the lack of quality time together

that caused you to drift apart? Was he overly committed to his career as king of Mycenae and commander
of the Argive expedition against Troy?

CLYTEMNESTRA: It was a little more direct than
that, Mollie. He murdered our daughter.

AGAMEMNON: It wasn't a murder. It was a sacrifice
to the gods.

CLYTEMNESTRA: So you could get a favorable
wind to take your (bleep)ing fleet to Troy!

MOLLIE: Clytemnestra, watch your language, please;
remember that this is daytime television. Besides,
Agamemnon, hadn't you made an old promise to Artemis to sacrifice your daughter to atone for slaying
her favorite stag?

AGAMEMNON: Yes, but my wife talked me out of
it. That's why Artemis sent the winds against us. I was
just doing my civic duty. Anyway, it was Menelaus
who talked me into it. He wanted Helen back.

CLYTEMNESTRA: So for that blonde tramp and the
chance to get famous and to plunder the richest city
in the known world, you killed *your own daughter*!
Who *loved* you! And you told her you were making
a splendid marriage for her!

CASSANDRA: Not that Achilles would have been
any prize if she *had* married him. These Achaean
dudes are all alike; women are nothing but property
and prizes of war. Even the gods don't see us as *people*. At least Artemis spared Iphigeneia and substi-
tuted a hind in her place. Pallas Athene never did a
thing for me even though I had invoked her protection
in her own temple.

CLYTEMNESTRA: I'm not a feminist, but you're
making a lot of sense. I really wish now that I hadn't
murdered you, too.

CASSANDRA: Thanks for nothing.

MOLLIE: Later, Cassandra. Agamemnon and Clytemnestra, have you considered joining that couples' group that has helped Helen and Menelaus so much?

CLYTEMNESTRA: That would be about as much help as that temporary restraining order that Orestes took out against the Furies. My bimbo sister may have fooled around on her husband—although if you believe what she told Euripides on *Lifestyles of the Rich and Mythical* right after she did that *Playboy* layout, that wasn't even her but some evil twin that I for one never heard of before—but Agamemnon *murdered* Iphigeneia.

AGAMEMNON: You fooled around on me with Aegisthus!

CLYTEMNESTRA: And I suppose you spent ten years on the windy Scaean plain in a state of total celibacy?

MOLLIE: Surely the issue isn't adultery, but murder?

AEGISTHUS: The Atreids started it!

AGAMEMNON: I treated you like a brother, and you stabbed me in the bathtub!

AEGISTHUS: And I'd do it again given the chance. Your father did worse to mine.

CASSANDRA: Speaking as the only innocent victim in this whole mess, I just want to point out that you people have been killing each other for generations. Sons, daughters, fathers, mothers, sisters, brothers— you can't tell the slayers without a scorecard!

AEGISTHUS: ⎫
AGAMEMNON: ⎬ Later, Cassandra.
MOLLIE: ⎭

ESME: I wonder if any of you have read my book?

MOLLIE: We'll be right back.

(COMMERCIAL BREAK)

MOLLIE: We're back. I'm afraid that Clytemnestra, Agamemnon, and Aegisthus have had to leave to attend the auction of the movie rights to their books. But the next generation is here.

CASSANDRA: So am I.

MOLLIE: LATER, Cassandra. We need to finish up with the immediate family first. Our guests for this segment are Iphigeneia and Electra, the daughters of Clytemnestra and Agamemnon, and their brother Orestes. Orestes is, of course, accompanied by the Furies, these ladies with the smoldering torches and the snakes in their hair, and the Furies are accompanied by their lawyer.

ELECTRA: Can I change my seat? I asked not to be put next to the Furies; don't you people know anything about the dangers of secondhand smoke?

MOLLIE: Perhaps the Furies wouldn't mind extinguishing their torches?

(AGITATED HISSING)

Is that the Furies hissing, or their snakes?

LAWYER: Yes.

IPHIGENEIA: I'll switch seats with you, Electra. The Furies aren't going to change until they learn to take responsibility for their own behavior. Their pursuit of Orestes is just a way of avoiding their own issues.

CASSANDRA: You're in a twelve-step program, aren't you?

IPHIGENEIA: Why, yes, "Recovering Victims of Human Sacrifice." It's done wonders for me. However did you guess?

CASSANDRA: I'm psychic.

IPHIGENEIA: I'd like to take this opportunity to express my feelings to my parents, my siblings, and to Artemis who started the whole thing. I've written it all down. (Pulls out sheaf of papyrus.)

CASSANDRA: Oh, puh-leeze!

MOLLIE: I'm afraid we don't have time for that right now. But we're all really happy for you, Iphigeneia.

While most of our guests got into trouble with each other, and with the gods, by doing the wrong thing, Orestes, your problem was trying to do the right thing. You were caught between your sacred duty to avenge the murder of your father and your equally sacred duty not to harm your mother. You did your duty to your father, but you suffered madness and the pursuit of the Furies as a result.

ORESTES: I never wanted to kill anybody. Electra really pushed me. And Apollo commanded it. I was just following orders. Apollo was my witness and lawyer at my trial before the court of the Areopagus in Athens, and Pallas Athene herself cast the deciding vote for acquittal. I've been in intense psychotherapy with Asclepius, and I've been working out issues with the Furies. I think I can get them to promise not to intervene in the civil trial.

ELECTRA: Just because Mother always liked you best, you were willing to let our father and sister go unavenged. What a wimp! And all of you got more plays written about you than I did. It isn't fair!

ORESTES: Freud named a complex after you.

ELECTRA: Not the big one.

IPHIGENEIA: But Mom always liked *me* best! And Electra was Daddy's pet.

CASSANDRA: Now who's failing to own her own problems, Iffy dear?

IPHIGENEIA: Oh, shut up.

ESME: You'll none of you get anywhere while you're all playing the blame game. People, today is the first day of the rest of your mythological existence. Stop guilt-tripping and start living. And come on my radio show.

CASSANDRA: Doesn't it matter at all to you, Ms. Timberlake, that a lot of people have gotten *killed* here? Me included, incidentally.

ESME: You're trapping yourself in your own negative reality, dear.

MOLLIE: Another question from the audience?

THIRD AUDIENCE MEMBER: This is for the Furies. You say that you are pursuing this poor guy Orestes because it's your moral duty, assigned you by the gods—who have refused to be here, as I recall—to punish criminals and uphold divine and human law?

LAWYER: That is essentially correct. The Erinyes, or Eumenides as I prefer to call them, function as defenders of the natural order. There is nothing personal in their torturing people; they are official representatives of the power structure. Just like the IRS, only with snakes.

SAME AUDIENCE MEMBER: Well, I don't believe that for a moment. I don't think they're doing it out of a sense of duty. I think the Furies suffer from low self-esteem.

LAWYER: Oops! I really wish you hadn't said that. (More agitated hissing) Now, girls, remember you're on TV. (THE FURIES leap from their seats and fling themselves upon the hapless AUDIENCE MEMBER. More and louder hissing, interspersed with shrieks.) Allecto, NO! Megaera, don't! Tisiphone, remember your image! Remember the book deal! Ladies! Ladies! You're on TV!

MOLLIE: Go to commercial! SECURITY!
               (COMMERCIAL BREAK)

MOLLIE: Oh, this is terrible! The Furies have just torn several of the audience members limb from limb! This is entirely the responsibility of my associate producers, all of whom I have just fired. Fortunately we have insurance for this, but I want to apologize to everybody. Our security officers have removed the Furies, and the Atreids have left in a huff. To close out the program we just have you, Esme, and the Furies' lawyer, who will join us in a moment. Ah, here he is.

CASSANDRA: *I'm* still here. You kept saying "later"; this *is* later.

MOLLIE: Oh, yes, Cassandra. Forgive me, but I've forgotten just how you come into this story. I do remember that you were some sort of prophetess, but nobody ever believed you. How come?

CASSANDRA: I was Priam of Troy's most beautiful daughter. I had more suitors than I could count, but I wanted a career; I didn't want to get stuck on the mommy track. Then Apollo showed up and started sexually harassing me. I thought I could get rid of him by demanding the gift of prophecy before I would sleep with him, but he agreed, darn it! I got Mnemosyne to record our conversations and threatened him with a lawsuit, and he backed off; but he did put a curse on me so that everybody thought I was crazy and refused to believe me, even though all my prophecies came true.

MOLLIE: You predicted most of the events of the Trojan War, didn't you?

CASSANDRA: Yes. Also the murders of Agamemnon and myself by Clytemnestra and Aegisthus, Orestes' murder of his mother, and that Buffalo would never win a Super Bowl. When Troy fell, I took refuge in Pallas Athene's temple. I was clinging to her statue when a Locrian thug called Ajax the Less dragged me away and raped me. The Achaeans didn't do a thing to him, even though he knocked over the divine image, which is why most of them never made it home. You don't mess with Athene.

MOLLIE: I remember now. The Achaean army gave you to Agamemnon as a prize of war, and he took you back to Mycenae where you were both slain.

CASSANDRA: I was a loyal and devoted worshiper

of Pallas Athene, but she didn't protect me from
Apollo or the Achaeans. She avenged the slight to
herself, but she didn't care what happened to me.

LAWYER: You have a pretty good theological mal-
practice case there. I work on contingency, you know.

ESME: No, no, that's not the way to go. Cassandra
needs to mother her own inner child. The best way to
do this would be intensive long-term therapy. I suspect
Repressed Memory Syndrome may be involved here,
too. I notice Priam hasn't shown up today. Any man
with fifty sons and fifty daughters obviously suffers
from some sort of sexual dysfunction. Have you ever
been hypnotized? Would you like to be on my radio
program?

CASSANDRA: Don't you people ever listen to yourselves? The Furies are the only ones who've made
any sense here. The answer isn't feel-good therapy or
monetary compensation; the issues we're dealing with
are power and justice.

MOLLIE: Are you saying we should leave it up to
the gods?

CASSANDRA: No! The gods are the *problem,* not
the solution. They keep messing us up. Look at all the
women who got seduced by them. Did any of those
supernatural S.O.B.s ever ask politely? And the poor
things usually got turned into some sort of livestock
afterward by Hera, even though they'd had no choice.
And what about poor Medusa? She was a beautiful
girl, a priestess of Athene, but when Poseidon came
on to her, she couldn't say no. So Athene, who had
never bothered to protect her, first turned her into a
horrible monster and then, after she was murdered,
carried her head around on her shield as a trophy.
Clytemnestra was badmouthing her sister Helen a
while ago; well, Helen and I were close. We used to
hang out together at the Mall of Troy. She told me

she never wanted to run off with my rotten brother Paris; it was forced on her by Aphrodite. Menelaus was a much nicer guy, even though he was kind of wimpy; but I bet he really wanted her back because he was king of Sparta only by virtue of being married to her. Slaves and prizes, never people.

MOLLIE: You sound like you're even madder at the goddesses than at the gods.

CASSANDRA: Because they've bought into the patriarchal power structure, that's why. Look at Pallas Athene, so busy being Daddy's perfect little girl that she's forgotten her feminine identity—*and* how to think for herself. She's even managed to forget just why she was born fully-armed from the brow of Zeus.

FOURTH AUDIENCE MEMBER: Why is that? I've always wondered.

CASSANDRA: Because Zeus *ate* her mother, that's why! She was Metis, the goddess of prudence, his first wife. He swallowed her because she warned him that if she bore him a child, it would be greater than he. Then he got this industrial-strength Excedrin headache, so Hephaestus clove his skull open with an ax. And out popped Athene, who hasn't given him any headaches since. Unfortunately.

MOLLIE: So the prophecy of Metis came true?

LAWYER: Cassandra was a little inaccurate there. The prophecy was that she would bear him a *son* greater than he. So it didn't come true.

CASSANDRA: Typical patriarchal chauvinist malarkey! Athene is a goddess of wisdom as well as war, of both ethical and natural purity. She gave humankind the arts of weaving and spinning, of shipbuilding and horse-taming. She invented the plough, the ox-yoke, the olive-tree, and a whole bunch of musical instruments. What did her father ever do but hurl thunderbolts—which she can do, too—and mess around with unwilling women?

ESME: It sounds like you're really conflicted about her, Cassandra. You admire and worship her as a goddess but feel she's let you down as your own personal deity.

CASSANDRA: Why doesn't she ever show up when I invoke her? When I really need her?

(RUMBLING NOISE OFF)

MOLLIE: What's that noise? Who's out there? *Security!*

VOICE FROM BOOTH: There aren't any left!

MOLLIE: People, I'm not sure just what's going on here. There's a rider coming down the aisle on a great big motorcycle. He's wearing leathers and there is a terrified owl clutching the handlebars for dear life. People, I do believe it's a genuine *deus ex machina*— a god from the machine. Oh, I feel just so privileged to have this happen on THE MOLLIE! SHOW. He's taking off his helmet—wait! It's a woman! A *dea ex machina*.

MOTORCYCLIST: A goddess *on* a machine, actually.

CASSANDRA: Pallas Athene!

ATHENE: Better late than never, I hope. Cassie, I really owe you one. Or more than one. You are absolutely right about my buying into the patriarchal mindset. But I've spent most of the last aeon in therapy with Susan Forward, learning to separate from my toxic father. I'm totally empowered now. I've been networking with the Fates and Persephone—she's packed up her gardening tools, her collection of seed catalogues, and her pet mole and split from Hades, by the way—and we're going to hack our way through the Olympian glass ceiling. Hera's divorcing Zeus and he's been hit with a couple of dozen palimony suits from assorted wildlife and farm animals. And Demeter's running for head god on a reform ticket.

LAWYER: Why are you riding a motorcycle?

ATHENE: It's not "a motorcycle," dim bulb; it's a Harley—a 1955 panhead rigid-frame with SU carburetor generator, bottom-end, stroked to 93 cubic inches. A real chariot of the gods. What else would a goddess of war and invention ride? You were expecting maybe a moped? Got to get a safety carrier for the owl, though. Cassandra, there's a spare helmet on the back, under the aegis. Climb on and we'll split for the Elysian Fields. The Furies are organizing a Million Maenad March on Olympus.

MOLLIE: Cassandra, you can't leave now! You're the only mythical guest I have left!

LAWYER: Wait, Cassandra! What about the lawsuit? I work on contingency, you know!

ESME: Cassandra, you need to talk this out. Preferably on my radio show! And Pallas Athene, all this acting out can't be good for you. If you would just read my book—

ATHENE: Enough! Cassandra told you that it's about justice and empowerment, not lawsuits and therapy. Why didn't you listen to her?

CASSANDRA: Probably the curse again.

ATHENE: Oh. Yeah. Right. Artemis and I will deal with Apollo real soon now. And Aphrodite can straighten out Ares if we can ever get *her* consciousness raised; it's not easy to discredit the beauty myth to the very goddess who invented it.

CASSANDRA: Ares may be beyond redemption even by Robert Bly. Anyway, do we really need another god of war when we have you? Shouldn't there be a quota?

ATHENE: Cassie, how would you like a job as my executive assistant? I like the way your mind works.

CASSANDRA: Do you have a dental plan?

ATHENE: Yes. It involves kicking chauvinist gods and Achaeans in the teeth.

CASSANDRA: Right on!

MOLLIE: You can't just take off like this. What about my show?

ESME and LAWYER: We can solve your problems for you.

ATHENE: The whole point of being a *dea ex machina* is that you get to be the one who hands out the solutions. Speaking of which— (Thunderbolts. All cameras cease to function.)

MOLLIE: . . . security . . .

VOICE FROM BOOTH: Go to commercial! Go to commercial!

(COMMERCIAL BREAK)

VOICE FROM BOOTH: I'm afraid we've lost our visuals. Will one of the assistant producers please come to the greenroom mike?

ANOTHER VOICE FROM BOOTH: They've all been fired.

FIRST VOICE: Right. Vince, get down there with a hand mike and eyeball the situation. I'll fill in from here until we get Mollie back online. People, this is the point in the show where Mollie and the experts usually sum up what we've learned from today's discussion. Yeah, Vince?

VINCE: We've got a real bad scene here, Larry. There's this shield lying on the stage, with a horrible face on it, and the audience appears to have been turned to stone. Fortunately, most of them left after the Furies got loose. I can't find Mollie or the lawyer or the shrink anywhere; but there are three of the biggest, butt-ugliest frogs you ever saw hopping around the stage. Wait! They're going after my mike!

MOLLIE:
ESME: } Brek-kek-kek-kek, co-ax! co-ax! Brek-kek-
LAWYER: kek-kek, co-ax! co-ax!

LARRY: Turn off the mike, Vince! Turn off the mike! Well, folks, that will do it for THE MOLLIE! SHOW for this week. Tune in Monday, when our subject will be "Saints Being Stalked by Sluts," with guests John the Baptist and Salome. Vince! Lose the livestock! Cut! Cue GERALDO promo! Out!

ANNOUNCER: This program is copyrighted by Mollie Drake Productions. All rights reserved. For a transcript, send five dollars to Mollie Drake Publications at the address shown on your screen.

TELOS

NOTE: The Mollie Drake Productions staff philologist (formerly assistant producer) has determined that "Brek-kek-kek-kek, co-ax! co-ax!" is Ancient Greek for "Ribit! ribit! ribit!"

KIN
by Michelle West

Michelle West is another native of Ontario, Canada. She is the author of *Hunter's Oath, Hunter's Death,* and *The Broken Crown,* all published by DAW Books.

She stood by the side of the damp-eaten wood, holding the bridle as if it were a dangerous weapon, as if, in fact, she knew how to wield it. She did not, of course, and had she, she would not have attempted it; she had lived in the mountain's heights for all of her youth. The cold of those years was reflected in everything; snow brought it back easily, as did the wind's piercing cold, but the summer's heat and the spring's thaw reminded her of the dark years by their absence; in all things, she was what her past made her.

Still, from those years, the myths had made her whole; she had lived and died and lived and died at the whim of countless tellings, until the tellings themselves had become so little echoed—and so little believed—that both she and her sister were freed.

And this was their freedom, or at least hers: To stand in this weed-strewn pasture, the sun browning her skin, the past alive by its absence, diminishing her, aging her, who had no need to feel age. Her breath was an odd wheeze as she dismissed thoughts that had, of late, become less easy to dismiss. She was tired, that was all.

They did not speak of the one whom death had delivered to other realms, but they had a memory that was long indeed, and forgave nothing.

She waited, and after some time, the boy came; the boy had to come first. His eyes were darkened by something other than exhaustion or lack of sleep; his arms too thin, his legs too thin.

This one, she thought coolly, *won't last long.*

He had the look of fragility about him; she thought, perhaps, he had found the street too long ago to be of use to her, or to the child that she had come to seek. Her nephew, the difficult one.

But there was, in his boyish step, some hopeful brightness, some spark that all beating, all neglect had not yet dimmed; it would have to do.

She whispered his name, or rather, she whispered and he heard his name, expected to hear it in the sibilance of the syllables that were spoken just out of hearing's reach. He stopped at once, his eyes wide at the sight of her. The flattery pleased her; she kept him frozen there, in awe of what was no longer legendary appearance, until she remembered why she had come.

And besides, she thought, she had no taste for a child of his kind; they were unpleasant, in ways that were often fatal.

She held the bridle; as it caught the sunlight it absorbed the color, becoming links of fine gold, a thing not meant for a horse.

For you, she said, and the wind took the words. *You will need it.* It did not please her to hold it, but he was still transfixed; she knew a moment of panic before he moved and she realized that it was not inadvertent use of her power, but his youth, that had kept him in place.

The bridle exchanged hands, and she leaned forward, brushing his cheeks with the tendrils of her living hair. *Go on,* she told him, without speaking, *and you will find what you were promised.*

But promised by what, or by who, she did not say.

As if in stupor, he began to climb the rotting fence. It was a miracle that the fence supported his weight; she knew it for fact, because she had asked for it; long years had given her more than a passing familiarity with miracles of all nature. This was a minor one, and her sister, younger than she by a very small measure, and given to whining about these things, would have pronounced it a solid waste of effort; she did not much like boys of this one's bent, and for good reason.

Such a child had, after all, killed the eldest. But she would have consented to its use, not for the nameless boy's sake, but for the sake of the nephew.

It was hard for the sisters to come together to these pastures, this brook, this sight; in the hills beyond it, the stench of industry rose, the sight of the cities they had both grown to love in the same wary way they had loved their cave: not at all, and with a growing weariness and vexation that caused no small amount of friction between them.

The boys were harder to find; they went missing, and what had once been the age of a manhood ready for war and war's death was now not even the age of consent. The boys best for her nephew were boys who did not stray far from the folds of their parents' grim watch; who did not, indeed, know how to stray far, although they were so very bright and shiny the shadows did not scare them so much as challenge them.

Active boys with causes.

No, all that was left to either sister, as easy picking, were those boys who had been battered by life until only a little spark remained, if even that, of childhood's hope, the desire for justice that betrayed all children, and was in the end betrayed by them.

There were some that yearned for a place to belong, and they would often do anything, beneath the cruelty of their angry facade, to get it; these, the sisters took.

But among them there were those who harbored dreams of justice, of being more than just a child of pleasure—and pain—in the tarnished glow of neon and fluorescent signs, in the streets paved with asphalt and oil, with their offered oblations of urine and blood. The girls were discarded—for reasons of sisterhood, but also because the sisters themselves were created, and sustained, by a principal that did not easily allow them to seek out others who were once almost of their kind. In youth, especially, the girls had a faint glow of the sisters' power, some hint of their hidden beauty, some hope or promise.

And what is that promise to us? she thought, as she thought of young girls in the streets that would age them. *And what is their aging, after all? All things age and die.*

The bridle, the boy took, denying the truth of the words she had not spoken—at least hoped she had not spoken—aloud. He was not so stupid as to tell her all of his desire—in fact, he was wise enough to tell her none of it at all—but she understood it well enough, although it was no part of her nature.

Experience shaped even such as she, if slowly.

Go, she told the boy. *Follow the stream to the lake. He will be waiting there for you.*

She stayed to watch, because she had to, and she bitterly regretted the time spent. *I'm just as much of an addict,* she thought, *as you are. We are driven by compulsion, you and I; we are not so very different.*

Oh, but you are, the wind whispered in its singularly insolent voice. He will die.

She shrugged, not in the mood to be swayed by something as smug as a brisk breeze. It was starting, after all. It was beginning again.

The boy no longer saw her, although she saw him well enough; she had eyes, after all, that were not limited by the singular poverty of vision that marked humanity. As well, she could taste his scent on the wind, could hear the heave of his soft chest, his breath's rattle, thin and weak.

The bridle, she chose not to look at, although it swung in the child's hand like a noose. It was not necessary, not strictly speaking, but it was part of the ritual, and ritual governs many things long after the reason for its birth is forgotten. So had she learned.

There were no monsters left, of course.

No heights to climb to.

No terrors besides which the crash of falling snow, the rush of swollen river, the breaking of earth covered by the thinnest layer of human habitat, paled in comparison. Malice had descended, as had all else, into frail form, frail beauty; it was hidden in the hearts of man, and it burned like a weak flame.

Once, twice, she had seen it spark and light incandescent across the horizon; once or twice she had held her breath, feeling a moment the last days of her youth, the last years. But it was extinguished, always, one way or the other. No great ambition survived the span of a handful of small years. Ah, there, the boy had reached the pond.

What did he see, she wondered?

His breath caught and stopped a moment, his jaw fell open, his eyes grew wide with unblinking until dryness forced them to shut and water.

She knew what she saw: a white beast, on all fours, hooves old and cracked, a back bowed like a poor woman's laundry line in the summer heat. And there, like the glimmer of youth in a wizened old face, the shadows of what had once been his greatness, a whisper of things so long unseen that had they not once been so remarkable, they would be forgotten completely.

It was, of course, a bitter truth: She had seen them only once, at his birth, and they had been awash in the course of her sister's blood. The boy who'd killed her had not even left enough to bury, although it was not their custom; why would they have customs for death, after all, who so little understood its ways?

Still, death was faced, and with it came loss, and it was a loss that they did not understand completely, for the kin that they had that dwelled in the land of the dead were not, themselves, dead. It was a strangeness, the first of many, and it was complete, an act in and of itself. That boy was long dust, no doubt for the hubris of the act of killing; for the act of killing which was the only thing that could, in the end, give him the immortality that he had robbed her of. A bitter transfer.

Oh, yes, he was immortalized.

Her sister? Immortalized as well, but that act deprived where the first granted.

And the child born out of her sister's golden blood?

Ah, that child had flown, just once, glorious in his birth. It was, she knew, the most beautiful thing that she had ever seen, and she a god's kin, and she an immortal.

Flight. Freedom. Those two words had never meant as much as they had on that single still memory-bright day.

She heard that the child's wings had served the gods' will—as they all had, she thought, with bitterness, with satisfaction—that they had carried a boy, another dream-filled, hopeful child, to the heights to do battle with the Chimera. A distant cousin, and an envied one, to be so feared and so little hunted, these three heads all of one body, that they might comfort and never be parted.

She heard the intake of a boy's breath, the newness of one whom the streets had yet failed to make old, and her lips set in a line so thin their edge cut any words that attempted to escape.

What do you see? she thought.

Her sister came to the clearing hours after the boy and the child had left, no doubt to play their games. Hours after the golden links of bridle had been awkwardly—had been incorrectly—placed around the head and mouth of her sullen nephew.

Was it imagination, or did his eyes clear, for the first time in decades? Was it desire on her part, something old and foolish, or did the shadow of a glory that she could remember but could never partake in, did that shadow of that glory flicker into life? She watched with bitterer hunger than ever she fed, hoping for a truth in a vision of thin boy, old child.

She wanted the boy to mount, but her nephew threw back his bramble twisted mane, his veined head, and pierced her with his stare. Between them, she and he, there was no friendliness; could never be.

He was born to carry heroes, and she, to hone them.

He led the boy away—or perhaps the boy, responding to his unspoken desire, led him—and she stood alone a long time, in the twist of bitter wind and an ache that had been growing.

"You do yourself no good by this, sister."

"Stheno, leave be."

She never did; sisters were seldom that considerate.

"You've been too long in the day," she continued, her face turned away from the pond that lay beyond rotted fence. Still, as if she could see it—and of course, she could, the stance was meant as statement, not as practical act—she said, "You felt you must waste a miracle here, I presume. The boy was so close to being a complete loss that he couldn't climb a fence without hurting himself?"

"The fence was rotting."

"Everything does."

Euryale said nothing. After a moment, she turned and began to walk. Her sister trailed her, a shadow on the ground, very like the serpents that they were both so fond of in these diminished days.

"You've got that look about you," Stheno said. She was worried, and when she worried, she was unbearable. Very human. "Euryale, won't you speak?"

"I've nothing to say."

"You're dreaming of the old days."

"Neither of us dreams," the older sister said coolly. "Neither of us knows how to sleep."

"We slept," Stheno said, coldly and bitterly, "once."

"Yes. And look at what it cost us."

These words were rote, between them; they took turns playing their parts, blending and mingling until it did not matter at all who said what. Euryale brightened, although the brightness was false, and caught her sister by the arm; they walked together from the empty pasture, the empty past.

Look at what it cost us.

The words themselves felt wrong, awkward as she turned them over, and over again. She felt the loss of her sister keenly, for her sister had been the only mortal among them, and therefore the most powerful. Death, the ability to approach it—there was a strength in that.

As if she could hear the thoughts, Stheno held on

the more tightly. There was an anger in her that the evenings' killing did not dismiss.

The killings were simple, in the here and now; sometimes they were obvious and unsubtle and sometimes they took longer, for many things could be turned to stone, and the figurative heart over which so many mortals lost their minds, if only for brief bursts of time, was as good as any.

But her heart, as it were, was not in it, and in the end, much exasperated, Stheno had left her kill, and her pleasure, to take umbrage at her sister's lack.

"You have wasted that child," she said, disapproving.

"I am not in the mood."

"Euryale, you have killed four men in three days, because you are not, as you've said, in the mood. We have hardly been here a few months and we will already be forced to move on if we do not want the undue attention of the local authorities."

"In the old days," the older sister said, "we did not run."

"In the old days," was the pert reply, "we lived in a cave in the side of a large rock with only the passersby for company."

"Weren't we happier then?"

"Euryale, I forbid you to see the child. Is that clear? You are—you are not ever in your right mind afterward."

"I cannot," Euryale replied. "He is all that is left of her."

"She was mortal," Stheno replied. "It tells you much, that the love of a mortal was so dangerous. Forget about it. Do as I have done."

And have you done, sister? Have you truly forgotten? Have you forgotten the day she came to us, trans-

formed by the rage of a jealous god for suffering the
unwanted attentions of the Lord of the Ocean? Have
you forgotten her fear, at both herself and us, the way
she huddled in terror unable to even clean herself for
days on end, afraid to weep because the hiss of her
voice was so terrible to her ears? The lament for lost
beauty, as if beauty is something that is not entirely
controlled by the viewer, and not the one viewed.

I remember.

I remember it all.

She went out that night without her sister, seeking
not the lights of the city, but the darkness they illumi-
nated. Or at least so she believed, but the lights were
too harsh, this one night, and the darkness a pathetic
thing, truly, a thing to be pitied. Oh, it claimed lives,
and some of those lives were lost in a fashion humanity deemed horrible—but what of it? The darkness
was spawned in smallness, contained by smallness, defeated by smallness.

Or perhaps not.

They had given each other solace for centuries. She
did not remember what it was to be beautiful, although she remembered, vaguely, that she had been;
what she best remembered was Medusa's perfect skin,
the happiness with which she sang, the stories she told, the
way she had moved, so very like a mortal. Perhaps the
shadows had been upon her even then, and they had not
seen it, had not chosen to see it. She had become
something greater than she had been, and they all knew
it. In the darkness, they did not see each other, and yet
they adapted; they learned to draw happiness from each
other. And in the darkness, away from the aegis, away
from their parents, away from the attentions of unwanted gods, they slept. They dreamed.

Euryale wanted to sleep again; she wanted the

depth of darkness that not even her sisters perturbed
except by the subconscious certainty of their presence,
their affection.

"Euryale."

She stirred.

"Euryale!"

Blinked. Turned in the direction of her sister's
voice, the one that remained. She loved Stheno, truly;
Stheno was her history, the knowledge of her past, the
one who understood what she had lost—for they were
halves of a whole. Or had been. Closing her eyes, she
turned again.

"Why are you doing this to me?"

"I do nothing, sister."

"You do, and you know it, and you don't want to
know it. Why? You know what happened the last
time. The last time we slept."

"I wasn't sleeping."

"No. But you wanted it. I could taste it half the city
away. This is not the place, Euryale."

"And where *is* the place?" The moment the question left her lips, she knew.

Stheno was angry. "If you do this thing, you will do
it alone."

"Yes."

Very angry. "Listen to me! Do you know what
you'll lose? Haven't you learned from her—" Stopped,
her anger growing. "It's that boy. And the child. Her
child. You always fall into melancholy when you've
seen the child."

Euryale said nothing.

"I've half a mind to kill him."

"But you will not."

Silence. Then, "No."

That would bring back a moment of the age of

greatness. The sisters were silent. At last, Stheno rose, her anger contained perfectly except for the clicking of her fingernails, the clattering of multiple claws. She would go out, tonight, Euryale thought, suddenly tired. She would go out and rampage, as she did when she was angry.

The boy's friends were the only group they had cultivated, taking them aside in ones and twos, preparing them for the fate they little understood they had chosen.

"You warned me," she told her sister mildly, "that I had taken too many lives this past month. You will do worse."

"Does it matter?" Stheno snapped back. "We will move, as we always move, one way or the other." Her anger brought her back to herself in a way nothing else could; it was as if, at core, all they had was their anger—and each other.

She went. She was gone. Euryale was alone, and she could not rouse herself to join her sister.

Almost, she did not do it.

She could see it now; she had a vision that had been wakened by her sister's momentary, her sister's ancient, rage.

But she had more than vision; she had the responsibility that came with it. Eldest after the death of the eldest, she had done what she could to maintain the family traditions, but she was flagging, and she accepted it here, in the pathetic darkness of mortal night, in a world of ash and colors so pale they might all be gray.

Who would be left, if she did as she desired? Who would be left to comfort Stheno, to feed the child those things that sustained him? There had been only one answer, each time she asked the question; there was only one answer now.

And it was not strong enough.

Euryale shook herself. She desired sleep, but before she could sleep, it was time to awaken.

She had seen him once. She had seen him in the shock of the realization that where they had been three, they would be two, forever. Or for as long as they woke, as long as they were vigilant. Medusa was the deep one, the lover of the depths, and with her, they lost what they were to two things: the winged child and the golden warrior. They were her heart laid bare by the malice of Poseidon, given life by advances that none—not even the goddesses themselves—could in the end deny. And yet she could not bring herself to hate them; they were of her sister, after all, her blood.

She had come to realize that Chrysaor was a monster's son, but the winged one was different, a difficult child. And as any adolescent, she dreamed of riding him. But she could not seek him out until the gods had drifted, lifeless themselves, from the halls of Olympus, and when she had at least caught sight of him again, she knew him only by the bridle; all glory had passed with the gods.

And yet.

And yet she found that he made his way, as if drawn, toward the young men. Toward their battles, toward their glories, and toward the hubris of their untimely deaths. He carried them, and they accepted what he offered, slow at first to see the shadow of beating wings that would carry them forever from the touch of stale ground.

Afterward, he was stronger, his coat sleeker, his back less bowed; his hooves were strong and dark, and they did not have the cracks and chips that the ground forced upon them year after year. Youth, as if youth were only an ignorant boy's heroics, settled about this child, this difficult child, and she could almost imagine—

—she could almost imagine that she could see the wings that lay folded across his back.

But they were not for her, and she knew it; knew it bitterly. They were a present for the young heroes of the ancient world.

As if, by carrying them to do battle with their monsters, he was thanking the breed for his birth. His mother's death.

And Euryale knew one thing well, although the knowledge had been buried with effort and time and the dimming of the world. She knew how to be that monster, that terrible death. Uncloaking herself as even her sister in her rage had not dared, Euryale walked the streets of the city, unaware now of which city it was, unaware of its modern name—for modern names had so little meaning, so little history, they were tossed in the sea change of mortality. She threw back the skin that she labored under; opened her eyes, let loose the roar of her breath, the piercing sweet beauty of her claws, the fullness of glance that had petrified all those would-be heroes. All those sword-wielding midwives who had come to better Perseus, had come to become legend, a bit of life that could somehow be held onto when teeth and hair and youth could not.

Here, she caught the eyes of the men—it was the men, always, that enraged her in their duplicity and their easy use of power, no matter that the modern world had taken so much of their power—and made of them statues; trapped them within themselves, forced them into the poverty of their existence, just once, the madness of their small, small lives. She called the night, and the shadows came, she called the fire and it limned the darkness with its orange light.

Death she called, and if Hermes did not crest its wave with winged foot, death came nonetheless.

Half a city away, Stheno heard her, and even over the roar of ancient breath, Euryale could not drive away the sound of her weeping.

But above the sound of weeping, she heard it, sharp as the clean sound of sheath and sword being parted: the beating of wings.

Her hero was coming.

She did not read the news the next day; she'd forgotten how. She'd forgotten much but the sound of weeping, the terrible sound of her own voice raised in a cry of pain that the mountains, surely, remembered. She did not wear clothing; did not dress for the neon of street, the bright light of restaurant, the travel between men that had marked the modern life. Cast off, like the fashion it was, she returned to her roots; Euryale, Gorgon, the middle child.

She heard Stheno's weak wail, the voice was shredded by wind and lost; it confused her a moment before she remembered, herself, how far away from the cave she must have wandered, searching, always searching, for that one thing that they had lost: Her sister's head.

She found stone and statues in its stead, fat ones, rounded with food and wine, surprised in laughter or merriment or the first—if they were smart enough— hint of horror; she found no Gorgon's head. Had she, she was not certain what she would have done; but she felt compelled to search; the emptiness was like a hunger that demanded feeding.

And at last, empty-handed, she returned to the cave.

When had the courts become so large and so empty, the chariots so ugly and so confining? When had youth been swept aside for age and a power that she did not see as power, even if she felt its passing?

Stheno, she cried, but her sister, weeping, could not answer. She must, she must be at the cave.

The mountains.

The heights.

Had she wings—had she wings, she would find purchase in the air; she had claws, and the strength of ten men—such a quaint phrase that, as if men had strength at all—and the rock gave way where stubborn air would not. Ah, she was tired, and she had failed, and she had experienced the first—the only—loss.

No bright messenger came for her sister.

What happened to dead monsters, after all? Did sleep just claim them, take them all? Did they become the dreams of mortal men, or did they fully and finally have dreams of their own?

The rocks tried twice to kill her, but she was not so easily dislodged, and besides, she had loosed her form; the fall itself was not the thing which was destined to be her death. It was not from accident or mishap that monsters met their deaths. Not from those.

She looked over her shoulder, seeing in the sky a speck of light, a thing brighter than sunlight, brighter than starlight, a thing that was steadier than the sudden lurch of heart and breath. She was not in the right place, not yet; she must hurry.

The mountains had never seemed so high; never so remote; they were merciless. And she was merciless, and understood that she and the mountains were not dissimilar, excepting in this one, this significant thing: She was tiring. She was so tired.

Home beckoned. Home, darkness, a place of blessed isolation. No sisters here, and she would regret that, she thought, for if she could have one thing, and only one thing, it would be to sleep in the arms of her sisters. Stheno was not yet ready to sleep, and Medusa had passed on; she felt the loss keenly as her feet, scratched by the newness of sharp rock where she'd been forced to tear out a chunk or two to gain purchase, touched the gentle incline that led into the darkness. No mirrors here. No reflective waters. No gold, no thing to catch the light and return with both it and the image of serpents.

Now, she thought, as she turned to face the mouth of the cave. I am ready for you, nephew.

No prayer passed her lips, and only a single word: *Stheno.*

She heard the wail of her sister, weighted by mortal concern, by mortal conceit, trapped by life and the living of life. She did not ask her sister to take what was left of the family responsibility onto her own shoulders; it was too harsh a burden, or rather, it would be, for at least some centuries.

But in the end, Stheno would be drawn, as Euryale had been—as, perhaps, Medusa had—into the folds of the past, and pressed there like forming layers of rock. The sadness colored her thoughts while she could hold it—but she could not hold it long.

For the sight came sudden and unlooked for.

She had thought to be sleeping when they arrived, he carrying the boy, and the boy the shiny shield, the sharpened sword.

Winged and white and glorious, he carried the hero, as he was born to do. His brother had birthed monsters, as *he* had been born to do. What glory, what brilliance greater than this? She saw, or thought she saw, the flash of swordlight in the hands of the spindly, undeterred youth whose hand clutched mane and not bridle, whose confidence spoke of a bond of trust that had been built between them, immortal and mortal, child and child. A cause seemed writ across both their features.

Did she cry?

No; she could not; it was not in her nature. For sorrow, yes, but for joy—no. And it was joy she felt, and sleep coming, for she saw the child of her dreams, her sister's bright heart, a purity that she could not stain.

Who will feed you? she thought, and then did not think it; she knew that heroes would rise and fall, greater and lesser, and that they would find him, somehow, feed him, somehow, borrow his greatness and give it to him at one and the same time.

But they would not feed him as she had, this day, for there were hardly any of her kind left to give him occasion to rise to.

Come, she thought. She coiled there, at the cave's mouth, the sleep heavy and thick in her mouth, across her many eyes. One by one they shut, and fight for vision of her nephew or no, she could not keep them open.

Come.

Like dream, like sleep, he did, and he would do her the mercy of never asking her to rise again in the diminished world that had somehow conspired to become her home.

Stheno . . .

THE DIVINE COMEDY
by Dennis L. McKiernan

Dennis McKiernan, one of a growing number of writers choosing Tucson, Arizona, as their home, is a best-selling fantasy writer. His most recent book is *Into the Forge*.

Of his story, Dennis says: "One might wonder what happens to all gods in the end, even those denizens of Olympus. Do old gods never die but just sparkle away? Or is there a more fitting finale?"

Wha—? *What in mud am I doing here?*
     I stood there dripping, saltwater falling away from me into the gray mist.

Something's wrong.

A free-standing door stood before me.

Unemployment Office.

That's what it said on the frosted glass: *Unemployment Office.*

There was no building behind . . . just a free-standing door.

Something is definitely wrong. One minute I was cruising through the trench; the next minute . . . here . . . wherever in chaos "here" is.

Oh, well.

I opened the door.

A blast of hot air and angry, shouting voices and a stench of incense and flowers and honey mingled with sweat and sour wine and unwashed bodies whelmed into me, knocking me backward.

Holy mud!

Taking a deep breath, I stepped through the door and stood gaping at the madhouse I'd entered. It was an office, all right, packed with beings—shouting angry beings. It was dirty and hot, seedy, crowded, crowded with all sorts, milling about, dressed in togas and robes, in fur and loincloths, with elephant-heads and wings and many arms and sheer veils, and in all sorts of other gorgeous, bizarre, and peculiar raiments, as if attired for some kind of costume ball. Some were sitting on benches against the wall, filling out papers. Others were sitting at desks, yelling at various clerks. Harsh fluorescent lights glared down upon this chaos. Somewhere in the background I could hear wild laughter.

As I stood there looking, taking it all in, water puddling about my feet—"Shut the door, buttbrain"—a voice cut through the bedlam.

It was the thin-lipped male receptionist, black slicked-down hair center parted, dressed in a tight-fitting, narrow-lapelled black suit, buttoned vest, white shirt with a high celluloid collar and cuffs, and glaring at me over his Ben Franklins, his desk covered with stacks of paper.

As I swung the door to, I took another look outside—still the same featureless fog, stretching endlessly into a gray void, as far as the eye could see.

I shut the door . . . it disappeared.

I stepped to the desk and stood dripping and waiting while the receptionist continued to scribble on a piece of paper before him.

There were no windows to the outside, though to my left, jutting in through the wall was an air conditioner with an *Out of Order* sign hanging from it.

To my right in the far corner stood a large bottled-water cooler. *At least* something *in this office is right*!

High on the wall to the left of the water cooler was a sign proclaiming *Exit,* but no door stood below. Just like the sign saying *Entrance* above where I had entered, nothing but a blank wall beneath.

On the far wall was a clock—broken, the pendulum hanging at an odd angle, *1990 AD* showing on its display—mounted above a windowed door to another office, *Top Dog* etched on the glass; I could see there was someone inside.

Behind me were the benches along the wall, occupied, costumed entities filling out forms, cursing.

And the stench and noise and heat beat at me like a hammer as I stood before the desk.

I cleared my throat.

"What do you want, butthead?" asked the receptionist without looking up.

Butthead! Butthead! By the depths! This is too much! I reached out a hand and made the gesture to open the chasm below and bring on the maelstrom and suck this blasphemer down into the black abyss forever.

The water cooler went *Glug*!

Otherwise, nothing happened.

I looked at my hand.

"You can't do that crap anymore, fishbreath," said the clerk.

"I can't do . . . ?"

"That's right. You can't do diddlysquat, turkey."

I tried again. This time the water cooler didn't even go *glug*.

"You don't get it, do you, stupid?"

I shook my head, *No*.

"You're unemployed. Your flock has dwindled below critical mass, cretin. Why the hell else would you be here?"

I stood there dumbfounded.

He shoved a sheaf of papers my way. "Fill these out, dork."

Confused—*Is this any way to treat a god? Just wait until Poseidon hears of this . . . wherever he's gotten to*—I took the forms and backed away from the desk. *Squish!* I stepped into a pile of horse manure.

"We get all kinds of horses' butts in here," sneered the clerk, as he transformed into a punk dressed in a black leather jacket, his hair a tall, upright row of orange spikes down the center of an otherwise bald head, a black upside-down cross dangling from his left ear.

I stumbled down to the water cooler and poured several cupfuls over myself. *Damn tiny cups! Hardly large enough to do the job.* Still, I persisted.

Refreshed, dripping, I sat down, muscling my way in between these two guys on the same bench. One wore a black mask and gold robes, the only flesh showing was on his terribly scarred hands; the other guy was a big blond dressed in a loin cloth and wearing soft leather buskins. He had these blue stripes across his chest, and a couple of blue daubs on his cheeks.

"*Fwccing* clerk from hell," growled Blue-daub under his breath.

Ping!

A loud ding knelled through the office. Silence fell. All heads looked up.

"Broads' time," shouted the punk. "Venus! Aphrodite!"

Aphrodite? Clacking scallops, even though I had never actually met her, I knew of Aphrodite from The Mountain even though I had never actually been there—too high and dry for the likes of me. And Venus . . . I seem to recall tales of her bobbing about on a bivalve, but that was before my time, and you know how dolphins can mess up a perfectly good tale.

Two buxom females dressed in diaphanous togas stepped to his desk, bedlam returning as the other occupants resumed their complaining and cursing and shouting. The two women could have been sisters, even twins, they looked so much alike as to be virtually identical—except one had her hair up in Greek ribbons while the other seemed more . . . more Romanesque.

I looked down at my forms. *Damn!* I needed a pencil.

I stood and stepped to the receptionist.

"Where *is* this ranch?" asked one of the ladies, the Greek, Aphrodite I would think.

"Nevada, broad," came the answer.

"We're not going to have to cook, are we?" The Roman lady's eyes narrowed. "My skills lie elsewhere."

"Mine, too," added the Greek. "Oh, I wish I were back on The Mountain, doing what I do so well, instead of going to this, this—"

"You won't notice the difference, bubblehead," interrupted the punk receptionist.

As I got my pencil, the ladies stepped toward the wall to the right. When they approached, a section below the *Exit* sign glowed with a green fire, witch fire, and there stood a portal . . . to elsewhere.

Beyond, through shimmering heat waves, I could see a long road curving toward a low mansion in the distance. Gack! It was in an arid desert. I shuddered in revulsion.

"But I don't know *anything* about ranches!" complained the Roman.

"Much less mustangs," chimed in the other.

Wild laughter sounded from somewhere, cutting through the noise.

Hand in hand, they stepped through, heading toward the distant mansion, while the opening behind dissolved, leaving blank wall where portal had been.

TICK!

All heads whipped about, eyes staring at the . . . at the . . . clock?

I looked, too.

The pendulum hung at a different angle; the display now read *2000 AD.*

Wham! The door below the *Entrance* sign blasted open, and a skull-headed rider astride a fire-breathing dragon came screaming through. "Save me! Save me!"

The punk sneered and clenched his fist upright, all but the vertically pointing middle finger. In that instant, the dragon and rider dissolved in sparkles of light, shrieking.

I turned to Blue-daub. "What the . . . ?"

"The game broke up."

"Game?"

"Yeah. Some gods are born during games on earth. When the game breaks up . . ." He drew his finger across his throat, going *Kkkkkk!*

Ping!

"Next buttbrain!" shrilled the receptionist, now a hatchet-faced lady in a black dress with a high collar, her hair pulled into a severe bun.

This big Roman in a crested gold helmet with a nose guard and cheek plates, wearing a gold breastplate and arm and leg greaves, and a short, pleated skirt, and sandals, and bearing a short sword, stepped up to the desk, only to be shouldered aside by an equally big Nordic guy in a horned helmet and leather vest and pants and buskins, and carrying a big hammer.

"Out of the way, buttbrain, I'm the next buttbrain here."

"Like Hades!" shouted the Roman, shoving back.

The two of them went at it tooth and nail, smashing into desks and chairs, scattering the occupants, crashing into walls, hammer blanging upon sword. No one tried to separate them. Maybe this sort of thing happened all the time.

I ran to protect the water cooler.

TOCK!

Immediately the fight stopped, each warrior—what else *would* they be—staring in panic at the clock.

The pendulum now hung at a new angle, the display reading *2010 AD*.

Someone screamed, and among the beings at the desks I could see bright sparkling lights fading into nothingness, matching a thin wail also fading into nothingness—just as had the dragon and rider.

The two former combatants scrambled up to stand before Hatchet Face's desk.

She handed each a paper, sneering, "Pinheads. We'll see how well you do in the NWWF."

The portal reappeared, and I could see an arena filled with thousands of screaming, cheering humans, all focused on a brightly-lit, roped-off platform, where two guys grappled and kicked and bit, trying it seems to murder one another.

As they passed by me, the big Norseman, reading his paper, said, "What in Hèl is a contract? And what does it mean when it says that we're a tag team?"

The Roman shrugged, and they stepped through into the top rows of the arena, the exit disappearing after, solid wall returning, as an uninhibited giggling tittered through the office.

I dumped more water over my head, then returned to my place on the bench.

"What, by the Great Kraken, is going on here?" I asked the blue-daubed guy.

He cocked an eyebrow at me.

"I mean, that clock, for instance."

He looked frightened and lowered his head into his hands, saying nothing, but the guy in the black mask and gold robes, the guy with the scarred hands answered.

"It's ticking off the years on Earth," he replied, his voice muffled by his facial covering.

"But . . ."

"Each tick is worth ten."

"Ten ticks?"

"No, ten years; each tick is worth ten years."

"But it's ticked twice since I've been here, and that's only been some ten minutes or so . . . not twenty years."

"Time runs differently here."

"Holy tides."

I thought over what he said, watching the clock. Now I could see that the pendulum was actually moving, eking downward in an arc. "What does the AD mean?"

"Some say it means *'anno Domini,'* whereas others claim it means *'after date.'* It all started when this guy was crucified; ultimately, he became a god to some; they reckon AD based on his probable birth date, a virgin birth, or so they say. In any event—" he glanced at the clock, "—it's been some 2010 years since this method of keeping count of the years began."

He paused a moment, glancing down at his hands and said, "Before that, I am told the display showed years denoted by an Egyptian system . . . or Chinese. I don't know which. The clock was on AD 350 when I got here, most of my acolytes having been converted to the god on the cross."

"Then you've been here—"

Another scream sounded, and more sparkles glittered up into the air.

Blue-daub winced.

I looked at Black Mask. His eyes were wide. Perhaps with fear.

He glanced at me, and answered my next unspoken question. "The one who went up in sparkles—his last worshipers died . . . or stopped believing."

Holy Whale! So that's it! Thank the waves, there's plenty of dolphins and porpoises in the sea.

Ping!

The receptionist, now an obese, sweating, cigar-smoking, red-necked, crew-cut slob dressed in a buttoned shirt, strained to its limits, with loose tie hanging from the limp-collared neck bellowed, "Next jerk!"

As the slob took care of this jackal-headed guy, I turned to Black Mask. "Who is this tube worm of a receptionist?"

"I heard that, buttface!" yelled the clerk. "That's for me to know and you to . . . never know."

My pencil point snapped off.

I got up to get another pencil from the desk, but the slob scooped them all into his top drawer, locking it and slipping the key in with a hundred others on a key chain fastened to his belt and then grinning wickedly at me, his yellow-stained teeth glistening with tobacco juice from the chomped cigar.

To the great abyss with you, you tubeworm. I didn't say it out loud.

As I sat back down, Blue-daub handed me his sword. "Here, perhaps you can sharpen it with this, though I ween it's no longer enchanted."

Struggling—what the mud, did you ever try to sharpen a stub of a pencil with a disenchanted sword?—I dully hacked away at the stump. I ended up with a butchered something that I could barely hold with my fingertips.

Laughter sounded above the background.

TICK!

The display now read *2020 AD*.

In quick succession, the entrance slammed open three times, ephemeral figures rushing inward, only to vanish in sparkles.

Games broke up, I thought.

Then it struck me. Mud! That's all it ever was. Just a game. A grand and glorious game. No matter which "god" we are, it's just a game.

And we are born when there are enough "true believers," and we die when the believers—

Ping!

"Next buttbrain!"

—we die when the believers are no more, when they either lose faith or when the last one passes on or when another faith supersedes our own.

And if the clerk from hell is right, when the number of believers falls below critical mass, then we come here.

Enlightenment! That's it. That's the reason that most of the gods are out of work: enlightenment—on land it's an age of enlightenment. Belief falters. Gods are stripped of their divinity, their powers dwindling to nothing, now that there aren't enough of the faithful to sustain them. It's got to be deep, black mud for them, the gods of the land dwellers, this age of enlightenment. Huah! Maybe that's where Poseidon disappeared to; I mean, most of his worshippers were land dwellers. They diminished, fell away, he came here, and now perhaps he's on earth . . . either that or he went up in sparkles. Triton and the others, too. All but me. I am worshiped by—

—Oh, wait a minute! If losing believers means you

come here—holy waves!—that must mean that the numbers of true believers for me have fallen below critical mass, too. How can that be? Porpoises and dolphins don't just vanish. And sure as the Great Kraken, there's been no age of enlightenment for the porpoises, for the dolphins.

I went to the water cooler and dumped more liquid over my head.

Tuna boats! What else could it be? Damn netters! And they had claimed that they were dolphin safe! That's got to be it! . . . I think.

Wait a minute! Wait a minute! There *are* those experiments with dolphins at those human institutes, both academic and military. And some of the captives had escaped; others had been released. And they had returned to the ocean, bringing their newfound knowledge with them. Maybe the age of dolphin enlightenment had come after all.

TOCK!

2030 AD.

A brown-skinned, elephant-headed guy, his loins wrapped in a yellow dhoti cinched with a red sash, stood before the snuff-sniffing receptionist, now a powdered-wigged, ruffled-shirted fop.

Elephant-head's voice was hollow, nasal, as if he were speaking through a long tube. "Select one of three?" he honked, puzzled. I thought I could hear tiny echoes reverberating up and down his trunk. "You must please explain."

"What's to explain, hosenose? Unlike that homicidal, multi-armed broad you came in here with, at least you've got choices: you can be a capering, clowning team mascot for the Pittsburgh Pachyderms, or work as a greeter at a theme park in Orlando or Anaheim, or be a figurehead for the Republican party."

As if in counterpoint, again I heard mad laughter

rising up above the level of strident cursing and shouted frustration within the office.

Elephant-head tootled softly, mournfully, then grasped a pen with his trunk, closed his eyes, and jabbed it down onto the paper before him.

"Good choice, Dumbo . . ."

I didn't hear what he had selected, for at that moment the insanity of it all struck me, and I turned to Black Mask. "Why are we here?" I asked. "Oh, I don't mean in the general metaphysical sense, but rather, why are we in an unemployment office? Why are we seeking jobs?"

"To live longer," he responded. "By getting a job on the earth, we escape this place. There, we'll live out a goodly span of years. Whereas, since time runs differently here, if we stay, we'll live but a few minutes or a few hours, several hundred ticks of that clock at most, until all believers are gone. Then so will we be gone."

As if to underscore Black Mask's prophetic words— *Yaggghhh* . . . !—someone else vanished in a sparkle of light.

When next I looked up, there was another exgod at the desk. An older guy. In a toga, his hair and beard long-curled and oiled. Holy mud, it could have been Poseidon, himself . . . but was not. Poseidon was a bit older, I think. Wait a moment now, Poseidon had a younger brother: Zeus, the most powerful of all. Fish! Can it be that even *he* has sunk to such depths?

The clerk, now a slicked back, greased hair, pencil-thin-mustached man in an overlarge dark pinstriped silk suit and black-and-white pointed-toe shoes and a wide-brimmed hat and a watch chain that dangled down from his vest to the floor and back up again sneered, "Zeus, you old fart, what are you good for?

I mean, this hep cat wants to know what did you ever do that showed any talent?"

By the Gulf of Eternity, it is *Zeus!*

"Well, ah, let me see . . ." the old guy pondered a bit, one eye on the clock. "Oh, I know! I used to, ah, seduce young ladies. . . ." He looked hopefully at the hep cat.

The man flipped through a rolodex, all the while mumbling under his breath: "Chippendale's . . . Loveboat . . . Hollywood . . . Hollywood? Well all reet and gimme some skin. Hollywood! That's Jake. They do some porno there."

A gleam glistened in Zeus' eye, then died. "Hera would object," he mumbled.

"She's gone on to her sparkly reward," sniggered the hep cat. "Look, numbskull, novelty acts are big out there. I think you'd go big, too. But listen, there's a small danger. A lotta guys in that line of work have bitten the big one, so—"

"Hey! I don't do that sort of stuff!"

"No, buttbrain, I'm talking about catching fatal diseases. I'm talking about, you gotta use a condom." The cat shoved a small package at Zeus. "You gotta wear these, loverboy."

"What! What! Me? Meee? Use these things—" Zeus peered at the label on the packet, "—from Troy?"

A joyous giggling tittered throughout the office.

TICK!

I returned to my form.

Name: *Tk-tk!cht,tkatkachr;chr-gok-ok'psieuwww-nnunk!gnk-gnk* . . . I gave up on the name thing. *Fish! There's just no way to translate all the dolphin clicks and chirps and whistles and grunts and . . .* I erased everything but the *Tk-tk!*

Then I erased that and put down the name the Nereids and Sisyphus had given me: *Palaemon.*

Tides! I hadn't used that name in aeons. And before Palaemon I was known as Melicertes, son of Athamas and Ino. There was even an old legend about me, but they got it wrong, saying that my mother had jumped into the sea with me when I was but a babe, fleeing the Hera-induced madness of my father, and the tale had it that I had drowned. Not so! A dolphin had saved me. There's even some statues of me as a youngster commemorating that rescue—the boy on the dolphin, they call them, I believe.

I shook my head to clear it of these vagaries and returned to the form.

Occupation: *unemployed god.*

Skills: *I do miracles—*

—Oops, gotta erase that.

Skills: *I used to do miracles.*

What on earth can you do; where might you be employed? *I could jump through hoops at any SeaWorld.*

Jump through hoops? How undignified. How degrading. . . . To mud with that! I'd rather be crucified—No, wait a minute, I just remembered, that's already been done.

I sighed.

Again the door whammed open, and this short guy wearing a crown engraved with a *Z* came running in. He started slamming stuff onto the Zulu-warrior receptionist's desk: a platinum bar, a painting of himself, a jewel-encrusted egg, an ivory torch, a pile of Zorkmids, and more, lots more, all the while babbling about getting to the head of the line. But with a flash and a bang and a puff of smoke, he vanished.

"Finally obsolete," grunted Black Mask.

I didn't ask him what he meant.

Ping!
"Next buttbrain!"

Some three hours later, the office was cleared of all exgods, but for me. And the place was incredibly quiet, except for the giggling in the background.

The clock now read *2360 AD*.

Many times the door had slammed open, but only vanishing remains of ephemeral wraiths sparkled inward, the gods dying even as they entered.

Some of those already inside had gone aglimmering as well.

For them, the grand and glorious game was over.

And now the place was empty, except for me, and the clerk from hell . . . and whoever it was behind that windowed door along the far wall. What had happened to the other clerks, where they had gone, I didn't know. Perhaps they ebb and flow as the need ebbs and flows, and since the crowd was now gone . . . Even so, the place was still dirty and hot and seedy and the air conditioner still didn't work and the room seemed somehow more cramped, as if the perverse dimensions of the office had shifted, had shrunk, the very walls crowding inward. And the water in the cooler was getting dangerously low.

Ping!
"Next buttbrain!"

I stepped to the desk with my papers.

"What now, fishface?" asked the Mandarin receptionist, stroking his long, long mustache with a lacquer-nailed hand that just moments before had been a wet flipper.

I lost my temper. "Listen, you jerk, I'm here for a job! I didn't know that when I came in, but now I do. So you, butthead, *you* get to work!"

I shoved my papers at him.

"Where's your number, dork?"

"What number?"

"You have to take a number, droolmouth!" He pointed at a number-ticket dispenser hanging from the wall near the entrance sign.

"What? What! What do you mean, take a number? I'm the only one here!"

"Procedure, buttbrain. Procedure."

Wild laughter rose up in the background. And now I could tell that it was coming from the office across the room.

"Look," I said in a reasonable tone, "I'm the only, *the only* one here. I don't *need* a number."

"Look yourself, dork. I don't set the rules. The Boss does. *He* does." The clerk jerked his thumb over his shoulder at the office behind, the one with the laughter. "Now take a number, dog poop."

Sighing, I took a number. It was 247.

"Fifty-three!" called out the receptionist, flipping one of the cards on his desk, the number 53 now showing.

"Fifty-three?" I shouted, pointing at the number dispenser at the entrance. "Fifty-three? I got 247! What the mud happened to all the numbers between?"

"They were sparklers, boob, sparklers."

TICK!

2370 AD.

Damn! My number won't come up for another fifteen or sixteen hours, and by that time the clock will be reading . . . reading . . . 4210 AD!

Can I last that long?

Joyous laughter tittered forth from the office.

What kind of a jerk is running this place? Just who in mud is this "Top Dog?"

I got up and strolled to the office door. Inside was

a great desk, and sitting behind was what looked to be a man. He was eating something, from a shallow wooden bowl, finger food, and smoking a great long pipe. So *this* was the guy who was responsible for that damn clerk, the clerk from hell, no doubt thinking that it'd be hilarious to treat gods—ex-gods—in such a cavalier, disrespectful, rude, blasphemous . . .

He glanced up, then stood and came to the window and looked me in the face. There was laughter deep within his dark, dark eyes—black, some would say— eyes set within a lean, long-nosed, pointed face. A red face. Amerind red.

He didn't look crazy. Just crafty. And happy. As if enjoying a huge, clever, secret joke.

And he smiled at me, a great, white, toothy smile.

I couldn't help it; I smiled back.

I glanced at the nameplate on the desk—

Ping!

"Fifty-four!"

Stumbling back to my bench, I pondered cruel fate.

Would the faith of the dolphins and porpoises last? For sixteen more hours? For a couple of millennia?

TOCK!

I glanced up at the clock. *What the . . . ? It now read 430 LL.*

"The clock," I called to the hobo clerk.

He turned and looked. "Crap! Some new buttbrain, some new religion. This is gonna mean more work."

Wild giggling came from the boss's office.

Ping!

"Fifty-five."

TICK!

440 LL.

The door opened and in came a bearded, breech-clothed, Jewish-looking guy dragging a big cross, followed by a dark, hawknosed Arab with a crescent and star emblazoned on his robes. As they stepped to the emaciated, brown, turbaned clerk from hell, another guy entered, this one an Oriental, and finally there came this old white-beard—a big, angry, jealous-looking bastard.

Mud! I'd heard from Blue-daub and Black Mask about these guys. *By the Great Whale, if they've been displaced . . . This* LL *religion must be a powerful one, indeed. Maybe powerful enough to affect even dolphins, even porpoises.*

Ping!

"Fifty-six!"

TOCK!

450 LL.

I began to do something that I'd never done before: I began to sweat!

Wild laughter rang out.

Crazy redskin. Sitting in there, eating those dried-up mushrooms, smoking that great long pipe. Giggling. Laughing. As if enjoying a vast, elaborate trick, an immense joke of his own making, a divine comedy rare. Like he's got nothing at all to be worried about. Like whoever believes in him will never lose faith.

The son of a bitch.

And his name! What kind of a name is "Coyoté," anyhow?

Ping!

"Fifty-seven!"

TICK!

FANTASY ANTHOLOGIES

Don't Miss These Exciting DAW Anthologies

SWORD AND SORCERESS
Marion Zimmer Bradley, editor
☐ Book XV   UE2741—$5.99

OTHER ORIGINAL ANTHOLOGIES
Mercedes Lackey, editor
☐ SWORD OF ICE: And Other Tales of Valdemar   UE2720—$5.99

Jennifer Roberson, editor
☐ HIGHWAYMEN: Robbers and Rouges   UE2732—$5.99

Martin H. Greenberg, editor
☐ ELF MAGIC   UE2761—$5.99
☐ ELF FANTASTIC   UE2736—$5.99
☐ WIZARD FANTASTIC   UE2756—$5.50
☐ WHITE HOUSE HORRORS   UE2659—$5.99

Martin H. Greenberg & Lawrence Schimel, editors
☐ TAROT FANTASTIC   UE2729—$5.99
☐ THE FORTUNE TELLER   UE2748—$5.99

Mike Resnick & Martin Greenberg, editors
☐ RETURN OF THE DINOSAURS   UE2753—$5.99
☐ SHERLOCK HOLMES IN ORBIT   UE2636—$5.50

Richard Gilliam & Martin H. Greenberg, editors
☐ PHANTOMS OF THE NIGHT   UE2696—$5.99

Norman Partridge & Martin H. Greenberg, editors
☐ IT CAME FROM THE DRIVE-IN   UE2680—$5.50

Buy them at your local bookstore or use this convenient coupon for ordering.

PENGUIN USA   P.O. Box 999—Dep. #17109, Bergenfield, New Jersey 07621

Please send me the DAW BOOKS I have checked above, for which I am enclosing
$_____ (please add $2.00 to cover postage and handling). Send check or money
order (no cash or C.O.D.'s) or charge by Mastercard or VISA (with a $15.00 minimum). Prices and
numbers are subject to change without notice.

Card #_____ Exp. Date _____
Signature_____
Name_____
Address_____
City _____ State _____ Zip Code _____

For faster service when ordering by credit card call **1-800-253-6476**

Allow a minimum of 4-6 weeks for delivery. This offer is subject to change without notice.

Science Fiction Anthologies

☐ **FIRST CONTACT**
Martin H. Greenberg and Larry Segriff, editors

UE2757—$5.99

In the tradition of the hit television show "The X-Files" comes a fascinating collection of original stories by some of the premier writers of the genre, such as Jody Lynn Nye, Kristine Kathryn Rusch, and Jack Haldeman.

☐ **RETURN OF THE DINOSAURS**
Mike Resnick and Martin H. Greenberg, editors

UE2753—$5.99

Dinosaurs walk the Earth once again in these all-new tales that dig deep into the past and blaze trails into the possible future. Join Gene Wolfe, Melanie Rawn, David Gerrold, Mike Resnick, and others as they breathe new life into ancient bones.

☐ **BLACK MIST:** and Other Japanese Futures
Orson Scott Card and Keith Ferrell, editors

UE2767—$5.99

Original novellas by Richard Lupoff, Patric Helmaan, Pat Cadigan, Paul Levinson, and Janeen Webb & Jack Dann envision how the wide-ranging influence of Japanese culture will change the world.